Praise for

Medusa's Ankles

and Other Short Fiction of A. S. Byatt

"Byatt's stories are provoking and alarming, richly yet tautly rendered. They feed our primitive readerly desires as well as our reflective impulses. . . . Byatt has the sheer narrative skill to raise the hairs on the back of your neck and make your pulse race."

—Claire Messud, *The New York Times Book Review*

"Amongst the many prizes that A. S. Byatt has won in a stellar career spanning nearly six decades, a late accolade, the Hans Christian Andersen Literature [Award], cites her 'belief in the true value of fairy tales, fables, and poetry.' It's an award that perceptively understands much of the foundation and inspirations for Byatt's work; for running like an underground river, or a life-giving stream, in her oeuvre is a cogent, intricate, enriching conversation going on with some of the oldest genres known to human civilization."

—Neel Mukherjee, *Electric Literature*

"If Scheherazade ever needs a break, Byatt can step in, indefinitely."

—*Chicago Tribune*

"*Medusa's Ankles* collects mesmeric, tantalizing short stories from over the course of Man Booker Prize–winning author A. S. Byatt's career. . . . As in her novels, Byatt's shorter works display her fluent, luminous prose. Even in her most realistic stories, dark and glittering descriptions . . . bewitch readers into an otherworldly experience."

—*Shelf Awareness*

"[Byatt's] stories display all her talents as a novelist, but spiced with an additional friskiness . . . a bright, sensual prose that seems to paint rather than describe, giving a teacup, a mountainside, or the night sky a texture and density that go beyond words on a page."

—Penelope Lively, *Evening Standard*

"*Medusa's Ankles* opens with a haunting and strangely gentle ghost story ('The July Ghost') and ends with a terse contemporary fable about our feckless destruction of the planet ('Sea Story'). In between are worlds and characters, actual and magical, that the reader will not soon forget." —*New York Journal of Books*

"The short story format suits [Byatt] beautifully. . . . She favors adjective-spangled cascades of images, excavates the dictionary for rare specimens, and sends iambs and anapests cavorting across the paragraphs. . . . Exquisite. . . . Beautifully evocative."

—*Kirkus Reviews*

"A scintillating look at three decades of the author's work. Her stories transcend genre and stylistic limits, traversing through landscapes fantastical and real, as they bewitch, unnerve, and comfort the reader. . . . Each story showcases Byatt's exquisite prose and her wide-ranging mastery of the short story form. For the uninitiated, this makes for a perfect entry point." —*Publishers Weekly*

A. S. BYATT

Medusa's Ankles

A. S. Byatt is the author of numerous novels, including *The Children's Book*, *The Biographer's Tale*, and *Possession*, which was awarded the Booker Prize. She has also written two novellas published together as *Angels & Insects*, five collections of short stories, and several works of nonfiction. She lives in London.

ALSO BY A. S. BYATT

FICTION

The Shadow of the Sun

The Game

The Virgin in the Garden

Still Life

Sugar and Other Stories

Possession: A Romance

Angels & Insects

The Matisse Stories

The Djinn in the Nightingale's Eye

Babel Tower

Elementals

The Biographer's Tale

A Whistling Woman

Little Black Book of Stories

The Children's Book

CRITICISM

Degrees of Freedom: The Novels of Iris Murdoch

Unruly Times: Wordsworth and Coleridge in Their Time

Passions of the Mind: Selected Writings

Imagining Characters (with Ignês Sodré)

On Histories and Stories: Selected Essays

Portraits in Fiction

Memory: An Anthology (ed. with Harriet Harvey Wood)

Peacock & Vine: Fortuny and Morris in Life and at Work

Medusa's Ankles

Selected Stories

A. S. BYATT

With an introduction by
DAVID MITCHELL

VINTAGE INTERNATIONAL
Vintage Books
A Division of Penguin Random House LLC
New York

FIRST VINTAGE INTERNATIONAL EDITION 2022

The Library of Congress has cataloged the Knopf edition as follows:
Names: Byatt, A. S. (Antonia Susan), [date] author.
Title: Medusa's ankles : selected stories / A. S. Byatt ;
with an introduction by David Mitchell.
Description: First United States edition. | New York : Alfred A. Knopf, 2021.
Identifiers: LCCN 2021016813 (print) | LCCN 2021016814 (ebook)
Subjects: LCGFT: Short stories.
Classification: LCC PR6052.Y2 M43 2021 (print) | LCC PR6052.Y2 (ebook) |
DDC 823/.914—dc23
LC record available at https://lccn.loc.gov/2021016813
LC ebook record available at https://lccn.loc.gov/2021016814

Vintage International Trade Paperback ISBN: 978-0-593-46685-8
eBook ISBN: 978-0-593-32159-1

vintagebooks.com

Printed in the United States of America
10 9 8 7 6 5 4 3 2 1

CONTENTS

INTRODUCTION

A. S. Byatt's reputation as a master of the long form has been crystallised by *Possession,* a novel of depth, breadth, and heft; the "Frederica Quartet," a prose tapestry of postwar England; and *The Children's Book,* a many-chambered country house of a narrative. This timely collection showcases Byatt's gifts as a master of the short story. To my mind, she belongs in that select club of writers whose members include Dickens, John Cheever, Sylvia Townsend Warner, and Elizabeth Bowen, and who achieve virtuosity in both short- and long-form fiction. The stories in this volume beguile, illuminate, immerse, unsettle, console, and evoke. They buzz with wit, shimmer with nuance, and misdirect like a street conjuror. They amend, or even rewrite, any putative Rules of the Short Story time and again. They possess a sentient quality. If *Medusa's Ankles* was a retrospective exhibition, the gallery would need no guide or "explainer" cards stuck next to the paintings—the stories are perfect and lucid as they stand. For this introduction, however, I've settled on three qualities of Byatt's writing that have a particular glow for me. A brief discussion of these, following a thumbnail biography, are what I'd like to offer the reader, here at the doors of the gallery.

A. S. Byatt was born Susan Drabble in Sheffield in 1936, the eldest daughter of a county court judge and a scholar of Victorian poetry. I hereby succumb to the biographical temptation to locate the sources of thematic streams in Byatt's fiction in her upbringing: notably, a deep moral engagement; the effect of domineering patriarchs; due reverence for intellect; and a friction between the life of the mind and the life of the housewife. All four Drabble children were educated in Sheffield and York, though the communal confines of boarding school did not suit the bookish future author, and the loneliness of her school years informs one story in this volume, "Racine and the Tablecloth." Byatt has written approvingly, however, of her Quaker schooling's respect for silence and listening, and an outsider's perspective is also a novelist's perspective. Byatt's horizons broadened and brightened upon going up to Cambridge to read English in 1954. The emancipations of fifties undergraduate life are fictionalised in her novel *Still Life* (1978)—as are the casual sexism and taken-as-read elitism. Spells of postgraduate study followed at Bryn Mawr College, Philadelphia, and Somerville College, Oxford. These, too, would be creatively fruitful: few authors engage with the pleasures of scholarship as persuasively as Byatt. Several academics inhabit *Medusa's Ankles*, and even if jaded or satirical, they love their work. A. S. Byatt married in 1959 and combined raising a family, lecturing in art, and writing her debut novel, *The Shadow of the Sun,* published in 1964. She became a full-time writer only in 1983. Despite living in London, her Yorkshire roots assert themselves throughout her oeuvre: Byatt's literary England has a magnetic north and a cosmopolitan south. *Possession* won the Booker Prize in 1990 and made A. S. Byatt a household name, in book-reading households at least. The novel remains the author's best-known work, and ushered in a remarkably industrious decade. In addition to serving on boards for the British Council and the Society of Authors, she travelled widely and wrote *Angels and Insects* (1992), a diptych of lush, learned novellas; the third novel in the "Frederica Quartet," *Babel Tower* (1996); three collections of short stories; and a highly original novel, *The Biographer's Tale* (2000). She was made a Dame of the British Empire for services to literature in 1999. The "Frederica Quartet" was concluded with *A Whistling Woman* in 2002, followed by a fourth story collection, *The Little Black Book of Stories* (2003), her most recent full-length novel, the Booker-shortlisted *The Children's Book* (2009), and a novella of reworked mythology, *Ragnarok* (2011). Throughout her career, Byatt has written essays, journalism, art criticism, and biography, the latter including books on Iris Murdoch,

Wordsworth, and Coleridge, William Morris and the Spanish designer Mariano Fortuny. Her life of scholarship, literature, art, and ideas informs, and is reflected in, the stories in these pages. All writers turn their lives and selves into writing: it's the "how" and the "what" of this act of alchemy that is unique to each writer; and it is to a trio of qualities of A. S. Byatt's particular alchemy to which I now turn.

Firstly, note the sheer range. Most great short-story writers are distinctive stylists more than they are stylistic chameleons. Most habitual readers of short stories could pass a "Name That Author" test and identify, say, Raymond Carver, Anton Chekhov, or Alice Munro by a single page of their prose. As a rule of thumb, however, the more readily identifiable the author, the narrower the world of the author's literary corpus. Narrowness of world does not equate with narrowness of vision, or mind, or skill. Infinity can indeed be held in the palm of a hand, and eternity in an hour. A. S. Byatt's stories bypass this rule of thumb with relish. She is both a highly distinctive stylist—ornate, cerebral, "Byatty"—and a short-story writer whose menu of answers to the question "What form can a story take?" is long, varied, and rich. "The July Ghost" is a portrait of a mother who has lost a child and an agnostic ghost story. It is subtle, poignant, and ever so slightly trippy. In contrast, "Sugar" is a meandering clamber around a family tree, ripe with memorable anecdote and northern-hued. "Precipice-Encurled" is a set of framed narratives about the poet Robert Browning, a family he knew in Italy, a young artist and a woman who models for him. It is sumptuous, expectation-busting, heartbreaking, and immune to classification. "Racine and the Tablecloth" is a tale of a vulnerable pupil and her ambiguously predatory schoolmistress set in an all-girls' boarding school. This may be Muriel Spark turf, but Byatt's story reads like biography and feels shot in black and white.

So much for the first four stories of *Medusa's Ankles:* my point is, I could describe the next fourteen in the collection, and none would much resemble the others. When I encounter this degree of writerly omnivorousness, I speculate about its source. Kipling's formidable range came from a peripatetic life spent in (and between) different worlds; and from, to use a now-quaint word, his adventures. I wonder if Byatt's range comes from inner conversations with what she reads; from a scholar's delight in exploring the rabbit warrens of research; and from a likeable openness to genre fiction. It was traditional for literary figures of Byatt's generation and altitude on the literary ladder to distinguish between serious literary fiction and genre fiction, and to allot respect, study, and awards only to the former. As I write in the early 2020s, this distinction is fading—Bob Dylan has won the Nobel Prize in Literature and Booker longlists may now include graphic novels—but genre snobbery is still alive, well, and writing reviews. (I have the bruises to prove it.) A. S. Byatt is the opposite of a genre snob. In this collection, "Dragons' Breath" uses, well, dragons, in the service of a fever-dream parable. "Cold" is a fairy story with a feminist twist. "Dolls' Eyes" flirts with Gothic horror, and is steeped in the genre's history cleverly enough to outwit the reader. "A Stone Woman" melds fantasy, psychology, Ovid, and Scandinavian myth to delineate both the metamorphosis of a widow into a crystal she-troll and the stages of grief. "The Lucid Dreamer," a tale of an experimental psychonaut entering free fall, occupies that zone of British science fiction staked out by J. G. Ballard and John Wyndham. I'm not claiming that Byatt is a genre writer, or that *Medusa's Ankles* should be exiled to the SF/Fantasy section (shudder!). The full spectrum of the English literary canon, in all its realist glory, is present and correct too—George Eliot, Henry James, Proust, Virginia Woolf, D. H. Lawrence, Iris Murdoch. As a literary traveller, however, Byatt engages with writers as far off the Leavisite road map as the Brothers Grimm, Italo Calvino, Ursula le Guin, Neil Gaiman. (During a conversation with Gaiman I told him how much A. S. Byatt enjoyed his fantasy novel *Coraline.* He replied without hesitation, "Antonia's one of us.") Byatt's scholarly knowledge of English literature, combined with her freethinking attitude to genre, produces magnificent hybrids. The longest story here, "The Djinn in the Nightingale's Eye," is built of distinct modes of writing that are rarely found in the same room. We begin with middle-class kitchen-sink drama: Gillian Perholt, the protagonist, has been dumped by her husband for a younger woman. The story segues into literary theory when Gillian, a narratologist, presents a paper at a conference in Ankara. Next up is travel writing, as Gillian visits museums and mosques. Then, stunningly, this near-novella veers into fantasy, when a djinn is freed by Gillian from an old bottle acquired in a bazaar. Surreal comedy—no spoilers, but watch out for a cameo by tennis player Boris Becker—is followed by a wholly persuasive interspecies romance. The story's breathtaking genre shifts make "The Djinn in the Nightingale's Eye" utterly unpredictable, and its themes dynamic and various. It is Byatt at her magpie-minded, ideas-studded, plot-driven best.

To an art historian, angels, dragons, and dreamscapes are as legitimate subjects as sunflowers, haystacks, and realist portraits. A. S. Byatt's scholarly knowledge of art informs her prose as pervasively as (Doctor) Chekhov's knowledge of medicine and human malaises informs his. Certainly, Byatt's characters are introduced with a portraitist's eye. Of Ines's mother in "A Stone Woman" we are told, "[She]—a strong bright woman—had liked to live amongst shades of mole and dove." Some of Byatt's most vivid creations are painters, like Joshua Riddell, the artist in "Precipice-Encurled"; or art lecturers, like Professor Perry Diss ("Bury this?") in "The Chinese Lobster" who falls foul of campus politics; or artists in the broader senses, like Hew the architect in "The Narrow Jet," Thorsteinn the sculptor from "A Stone Woman," or the oneiric artist in "The Lucid Dreamer." Such characters are Byatt's conduits for ideas about making art, looking at art and art's centrality to the mind and the world. "Precipice-Encurled" features John Ruskin—from whom art lecturers claim professional descent—and Joshua Riddell, engaging with Ruskin's idea's before our very eyes:

> Monsieur Monet had found a solution to the problem posed by Ruskin, of how to paint light, with the small range of colours available: he had trapped light in his surface, light itself was his subject. His paint was light. He had painted, not the thing seen, but the act of seeing.

This conversation happens across years and ontological boundaries. Few writers embed theory in their fiction with Byatt's boldness and success. The theories of art are sometimes illustrated by the very story that houses them. The line quoted above—"He had painted, not the thing seen, but the act of seeing"—is embedded in "Precipice-Encurled" as much by characters' *perceptions* of what happens, as by what actually happens. Art powered by the dissonance between characters' interiors and the world's exteriority is as old as Shakespeare and Cervantes, but Byatt elevates this dissonance itself to subject and theme. And plot and structure, when occasion permits. "Ekphrasis"—the use of a work of visual art as a literary device—is a word seldom reached for in everyday conversation, but it's a perfect fit for "Christ in the House of Martha and Mary." The story imagines the circumstances around the titular painting by Diego Velázquez—a picture that encloses a picture—from the viewpoint of Concepción, the cook who appears in the Velázquez painting. This story is unfussy about those oft-mystified concepts "inspiration" and "the creative process." It bestows dignity upon art in all its manifestations, including cooking. Byatt's Velázquez addresses Concepción not as a disposable domestic but as a respected equal:

> The cook, as much as the painter, looks into the essence of the creation not, as I do, in light and on surfaces, but with all the other senses, with taste, and smell, and touch, which God also made in us for purposes . . . the world is full of light and life, and the true crime is not to be interested in it. You have a way in. Take it. It may incidentally be a way out, as all skills are.

Byatt can describe a painter at work with the vivacity and precision of a skilled football pundit. I would call these passages "notoriously difficult" to write, but the phrase feels misleading—so few writers even try. In this sensuous passage from "Precipice-Encurled," artist Joshua Riddell sketches Juliana Fishwick, daughter in the family with whom he is staying in Italy. It is a double love scene between Joshua and Juliana, and between artist and vocation:

> His pencil point hovered, thinking, and Juliana's pupils contracted in the greenish halo of the iris, as she looked into the light, and blinked, involuntarily. She did not want to stare at him; it was unnatural, though his considering gaze, measuring, drawing back, turning to one side and the other, seemed natural enough. A flood of colour moved darkly up her throat, along her chin, into the planes and complexities of her cheeks.

If Velázquez is an established artist and Joshua Riddell a wunderkind, Bernard Lycett-Kean in "A Lamia in the Cévennes" is an artist-in-progress. The story is comic—a lamia gets trapped in an English expat's swimming pool—and cerebral, as we watch Bernard fall in love not with the mythological seductress, but with art itself. The story is a kind of serio-comedic miniature of Van Gogh's collected letters to his brother Theo—a self-drawn road map of artistic growth. In this passage, Bernard notices that reality represents itself as shifting fields of colours and luminosities, mirrored by Byatt in her prose:

> The best days were under racing cloud, when the aquamarine took on a cool grey tone, which was then chased back, or rolled away, by the flickering gold-in-blue of yellow light in liquid. In front of his prow or chin in the brightest lights moved a mesh of hexagonal threads, flashing rainbow colours, flashing liquid silver-gilt, with a hint of molten glass; on

> such days liquid fire, rosy and yellow and clear, rain across the dolphin, who lent it a thread of intense blue.

It is not easy to think of another writer with so painterly and exact an eye for the colours, textures, and appearances of things. The visual is in constant dialogue with the textual. One aftereffect of reading Byatt resembles the aftereffect of a morning in an art gallery whereby, upon leaving, I find myself framing rectangles in my field of vision and looking at them—at the world—as I might a painting. These stories are in constant dialogue with readers, asking, "What is art?" and "Why do we need it?" and "What does it do to us?" and "Why make the damn stuff?" These questions linger long after putting the book down. This thought-bubble of Bernard's could feasibly puff out of the skull of any writer, or artist of any bent:

> He muttered to himself. Why bother. Why does this *matter* so much. *What difference does it make to anything if I solve this blue* and just start again. I could just sit down and drink wine. I could go and be useful in a cholera camp in Colombia or Ethiopia. *Why bother to render the transparency in solid paint on a bit of board.* I could *just stop.*
>
> He could not.

Art is a mercurial lover. One artist you'll meet in these pages pays a truly shocking final price for his devotion to his art. Yet art is also what saves Bernard from the titular lamia. For Velázquez, art is the key that unlocks life. Whatever chord the stories end on, the artists can no more ignore their art than a character can change the story they appear in, or a Greek hero outwit the Fates.

Metafiction, my dictionary tells me, is "fiction in which the author self-consciously alludes to the artificiality or literariness of a work by parodying or departing from novelistic conventions and traditional narrative techniques." Quite a mouthful, and not an overly appetising one. Metafiction as practised during 1980s "peak-post-modernism" led up some sterile cul-de-sacs. How can a reader care about a character who discusses his own fictionality? Metafiction in A. S. Byatt's stories is subtler, however, often wrapped up with voice, and is an urbane pleasure of her work. First-person narratives are the "home viewpoint" for many a fine writer, but they require an extra act of complicity from the reader, who must "believe" not only the story but also in the reality of its fictional narrator. Byatt's stories are all third-person, told by a narrator who balances the needs of the story—keep that disbelief suspended, keep the reader caring—with the "insider information" that only a sentient narrator can impart. On occasion, the narrator is chatty, pondering aloud at the start of "Racine and the Tablecloth," "When was it clear that Martha Crichton-Walker was the antagonist?" Since we, the readers of said story, can't be expected to know the answer, the narrator elaborates: "Emily found this word for her much later, when she was a grown woman." Sometimes the narrator alludes to the reader's role in fiction by inviting us to fill in an onerous blank, as in the story of Gillian Perholt's dumping, by fax, by her husband. "It was long and self-exculpatory, but there is no need for me to recount it to you, you can very well imagine it for yourself." From time to time the narrator will philosophise, noting that if the newly-wed Fiammarosa (from "Cold") was sometimes lonely in her glass palace, "this was not unusual, for no one has everything they can desire." Such remarks bridge Fiammarosa's fantastical reality with our own less fantastical one, and make the point that the workings of the heart—and marriage—are pretty much the same, whether they reside in an enchanted palace or a house with a postcode. Elsewhere, the narrator offers cinematic "fore-flashes": in one of the frame narratives in "Precipice-Encurled," a woman is waiting for the poet Robert Browning. "She . . . will do this for many years," prophesies the authorial voice, thereby elongating this character's sad arc, and shading her in tones of Miss Havisham and *The Aspern Papers.* The effect reminds me of watching a film with a taciturn director's commentary; or, more precisely, a film whose script includes a few remarks spoken by the director from behind the camera. Narrators clued up on the act of narration are, of course, nothing new. Chaucer was at it in the 1300s—but there's a self-knowing quality to Byatt's narrator's self-knowledge that renders the mechanisms of these stories sporadically visible. At these moments I even sense Byatt observing the reader through her narrator, like Dutch painters painting their own reflections in mirrors.

As "The Djinn in the Nightingale's Eye" is metafictional by way of being a Narratologist's Tale, so the story "Raw Material" is fiction about fiction. Jack Smollett (the names of Byatt's characters hum with allusion) is a one-hit-wonder, ex–Angry Young Man novelist who, in the 1960s, "left for London and fame, and returned quietly, ten years later." Jack lives off a circle of students who are unencumbered by a surfeit of talent. One week, the octogenarian Cicely Fox appears in his class with a brief essay, "How We Used to Black-Lead Stoves." The essay itself is included in "Raw Material," as are a couple of follow-ups. Jack sees the merit and authenticity in Cicely's work as "the real thing." Artistically, the semi-washed-up youngish writer is smitten and reignited by the senior. The essays, the narrator tells us, "made Jack want to write. They made him see the world as something to be written." If the "painter" stories allow Byatt to depict a painter painting, "Raw Material" enables Byatt to write a writer discussing writing. Byatt ricochets ideas between these metafictional levels. "He had given up telling them that Creative Writing was not a form of psychotherapy. In ways both sublime and ridiculous it clearly was, precisely, that." Tonally, "sublime and ridiculous" would be a fair description of the whole story. It is about the clarity offered by poetry and prose; about why writers write what writers write about. It is dark, shocking, and exhibits Byatt's ticklish sense of the ridiculous. It is a counterpoint to death, which arrives with all the warning an owl gives a vole. The narrative eye of "Sea Story" has the godlike precision of a GPS satellite, tracking the voyage of a message in a bottle from Filey to its (un-Romantic) destination in the Great Caribbean Trash Vortex. Meditatively, brilliantly, the story gives form to Byatt's recurring theme of epistemology: What are the limits of knowledge? What do we know is true, and what do we merely believe is true? Is truth a constant, or a lover's words on a page of paper rolled up in a plastic Perrier bottle doomed to split open, disintegrate, and end up inside a mollyhawk's chicks?

About 170 pages from this one you'll meet Orhan Rifat, a cosmopolitan Turkish academic, waiting for Gillian Perholt at Ankara airport. Orhan will refer to a statue's breasts, explaining: "They are metaphors. They are many things at once, as the sphinxes and winged bulls are many things at once." These remarkable stories, too, are many things at once. Chains of cause and effect. Puzzle boxes. Meditations. Learned discourses. Statements of regret and offerings of solace. X-rays of the heart. Showcases of beauty for beauty's own sake. Views of a world where, to be sure, bad things can happen to good people; but also where happy-ish endings, qualified by realism, are not beyond hope. Step inside. Take your time. Savour your discoveries. "They sat in silence and were amazed, briefly and forever."

—David Mitchell
May 2021

MEDUSA'S ANKLES

THE JULY GHOST

"I think I must move out of where I'm living," he said. "I have this problem with my landlady."

He picked a long, bright hair off the back of her dress, so deftly that the act seemed simply considerate. He had been skilful at balancing glass, plate, and cutlery, too. He had a look of dignified misery, like a dejected hawk. She was interested.

"What sort of problem? Amatory, financial, or domestic?"

"None of those, really. Well, not financial."

He turned the hair on his finger, examining it intently, not meeting her eye.

"Not financial. Can you tell me? I might know somewhere you could stay. I know a lot of people."

"You would." He smiled shyly. "It's not an easy problem to describe. There's just the two of us. I occupy the attics. Mostly."

He came to a stop. He was obviously reserved and secretive. But he was telling her something. This is usually attractive.

"Mostly?" Encouraging him.

"Oh, it's not like *that*. Well, not . . . Shall we sit down?"

They moved across the party, which was a big party, on a hot day. He stopped and found a bottle and filled her glass. He had not needed to ask what she was drinking. They sat side by side on a sofa: he admired the brilliant poppies bold on her emerald dress, and her pretty sandals. She had come to London for the summer to work in the British Museum. She could really have managed with microfilm in Tucson for what little manuscript research was needed, but there was a dragging love affair to end. There is an age at which, however desperately happy one is in stolen moments, days, or weekends with one's married professor, one either prises him loose or cuts and runs. She had had a stab at both, and now considered she had successfully cut and run. So it was nice to be immediately appreciated. Problems are capable of solution. She said as much to him, turning her soft face to his ravaged one, swinging the long bright hair. It had begun a year ago, he told her in a rush, at another party actually; he had met this woman, the landlady in question, and had made, not immediately, a kind of *faux pas,* he now saw, and she had been very decent, all things considered, and so . . .

He had said, "I think I must move out of where I'm living." He had been quite wild, had nearly not come to the party, but could not go on drinking alone. The woman had considered him coolly and asked, "Why?" One could not, he said, go on in a place where one had once been blissfully happy, and was now miserable, however convenient the place. Convenient, that was, for work, and friends, and things that seemed, as he mentioned them, ashy and insubstantial compared to the memory and the hope of opening the door and finding Anne outside it, laughing and breathless, waiting to be told what he had read, or thought, or eaten, or felt that day. Someone I loved left, he told the woman. Reticent on that occasion too, he bit back the flurry of sentences about the total unexpectedness of it, the arriving back and finding only an envelope on a clean table, and spaces in the bookshelves, the record stack, the kitchen cupboard. It must have been planned for weeks, she must have been thinking it out while he rolled on her, while she poured wine for him, while . . . No, no. Vituperation is undignified and in this case what he felt was lower and worse than rage: just pure, childlike loss. "One ought not to mind places," he said to the woman. "But one does," she had said. "I know."

She had suggested to him that he could come and be her lodger, then; she had, she said, a lot of spare space going to waste, and her husband wasn't there much. "We've not had a lot to say to each other, lately." He could be quite self-contained, there was a kitchen and a bathroom in the attics; she wouldn't bother him. There was a large garden. It was possibly this that decided him: it was very hot, central

London, the time of year when a man feels he would give anything to live in a room opening onto grass and trees, not a high flat in a dusty street. And if Anne came back, the door would be locked and mortice-locked. He could stop thinking about Anne coming back. That was a decisive move: Anne thought he wasn't decisive. He would live without Anne.

For some weeks after he moved in he had seen very little of the woman. They met on the stairs, and once she came up, on a hot Sunday, to tell him he must feel free to use the garden. He had offered to do some weeding and mowing and she had accepted. That was the weekend her husband came back, driving furiously up to the front door, running in, and calling in the empty hall, "Imogen, Imogen!" To which she had replied, uncharacteristically, by screaming hysterically. There was nothing in her husband, Noel's, appearance to warrant this reaction; their lodger, peering over the banister at the sound, had seen their upturned faces in the stairwell and watched hers settle into its usual prim and placid expression as he did so. Seeing Noel, a balding, fluffy-templed, stooping thirty-five or so, shabby corduroy suit, cotton polo neck, he realised he was now able to guess her age, as he had not been. She was a very neat woman, faded blond, her hair in a knot on the back of her head, her legs long and slender, her eyes downcast. Mild was not quite the right word for her, though. She explained then that she had screamed because Noel had come home unexpectedly and startled her: she was sorry. It seemed a reasonable explanation. The extraordinary vehemence of the screaming was probably an echo in the stairwell. Noel seemed wholly downcast by it, all the same.

He had kept out of the way, that weekend, taking the stairs two at a time and lightly, feeling a little aggrieved, looking out of his kitchen window into the lovely, overgrown garden, that they were lurking indoors, wasting all the summer sun. At Sunday lunchtime he had heard the husband, Noel, shouting on the stairs.

"I can't go on, if you go on like that. I've done my best, I've tried to get through. Nothing will shift you, will it, you won't *try,* will you, you just go on and on. Well, I have my life to live, you can't throw a life away . . . can you?"

He had crept out again onto the dark upper landing and seen her standing, halfway down the stairs, quite still, watching Noel wave his arms and roar, or almost roar, with a look of impassive patience, as though this nuisance must pass off. Noel swallowed and gasped; he turned his face up to her and said plaintively,

"You do see I can't stand it? I'll be in touch, shall I? You must want . . . you must need . . . you must . . ."

She didn't speak.

"If you need anything, you know where to get me."

"Yes."

"Oh, well . . ." said Noel, and went to the door. She watched him, from the stairs, until it was shut, and then came up again, step by step, as though it was an effort, a little, and went on coming, past her bedroom, to his landing, to come in and ask him, entirely naturally, please to use the garden if he wanted to, and please not to mind marital rows. She was sure he understood . . . things were difficult . . . Noel wouldn't be back for some time. He was a journalist: his work took him away a lot. Just as well. She committed herself to that "just as well." She was a very economical speaker.

So he took to sitting in the garden. It was a lovely place: a huge, hidden, walled south London garden, with old fruit trees at the end, a wildly waving disorderly buddleia, curving beds full of old roses, and a lawn of overgrown, dense ryegrass. Over the wall at the foot was the Common, with a footpath running behind all the gardens. She came out to the shed and helped him to assemble and oil the lawn mower, standing on the little path under the apple branches while he cut an experimental serpentine across her hay. Over the wall came the high sound of children's voices, and the thunk and thud of a football. He asked her how to raise the blades: he was not mechanically minded.

"The children get quite noisy," she said. "And dogs. I hope they don't bother you. There aren't many safe places for children, round here."

He replied truthfully that he never heard sounds that didn't concern him, when he was concentrating. When he'd got the lawn into shape, he was going to sit on it and do a lot of reading, try to get his mind in trim again, to write a paper on Hardy's poems, on their curiously archaic vocabulary.

"It isn't very far to the road on the other side, really," she said. "It just seems to be. The Common is an illusion of space, really. Just a spur of brambles and gorse bushes and bits of football pitch between two fast four-laned main roads. I hate London commons."

"There's a lovely smell, though, from the gorse and the wet grass. It's a pleasant illusion."

"No illusions are pleasant," she said, decisively, and went in. He wondered what she did with her time: apart from little shopping expeditions she seemed to be always in the house. He was sure that when he'd met her she'd been introduced as having some profession: vaguely literary, vaguely academic, like everyone he knew. Perhaps she wrote poetry in her north-facing living room. He had no idea what it would be like. Women generally wrote emotional poetry, much nicer than men, as Kingsley Amis has stated, but she seemed, despite her placid stillness, too spare and too fierce—grim?—for that. He remembered the screaming. Perhaps she wrote Plath-like chants of violence. He didn't think that quite fitted the bill, either. Perhaps she was a freelance radio journalist. He didn't bother to ask anyone who might be a common acquaintance. During the whole year, he explained to the American at the party, he hadn't actually *discussed* her with anyone. Of course he wouldn't, she agreed vaguely and warmly. She knew he wouldn't. He didn't see why he shouldn't, in fact, but went on, for the time, with his narrative.

They had got to know each other a little better over the next few weeks, at least on the level of borrowing tea, or even sharing pots of it. The weather had got hotter. He had found an old-fashioned deck chair, with faded striped canvas, in the shed, and had brushed it over and brought it out on to his mown lawn, where he sat writing a little, reading a little, getting up and pulling up a tuft of couch grass. He had been wrong about the children not bothering him: there was a succession of incursions by all sizes of children looking for all sizes of balls, which bounced to his feet, or crashed in the shrubs, or vanished in the herbaceous border, black and white footballs, beach balls with concentric circles of primary colours, acid-yellow tennis balls. The children came over the wall: black faces, brown faces, floppy long hair, shaven heads, respectable dotted sun hats and camouflaged cotton army hats from Milletts. They came over easily, as though they were used to it, sandals, training shoes, a few bare toes, grubby sunburned legs, cotton skirts, jeans, football shorts. Sometimes, perched on the top, they saw him and gestured at the balls; one or two asked permission. Sometimes he threw a ball back, but was apt to knock down a few knobby little unripe apples or pears. There was a gate in the wall, under the fringing trees, which he once tried to open, spending time on rusty bolts only to discover that the lock was new and secure, and the key not in it.

The boy sitting in the tree did not seem to be looking for a ball. He was in a fork of the tree nearest the gate, swinging his legs, doing something to a knot in a frayed end of rope that was attached to the branch he sat on. He wore blue jeans and training shoes, and a brilliant tee shirt, striped in the colours of the spectrum, arranged in the right order, which the man on the grass found visually pleasing. He had rather long blond hair, falling over his eyes, so that his face was obscured.

"Hey, you. Do you think you ought to be up there? It might not be safe."

The boy looked up, grinned, and vanished monkey-like over the wall. He had a nice, frank grin, friendly, not cheeky.

He was there again, the next day, leaning back in the crook of the tree, arms crossed. He had on the same shirt and jeans. The man watched him, expecting him to move again, but he sat, immobile, smiling down pleasantly, and then staring up at the sky. The man read a little, looked up, saw him still there, and said,

"Have you lost anything?"

The child did not reply: after a moment he climbed down a little, swung along the branch hand over hand, dropped to the ground, raised an arm in salute, and was up over the usual route over the wall.

Two days later he was lying on his stomach on the edge of the lawn, out of the shade, this time in a white tee shirt with a pattern of blue ships and water-lines on it, his bare feet and legs stretched in the sun. He was chewing a grass stem, and studying the earth, as though watching for insects. The man said, "Hi, there," and the boy looked up, met his look with intensely blue eyes under long lashes, smiled with the same complete warmth and openness, and returned his look to the earth.

He felt reluctant to inform on the boy, who seemed so harmless and considerate: but when he met him walking out of the kitchen door, spoke to him, and got no answer but the gentle smile before the boy ran off towards the wall, he wondered if he should speak to his landlady. So he asked her, did she mind the children coming in the garden. She said no, children must look for balls, that was part of being children. He persisted—they sat there, too, and he had met one coming out of the house. He hadn't seemed to be doing any harm, the boy, but you couldn't tell. He thought she should know.

He was probably a friend of her son's, she said. She looked at him kindly and explained. Her son had run off the Common with some other children, two years ago, in the summer, in July, and had been killed on the road. More or less instantly, she had added drily, as though calculating that just *enough* information would preclude the need for further questions. He said he was sorry, very sorry, feeling to blame, which was ridiculous, and a little injured, because he had not known about her son, and might inadvertently have made a fool of himself with some casual reference whose ignorance would be embarrassing.

What was the boy like, she said. The one in the house? "I don't—talk to his friends. I find it painful. It could be Timmy, or Martin. They might have lost something, or want . . ."

He described the boy. Blond, about ten at a guess, he was not very good at children's ages, very blue eyes, slightly built, with a rainbow-striped tee shirt and blue jeans, mostly though not always—oh, and those football practice shoes, black and green. And the other tee shirt, with the ships and wavy lines. And an extraordinarily nice smile. A really *warm* smile. A nice-looking boy.

He was used to her being silent. But this silence went on and on and on. She was just staring into the garden. After a time, she said, in her precise conversational tone,

"The only thing I want, the only thing I want at all in this world, is to see that boy."

She stared at the garden and he stared with her, until the grass began to dance with empty light, and the edges of the shrubbery wavered. For a brief moment he shared the strain of not seeing the boy. Then she gave a little sigh, sat down, neatly as always, and passed out at his feet.

After this she became, for her, voluble. He didn't move her after she fainted, but sat patiently by her, until she stirred and sat up; then he fetched her some water, and would have gone away, but she talked.

"I'm too rational to see ghosts, I'm not someone who would see anything there was to see, I don't believe in an afterlife, I don't see how anyone can, I always found a kind of satisfaction for myself in the idea that one just came to an end, to a sliced-off stop. But that was myself; I didn't think *he*—not *he*—I thought ghosts were—what people *wanted* to see, or were afraid to see . . . and after he died, the best hope I had, it sounds silly, was that I would go mad enough so that instead of waiting every day for him to come home from school and rattle the letter box I might actually have the illusion of seeing or hearing him come in. Because I can't stop my body and mind waiting, every day, every day, I can't let go. And his bedroom, sometimes at night I go in, I think I might just for a moment forget he *wasn't* in there sleeping, I think I would pay almost anything—anything at all—for a moment of seeing him like I used to. In his pyjamas, with his—his—his hair . . . ruffled, and, his . . . you said, his . . . that *smile.*

"When it happened, they got Noel, and Noel came in and shouted my name, like he did the other day, that's why I screamed, because it—seemed the same—and then they said, he is dead, and I thought coolly, *is* dead, that will go on and on and on till the end of time, it's a continuous present tense, one thinks the most ridiculous things, there I was thinking about grammar, the verb to be, when it ends to be dead . . . And then I came out into the garden, and I half saw, in my mind's eye, a kind of ghost of his face, just the eyes and hair, coming towards me—like every day waiting for him to come home, the way you think of your son, with such pleasure, when he's—not there—and I—I thought—no, I won't *see* him, because he is dead, and I won't dream about him because he is dead, I'll be rational and practical and continue to live because one must, and there was Noel . . .

"I got it wrong, you see, I was so *sensible,* and then I was so shocked because I couldn't get to want anything—I couldn't *talk* to Noel—I—I—made Noel take away, destroy, all the photos, I—didn't dream, you can will not to dream, I didn't . . . visit a grave, flowers, there isn't any point. I was so sensible. Only my body wouldn't stop waiting and all it wants is to—to see that boy. *That* boy. That boy you—saw."

He did not say that he might have seen another boy, maybe even a boy who had been given the tee shirts and jeans afterwards. He did not say, though the idea crossed his mind, that maybe what he had seen was some kind of impression from her terrible desire to see a boy where nothing was. The boy had had nothing terrible, no aura of pain about him: he had been, his memory insisted, such a pleasant, courteous, self-contained boy, with his own purposes. And in fact the woman herself almost immediately raised the possibility that what he had seen was what she desired to see, a kind of mix-up of radio waves, like when you overheard police messages on the radio, or got BBC One on a switch that said ITV. She was thinking fast, and went on almost immediately to say that perhaps his sense of loss, his loss of Anne, which was what had led her to feel she could bear his presence in her house, was what had brought them—dare she say—near enough, for their wavelengths to mingle, perhaps, had made him susceptible . . . You mean, he had said, we are a kind of emotional vacuum, between us, that must be filled. Something like that, she had said, and had added, "But I don't believe in ghosts."

Anne, he thought, could not be a ghost, because she was elsewhere, with someone else, doing for someone else those little things she had done so gaily for him, tasty little suppers, bits of research, a sudden vase of unusual flowers, a new bold shirt, unlike his own cautious taste, but suiting him, suiting him. In a sense, Anne was worse lost because voluntarily absent, an absence that could not be loved because love was at an end, for Anne.

"I don't suppose you will, now," the woman was saying. "I think talking would probably stop any—mixing of messages, if that's what it is, don't you? But—if—*if* he comes again"—and here for the first time her eyes were full of tears—"if—you must promise, you will *tell* me, you must promise."

He had promised, easily enough, because he was fairly sure she was right, the boy would not be seen again. But the next day he was on the lawn, nearer than ever, sitting on the grass beside the deck chair, his arms clasping his bent, warm brown knees, the thick, pale hair glittering in the sun. He was wearing a football shirt, this time, Chelsea's colours. Sitting down in the deck chair, the man could have put out a hand and touched him, but did not: it was not, it seemed, a possible gesture to make. But the boy looked up and smiled, with a pleasant complicity, as though they now understood each other very well. The man tried speech: he said, "It's nice to see you again," and the boy nodded acknowledgement of this remark, without speaking himself. This was the beginning of communication between them, or what the man supposed to be communication. He did not think of fetching the woman. He became aware that he was in some strange way *enjoying the boy's company.* His pleasant stillness—and he sat there all morning, occasionally lying back on the grass, occasionally staring thoughtfully at the house—was calming and comfortable. The man did quite a lot of work—wrote about three reasonable pages on Hardy's original air-blue gown—and looked up now and then to make sure the boy was still there and happy.

He went to report to the woman—as he had after all promised to do—that evening. She had obviously been waiting and hoping—her unnatural calm had given way to agitated pacing, and her eyes were dark and deeper in. At this point in the story he found in himself a necessity to bowdlerise for the sympathetic American, as he had indeed already begun to do. He had mentioned only a child who had "seemed like" the woman's lost son, and he now ceased to mention the child at all, as an actor in the story, with the result that what the American woman heard was a tale of how he, the man, had become increasingly involved in the woman's solitary grief, how their two losses had become a kind of *folie à deux* from which he could not extricate himself. What follows is not what he told the American girl, though it may be clear at which points the bowdlerised version coincided with what he really believed to have happened. There was a sense he could not at first analyse that it was improper to talk about the boy—not because he might not be believed; that did not come into it; but because something dreadful might happen.

"He sat on the lawn all morning. In a football shirt."

"Chelsea?"

"Chelsea."

"What did he do? Does he look happy? Did he speak?" Her desire to know was terrible.

"He doesn't speak. He didn't move much. He seemed—very calm. He stayed a long time."

"This is terrible. This is ludicrous. There *is no boy*."

"No. But I saw him."

"Why you?"

"I don't know." A pause. "I do *like* him."

"He is—was—a most likeable boy."

Some days later he saw the boy running along the landing in the evening, wearing what might have been pyjamas, in peacock towelling, or might have been a track suit. Pyjamas, the woman stated confidently, when he told her: his new pyjamas. With white ribbed cuffs, weren't they? and a white polo neck? He corroborated this, watching her cry—she cried more easily now—finding her anxiety and disturbance very hard to bear. But it never occurred to him that it was possible to break his promise to tell her when he saw the boy. That was another curious imperative from some undefined authority.

They discussed clothes. If there were ghosts, how could they appear in clothes long burned, or rotted, or worn away by other people? You could imagine, they agreed, that something of a person might linger—as the Tibetans and others believe the soul lingers near the body before setting out on its long journey. But clothes? And in this case so many clothes? I must be seeing your memories, he told her, and she nodded fiercely, compressing her lips, agreeing that this was likely, adding, "I am too rational to go mad, so I seem to be putting it on you."

He tried a joke. "That isn't very kind to me, to imply that madness comes more easily to me."

"No, sensitivity. I am insensible. I was always a bit like that, and this made it worse. I am the *last* person to see any ghost that was trying to haunt me."

"We agreed it was your memories I saw."

"Yes. We agreed. That's rational. As rational as we can be, considering."

All the same, the brilliance of the boy's blue regard, his gravely smiling salutation in the garden next morning, did not seem like anyone's tortured memories of earlier happiness. The man spoke to him directly then:

"Is there anything I can *do* for you? Anything you want? Can I help you?"

The boy seemed to puzzle about this for a while, inclining his head as though hearing was difficult. Then he nodded, quickly and perhaps urgently, turned, and ran into the house, looking back to make sure he was followed. The man entered the living room through the French windows, behind the running boy, who stopped for a moment in the centre of the room, with the man blinking behind him at the sudden transition from sunlight to comparative dark. The woman was sitting in an armchair, looking at nothing there. She often sat like that. She looked up, across the boy, at the man; and the boy, his face for the first time anxious, met the man's eyes again, asking, before he went out into the house.

"What is it? What is it? Have you seen him again? Why are you . . . ?"

"He came in here. He went—out through the door."

"I didn't see him."

"No."

"Did he—oh, this is so *silly*—did he see me?"

He could not remember. He told the only truth he knew.

"He brought me in here."

"Oh, what can I do, what am I going to *do?* If I killed myself—I have thought of that—but the idea that I should be with him is an illusion I . . . this silly situation is the nearest I shall ever get. To him. He was *in here with me*?"

"Yes."

And she was crying again. Out in the garden he could see the boy, swinging agile on the apple branch.

He was not quite sure, looking back, when he had thought he had realized what the boy had wanted him to do. This was also, at the party, his worst piece of what he called bowdlerisation, though in some sense it was clearly the opposite of bowdlerisation. He told the American girl that he had come to the conclusion that it was the woman herself who had wanted it, though there was in fact, throughout, no sign of her wanting anything except to see the boy, as she said. The boy, bolder and more frequent, had appeared several nights running on the landing, wandering in and out of bathrooms and bedrooms, restlessly, a little agitated, questing almost, until it had "come to" the man that what he required was to be reengendered, for him, the man, to give to his mother another child, into which he could peacefully vanish. The idea was so clear that it was like another imperative, though he did not have the courage to ask the child to confirm it. Possibly this was out of delicacy—the child was too young to be talked to about sex. Possibly there were other reasons. Possibly he was mistaken: the situation was making him hysterical, he felt action of some kind was required and must be possible. He could not spend the rest of the summer, the rest of his life, describing nonexistent tee shirts and blond smiles.

He could think of no sensible way of embarking on his venture, so in the end simply walked into her bedroom one night. She was lying there, reading; when she saw him her instinctive gesture was to hide, not her bare arms and throat, but her book. She seemed, in fact, quite unsurprised to see his pyjamaed figure, and, after she had recovered her coolness, brought out the book definitely and laid it on the bedspread.

"My new taste in illegitimate literature. I keep them in a box under the bed."

Ena Twigg, Medium. The Infinite Hive. The Spirit World. Is There Life After Death?

"Pathetic," she proffered.

He sat down delicately on the bed.

"Please, don't grieve so. Please, let yourself be comforted. Please . . ."

He put an arm round her. She shuddered. He pulled her closer. He asked why she had had only the one son, and she seemed to understand the purport of his question, for she tried, angular and chilly, to lean on him a little, she became apparently compliant. "No real reason," she assured him, no material reason. Just her husband's profession and lack of inclination: that covered it.

Perhaps, he suggested, if she would be comforted a little, perhaps she could hope, perhaps . . .

For comfort then, she said, dolefully, and lay back, pushing Ena Twigg off the bed with one fierce gesture, then lying placidly. He got in beside her, put his arms round her, kissed her cold cheek, thought of Anne, of what was never to be again. Come on, he said to the woman, you must live, you must try to live, let us hold each other for comfort.

She hissed at him, "Don't *talk*" between clenched teeth, so he stroked her lightly, over her nightdress, breasts and buttocks and long stiff legs, composed like an effigy on an Elizabethan tomb. She allowed this, trembling slightly, and then trembling violently: he took this to be a sign of some mixture of pleasure and pain, of the return of life to stone. He put a hand between her legs and she moved them heavily apart; he heaved himself over her and pushed, unsuccessfully. She was contorted and locked tight: frigid, he thought grimly, was not the word. Rigor mortis, his mind said to him, before she began to scream.

He was ridiculously cross about this. He jumped away and said quite rudely, "Shut up," and then ungraciously, "I'm sorry." She stopped screaming as suddenly as she had begun and made one of her painstaking economical explanations.

"Sex and death don't go. I can't afford to let go of my grip on myself. I hoped. What you hoped. It was a bad idea. I apologise."

"Oh, never mind," he said and rushed out again onto the landing, feeling foolish and almost in tears for warm, lovely Anne.

The child was on the landing, waiting. When the man saw him, he looked questioning, and then turned his face against the wall and leant there, rigid, his shoulders hunched, his hair hiding his expression. There was a similarity between woman and child. The man felt, for the first time, almost uncharitable towards the boy, and then felt something else.

"Look, I'm sorry. I tried. I did try. Please turn round."

Uncompromising, rigid, clenched back view.

"Oh well," said the man, and went into his bedroom.

So now, he said to the American woman at the party, I feel a fool, I feel embarrassed, I feel we are hurting, not helping each other, I feel it isn't a refuge. Of course you feel that, she said, of course you're right—it was temporarily necessary, it helped both of you, but you've got to live your life. Yes, he said, I've done my best, I've tried to get through, I have my life to live. Look, she said, I want to help, I really do, I have these wonderful friends I'm renting this flat from, why don't you come, just for a few days, just for a break, why don't you? They're real sympathetic people, you'd like them, I like them, you could get your emotions kind of straightened out. She'd probably be glad to see the back of you, she must feel as bad as you do, she's got to relate to her situation in her own way in the end. We all have.

He said he would think about it. He knew he had elected to tell the sympathetic American because he had sensed she would be—would offer—a way out. He had to get out. He took her home from the party and went back to his house and landlady without seeing her into her flat. They both knew that this reticence was promising—that he hadn't come in then, because he meant to come later. Her warmth and readiness were like sunshine, she was open. He did not know what to say to the woman.

In fact, she made it easy for him: she asked, briskly, if he now found it perhaps uncomfortable to stay, and he replied that he had felt he should move on, he was of so little use . . . Very well, she had agreed, and had added crisply that it had to be better for everyone if "all this" came to an end. He remembered the firmness with which she had told him that no illusions were pleasant. She was strong: too strong for her own good. It would take years to wear away that stony, closed, simply surviving insensibility. It was not his job. He would go. All the same, he felt bad.

He got out his suitcases and put some things in them. He went down to the garden, nervously, and put away the deck chair. The garden was empty. There were no voices over the wall. The silence was thick and deadening. He wondered, knowing he would not see the boy again, if anyone else would do so, or if, now he was gone, no one would describe a tee shirt, a sandal, a smile, seen, remembered, or desired. He went slowly up to his room again.

The boy was sitting on his suitcase, arms crossed, face frowning and serious. He held the man's look for a long moment, and then the man went and sat on his bed. The boy continued to sit. The man found himself speaking.

"You do see I have to go? I've tried to get through. I can't get through. I'm no use to you, am I?"

The boy remained immobile, his head on one side, considering. The man stood up and walked towards him.

"Please. Let me go. What are we, in this house? A man and a woman and a child, and none of us can get through. You can't want that?"

He went as close as he dared. He had, he thought, the intention of putting his hand on or through the child. But could not bring himself to feel there was no boy. So he stood, and repeated,

"I can't get through. Do you want me to stay?"

Upon which, as he stood helplessly there, the boy turned on him again the brilliant, open, confiding, beautiful desired smile.

SUGAR

Vom Vater hab' ich die Statur
Des Lebens ernstes Führen;
Von Mütterchen die Frohnatur
Die Lust zu fabulieren.
Urahnherr war der Schönsten hold
Das spukt so hin und wieder;
Urahnfrau liebte Schmuck und Gold
Das zuckt wohl durch die Glieder.
Sind nun die Elemente nicht
Aus dem Complex zu trennen
Was ist denn an dem ganzen Wicht
Original zu nennen?

—GOETHE

My mother had a respect for truth, but she was not a truthful woman. She once said to me, her lip trembling, her eyes sharp to detect my opinion, "Your father says I am a terrible liar. But I'm not a liar, am I? I'm not." Of course she was not, I agreed, colluding, as we all always did, for the sake of peace and of something else, a half-desire to help her, for things to be as she said they were. But she was. She lied in small matters, to tidy up embarrassments, and in larger matters, to avoid unpalatable truths. She lied floridly and beautifully, in her rare moments of relaxation, to make a story better. She was a breathless and breathtaking raconteur, not often, and sometimes overinsistently, but at her best reducing her audience to tears of helpless laughter. She also told other kinds of story, all the time latterly, all the time we were in her company, monotonous, malevolent, unstructured plaints, full of increasingly fabricated evidence of nonexistent wickedness. But that is another matter. I did not set out to write about that. I set out to write about my grandfather. About my paternal grandfather, whom I hardly knew, and about whom I know very little.

When my father was dying, I came into his hospital room once, and he sat up against his pillows and looked at me out of his father's face. I had never thought of them as being alike. My father was a handsome man, in a very English way, blue-eyed, fair-skinned, with fine red-gold hair that very slowly lost its fire and turned rusty and then white. He had quite a lot of it still left when he died, very lively silvery hair, floating. He had a wide, straight, decisive mouth. None of these words recall him. His father, my grandfather, never had any hair that I can remember, and had heavy cheeks and a fuller, more petulant mouth. It occurred to me for the first time, seeing his face in my father's, to wonder if his hair had been red. He had had six children, of whom my father was the youngest, all of whom had the fiery hair. My grandmother, I am fairly sure, was dark brown. I did not tell my father that I had seen this semblance, partly because it vanished when he spoke, partly because I thought of it as unflattering, having as a small child seen my grandfather as someone off-putting, stout and old. The old were old in my early childhood, in the war years: there was an absolute barrier. My father never came to seem old as my grandfather was, though he was seventy-seven when he died. At the time when I saw my grandfather in him he must have had about three months left to live. He was, by accident, in hospital in Amsterdam. It was a spotless and civilised hospital, full of seriously gentle doctors and nurses all of whom spoke an English more perfect than might have been found in any hospital at home. My father disliked his dependence and they made it decorous for him. Whilst he was there, which was several weeks, we all, my sisters and brother and I, visited him. The visiting hours were long, most of the afternoon and evening, and for most of this time on most of these days, he talked to us. All my life, I had held it against him that he never talked to us. He worked with steady concentration, long long hours, and was often away on circuit. During my early childhood, when his parents were alive, he had been away altogether, in the Air Force, in the Mediterranean, in the war. He was called back from the Nuremberg trials to his father's deathbed, or so my mother had always said. What exactly he was doing there, if indeed he was there, I have never heard and cannot imagine. In those weeks in Amsterdam he talked a great deal, about his father, about his mother, about his childhood, as he had never done. I don't know if he realised how very little he had ever said. He was a silent man but by no means a cold or distant man, not as you might think of a distant man, if you read that word, immediately.

He was a judge. When I say that of him, I do not think of him as sitting in judgment. I think of him as a man with an unwavering instilled respect for evidence, for truth, for justice. When he delivered moral opinions, you could see that he was of his generation, time and place, a good man, a Yorkshireman, ambitious to better himself, aware, largely from outside, of social discriminations and niceties of class, a late-convinced Quaker, a socialist-turned-social-democrat. I respected his moral opinions, I share most of them, I am his child. But more than these opinions I respect in him his wish to be exact, a kind of abstract need which is somehow the essence of virtue. You might say, love is the essence of virtue. We were very inhibited people. Even my mother, with her indisciplined rush of speech, fantasy, embarrassing candour, endless barbed outrage, even my mother was essentially inhibited in that sense. We didn't know how to talk about love. But truthfulness, yes. All those weeks, he kept looking at what was happening, with his respect for evidence. Once, towards the end, it faltered a little. He argued quite fiercely about the inexactness of the terms benign and malignant. All growths are malignant, he said, if they are hurting you, if they are engrossing themselves at your expense. I could see he knew what he was doing, playing with words; his eyes were not taking his speech seriously. His father died of cancer of the prostate, or so my mother said. During this curious excursus about these adjectives he said, as though I knew, which I didn't, that when he had had "that growth" removed from his own prostate some years ago it had been entered on his record as "benign." "What do they mean, benign?" he said cunningly, deliberately confusing himself, looking at me to see if I too could be confused. By the time of this conversation he was back in London. I think he had been told what his expectations were. They were then in fact a bare three weeks, though I believed, and he may have believed, that he still had many months, maybe a year. He was partly being kind to me too, confusing us both. He thought at that time a great deal about his father's death. He told me once, I am now almost sure that it was he who told me and not my mother, that his father's sufferings had been terrible. My father did not die of cancer of the prostate, nor even, as far as we can tell, of the wholly unsuspected voracious lymphoma whose cells the Dutch surgeons had discovered in the fluids drained from him in the coronary ward to which he was taken after collapsing in Schiphol Airport from the heart disease which he knew very well he had. He did not suffer in his father's way.

It was his father's death that was one of the main points of dispute in his relations with my mother, during their last troubled years. I am nearly sure it was this dispute that gave rise to the direct accusation of lying which so distressed my mother. She had always maintained that she had been present at my grandfather's deathbed; she had been present, she led us to suppose, at the moment of his death. The events of my grandfather's passing, the family intrigues and stresses, the testamentary injustices only righted by the hurried return of my father, the lawyer, were one of my mother's best tales. They had become part of my own shaky sense of my origins, a kind of Dickensian melodrama of which my mother had been a brisk and humane witness and my father a practical hero. I had a vision of this scene derived largely from Victorian novels and a little from my infant memories of my grandfather's house, huge, bleak, dark, polished, and gauntly uncomfortable. It all took place, in my imagination, in a kind of burnt umber light, thick and brown. Various surrounding persons wore frilled and starched caps and aprons over black stuff dresses. There was a carafe and a finely etched water glass on a bedside cupboard and my shrunk bald grandfather in a huge mound of feather pillows and mattresses, suffering an ultimate drowsiness of too much painkiller and mortal weakness. The brown light drifted like heavy dust. I do not know where this vision came from: not from my mother, though it was indissolubly connected to her eyewitness narrative. In his last years my father maintained more and more stubbornly and acrimoniously that this account was a fabrication, that only he himself had been present, that my mother had kept well away. He adduced her behaviour during other family disasters and crises, and the evidence was on his side. My mother had a terror of direct confrontation with grief and pain. She avoided her own mother's dying; she did not attend her grandson's funeral. Nor did she come to Amsterdam. She affected to believe that this crisis was temporary and inconvenient. I have no idea what she thought in her heart. In any case, my father's evidence seemed on all logical grounds almost wholly preferable. It was just that I discovered, during those weeks in Amsterdam, that I needed an idea of the past, of those long-dead grandparents, and that the idea I had, which was derived from my mother's accounts, was not to be trusted and bore no very clear relation to truth or reality. It was also clear that my father, during those last weeks, was trying to form a just and generous idea of his own father, whom he had fought, at a cost to both of them. So his account had also its bias.

Perhaps I should now set out the elements of the family myth derived from my mother's accounts of my father's family. These accounts are dyed with her own perpetual anxiety as to whether she herself was, in the last resort, acceptable or unacceptable to them. Also by her own most necessary, most comfortable myth that she herself had represented to my father a human normality, a domestic warmth, an ease of communion quite absent from the chill household and extravagant passions amongst which he had grown up. As a small girl I believed what I was told, including this myth, despite having lived for months with my querulous and cross maternal grandmother, despite daily exhibitions of my mother's frustration and rage.

The idea she gave me of the family in Conisborough is skeletal and discontinuous. She liked to tell the same few exemplary episodes over and over: the strange behaviour of my grandmother with the teapot, my own first wintry visit to the dark Blythe House, the never-quite-explained indifference or aloofness of my father's family to my parents' wedding. She faltered in telling this, and I think told differing versions, in some of which my paternal grandfather attended briefly and in some not at all. Something had hurt her badly, and when my mother was hurt to the quick the narrative power became disjunct, the odd sentence failed to reach its verb and died on a question mark. The hero of the wedding story was her own father, a red-whiskered, extravagantly open workingman who had done her proud and had also in some way been hurt, or so I deduce. I remember that grandfather well, my only relation given to loud laughter, practical jokes, and a disrespect for reticence. He was kind and frightening, and ambitious for his daughters in a practical way, though admitting to a regret that he had no vigorous, mechanically minded son.

The central figure of the Conisboro' family was in one sense my grandfather, who is presented as a Victorian despot, purblind to the feelings of his wife and children, wholly devoted to his business which was the manufacture and sale of boiled sweets. He seems to have spent no time in the company of his six children, and to have had no thought for their future other than that they should be incorporated, in due course, into the family business, which was their life. My grandmother, a devout Methodist, was characterised, always, by both my parents, as "a saint." My mother went in considerable awe of her, though she would also utter witty and disparaging comments on her ungainly housekeeping, and imply that they had, in the end, come to love and respect each other. The eldest son, my uncle Barnet, was crippled at birth, and spent his twenty-nine years confined to a wheelchair. My grandmother, my mother said, had devoted herself wholly to this helpless son, "did everything for him herself," insisted on lifting and changing and pushing even when her strength was unequal to it. As a result, my mother implied, the other five were neglected, were, in her phrase, "left to drag themselves up as best they might." They were all, also, my mother claimed, extraordinarily gifted, intelligent, creative, vital, stunted, apart from my father, by my grandfather's incapacity to imagine that education conferred any benefits, or that any life other than the making of boiled sweets could possibly be desirable. They went to the local grammar school, where my mother indeed met my father, in the eleven-plus intake. From there they were removed as early as possible, given, in my mother's phrase, "any *material* thing they desired" and set to work for the sugar-boiling.

Barnet, Arthur, Gladys, Sylvia, Lucy, and Freddie, who was my father. I met some of them, extremely briefly, though not Barnet and Sylvia. They are not part of my life, only of stories and sharp pictures, which, if they have anything in common, have the idea of furious energy, unmanaged passion, thwarted and gone to waste. The Arthur I saw I associate with thick carpets and golf clubs: the Arthur of the myth wanted to live dangerously, was a skilled pilot, a motorcycle speedway racer in the Isle of Man, a volunteer rear gunner in the First War. He flew, my mother said, round Conisborough Castle, a gloomy circular ruined tower, visible in my childish imagination from the upper windows of Blythe House. I see him roaring and dipping, looping the loop and circling, watched by the redheaded siblings envying the brief speed and freedom. The only other thing I know about Arthur is the manner of his death. This story is my father's, unusually. He had a heart attack from which he recovered, assumed, without evidence, that he had an undivulged cancer and a short life expectancy, and went out, belatedly, to live dangerously again, thus precipitating another heart attack and a fatal collision with the back of a stationary bus. "Wine, women, and song," my father said darkly, partly shocked by his brother's failure to examine the evidence properly, partly envious of the extravagance. Arthur never left Conisboro' and the boiled sweets, however. I remember him red and solid and a little bluff. I remember a resemblance to his father.

Gladys married young, and briefly, because she had to, my mother said. She married a coal miner and divorced him with considerable firmness once the immediate need for respectability was past. My mother did not expatiate on Gladys, whom she clearly disliked. I can't remember how old I was when she first told me these few facts—old enough to have read some Lawrence as well as suffering *Jane Eyre,* old enough to imagine a romantic red-haired girl in a long serge skirt running through fields, hiding behind hedges, with courage and fear, to a place of secret and absolute emotion. I see always a dry stone wall and grey-green, slightly sooty Yorkshire hill grass. This imagination was daunted by my incapacity to connect this girl with the wild, ageing aunt who visited us briefly, in Sheffield, when I was thirteen, and presented us with two huge, pink-cheeked, rose-pouting, lace-frilled dolls in cellophane-covered boxes, and a diverse and lavish set of manicuring tools in a soft red leather case. My mother made this transient visitor most unwelcome and she never came again. My mother in fact hated any incursion by any guest into her fenced and indomitably comfortable domestic territory. I remember them sitting at tea, on two corners of the dining table, my mother's mouth pinched with disapproval and distaste. My aunt was large and alarming. She wore an odd hat, which I have re-created as a bright purple silken turban, though I think that is my invention, and had a great unruly mass of wiry gingery hair and very pale sharp blue eyes, close to the sides of a prominent beaked nose. My mother poured tea, and waited very obviously for the visit to be over. My aunt began various jerky speeches which trailed away; her movements were abrupt and awkward. After she had gone, my mother spoke with concentrated and sharply expressed distaste of the vulgarity and unnecessary extravagance of the silly presents. It was only this year that my younger sister told me that she had found the dolls magical and beautiful. Later, this aunt spent several years in a caravan perched on the North Yorkshire coast. I remember my father's alarm when the radio reported that part of these cliffs had been swept away, perhaps in the terrible storms of 1953. I remember him going north to sort out some trouble in which she had threatened a neighbour with a garden fork. She was, my mother said, "quite mad." Certainly she died after some years in a mental hospital. My father went to visit her, during her last years, and reported that she failed to recognise him. He never I think described her, or her acts, to me, except during those last null years, when he would say sadly that it made you wonder what it was all for. I found her story hopeful and exciting, against the evidence. What I was afraid of, in the days when I first learned about her, was the "normal," the respectable, the quotidian domesticity which my mother claimed to be happiness, suffered with savage resentment, and exacted payment for, from those she cared for.

My grandfather's two youngest children carried out acts of considered rebellion and escape. My mother's favourite tale, apart from the tale of the teapot perhaps, was the tale of my father's act of severance. She herself, a girl from the working class, from a back-to-back house with no inside plumbing, but supported by her father, had won unprecedented scholarships to Cambridge, where she went in what I imagine as a frail tremor of intellectual will and unimaginable social terror to read English. Her Cambridge was the Earthly Paradise and the Queen of Hearts' garden of arbitrary obstacles and disgraces rolled into one. Until she died she went over and over moments of solecism she had too late detected in those years. She dreamed at least yearly, perhaps more often, that she was to be forced to resit her finals with no warning, and consequently to be exposed as a fraud. My father, who was, my mother acknowledged, the only student in her year who did better than she did in exams, had been briskly removed from school by his father to become a commercial traveller in boiled sweets. My mother said that this was a black time of his life, and that he became very ill, frightening his mother once or twice by fainting into the coal bucket. The "into" was part of her graphic style. As a little girl I had a clear vision of his pale limbs somehow telescoped and contracted into this dirty receptacle, like a discarded dead root, though I think now that he was probably trying to lift it, that the blood ran to his head. I knew exactly where this coal bucket stood in Blythe House. It stood on the threshold between the kitchen and the cellar, whose dark door led into a frightening blackness I remember stepping nervously back from. I must have been three. The coal bucket can never have been there, but I associate the two blacknesses, the fear of uncontrolled falling. My mother said my father would never afterwards talk about this time. In Amsterdam he did, a little, half-apologizing to some unseen presence for the great trouble he had caused by his mixture of deviousness and distress. He had worked, my mother said, secretly and alone and late at night, unknown to his father, to take the Cambridge entrance exam, had saved and skimped every penny of what she called his "pocket money" and he later, in the hospital, called "my wages" and had finally won an exhibition to read law. So he had confronted his father, and had explained that he had saved, from this allowance, enough money for his first year's fees and lodging, and that he meant now to go to Cambridge, because that was what he wanted to do.

The end of this tale always puzzled my imagination. My grandfather, my mother said, had been filled with pride and delight at this announcement, and had "fallen upon your father's neck"—an unlikely motion, I always thought, in that portly and rigid trunk. I think now the phrase derives from the good father's reception of the Prodigal Son, but that is confusing, for my grandfather's hypothetical embrace welcomed revolt and prodigality. In any case, my mother said, Pa had immediately put £1,000 into my father's bank, in order that he should live comfortably at Cambridge. No sentence of my grandfather's speech was recorded in my mother's account of this episode, which, although dramatically delightful, causes problems about his nature, and the true nature of his unreasonable rigidity and his children's incapacity to communicate with him. How could they have had no inkling that he would have been proud or pleased? Was he capricious? Stubborn? Easily enraged? Had his children ever tried to explain to him what they wanted or hoped for? Had they inherited from my saintly grandmother an expectation of self-denial and strict obedience which precluded any attempt at dialogue? Was he formidable, was he wrathful, was he stony, was he emotional? No one has told me, I do not know anything about him. My father said, "Pa tried to do the best for us according to his lights, but he couldn't conceive of things outside his business." Where did it all come from then, the drive, the ambition, the passions of his offspring? I associate him with Dombey, if only because I think my father did. He once said that Dickens's observation of Florence Dombey was a miracle, that a child neglected and passed over and denigrated does indeed become more and more self-critical, more anxious to please, to find authority reasonable. But he himself did not submit for long. He went to Cambridge, and did well, and had tea in punts with my pretty and fragile mother.

The story of Lucy parallels that of my father, in some ways. This again is my mother's version. At some point my grandfather had sent Lucy and Sylvia on a world cruise, for what reason my mother did not say, though she made it clear that in her view a world cruise was a poor substitute for higher education and some degree of financial independence. Lucy had been ravished by the open spaces and free life of Australia during this journey. It was an idea that at second-hand moved my father, too. When I was myself sitting Cambridge entrance and he a very successful junior barrister, or perhaps during the first slacker year after he took silk, he found time to write a thick, escapist novel, in which the hero moved from the dark, dirty, and dangerous world of Sheffield steel mills to a land of clear, clean deserts and great flocks of wheeling, pearly parrakeets. He threatened occasionally to emigrate. It was his generation's dream in the years of austerity and the choking class structure and battle fatigue. Lucy did in fact carry out this postwar dream, appearing one morning at breakfast in Blythe House to announce that she and a young woman friend had passages booked to sail that very day. "That very day" is my mother's contribution, and perhaps suspect, but the tale is the same. My grandfather could only tolerably be dealt with by faits accomplis. His reactions to this announcement are not known to me. Lucy went to a life of violin playing and the breeding of Airedales. In the early years of his retirement my father went out to see the deserts for himself and came back troubled about the corruption of the aborigines by alcohol, and perhaps a little lowered, as a man is whose dream vision has been replaced by a solid and limited reality. I was glad he never emigrated for I early developed a passion for languages, and thus for Europe. My father died European, despite his vision of deserts, as a direct consequence of a journey up the Rhine, which he thought over, as he sat in his high Dutch hospital room, talking to the Humanist visitor about the novels of Conrad and Charlotte Brontë she brought him, and to a young surgeon about the kinds of hawk planing over the roofs which were all he could see. "It was civilised," he said with satisfaction, of his last painful venture. He described cranes and herons and castles and the moonlit water. And his own defeat by a brief climb from mooring place to town centre. He was also a good raconteur, not like my mother, deliberate, weighing his words, judicious, telling you some things and holding others back.

When did my mother first tell me the story of Sylvia? I must have been too young to be told it, whenever it was, for I remember it as my first absolute confirmation that my mother's myth was untrue, that the hearth's warmth did not keep off the cold blast, that there was no safety. Before, I thought there were two sorts of people in the world, those to whom terrible things happened, as in books and the news, and those condemned to the protection of normality and the threat of boredom and custom. I believe my mother told me this story in the war itself, in Pontefract, where she kept house miserably whilst my father was away, except for a brief period of anxious and exalted activity when she taught English to grammar school boys. I loved her then. She talked to me about subjects and predicates, Tennyson and Browning, the Lady of Shalott, and not about household dirt and failures of attentiveness. I should already have known about uncertainty. I was a gloomy child and was in my secret soul certain that my father would never return from wherever he had abruptly vanished to, his red hair shorn, hung around with canvas buckets and kitbags under his ugly folded blue cap. There was a boy, too, at school, who died one night of diabetes. I remember being distressed that I couldn't really *know* he was dead, that everything went on just as if this wasn't so. Perhaps I only really learned about Sylvia later, but associate the learning with these other losses. Sylvia had fallen in love, on that fated world cruise, with someone whom my mother described as a "remittance man" in South Africa. They had married, and my grandfather had provided for them by offering them a workman's cottage he owned, in Conisboro'. There was a child, another Sylvia, who was, I believe, more or less my own age. They were very unhappy. The remittance man, according to my mother, was "very cold. Pa didn't understand. He came from a warm country. He was desperately cold." My saintly grandmother visited, furtively my mother managed to imply, with blankets and hot soup. She provided these also for the local poor. Quite what happened to the remittance man I never dared to ask. As a little girl I thought the word meant that he was somehow provisional and not to be considered. Perhaps he went home, to the hot sun and the gold mines and his life before the incursion of my tragic aunts. I have given him, in my imagination, the features of a South African novelist I know, thoughtful, considerate, secretive, withdrawn. When I was little I saw him as a Gilded Youth, in a boater.

At some point in her own history, and certainly when I was only just born, Sylvia killed both herself and her small daughter. I know this, because I inherited certain toys belonging to this destroyed cousin. There was a dog, or nightdress-case, zipped, furry, black and white, and peaceably couchant, whom I loved for years before I discovered his provenance. And after. I remember with terrible courage shouting, when some clearance of outgrown toys was proposed, "You can't throw Wops away. He was Sylvia's." Knowing I did not know what this sentence meant to them, using it to save my dog, shamed. "Your father smoked terribly for two years after Sylvia died," my mother said once. This at least explained why he, who never smoked, owned a chased silver cigarette case. I could not imagine his feelings. My mother had reduced her accounts of Sylvia to various manageable dicta. Sylvia, she gave the impression, was the most gifted of the gifted gaggle. She could have done all sorts of things, my mother said, and always added, "It was like putting a racehorse to draw a milk cart." She said also, scornfully, "She was no housewife, she had no idea." I imagined a hutlike house, stone-floored, coal-fired, with barely room to turn round in. There must, however, have been a gas oven. I think I took Sylvia's fate as a warning against both brilliance and sexual passion. My father used to be partly amused, but ultimately more alarmed, by any evidence of extravagant passions in his daughters. He was a romantically-minded man, and believed that the first lover is always the most important. He was a virtuous man, and was, it seems clear, steadfastly faithful to my mother. He spoke of his brother Arthur, in Amsterdam, with a kind of mild envy. He felt he had always been too cautious. "When I come before my Maker," he said, sipping the glass of wine the doctors, despairing of cure, had permitted him, "which I do not expect will happen, I shall have to beg him to forgive me my virtues." My mother said he had learned from the others' disasters, he had learned to be careful and to value security and domestic peace.

My mother's accounts of my grandmother's selflessness were like pearls, or sugar-coated pills, grit and bitterness polished into roundness by comedy and my mother's worked-upon understanding of my grandmother's real meaning. Whilst I cannot remember any quoted instance of my grandfather's speech I can remember various sayings of my grandmother, including her welcome of my infant self, on my first visit. There she stood on the doorstep, my mother said, rigid and doubtful—I imagine it for some reason taking place on a snowy evening, in the early dark. She did not say, how lovely to see you, or let me see the baby, or come in and get warm, but "It hardly seems worth the trouble of all that packing just to come here. Babies are always best in their own house, I think." My mother would always add a long explanation of this ungraciousness—my grandmother was genuinely self-deprecating, she was very well aware of the real trouble of transporting a baby with all her equipment, she was thanking my mother for having made the effort. The grit inside the pearly sugarcoating was a fear of rejection by both women, perhaps. "I nearly just turned round and went home," my mother always said, and always added, "but it was just her manner, she meant very well, really." And "she was really very fond of me, she came to see me as a daughter, I was a favourite." The famous teapot story is another such instance. It took place, I think, in the war, during petrol rationing. My grandmother was driven over by the chauffeur, from Conisboro' to Sheffield, to take tea with my mother and to see another baby. She sat briefly, talking to my mother. But when offered tea, she stood up abruptly and said no, no thank you, she had stayed too long, she must get back to pour my grandfather's tea for him, he expected it. My mother's emphasis in this story was on the childish helplessness of my grandfather, who, with a houseful of servants, could not stretch out a hand and lift his own teapot. My grandmother's formidable manner and her excessive dutifulness were part of each other, in my mother's vision, a kind of folly of decorum in which the result was the rejection of my own mother's carefully prepared tea and cakes. "All that way, and the petrol, and the chauffeur's time, wasted just to pour a cup of tea," my mother would say scornfully and yet with fear. This story runs into the story of my grandmother's death. Even in her last illness, my mother would say, when she was weak and in great pain, my grandfather would not allow her to sleep alone in a spare bedroom. She gave the impression, my mother, of the elderly man howling like a lost child, "creating" on landings until my grandmother wearily "dragged herself" downstairs again, to his side. "He couldn't sleep without her," my mother said. And "he had no consideration." This inarticulate crying out is the only image of his speech I have. I see him pacing in an improbable nightshirt, beside himself. My mother's contempt for male helplessness was edged with savagery. This operated even during my father's last illness, which she persisted in seeing as a fantasy and a betrayal, which could have been better handled. Her original announcement of his collapse included the authoritative and unfounded assertion that he'd be perfectly all right in a day or two, there was no need for anyone to bother. Her account of my grandmother's death is riddled with doubt, but I have nothing else certain to hold, or imagine, my father never got round to telling his version of that story, so the enraged and frantically obtuse old man persists in my memory.

I had almost forgotten what was perhaps her favourite tale, the perfect example of the fecklessness and neglect to which my father, before he found her, had been subject. Two of the sisters—she was never quite sure which—Gladys and Sylvia, Sylvia and Lucy—had gone out into the fields to play, taking with them the baby, my father, whom they had put, for safety, into a horse trough and had wholly forgotten, returning without him, remembering his whereabouts only when, many hours later, my grandmother asked where he was. The child had been discovered, my mother said, by searchers, lying half in and half out of the water in the stone trough, as the dark fell, quite abandoned. She always affected to find this story amusing, and always instilled into it a very understandable note of bitter indignation against everyone, the girls, the mother, the father, the state of affairs that could allow this to happen. When my father returned to it in Amsterdam it was with a kind of Arcadian pleasure. "We ran wild," he said with retrospective delight, "we had so few restrictions, we had each other and the fields and the stables—we had an amazingly free childhood, we ran wild." His little room in the Dutch hospital was warmly lit, for a hospital room. He had bad days when he huddled under the blankets and shivered with final cold. He had good days when he sat up and talked about the world of his childhood, the pony and trap, the taste of real fresh bread, the journeys they made in the pony trap to the races and came back in the dusk singing all together, the poems they wrote, the amazing variety of wildflowers there then were. "I grew up before the motorcar," he said. "You won't really be able to imagine. It was a world of horses. Everything smelled, rather pleasantly, of horses. The milk was fresh and tasty. There were real apples and plums."

During those weeks, during that unaccustomed talking, which despite everything was pleasant and civilised, as he meant it to be, he did try to construct a tale, a myth, a satisfactory narrative of his life. He talked about what it was like to be part of a generation twice disrupted by world war; he talked about his own ambitions, and more generally about how he had noticed that it was harder for those who felt they had achieved nothing to die. He talked above all about his childhood and particularly, perhaps, though not illuminatingly, about his father. He talked of how his aunt Flora's coffin had been refused houseroom, even for a night, by relatives who disapproved of her religious views. He knew he was dying. He had set out because he sensed he was very ill. But we were told before him, and more specifically, how fast and of what he was dying. He was surprised about the cancer. "I had no idea," he said to me, with a kind of grave amusement at having been caught out in ignorance, ignoring evidence. "It never occurred to me that that was what they were worried about." And, on another occasion, casually, but with a certain natural rhetorical dignity that was part of him, "You mustn't think I mind. I've nothing to regret and I feel I've come to the end. Don't misunderstand me—no doubt in the near future there will be moments of panic and terror. But you mustn't think I mind." He said that for my sake, but he was a truthful man. He was already steeling himself against the panic and terror, which were in the event much briefer and more cramped than we then supposed.

He had often said before, though he didn't repeat it, at least to me, during those weeks, that a man's children are his true and only immortality. As a girl I had been made uncomfortable by that idea. I craved separation. "Each man is an island" was my version of a delightful if melancholy truth. I was like Auden's version of Prospero's rejecting brother, Antonio, "By choice myself alone." But during those extreme weeks in Amsterdam I thought about origins. I thought about my grandfather. I thought also about certain myths of origin which I had pieced together in childhood, to explain things that were important, my sense of northernness, my fear of art, the promised end. By a series of elaborate coincidences two of these had become inextricably involved in what was happening. The first was the Norse Ragnarök, and the second was Vincent Van Gogh.

We went to see the *Götterdämmerung,* in Covent Garden, on the last night of my father's doomed Rhine journey. I had a bad cough, which embarrassed me. Now whenever I cough I see Gunter and Gutrune like proto-Nazis in their heavy palace beside the broad and glittering artificial water, and think as I thought then, as I always think, when I think of the 1930s, of my father in those first years of my life knowing and fearing what was coming, appalled by appeasement, volunteering for the RAF. When I was clearing his things I found a copy of the "Speech Delivered in the Reichstag, April 28th 1939, by Adolf Hitler, Führer and Chancellor." It was stored in a box of family photographs, the only thing in there that was not a photograph, as though it was an intimate part of our family history. At the time, because I was thinking about islands, I remember very clearly thinking about the similarities and dissimilarities between Prospero and Wotan. I thought, in the red dark, that the nineteenth-century Allfather, compared to the Renaissance rough magician, was enclosed in Victorian family claustrophobia, was essentially, by extension, a social being, though both had broken rods. When Fricka berated Wotan, I thought with pleasure of my father, proceeding slowly and freely along the great river.

My favourite book, the book which set my imagination working, as a small child in Pontefract in the early years of the war, was *Asgard and the Gods: Tales and Traditions of Our Northern Ancestors.* 1880. It was illustrated with steel engravings, of Wodan's Wild Hunt, of Odin tied between two fires, his face threatening and beautiful, of Ragnarök, the Last Battle, with Surtur with his flaming head, come out of Muspelheim, the gaping Fenris Wolf about to destroy Odin himself, Thor thrusting his shield-arm into the maw of the risen sea-serpent Jörmungander. I remember the shock of reading about the Last Battle in which all the heroes, all the gods, were destroyed forever. It had not until then occurred to me that a story could end like that. Though I had suspected that real life might, my expectations were gloomy. I found it exciting. I knew *Asgard* backwards before my mother told me about Sylvia, that is certain. I remember sitting in church, listening to the story of Joseph and his coat of many colours and thinking that this story was no different from the stories in *Asgard* and less moving than they were. I remember going on to think that Ragnarök seemed "truer" than the Resurrection. After Ragnarök, a very tentative, new, vegetable world began a new cycle, washed clean of blood and fire and gold. I may, I see now, rereading the book as I still do, have been influenced in these childish steps in literary theory and the Higher Criticism by the tone of the authors of *Asgard,* who rationalise Balder and Hodur into summer and winter, who turn giants into mountain ranges and Odin's wrath to wild weather, and who talk about the superior truths illustrated by the beautiful Christian stories. They are not Frazer, equating all gods gleefully with trees, but they set you on course for him. I identified Our Northern Ancestors in my mind with my father's family, wild, extravagant, stony, large, and frightening. They were something of which I was part. They were serious gods, as the Greeks, with their love affairs and capriciousness, were not. The book was, however, not my father's, but my mother's, bought as a crib for the Ancient Icelandic and Old Norse which formed an obligatory part of her degree course. I can't remember if she gave it to me to read, or if I found it. I do remember that she fed the hunger for reading, there was always a book and another book and another. She never underestimated what we could take. She was not kind to her children as social beings, she screamed at invited friends, she felt and communicated extremes of nervous terror. But to readers she was generous and resourceful. I knew she had been the kind of child I was, speechless and a reader. I knew.

It was with my mother, on the other hand, that the Van Gogh myth originated. Her family name had a Dutch shape and sound to it. Her family came, in part, from the Potteries, from the Five Towns, and a myth had grown up, with no foundation in evidence, that they were descended from Dutch Huguenots, who came here in the time of William the Silent, practical, warm, Protestant, hardworking craftsmen, with a buried and secret artistic strain. This Dutch quality was a kind of *Gemütlichkeit,* the quality with which my mother had hoped to warm and mitigate the wuthering and chill of my father's upbringing. In Sheffield, after the war, we had various reproductions of paintings by Vincent Van Gogh around our sitting room wall. There was one of the bridges at Arles, one of the sunnier ones, where the water is aquamarine and women are peacefully spreading washing. There were the boats on the beach at Les Saintes-Maries de la Mer, which I recognised with shock when I went there eight years later. There was a young man in a hat and yellow jacket whom I now know to have been the son of Roulin, the postman, and there was a Zouave in full oriental trousers and red fez, sitting on a bench on a floor whose perspective rose dizzily and improperly towards him. There were also two Japanese prints and what I think now must have been a print of Vermeer's *Little Street* in the Rijksmuseum, a housefront of great peace and steadiness, with a bending woman in a passageway on the left. I always, from the very earliest, associated these working women in Dutch streets with my mother. I associated the secret inwardness of the houses, de Hooch's houses even more than Vermeer's, with my mother's domestic myth, necessary tasks carried out in clear light, in their own confined but meaningful spaces. In my memory, I have superimposed a de Hooch on the Vermeer, for I remember in the picture a small blond Dutch child, with a cap and serious expression, close to the woman's skirts, who is my small blond self, gravely paying attention, as my mother would have liked. The Sheffield house, in whose sitting room these images were deployed, was one of a pair of semi-detached houses purchased as a wedding present for my father by his father, who could never, clearly, do things by halves, who thought, rightly, it would be an investment. We left one of these houses for Pontefract, during the war, for fear of bombs, and came back to the other. At the period when I most clearly remember the Van Goghs and the Vermeer/de Hooch the second house was in a state of renovation and redecoration. My grandfather had died, various large and dignified pieces of furniture had come to be fitted in, and there was money to spend on wallpapers and curtains. I remember one very domestic one, a kind of blush pink with regular cream dots on it, a sugar-sweet paper that my parents repeatedly expressed themselves surprised to like, and about which I was never sure. In my memory, the Van Goghs hang tamed on this delicately suburban ground, but in fact they cannot have done so. I am almost sure that paper was in the dining room, where my aunt Gladys was flustered by my enraged and aproned mother. In any case my earliest acquaintance with the paintings was as pleasantly light decoration round a three-piece suite. This was part of what he meant his work to be, sensuous pleasure for everyone. When did I discover differently? Certainly before I myself went to Arles, before Cambridge, in the 1950s, and saw that tortured and aspiring cypresses were exact truths, of their kind. When my father collapsed at Schiphol I was writing a novel in which the idea of Van Gogh stalked in and out of a text about puritanical northern domesticity. There was nowhere I would rather have found myself than the Van Gogh museum in Amsterdam. I was reading and rereading his letters. He wrote about the Dutch painters and their capacity to paint darkness, to paint the brightness of black. He wrote about the hunger for light, and about how his "northern brains" in that clear, heavy, sulphur yellow southern light were oppressed by its power. He was not cautious, he lived dangerously. He felt his brains were electric and his vision too much for his body. Yet he remained steadily intelligent and analytic, mixing his colours, *thinking* about the nature of light, of one man's energy, of one man's death. He painted the oppression of his fellow inmates in the hospital in St. Rémy. He was a decorous and melancholic northerner turned absolute and wild. He observed and reobserved his own grim redheaded skull and muscles without gentleness, without self-love, without evasion. He was truthful and mad. In the mornings I went and looked at his paintings, and in the afternoons I took the tram out to my father's echoing hospital, carrying little parcels of delicacies, smoked fish, fruits, chocolates. In the afternoons and the evenings he talked. He talked, amongst other things, about the Van Gogh prints, which were obviously his own, his choice, nothing to do with my "Dutch" mother. He talked particularly about the portrait of the Zouave. That was on one of his good days. I had bought him some freesias and some dahlias. I had not realised, in all those years, that he was one of the rare people who cannot smell freesias. He claimed that on this occasion he could. "Just a ghost of a smell, just a hint, I *think* I can smell it . . ." he said. He helped me to mend one of the dahlias with Sellotape, where I had bent its stem. "You can keep them alive," he said, "if you keep the water-channels open. I've often kept things alive successfully for surprisingly long periods, that way." He talked about Van Gogh's Zouave, the one of the family prints I had liked least, as a child, because the floor made me giddy and because the man was alien, both his clothes and his face. It was, said my father precisely, "a very powerful image of pure male sexuality. Absolutely straightforward and simple. It was always my favourite."

He looked at me over the tops of his little gold half-glasses and smiled. "Van Gogh went to find the Zouaves in the brothel in Arles," I said. I was going to go on to say that Van Gogh believed that the expense of energy in sex was bad for his, or anyone's, art. But he wasn't listening. He didn't really think I knew anything about Van Gogh. He had the idea that he might get well enough to go round the Rijksmuseum and see the Vermeers. He did. My sister took him, alarmingly unstable and determined. He wanted to hear music. He wanted to fit things in. Sometimes I think he meant to shorten his time by living well, so that he would die quickly. The Dutch doctors put life into him with nitroglycerine drips and blood transfusions. He told me one day, making a story out of it, how he had walked to the lavatory, lurching along walls, creeping along corridors, gripping bed foot and doorknob, only to find a queue of other frail pyjamaed men. He told this story with a detached, comic anger. He was saying, in effect, "This is what we come to." He was measuring his strength. On one of his better days he set out on the same journey quite gallantly. We had bought him some slippers. He was very troubled about the loss of his slippers and nail scissors, which had gone ahead of him, in the aeroplane he missed, to the home to which he never returned. My mother, who became obsessively angry about the taxi which had waited in vain for this aeroplane, was further enraged to receive someone else's suitcase, in the event. "With a dirty shirt, and someone else's dirty comb and used razor," she said. My mother drew back from all human dirt and muddle. My father sat on the edge of his hospital bed, scrupulously clipping his toenails. His ankle, between his pyjama and his new slippers, was white, and smooth, and somehow untouched, covered with young, unblemished skin. I looked at it and thought how alive it was.

In the mornings I walked along dark canals. I liked the city. I remembered that Camus had said that its concentric canals resembled the circles of Dante's Hell. I even bought a copy of *La Chute* to check the quotation, and carried it around with a paperback copy of Van Gogh's *Letters,* to read over my solitary lunches. Its hero calls himself a *juge-pénitent.* He recalls the wartime history of the city, with ironic detachment. He pleads (in the legal sense). Amsterdam is, he says, *"au coeur des choses. Avez-vous remarqúe que les canaux concentriques d'Amsterdam ressemblent aux cercles de l'enfer? L'enfer bourgeois, naturellement peuplé de mauvais rêves."* Despite my reason for being in the city, I didn't find it hellish, more reassuring in its persistent sea-fretted solidity. The people were kind and reasonable. The university teachers had agreed to take cuts in salary and working hours, in order to avoid redundancy. My father, who had not walked along the canals, nor studied the brick housefronts, sat in his concrete-walled cell and worked out the social background of everyone he met, the surgeon, the Humanist visitor, the nurses, the other patients. Unlike Camus, he did not suppose that to be bourgeois was to incline towards hell, bad dreams, and bad faith. But, in his generation, he found places on the social scale infinitely fascinating and important. The surgeon owned seagoing yachts and an empty piece of Scotland where he fished salmon and shot grouse. My father, even in those weeks, was delighted by this discovery, by this contact with good breeding and success. He said to me of his own father, diagnostically and matter-of-fact, "I suppose we were lower-middle-class really. That was what we were." He was being ruthlessly exact. He would have wished it otherwise. He talked to the surgeon in his professional voice, from behind his professional mask, more openly smiling than what I think of as his true self, the reflective, solitary face I watched, as he thought out his past, and his future. If he would have to ask his Maker to forgive his virtues, he was sure that they were virtues, and that he had exercised them. When he came home, to the London hospital, there was a strike on, the surgeons wore smeared gowns and the ancillary staff were brusque and sloppy. Amsterdam seemed a fitter place for him, somehow. Its strangeness was in a way life-giving.

To me, too. I took pleasure, despite everything, in mastering the train system, in reading words in a new language, in making friends with the Humanist, who was distressed by the approaching death of a teenage German heroin addict. I stumbled across the flower market, on the canal bank, where I bought him the dahlias. I sat in a restaurant in the Leidseplein and ate a huge bowl of mussels with a glass of good white wine, in the dying October sunlight. The table was in a little glazed front parlour, half outdoors, half in, which reminded me of the covered porch in my grandfather's Bridlington house, where I had spent a holiday bedridden with measles. The windows were finely etched with floral and geometric patterns. These, too, I associate with my grandfather. I see as I write that the etched drinking glass and carafe that stand by his bed in my vision of his death are those that stood in fact by my bed, on the only overnight visit to Blythe House. I remember that we inherited these objects at his death. My father was allergic to shellfish. He had collapsed in court in Naples, in 1944, after eating lobster, and had developed huge hives on the bench in Hull, twelve years later, after a prawn cocktail. A police surgeon, examining him privily in a cell, had told him he must never eat shellfish again, and he never had, though he had taken intense pleasure in them. I did not feel bad about eating the mussels. There was too much else to feel bad about, and I would not have eaten them if he had been there, I think. I did feel bad about the paintings. I experienced my one moment of desolation during those weeks in the middle of the Rijksmuseum, amongst all the darkly ingenious still lifes, the heaps of dead books, *mementoes mori,* the weight of the varying sameness of past endeavour, the silence, my own incapacity to stop and feel curious.

The Van Goghs were different. I could not like, I could not respond to the very last paintings, the tortured and incompetent cornfield, with the black despairing birds crowding over the paths which lead nowhere. But the great paintings of Arles and St. Rémy shone. The purple irises on gold. The perturbed bedroom. The solitary chair. The reaper, making his deathly way through white light in fields of shining corn. I knew what Vincent had said about this painting as the image of a cheerful death, a secular human image, of a man moving into the furnace of light. I stopped thoughts off. I thought of Vincent in front of Vincent's paintings. I brought postcards to my father for him to see, contained, faded diminutions of all this glory, and he painfully addressed them to my mother, her sister, his oldest friend, in trembling writing, saying that he was all right. We have all inherited his handwriting, which was cramped and nondescript. My mother's was generous and flowing and distinguished. We were all trained differently, yet we all write his small scrawl. How does that come about?

We talked about heredity during those long visits. He said my mother had come increasingly to resemble her mother, and that there was a lesson in that. We also talked about my mother's untruthfulness. My father felt that it was a failure in perfect good manners to complain about her narrative onslaughts on his own veracity. (This was complicated by a powerful fear they both had of failing memory, since accuracy meant so much to both of them, after all.) He said, not for the first time, anxious about the fact that it was not for the first time, that we had been over this ground, that she had claimed to have been at his father's deathbed, where she had not been.

"I should know," he said. "He was my father. I was certainly there. How can I be wrong?"

It was then that I saw that much of my past might be her confection.

"Have you ever thought," I said, "how much of what we think we know is made out of her stories? One challenges the large errors, like that one. But there are all the other *little* trivial myths that turn into memories."

He was struck by this, and produced an example, of how some flowers had died, and my mother had supposed that perhaps the cleaning lady might have watered them too little, or perhaps too much—probably too much, and that that was why they had died, because Mrs. Haines had overwatered them, and so hypothesis became the stuff of fact.

Earlier that year, when it had been she who was ill, we had had a similar conversation, and I had said, joking and serious, "It's all right for you. *You* didn't inherit those genes." Both of us, under stress, found this very funny, we laughed, in complicity. Later he told his housekeeper, over coffee, that I was the image of his mother, that I resembled that family, strikingly. But I don't think this is true, and the photographs I've seen don't bear it out. Now, in moments of fatigue, I feel my mother's face setting like a mask in or on my own. I have inherited much from her. I do make a profession out of fiction. I select and confect. What is all this, all this story so far, but a careful selection of things that can be told, things that can be arranged in the light of day? Alongside this fabrication are the long black shadows of the things left unsaid, because I don't want to say them, or dare not, or do not remember, or misunderstood or forgot or never knew. I left out, for instance, the tear gas. I wanted to write about Amsterdam as clean, and reasonable, and enduring, and so it was. But two of us came out of the airy space of the Van Gogh Museum into a cloud of drifting gas which burned our throats and scoured our lungs. There were black-armoured police and stone-throwing evicted squatters. Behind our hospital-headed tram was a smoking column of burning cars. For several nights we couldn't return to the hotel directly; it was cordoned by police and the paving stones were torn up. My father could not begin to be interested in these manifestations. He was fighting his own private battle. To omit them is a minor sin, and easy to correct. But what of all the others? What is the truth? I do have a respect for truth.

I remember one particular day at Blythe House, when both my grandparents were alive. I remember this day clearly, though it is not my only memory, possibly because I wrote about it at the time. Now I try to calculate how old I was, I see that I am already confused. It was during the war, during my father's Mediterranean absence, perhaps 1943 or 1944, certainly a very sunlit day during what I remember as a succession of burning still summers, the beginning of my hunger for sunlight. I had stayed at Blythe House in winter. It had seemed stiff and frightening and huge, whether because I was then very little, or because it was so much bigger than our wartime house I don't know. I remember an enormous cold bathroom, with a deep bath standing portentously in the middle of a huge empty space. I remember a view of dirty snow, a children's playground with slide and circular roundabout and swings on loops of chain. I remember the cellar mouth and a dark, frowsty kitchen. I remember my mother's pervasive anxiety. But this summer visit was different. I noticed things. I was not wholly passive.

At the beginning and end of the visit my grandparents stood formally side by side in front of the house, on a gravel drive, and I looked up at them. My grandmother wore a straight black dress, crêpy and square-necked. Her hair was iron-grey and caught up, I think, in a tight bun or roll. Her expression I remember as severe, judicious, unsmiling. Her stockings were thick and her shoes button-barred and pointed. She was composed, I could say, she made no unnecessary movements, no conciliatory speeches, no attempt at affectionate embrace. (My other grandmother rushed and enveloped us, smacking her lips.) My grandfather's face was obscured because it was tilted slightly backwards. He had a large protuberant belly, across which was looped a gold watch chain. I remember his belly most. He was not a fat man, nor a large man, but substantial. I thought—or if I did not think, I have since regularly thought, so that the ideas are bonded to this memory—both of Mr. Brocklehurst, the tall black pillar of *Jane Eyre,* and of Mr. Murdstone in *David Copperfield.* I did not expect my grandfather to do anything frightening or condemnatory, though I was afraid of committing a faux pas. He was identifiably a Victorian patriarch, that is all. Though in those days I had no idea of historical distance and supposed we were all threatened with Newgate prison for debt, and with Fagin's night in the condemned cell. I could tell, I think, that my grandfather was not very interested in me, and that he had nothing to say to me. But in some way I cannot now remember matters developed so that he escorted us to the works itself, to see the boiling of the sugar. On this journey we were accompanied by a tall man in a brown overall, with a lugubrious, respectful, and friendly face, and by some other forgotten man, who lingers in my memory only as the owner of a cloth cap.

The works was gaunt and bare. The floor I remember as mere earth, though it cannot have been: it was certainly dark, not tiled, and dusty. It was all like an enormous version of the outdoor wash-houses of the north, draughty and cold and echoing. On the left as we went in were large vessels I associated with the coppers my other grandmother boiled sheets in, stirring them with a huge wooden baton. I saw, or I remember, four of these. One was full of sulphurous yellow boiling sugar, one of a dark, cherry-red, one of bright green and one, which amazed me because it was an unusual colour for sugar, of a kind of pale inky colour, a molten sea of heaving, viscous blue glass. The colours and the surfaces were brilliant and enchanted. They undulated, they burst in thick, plopping bubbles, they swirled with curving streamers of trapped air like slivers of glass. There was a smell, not cloying but clear and appetizing, of browning sugar. We moved on and saw large buckets full of this gleaming fluid poured onto a huge metal table, or belt, which ran the length of the room. Smoking it hissed down and began to harden. Men with paddles manipulated and spread it, ever finer, more translucent, wider, like rolled pastry magnified numberless times, the colours paling so that magenta became clear peony-pink, so that indigo became dark sky-blue, so that topaz became straw-gold. And a kind of primitive mechanical tart cutter descended and stamped these gleaming sheets, making rows of rounded disks. The process had things in common with glassblowing, which then I had not seen, but which later, in Venice, in Biot, reminds me always of the urgent work with the hot sugar, before it cools. Humbugs ran not flat but in a long coiling serpent, thick as a man's trunk at one end, tapering to thumb-size, through an orifice which simultaneously gave it a half-twist and bit. The most miraculous moment was when my grandfather urged the man in the brown overall to show me how the stripes were made in humbugs. Now I have it, now, almost, I hear his voice. It was both hesitant and eager and wholly absorbed in its subject. I cannot remember the words, but I can remember his certainty that I would find this process, his work, as startling and satisfactory and amazing as he did himself. This is all I know about him at first hand, that his work fascinated and absorbed him. The humbug stripes were as extraordinary as he had promised. The humbug sugar lay, hot and soft, in a huge mass at one end of the table. The overall man pulled off an armful of it, which he rolled roughly into a fat serpent coil, a heavy skein, like my mother's knitting wool, on his two arms. We went out of the shed, into a yard, where a large hook protruded from the wall—very high up, it seemed to me, so that he had to reach up to it. But I was a very small child for my age, maybe it was not so high. The man hung the fat tube of brown sugar—dark, treacle-brown sugar—over this hook and began to whip it around, and around. I knew this motion, it was the regular turn of the playground skipping rope, twist and slap, twist and slap. And as I watched, the sugar lightened. From treacle to coffee, from coffee to a milky fawn, from fawn to a barley-sugar straw colour, and from there, through the gelatine colour of old dried egg white to pure white, no longer translucent but streaked and streaked with infinitely fine needles of air. "It's the air that does it," my grandfather said. "Nothing but whipping in air. There's no difference between the two stripes in a humbug but air: the sugar's exactly the same." I remember him saying, "It's the air that does it." I think I remember that. We took the white rope back into the factory, and laid it on a dark one, and the two were wound round and round each other, spiralling and decreasing in girth, by skilled slapping hands, until the tapered point could be inserted into the snapping machine. I remember the noise it made, moving on the metal, a kind of crunching and crackling of dried sugar, and a thump and slap of the main body of it—this last noise a magnified version of school plasticine rolling.

When it was over, my grandfather fetched out several conical paper bags and these were filled with the fragile slivers of sugar that fell away from the stamping machine. Those too I still remember. At first they were light and powdery and crystalline, palest of colours, rose, lemon, hyacinth, apple. Hot they tasted delectable, melting like sweet snowflakes in those days of sugar rationing. If rationed out and kept too long they settled, coagulated, and became a rocky mass undifferentiated, paper-smeared, sweating drops of saccharine moisture.

I wrote about this, at East Hardwick School. It is the first piece of writing I remember clearly as mine, the first time I remember choosing words, fixing something. I remember, still, two words I chose. Both were from my reading. One was from a description of birds on a Christmas tree, in, I think, Frances Hodgson-Burnett's *Little Princess*. The birds were German, delicate, and made of very fine "spun-glass." The word had always delighted me, with its contradiction between the brittle and the flexible thread produced. I remember I used it for the fragments in our conical paper bags. I remember also casting about for a way of telling how violent, how powerful were the colours in the sugar vats. I wrote that the green was "emerald" and I know where I found that word, in the reading endlessly supplied by my mother. "And ice, mast-high, came floating by / As green as emerald." As green as emerald. Did I go on to other jewels? I don't remember. But I do remember that I took the pleasure in writing my account of the boiling sugar that I usually took only in reading. Words were there to be used.

Later, my grandfather encouraged me to pick his flowers. He had a conservatory, on one side of the grey house, with a mature vine, and huge bunches—I remember many huge bunches—of black grapes hanging from the roof and the twisting stems. He gathered one of these, and encouraged us to taste and eat. "More," he said, when we took a tentative couple of fruit. "They are there to be eaten." Grapes were unknown in those dark days. I remember dissecting mine, the different pleasures of the greenish flesh inside the purple bloom of the skin, the subtle taste, the surprise of the texture and the way the juice ran. I was taken out and told to pick flowers. I took a few dubious daisies from the lawn. "No, no," he said, "anything, anything at all, you help yourself and make a really nice bunch." He liked giving, that too I am sure of, from my own experience. I made a Victorian nosegay. Everything went right, it formed itself, circles of white, round circles of blue, circles of rose, a few black-eyed Susans. And a palisade of leaves to hold its tight, circular form together. I ran up and down, selecting, rejecting, rich. My mother described the early age at which I had distinguished the names, phlox, antirrhinum, lupin. I don't remember her much that day; she must have been at ease. Or else I was. It was unusual for either of us to be at all settled, at all confident, at all happy. It was almost like my father's idea of his family life as Eden, though then I didn't know of that, knew only that these grandparents were to be regarded with awe. I don't think I saw them again. We did not go there often, and after a time my grandmother died, and then my grandfather, who could not, my mother said, live without her. "He was like a lost child. He was quite helpless, all the life gone out of him."

My mother only outlived my father for a little more than a year. She did not appear to grieve for him, going only so far as to remark that she missed having him around to agree with her about Mrs. Thatcher's treatment of the miners. She was curiously despondent about the prospect of dying herself under a government for which she felt pure, instinctive loathing. Immediately after the war she had once told me that when it began she had thought through, imagined through, all the worst possible things that could happen, to England, to my father. "Then I put it behind me and simply didn't think of it anymore," she said. "I had faced it." As a little girl, I found this exemplary and admirable. Action is possible if you stop off feeling. Some chill I had learned from my mother worked in Amsterdam when I stopped off the dangerous thoughts possible in the presence of Van Gogh's dying cornfields or his dark painting of his dead father's Bible. I could talk to my father about his father only by not loving him too much, not exactly at that moment, not thinking too precisely about his living ankle, cutting him off. My poor mother maybe—in part—cut him off too efficiently, too early, faced it all too absolutely and too soon. During the war, I have been told recently, the Air Force wrote to her relations begging them to influence her to desist from writing despairing letters to her husband in North Africa. Wives were asked to keep cheerful, to tell good news, not to distress the men. She faced his loss, I believe her, and then complained of her lot. She said when he had died, bewildered and uncertain, "I had got used to it already, you see, I had got used to him not being there, all the time he was in Amsterdam." She was explaining her apparent lack of feeling.

The day of his funeral was bitterly cold. It was just before Christmas. It was a Quaker cremation, attended mostly by non-Quakers, who did not break the tense silence. I felt nothing, I felt fear of feeling, I felt the rush of time. Outside my mother was pinched and tiny and stumbling. I said, "I remembered the day he came back from the war." "Yes," she said, very small and vague. He came back at midnight, or so my mother always said. He had sent a telegram which never arrived, so she had no idea. She went furiously to the door and burst out, "It's too bad," thinking he was the air-raid warden complaining about chinks in the blackout. What did they say to each other? I remember being woken—how much later? I remember the light being put on, a raw, dim, ceiling light, not reaching the gloomy corners. I remember the figure in the doorway, the uniform, the red hair, a smile as surprised and huge and half-afraid as I imagine my own was. I remember him holding his officer's hat. Why hadn't he put it down? Or am I wrong? I remember even an overcoat, but I confuse the memory of his return hopelessly with his parting. The hair was less red, more gold than I'd remembered. He had a hairy ruddy-ginger Harris tweed jacket which my mother had always said exactly matched his hair, and which I still think of as "matching" it, though I saw differently and remember better. (And how to be sure with all the years of fading between then and that last cold day?) I sat up, scrambled to my feet and leaped an enormous leap, over my bed, over the gap, over the bed with my small sleeping sister. I don't remember the trajectory of this leap. I remember its beginning but not its end, not my safe arrival. I do remember—this is surely memory, and no accretion—a terror of happiness. I was afraid to feel. This event was a storied event, already lived over and over, in imagination and hope, in the invented future. The real thing, the true moment, is as inaccessible as any point along that frantic leap. More things come back as I write; the gold-winged buttons on his jacket, forgotten between then and now. None of these words, none of these things recall him. The gold-winged, fire-haired figure in the doorway is and was myth, though he did come back, he was there, at that time, and I did make that leap. After things have happened, when we have taken a breath and a look, we begin to know what they are and were, we begin to tell them to ourselves. Fast, fast these things took and take their place beside other markers, the teapot, the horse trough, real apples and plums, a white ankle, the coalscuttle, two dolls in cellophane, a gas oven, a black and white dog, gold-winged buttons, the melded and twisting hanks of brown and white sugar.

PRECIPICE-ENCURLED

What's this then, which proves good yet seems untrue?
Is fiction, which makes fact alive, fact too?
The somehow may be thishow.

—ROBERT BROWNING

I

The woman sits in the window. Beneath her is the stink of the canal and on the skyline is a steel-grey sheet of cloud and an unswallowed setting sun. She watches the long lines of dark green seaweed moving on the thick surface of the water, and the strong sweeping gulls, fugitives from storms in the Adriatic. She is a plump woman in a tea gown. She wears a pretty lace cap and pearls. These things are known, are highly probable. She has fine features fleshed—a compressed, drooping little mouth, a sharp nose, sad eyes, an indefinable air of disappointment, a double chin. This we can read from portraits, more than one, tallying, still in existence. She has spent the afternoon in bed; her health is poor, but she rallies for parties, for outings, for occasions. There she sits, or might be supposed to sit, any autumn day on any of several years at the end of the last century. She commands the devoted services of three gondoliers, a handyman, a cook, a maid, and a kitchen maid. Also an accountant-housekeeper. She has a daughter, young and marriageable, and a husband, mysteriously ill in Paris, from whom she is estranged but not divorced. Her daughter is out on a party of pleasure, perhaps, and has been adjured to take her new umbrella, the one with the prettily carved crickets and butterflies on its handle. She has an eye for the execution of delicate objects: it has been said of her that she would exchange a Tintoretto for a cabinet of tiny gilded glasses. She has an eye for fashion: in this year where clothes are festooned with dead hummingbirds and more startling creatures, mice, moths, beetles, and lizards, she will give a dance where everyone must wear flights of birds pasted on ribbons—"awfully chic"—or streamers of butterflies. The room in which she sits is full of mother-of-pearl cabinets full of intricate little artefacts. She is the author of an unpublished and authoritative history of Venetian naval architecture. Also of some completely undistinguished poems. She is the central character in no story, but peripheral in many, where she may appear reduced to two or three bold identifying marks. She has a passion for pug dogs and for miniature Chinese spaniels: at her feet, on this gloomy day, lie, shall we say, Contenta, Trolley, Yahabibi, and Thisbe, snoring a little as such dogs do, replete. She also has a passion for peppermint creams; do the dogs enjoy these too, or are they disciplined? One account of her gives three characteristics only: plump, pug dogs, peppermint creams. Henry James, it is said, had the idea of making her the central character of a merely projected novel—did he mean to tackle the mysteriously absent husband, make of him one of those electric Jamesian force fields of unspecific significance? He did, it is also said, write her into *The Aspern Papers,* in a purely subordinate and structural role, the type of the well-to-do American woman friend of the narrator, an authorial device, what James called a *ficelle,* economically connecting us, the readers, to the necessary people and the developing drama. She lent the narrator her gondola. She was a generous woman. She is an enthusiast: she collects locks of hair, snipped from great poetic temples, which she enshrines in lockets of onyx. She is waiting for Robert Browning. She has done and will do this in many years. She has supervised and will supervise the excellent provision of sheets and bathroom facilities for his Venetian visits. She chides him for not recognising that servants know their place and are happy in it. She sends him quires of handmade Venetian paper which he distributes to artists and poets of his acquaintance. She selects brass salvers for him. She records his considered and unconsidered responses to scenery and atmosphere. She looks at the gulls with interest he has instilled. "I do not know why I never see in descriptions of Venice any mention of the seagulls; to me they are even more interesting than the doves of St. Mark." He said that, and she recorded it. She recorded that occasionally he would allow her daughter to give him a cup of tea "to our great delight." "As a rule, he abstained from what he considered a somewhat unhygienic beverage if taken before dinner."

II

Dear dead women, the scholar thinks, peering into the traces on the hooded green plane of the microfilm reader, or perhaps turning over browned packets of polite notes of gratitude, acceptance, anticipation, preserved perhaps in one of those fine boxes of which in her lifetime she had so many, containing delicate cigarettes on inlaid pearly octagonal tables, or precious fragments of verses copied out for autograph books. He has gleaned her words from Kansas and Cambridge, Florence, Venice and Oxford, he has read her essay on lace and her tributes to the condescension of genius, he has heard the flitting of young skirts at long-vanished festivities. He has stood, more or less, on the spot where she stood with the poet in Asolo in 1889, looking back to Browning's first contemplation of the place in 1838, looking back to the internecine passions of Guelphs and Ghibellines, listening to the chirrup of the contumacious grasshopper. He has seen her blood colour the cheeks of her noble Italian granddaughter who has opened to him those houses where the poet dined, recited, conversed, teased, reminisced. He likes her, partly because he now knows her, has pieced her together. Resuscitated, Browning might have said, did say, roundly, of his Roman murderers and biassed lawyers, child-wife, wise moribund Pope and gallant priest he found or invented in his dead and lively Yellow Book. A good scholar may permissibly invent, he may have a hypothesis, but fiction is barred. This scholar believes, plausibly, that his assiduous and fragile subject is the hidden heroine of a love story, the inapprehensive object, at the age of fifty-four, of a dormant passion in a handsome seventy-seven-year-old poet. He records the physical vigour, the beautiful hands and fine white head of hair of his hero. He records the probable feelings of his heroine, which stop short at exalted hero worship, the touch of talismanic mementos, not living flesh. He adduces a poem, "Inapprehensiveness," in which the poetic speaker reproves the inapprehensive stare of a companion intent on Ruskin's hypothetical observation of the waving form of certain weed growths on a ravaged wall, who ignores "the dormant passion needing but a look / To burst into immense life." The scholar's story combs the facts this way. They have a subtle, not too dramatic shape, lifelike in that. He scrutinises the microfilm, the yellowing letters, for little bright nuggets and filaments of fact to add to his mosaic. In 1882 the poet was in the Alps, with a visit to Venice in prospect after a proposed visit to another English family in Italy. She waited for him. In terms of this story she waited in vain. An "incident" elsewhere, an "unfortunate accident," the scholar wrote, following his thread, coupled with torrential rain in Bologna, caused the poet to return to London. He was in danger of allowing the friendship to cool, the scholar writes, perhaps anxious on her behalf, perhaps on the poet's, perhaps on his own.

III

A man, he always thought, was more himself alone in an hotel room. Unless, of course, he vanished altogether without the support of others' consciousness of him, and the solidity of his taste and his history in his possessions. To be itinerant suited and sharpened him. He liked this room. It was quiet, on the second floor, the last in a long corridor, its balcony face to face with a great, bristling primeval glacier. The hotel, he wrote, sitting at the table listening to the silent snow and the fraternising tinkle of unseen cattle, was "quite perfect, with every comfort desirable, and no drawback of any kind." The journey up had been rough—two hours carriage drive, and then seven continued hours of clambering and crawling on mule-back. He wrote letters partly out of courtesy to his large circle of solicitous friends and admirers, but more in order to pick up the pen, to see the pothooks and spider traces form, containing the world, the hotel, the mules, the paradise of coolness and quiet. The hotel was not absolutely perfect. "My very handwriting is affected by the lumpy ink and the skewery pen." Tomorrow he would walk. Four or five hours along the mountainside. Not bad for an old man, a hale old man. The mule jolting had played havoc with his hips and the long muscles in his back. At my age, he thought, you listen to every small hurt as though it may be the beginning of the last and worst hurt, which will come. So the two things continued in his consciousness side by side, a solicitous attention to twinges, and the waiting to be reinvested by his private self. Which was like a cloak, a cloak of invisibility that fell into comfortable warm folds around him, or like a disturbed well, whose inky waters chopped and swayed and settled into blackly reflecting lucidity. Or like a brilliant baroque chapel at the centre of a decorous and unremarkable house.

He liked his public self well enough. He was surprised, to tell the truth, that he had one that worked so well, was so thoroughgoing, so at home in the world, so like other public selves. As a very young man, in strictly nonconformist South London, erudite and indulged within the four walls of a Camberwell bibliomaniac's home, he had supposed that this would be denied him, the dining out, the gossip, the world. He wanted the world, because it was there, and he wanted everything. He had described his father, whom he loved, as a man of vast knowledge, reading, and memory—totally ignorant of the world. (This ignorance had extended to his having had to leave England perpetually, as an aged widower, on account of a breach of promise action brought, with cause, against him.) His father had with consummate idealism freed him for art. My father wished me to do what I liked, he had explained, adding: I should not so bring up a son.

French novelists, he claimed, were ignorant of the habits of the English upper classes, who kept themselves to themselves. He had seen and noted them. "I seem to know a good many—for some reason or other. Perhaps because I never had any occupation." Nevertheless, he desired his son to have an occupation, and the boy, amiable and feckless, brooded over by his own irreducible large shadow, showed little sign of vocation or application. He amused himself as a matter of course in the world in which the father dined out and visited, so assiduously, with a perpetually renewed surprise at his own facility. He was aware that Elizabeth would have wished it otherwise. Elizabeth had been a great poet, a captive princess liberated and turned wife, a moral force, silly over some things, such as her growing boy's long curls and the flimsy promises and fake visions of the séance. She too had not known this world that was so important. *One* such intimate knowledge as I have had with many a person would have taught her, he confided once, unguarded, had she been inclined to learn. Though I doubt if she would have dirtied her hands for any scientific purpose. His public self had a scientific purpose, and if his hands were dirty, he could wash them clean in a minute before he saw her, as he trusted to do. He had his reasonable doubts about this event, too, though he wrote bravely of it, the step from this world to that other world, the fog in the throat, the mist in the face, the snows, the blasts, the pain and then the peace out of pain and the loving arms. It was not a time of certainties, however he might assert them from time to time. It was a time of doubt, doubt was a man's business. But it was also hard to imagine all this tenacious sense of self, all this complexity of knowledge and battling, force and curiosity becoming nothing. What is a man, what is a man's soul?

Descartes believed, he noted down, that the seat of the soul is the pineal gland. The reason for this is a pretty reason—all else in our apparatus for apprehending the world is double, *viz.* two ears, two eyes, et cetera, and two lobes of our brain, moreover; Descartes requires that somewhere in our body all our diverse, our dual impressions must be unified before reaching the soul, which is one. He had thought often of writing a poem about Descartes, dreaming in his stove of sages and blasted churches, reducing all to the tenacity of the observing thinker, *cogito, ergo sum.* A man can inhabit another man's mind, or body, or senses, or history, can jerk it into a kind of life, as galvanism moves frogs: a good poet could inhabit Descartes, the bric-à-brac of stove and ill-health and wooden bowls of onion soup, perhaps, and one of those pork knuckles, and the melon offered to the philosopher by the sage in his feverish dream, all this paraphernalia spinning round the naked *cogito* as the planets spin in an orrery. The best part of my life, he told himself, the life I have lived most intensely, has been the fitting, the infiltrating, the inventing the self of another man or woman, explored and sleekly filled out, as fingers swell a glove. I have been webbed Caliban lying in the primeval ooze, I have been madman and saint, murderer and sensual prelate, inspired David and the cringing medium, Sludge, to whom I gave David's name, with what compulsion of irony or equivocation, David Sludge? The rooms in which his solitary self sat buzzed with other selves, crying for blood as the shades cried at the pit dug by Odysseus in his need to interrogate, to revive the dead. His father's encyclopaedias were the banks of such blood pits, bulging with paper lives and circumstances, no two the same, none insignificant. A set of views, a time-confined philosophy, a history of wounds and weaknesses, flowers, clothing, food and drink, light on Mont Blanc's horns of silver, fangs of crystal; these coalesce to make one self in one place. Then decompose. I catch them, he thought, I hold them together, I give them coherence and vitality, I. And what am I? Just such another concatenation, a language and its rhythms, a limited stock of learning, derived from my father's consumed books and a few experiments in life, my desires, my venture in dragon slaying, my love, my loathings also, the peculiar colours of the world through my two eyes, the blind tenacity of the small, the single driving centre, soul or self.

⋆

What he had written down, with the scratchy pen, were one or two ideas for Descartes and his metaphorical orrery: meaningless scraps. And this writing brought to life in him a kind of joy in greed. He would procure, he would soak in, he would comb his way through the Discourse on Method, and the Passions of the Soul: he would investigate Flemish stoves. His private self was now roused from its dormant state to furious activity. He felt the white hairs lift on his neck and his breath quickened. A bounded man, he had once written, may so project his surplusage of soul in search of body, so add self to self . . . so find, so fill full, so appropriate forms . . . In such a state a man became pure curiosity, pure interest in whatever presented itself of the creation, lovely or freakish, pusillanimous, wise or vile. Those of his creatures he most loved or most approved moved with such delighted and indifferent interest through the world. There was the tragic Duchess, destroyed by the cold egotism of a Duke who could not bear her equable pleasure in everything, a sunset, a bough of cherries, a white mule, his favour at her breast. There was Karshish the Arab physician, the not-incurious in God's handiwork, who noticed lynx and blue-flowering borage and recorded the acts of the risen Lazarus. There was David, seeing the whole earth shine with significance after soothing the passionate self-doubt of Saul; there was Christopher Smart, whose mad work of genius, his Song to David, a baroque chapel in a dull house, had recorded the particularity of the world, the whale's bulk in the waste of brine, the feather tufts of Wild Virgin's Bower, the habits of the polyanthus. There was the risen Lazarus himself, who had briefly been in the presence of God and inhabited eternity, and to whose resuscitated life he had been able to give no other characteristics than these, the lively, indifferent interest in everything, a mule with gourds, a child's death, the flowers of the field, some trifling fact at which he will gaze "rapt with stupor at its very littleness."

He felt for his idea of what was behind all this diversity, all this interest. *At the back* was an intricate and extravagantly prolific maker.

Sometimes, listening to silence, alone with himself, he heard the irregular but endlessly repeated crash of waves on a pebbled shore. His body was a porcelain-fine arched shell, sculpted who knew how, containing this roar and plash. And the drag of the moon, and the elliptical course of the planets. More often, a madly ingenious inner eye magnified small motions of flesh and blood. The twinge had become a tugging and raking in what he now feared, prophetically it turned out, was his liver. Livers were used for augury, the shining liver, the smoking liver, the Babylonians thought, was the seat of the soul: his own lay athwart him and was intimately and mysteriously connected with the lumpy pothooks. And with the inner eye which might or might not be seated in that pineal gland where Descartes located the soul. A man has no more measured the mysteries of his internal whistlings and flowings, he thought, than he has measured the foundations of the earth or of the whirlwind. It was his covert principle to give true opinions to great liars, and to that other fraudulent resuscitator of dead souls, and filler of mobile gloves, David Sludge the Medium, he had given a vision of the minutiae of intelligence which was near enough his own. "We find great things are made of little things," he had made Sludge say, "And little things go lessening till at last / Comes God behind them."

> "The Name comes close behind a stomach-cyst
> The simplest of creations, just a sac
> That's mouth, heart, legs and belly at once, yet lives
> And feels and could do neither, we conclude
> If simplified still further one degree."

"But go back and back, as you please, *at* the back, as Mr. Sludge is made to insist," he had written, "you find (*my* faith is as constant) creative intelligence, acting as matter but not resulting from it. Once set the balls rolling and ball may hit ball and send any number in any direction over the table; but I believe in the cue pushed by a hand." All the world speaks the Name, as the true David truly saw: even the uneasy inflamed cells of my twinges. *At* the back, is something simple, undifferentiated, indifferently intelligent, live.

My best times are those when I approximate most closely to that state.

She put her hand on the knob of his door, and pushed it open without knocking. It was dark, a light, smoky dark; the window curtains were not drawn and the windows were a couple of vague, star-lighted apertures. She saw things, a rug thrown over a chair, a valise, a dim shape hunched and silver-topped, which turned out to be her brother, back towards her, at the writing table. "Oh, if you're busy," she said, "I won't disturb you." And then, "You can't write in the dark, Robert, it is bad for your eyes." He shook himself, like a great seal coming up from the depths, and his eyes, dark spaces under craggy brows, turned unseeing in her direction. "I don't want to disturb you," she said again, patiently waiting for his return to the land of the living. "You don't," he said, "dear Sarianna. I was only thinking about Descartes. And it must be more than time for dinner." "There is a woman here," Sarianna confided, as they walked down the corridor, past a servant carrying candles, "with an aviary on her head, who is an admirer of your poems and wishes to join the Browning society." *"Il me semble que ce genre de chose frise le ridicule,"* he said, growlingly, and she smiled to herself, for she knew that when he was introduced to the formidable Mrs. Miller he would be everything that was agreeable and interested.

And the next day, on the hotel terrace, he was quite charming to his corseted and bustled admirer, who begged him to write in her birthday book, already graced by Lord Leighton and Thomas Trollope, who was indulgent when he professed not to remember on which of two days he had been born—was it May 7 or May 9, he never could be certain, he said, appealing to Sarianna, who could. He had found some better ink, and copied out, as he occasionally did, in microscopic handwriting, "All that I know of a certain star," adding with a bluff smile, "I always end up writing the same thing; I vary only the size. I should be more inventive." Mrs. Miller protested that his eyesight must be exquisitely fine, closing the scented leather over the hand-painted wreaths of pansies that encircled the precious script. Her hat was monumental, a circle of wings; the poet admired it, and asked detailed questions about its composition, owls, hawks, jays, swallows, encircling an entire dove. He showed considerable familiarity with Paris prints and the vagaries of modistes. His public self had its own version of the indiscriminate interest in everything which was the virtue of the last Duchess, Karshish, Lazarus, and Smart. He could not know how much this trait was to irritate Henry James, who labelled it bourgeois, whose fictional alter ego confessed to feeling a despair at his "way of liking one subject—so far as I could tell—precisely as much as another." He addressed himself to women exactly as he addressed himself to men, this affronted narrator complained; he gossiped to all men alike, talking no better to clever folk than to dull. He was loud and cheerful and copious. His opinions were sound and second-rate, and of his perceptions it was too mystifying to think. He seemed quite happy in the company of the insistent Mrs. Miller, telling her about the projected visit to the Fishwick family, who had a house in the Apennines. Mrs. Miller nodded vigorously under the wings of the dove, and leapt into vibrant recitation. "What I love best in all the world / Is a castle, precipice-encurled / In a gash of the wind-grieved Apennines." "Exactly so," said the benign old man, sipping his port, looking at the distant mountains, watched by Sarianna, who knew that he was braced against the Apennines as a test, that he had never since her death ventured so near the city in which he had been happy with his wife, in which he was never to set foot again. The Fishwicks' villa was in a remote village unvisited in that earlier time. He meant to attempt that climb, as he had attempted this. He needed to be undaunted. It was his idea of himself that he was undaunted. And so he was, Sarianna thought, with love. "Then we may proceed to Venice," said the poet to the lady in the hat, "where we have very kind friends and many fond memories. I should not be averse to dying in Venice. When my time comes."

IV

"What will he make of us?" Miss Juliana Fishwick enquired, speaking of the imminent Robert Browning, and in fact more concerned with what her companion, Mr. Joshua Riddell, did make of them, of the Fishwick family and way of life, of the Villa Colomba, perched in its coign of cliff, with its rough lawn and paved rooms and heavy ancient furnishings. She was perhaps the only person in the company to care greatly what anybody made of anybody; the others were all either too old and easygoing or too young and intent on their journeys of discovery and complicated games. Joshua Riddell replied truthfully that he found them all enchanting, and the place too, and was sure that Mr. Browning would be enchanted. He was a friend of Juliana's brother, Tom. They were at Balliol College, reading Greats. Joshua's father was a Canon of St. Paul's. Joshua lived a regular and circumspect life at home, where he was an only child, of whom much was expected. He expected very much of himself, too, though not in the line of his parents' hopes, the Bar, the House of Commons, the judiciary. He meant to be a great painter. He meant to do something quite new, which would have authority. He knew he should recognise this, when he had learned what it was, and how to do it. For the time being, living in its necessarily vague yet brilliant presence was both urgent and thwarting. He described it to no one; certainly not to Tom, with whom he was able, surprisingly, to share ordinary jokes and japes. He was entirely unused to the degree of playfulness and informality of Tom's family.

He was sketching Juliana. She was sitting, in her pink muslin, on the edge of the fountain basin. The fountain bubbled in an endless chuckling waterfall out of a cleft in the rockside. This was the lower fountain, furthest from the house, on a rough lawn on which stood an ancient stone table and chairs. Above the fountain someone had carved a round, sunlike face, flat and calmly beaming, with two uplifted, flat-palmed hands pushing through, or poised on, the rock face beside it. No one knew how old or new it was. In the upper garden, where there were flowerbeds and a slower, lead-piped fountain, was a pillar or herm surmounted with a head which, Solomon Fishwick had pointed out, was exactly the same as the heads on the covers of the hominiform Etruscan funerary urns. Joshua had made several drawings of these carvings. Juliana's living face, under her straw hat, was a different challenge. It was a face composed of softness and the smooth solid texture of young flesh, without pronounced bones, hard to capture. The blond eyebrows did not stand out; the eyes were not emphasised by long lashes, only by a silver-white fringe which caught the sunlight here and there. The upper lip sloped upwards; the mouth was always slightly parted, the expression gently questioning, not insisting on an answer. It was an extremely pleasant face, with no salient characteristics. How to draw softness, and youth, and sheer *pleasantness*? Her arms should be full of an abundance of something; apples, rosebuds, a cascade of corn. She held her little hands awkwardly, clasping and unclasping them over her pink skirts.

Juliana was more used to looking than to being looked at. She supposed she was not pretty, though passable, not by any means grotesque. She had an unfortunate body for this year's narrow styles, which required height, an imposing bosom, a flat stomach, an upright carriage. She was round and short, though she had a good enough waist; corseting did violence to her, and in the summer heat in Italy was impossible. So she was conscious of rolls and half-moons and sausages of flesh which she would dearly have wished otherwise. She had pretty ankles and wrists, she knew, and had stockings of a lovely rose pink with butterfly shells embroidered on them. Her elder sister, Annabel, visiting in Venice, was a beauty, much courted, much consulted about dashing little hats. Juliana supposed she might herself have trouble in finding a husband. She was not remarkable. She was afraid she might simply pass from being a shepherding elder sister to being a useful aunt. She was marvellous with the little ones. She played and tumbled and comforted and cleaned and sympathised, and wanted something of her own, some place, some thought, some silence that should be hers only. She did not expect to find it. She had a practical nature and liked comfort. She had been invaluable in helping to bestow the family goods and chattels in the two heavy carriages which had made their way up the hill, from the heat of Florence to this airy and sunny garden state. Everything had had to go in: baths and fish kettles, bolsters and jelly moulds, cats, dogs, birdcage and dolls' house. She had sat in the nursery carriage, with Nanny and Nurse and the restive little ones: Tom and Joshua had gone ahead with her parents and the household staff, English and Italian, had come behind. On the hot leather seat, she was impinged upon by Nurse's starched petticoats on one side, and the entwined, struggling limbs of Arthur and Gwendolen battling for space, for air on the other. When the climb became steep spare mules were attached, called *trapeli,* each with its attendant groom, groaning and coughing on the steeper and steeper turns, whilst the men went at strolling pace and the horses skidded and lay back in their collars leaving the toiling to the mules. She found their patient effort exemplary: she had given them all apples when they arrived.

She was in awe of Joshua, though not of Tom. Tom teased her, as he always had, amiably. Joshua spoke courteously to her as though she was as knowledgeable as Tom about Horace and Ruskin; this was probably because he had no experience of sisters and only a limited experience of young women. Her father had taught her a little Latin and Greek; her governess had taught her French, Italian, needlework, drawing, and the use of the globes, accomplishments she was now imparting to Gwendolen, and Arthur and little Edith. They seemed useless, not because they were uninteresting but because they were like feathers stitched onto a hat, dead decorations, not life. They were life to Joshua; she could see that. His manner was fastidious and aloof, but he had been visibly shaken, before the peregrination to the Villa Colomba, by the outing they had made from Florence to Vallombrosa, with its sweeping inclines and steep declivities all clothed with the chestnut trees, dark green shades "high overarched indeed, exactly," Joshua had said, and had added, "You can see that these leaves, being deciduous, will strow the brooks, thickly, like the dead souls in Virgil and Milton's fallen angels." She had looked at the chestnut trees, suddenly seeing them, because he asked her to. They clothed the mountains here, too. The peasants lived off chestnuts: their cottages had chestnut-drying lofts, their women ground chestnut flour in stone mortars.

When they had first rushed into the Villa Colomba, chirruping children and pinch-mouthed, disapproving cook, and had found nothing but echoing, cool space between the thick walls with their barred slit windows, she had looked to Joshua in alarm, whilst the children cried out, "Where are the chairs and tables?" He had found an immense hourglass, in a niche over the huge cavernous hearth, and said, smilingly, "We are indeed in another time, a Saturnine time." Civilisation, it turned out, existed upstairs, though cook complained mightily of ageing rusty iron pots and a ratcheted spit like a diabolical instrument of torture. Everything was massive and ancient: oak tables on a forest of oak pillars, huge leather-backed thrones, beds with heavy gilded hangings, chests ingeniously carved on clawed feet, too heavy to lift, tombs, Tom said, for curious girls. "A house for giants," Joshua said to Juliana, seeing her intrigue and anxiety both clearly. He drew her attention to the huge wrought-iron handles of the keys. "We are out of the nineteenth century entirely," he said. The walls of the *salone* were furnished with a series of portraits, silver-wigged and dark-eyed and rigid. Joshua's bedroom had a fearful and appalling painting of fruits and flowers so arranged as to form a kind of human form, bristling with pineapple spines, curvaceous with melons, staring through passionflower eyes. "*That,*" said Juliana, "is bound to appeal to Mr. Browning, who is interested in the grotesque."

Tom said he would not make much of the family portraits, which were so similar as to argue a significant want of skill in the painter. "Either that, or a striking family resemblance," said Joshua. "Or a painter whose efforts all turn out to resemble his own appearance. I have known one or two portraiture painters like that." Sitting now on the rim of the fountain trough, watching him frown over his drawing, look up, correct, frown, and scribble, she wondered if by some extraordinary process her undistinguished features might be brought to resemble his keen and handsome ones. He was gipsyish in colouring, and well-groomed by habit, a kind of contradiction. Here in the mountains he wore a loose jacket and a silk scarf knotted at his neck, but knotted too neatly. He was smaller and thinner than Tom.

Joshua worked on the mouth corner. He had chosen a very soft, silvery pencil for this very soft skin: he did not want to draw a caricature in a few sparing lines, he wanted somehow to convey the nature of the solidity of the flesh of cheek and chin. He had mapped in the rounds and ovals, of the whole head and the hat brim, and the descending curve of the looped plait in the nape of Juliana's neck, and the spot where her ear came, and parts of the calm wide forehead. The shadow cast on the flesh by the circumference of the hat was another pleasant problem in tone and shading. He worked in little, circling movements, feeling out little clefts with the stub of his pencil, isolating tiny white patches of light that shone on the ledge of the lip or the point of the chin, leaving this untouched paper to glitter by contrast with his working. He filled out the plump underthroat with love; *so* it gave a little, *so* it was taut.

"I wish I could see," said Juliana, "what you are doing."

"When it is done."

It was almost as if he was touching the face, watching its grey shape swim into existence out of a spiderweb of marks. His hand hovered over where the nose would be, curled a nostril, dented its flare. If anywhere he put dark marks where light should be, it was ruined. No two artists' marks are the same, no more than their thumbprints. Behind Juliana's head he did the edge, no more, of the flat stony texture of the solar face.

Juliana kept still. Her anxieties about Mr. Browning and the massive awkwardness of their temporary home were calmed. Joshua's tentative pencil began to explore the area of the eyes. The eyes were difficult. They must first be modelled—the life was conferred by the pinpoint of dark and the flecks of white light, and the exact distances between them. He had studied the amazing eyes created by Rembrandt van Rijn, a precise little bristling, fine, hairlike movement of the brush, a spot of crimson here, a thread of carmine there, a spiderweb paste of colour out of which a soul suddenly stared. "Please look at me," he said to Juliana, "please look at me—yes, like that—and don't move." His pencil point hovered, thinking, and Juliana's pupils contracted in the greenish halo of the iris, as she looked into the light, and blinked, involuntarily. She did not want to stare at him; it was unnatural, though his considering gaze, measuring, drawing back, turning to one side and the other, seemed natural enough. A flood of colour moved darkly up her throat, along her chin, into the planes and convexities of her cheeks. Tears collected, unbidden, without cause. Joshua noted the deepening of colour, and then the glisten, and ceased to caress the paper with the pencil. Their eyes met. What a complicated thing is this meeting of eyes, which disturbs the air between two still faces, which has its effects on the heartbeat, the hair on the wrists, the flow of blood. You can understand, Joshua thought, why poets talk of arrows, or of hooks thrown. He said, "How odd it is to look at someone, after all, and to see their soul looking back again. How can a pencil catch that? How do we know we see each other?"

Juliana said nothing, only blushed, rosier and rosier, flooded by moving blood under her hat, and one large tear brimmed over the line of lower lashes, with their wet silkiness which Joshua had been trying to render.

"Ah, Juliana. There is no need to cry. Please, don't. I'll stop."

"No. I am being silly. I—I am not used to be looked at so intently."

"You are beautiful to look at," said Joshua, comparing the flowing colours with the placid silver-grey of his attempt to feel out her face. He put down his drawing, and touched at her cheek with a clean handkerchief. The garden hummed with insect song and bubbled with water; he was somehow inside it, as he was when he was drawing; he looked down and there, under the tight pink muslin, was the generous round of a breast. It was all the same, all alive, the warm stone, the water, the rough grass, the swirl of pink muslin, the troubled young face. He put his two hands round the little ones that turned in her lap, stilling them like trapped birds.

"I have alarmed you, Juliana. I didn't mean that. I'm sorry."

"I don't want you to be sorry." Small but clear.

"Look at me again." It was said for him; it was what came next; they no sooner looked but they loved, a voice told him; the trouble was delightful, compelling, alarming. "Please look at me, Juliana. How often do we really look at each other?"

She had looked at him before, when he was not looking. Now she could not. And so it seemed natural for him to put his arms along the soft round shoulders, to push his face, briefly, briefly, under the brim of the hat, to rest his warm lips on the mouth corner his pencil had touched in its distance. Juliana could hear the sea, or her own life, swirling.

"Juliana," he said, "Juliana, Juliana." And then, prompted by some little local daemon of the grass plot and the carved smiler, "Juliana is the name of the lady in one of the poems I most love. Do you know it? It is by Andrew Marvell; it is the complaint of the mower, Damon."

Juliana said she did not know it. She would like to hear it. He recited.

> "My mind was once the true survey
> Of all these meadows fresh and gay;
> And in the greenness of the grass
> Did see my thoughts as in a glass
> 'Til Juliana came, and she,
> What I do to the grass, did to my thoughts and me."

"She was not very kind," said Juliana.

"We do not know what she was," said Joshua. "Only the effect she had upon the Mower."

He gripped the little fingers. The fingers gripped back. And then the children came bursting down the pathway under the trees, announcing an expedition to the village.

Juliana was in no doubt about what had happened. It was love. Love had blossomed, or struck, like lightning, like a hawk, as it was clearly seen to do in novels and poems, as it took no time to do, voracious or sunny, in the stories she lived on, the scenes her imagination and more, her moral expectations, naturally inhabited. Love visited all who were not ridiculous or religious. Simply, she had always supposed her own, when it came, would be unrequited and lowering, was unprepared for kisses and poetry. She went to bed that night and turned on her dusty bolster amongst her coarse sheets, all vaguely aflame, diffusely desirous, terribly unused to violent personal happiness.

Joshua was less sure of what had happened. He too burned that night, less vaguely, more locally, making a turmoil of his coverings and tormented by aches and tensions. He recognised the old cherub for what he was, and gave him his true name, the name Juliana gave him, honourably, not wriggling into demeaning her or himself by thinking simply of lust. He went over and over every detail with reverent pleasure, the pink muslin, the trusting tear-filled eyes, the flutter of a pulse, the soft mouth, the revelations of his questing pencil. But, unlike Juliana, he was already under the rule of another daemon or cherub; he was used to accommodating his body and mind to the currents of the dictates of another imperative; he felt a responsibility also to the empty greenness that had existed in his primitive innocence, before. He wanted, he loved; but did he want enough, did he love enough? Had he inadvertently behaved dishonourably to this young creature, certainly tonight the dearest to him in the world, certainly haloed with light and warm with charm and promise of affection?

He was twenty years old. He had no experience and was confused. He finally promised himself that tomorrow he would do as he had already promised himself he would do, set off early and alone up the mountain-side, to do some sketching—even painting. He would look at the land beyond habitation. He would explain to her: she would immediately understand all, since what he should say would be no more than the serious and honourable truth; that he must go away.

He rose very early, and went into the kitchen to beg sandwiches, and a flask of wine, from cook. Gianni was sent off to saddle his mule, to take him as far as the village, Lucchio, which could be seen clinging to the face of the mountain opposite. It was barely dawn, but Juliana was up, too; he encountered her in the dark corridor.

"I am going up the cliff, to paint," he said. "That was what I had intended to do, before.

"We must think a little," he said. "I must go up there, and think. You do understand? You will talk to me again—we will speak to each other—when I return?"

She could have said: it is nothing to me whether you go up the mountain or remain here. But she was honest.

"I shall look out for you coming back."

"Juliana," he said, "ah, Juliana."

The mule skidded on the stones. The road was paved, after a fashion, but the stones were upended, like rows of jagged teeth. Gianni walked stolidly and silently behind. The road circled the hill, under chestnuts, then out onto the craggier ascent. It twisted and the sun rose; the mule passed from cold shadow to whitish glare and back again. Hot stone was very hot, Joshua thought, and cold stone very cold. He could smell stone of both kinds, as well as the warm hairy sweating mule and the glossy rubbed ancient leather. He looked backwards and forwards, along the snaking line of the river that cut its way about and about between the great cones of the Apennines. The sky had a white clearness and emptiness, not yet gleaming, which was essentially Italian. He knew the mountains round: the Libro Aperto, or open book, the Prato Fiorito, velvety and enamelled with flowers, the Monte Pellegrino, covered with silvery edible thistles and inhabited, once, by hermits whose diet they were. He thought about the mountains, with reverence and curiosity, and his thoughts on the mountains, like those of many of his contemporaries, were in large part the thoughts of John Ruskin, who had seen them clearly, as no one else, it seemed, had ever seen them, and had declared that this clarity of vision was the essence of truth, virtue, and good art, which were, in this, one. Mountains are the bones of the earth, he had written. "But there is this difference between the action of the earth, and that of a living creature; that while the exerted limb marks its bones and tendons through the flesh, the excited earth casts off the flesh altogether, and its bones come out from beneath." Joshua thought about this, and looked at the working knobs of bone at the base of the mule-neck, under their thin layer of skin, and remembered, formally and then excitedly, the search for Juliana's bone under the round cheek. Ruskin was a geologist. His ideals of painting were founded on an intricate and analytical knowledge of how the movement of water shaped and unmade and shifted the eternal hills, of how clefts were formed, and precipices sheered. It had been a revelation to the young Joshua to read in *Modern Painters* how very young was man's interest in these ancient forms. The Greeks had seen them merely as threats or aids to the adventures of gods and heroes; mediaeval man had on the whole disliked anything wild or savage, preferring order and cultivation, trellised gardens and bowers to wild woods or louring cliffs. John Ruskin would have delighted in the mediaeval names of the hills through which he now travelled: the Open Book, the Flowery Meadow, the Pilgrim's Mount came straight out of Dante into the nineteenth century. Ruskin had characterised modern art, with some disparagement, as the "service of clouds." The mediaeval mind had taken pleasure in the steady, the definite, the luminous, but the moderns rejoiced in the dark, the sombre. Our time, Ruskin had said, and Joshua had joyfully learned, was the true Dark Ages, devoted to smokiness and burnt umber. Joshua had not understood about the necessity of brightness and colour until he came south this first time, until he saw the light, although intellectually he had been fired by Ruskin's diatribes against Victorian darkness and ugliness in all things, in dress, in manners, in machines and chimneys, in storm clouds and grottoes.

Only, in Paris, he had seen something which changed, not the desire for brightness, but the ideas about the steady, the definite, the luminous. Something which should have helped him with the soft expanse of Juliana's pink dress, which he remembered, turning a corner and seeing the village again, clutching the cliff like thorn-bushes with half their roots in air. It was to do with the flesh and the muslin, the tones in common, the tones that were not shared, a blue in the pink cloth . . . you could pick up in the vein or the eyelid, the wrist, a shimmer, a thread . . . The hot saddle shifted beneath him: the mule sighed: the man sighed. Gianni said, *"Lucchio, una mezz'ora."* The white air was also blue and the blue white light.

When they got there, there was something alarming about this tenacious and vertiginous assembly of buildings, peacefully white in the mounting heat, chill in their dark aspects, all blindly shuttered, their dark life inside their doors. Houses stood where they were planted, where a level floor, or floors, could be found for them—often they were different heights on different sides. Many had tiny gardens fronting the empty air, and Gianni pointed out to Joshua, in two different instances, a toddling child, stiff-skirted, bonneted, tethered at the waist by a length of linen to a hook in the doorpost. Even the church bells were grounded, caged in iron frames outside the church door, safe, Joshua could only suppose, from vibrating unstably against the overhanging rock shelf.

Here Joshua parted from Gianni and the mules; they would meet again near the bells on the roadway, an hour or so from sunset. He took the path that curved up out of the village, which passed the ancient fountain where the girls came and went barefoot, carrying great copper vessels on their heads, swaying. At the fountain he replenished his water bottle, and moistened his face and neck. Then he went on up. Above the village was a ruined and much decayed castle, its thick outer wall continuous with the rock face, its courtyard littered with shattered building blocks. He thought of stopping here to draw the ancient masonry, but after reflection went on up. He had a need to study the wholly inhuman. His path, a branching, vertiginous sheep track, now wound between whitish sheer pillars of stone; his feet dislodged rubble and a powdery dust. He liked the feeling of the difficult going-up, and his step was springy. If he got far enough up and round he would have a downwards vantage point for sketching the improbable village. He thought alternately about Ruskin and about Juliana.

Ruskin disliked the Apennines: he found their limestone monotonous in hue, grey and toneless, utterly melancholy. He had expended several pages of exact lyrical prose on this gloomy colouring, pointing out that it was the colouring Dante gave to his Evil-pits in the Inferno, malignant grey, he gleefully recorded, akin to the robes of the purgatorial angel which were of the colour of ashes, or earth dug dry. Ashes, to an Italian mind, wrote Ruskin beside his London coals, necessarily meant *wood ashes*—very pale—analogous to the hue seen on the sunny side of Italian hills, produced by the scorching of the ground, a dusty and lifeless whitish grey, utterly painful and oppressive. He preferred the strenuous, masculine, mossy, and complicated Alps, awesome and sublime. Joshua had not really seen the Alps, but he found these smaller mountains beautiful, not oppressive, and their chalky paleness interesting, not dulling. Ruskin believed the great artists were those who had never despised anything, however small, of God's making. If he was prepared to treat the Apennine rocks as though they had been created perhaps only by a minor daemon or demiurge, Joshua, on Ruskin's own principles, was not. If he could find a means of recording the effects of these ashy whitenesses, of the reddish iron stains in the stone, of the way one block stood against another, of the root-systems of the odd, wind-sculpted trees, he would be content. He would, if he could find his vantage, "do" the view of the village. He would also, for that love of the true forms of things desiderated by his master, do studies of the stones as they were, of the scrubby things that grew.

He found his perch, in time; a wideish ledge, in a cleft with a high triangular shadow bisecting it, diminishing as the sun climbed. He thought of it as his eyrie. From it he would see the village, a little lower, winding round the conical form of the mountain like a clinging wreath, crowned by a fantastic cluster of crags all sky-pointing like huge hot inverted icicles, white on the white-blue sky. These forms were paradoxical, strong yet aerial and delicate like needles, reminding him of the lightness of lace on the emptiness, yet stone of earth. He took out his sketching-glass and filled it, arranged his paints and his chalks and his pencils, became wholly involved in the conversion of estimated distances to perceived relative sizes and tones. The problem was to convey this blanched, bony world with shadows which should, by contrast, form and display its dazzle. He tried both with pencil and with washes of colour. Ruskin said: "Here we are, then, with white paper for our highest light, and visible illuminated surface for our deepest shadow, set to run the gauntlet against nature, with the sun for her light, and vacuity for her gloom." Joshua wrestled with these limitations, in a glare which made it hard for him to judge the brightness even of his own paper surface. He was very miserable; his efforts took shape and solidified into failures of vision. He was supremely happy; unaware of himself and wholly aware of rock formations, sunlight and visible empty air, of which he became part, moment by moment and then timelessly, the notation of things seen being no more than the flow of his blood, necessary for continuance in this state.

At some point he became quite suddenly hungry, and took out of his knapsack his oily but agreeable packages of bread, meat, eggs, cheese. He devoured all, exhausted, as though his life was in danger, and put away his chicken bones and eggshells, for had not Ruskin himself complained that modern man came to the mountains not to fast but to feast, leaving glaciers covered with bones and eggshells. He had an idea of himself tearing at his food like a young bird on its ledge. Wiping his fingers, pouring more water for his work, he remembered Juliana, confusedly and from a distance, a softness in the corner of his consciousness, a warmth to which he would return when he returned to himself. He could never hurt Juliana, never. Behind the stone he had chosen for his seat were the bleached remains of some other creature's meal; skeletal pinions and claws, a triangular pointed skull, a few snail shells, wrecked and pierced. He made a quick watercolour sketch of these, interested in the different whites and creams and greys of bone, shell, and stone. And shadow. He was particularly pleased with his rendering of a snail shell, the arch of its entrance intact, the dome of the cavern behind shattered to reveal the pearly interior involution. These small things occupied as much space on the paper as the mountains. Their shadows were as intricate, though different.

When he came to look out at the land again, the air had changed, Near, it danced; farther away, on the horizon, white cloud was piling itself up and throwing out long arms from peak to peak; under the arms were horizontal bars of black shadow which seemed impossible where the sky had been so bright, so even. He set himself to draw this advance, watching the cloud hang along the precipices, waiting to stoop, and then engulf them. A wind began to blow, fitfully, rattling his sketchbook. The riverbed darkened: sounds were stilled that he had hardly noticed, insect songs and the odd birdcall.

The thing that he had seen in Paris, the thing that he knew would change his ideas about painting, was a large canvas by Monsieur Monet, a painting precisely of mist and fog, *Vétheuil in the Fog*. It had been rejected by its prospective purchaser because it had not enough paint on the canvas. It was not clear and definite. It was vague, it painted little more than the swirl and shimmer of light on the curtain of white water particles through which the shapes of the small town were barely visible, a slaty upright stroke here, a pearly faint triangle of possible roof or spire there. You could see, miraculously, that if you could see the town, which you could not, it would be reflected in the expanse of river at the foot of the canvas, which you could also not see. Monsieur Monet had found a solution to the problem posed by Ruskin, of how to paint light, with the small range of colours available: he had trapped light in his surface, light itself was his subject. His paint was light. He had painted, not the thing seen, but the act of seeing. So now, Joshua thought, as the first thin films of mist began to approach his eyrie, I want to note down these shifting, these vanishing veils. Through them, in the valley on the other side, he could see a perpendicular race of falling arrows dark and glistening, the hailstorm sweeping. The speed of its approach was beautiful. He made a kind of pattern on his paper of the verticals and the fleeciness, the different thickness and thinness of the vapour infiltrating his own ledge. He must be ready to pack up fast when it descended or his work would be ruined. When it came, it came in one fierce onslaught, a blast in his face, an impenetrable white darkness. He staggered a little, under the blows of the ice-bullets, put up an arm, took a false step, still thinking of Ruskin and Monet, and fell. And it was all over. Except for one or two unimaginable moments, a clutch at life, a gasp of useless air, a rush of adrenaline, a shattering of bone and brain, the vanishing between instants of all that warmth and intelligence and aspiration.

Down at the Villa Colomba they had been grateful for their thick walls and windows. The garden had been whipped and the flowers flattened, the white dark impenetrable. It lasted only ten minutes, maybe a quarter of an hour. Afterwards the children went out and came back crying that it was like Aladdin's palace. Everywhere, in the courtyard, was a glittering mass of green and shining stones, chestnut leaves bright with wet and shredded, hailstones as large as hazelnuts. Arthur and Gwendolen ran here and there gathering handfuls of these, tossing them, crying, "Look at my diamonds." The solid, the enduring, the familiar landscape smiled again in the washed sunlight. Juliana went out with the children, looked up at the still shrouded peaks, and filled her hands too with the jewels, cold, wet, gleaming, running away between her outstretched fingers.

Sarianna Browning received a letter, and wrote a letter. It took time for both these letters to reach their destinations, for the weather had deteriorated rapidly after those first storms, the mules could travel neither down from the Villa Colomba nor up to the paradise of coolness and quiet. Whips of rain flung themselves around the smiling tops; lightning cracked; tracks were rivers; Robert complained of the deep grinding of the pain that might be rheumatism and might be his liver. The envelope when she opened it was damp and pliant. Phrases stood out: "terrible accident . . . taken from us at the height of his powers . . . we trust, with his Maker . . . our terrible responsibility to his father and mother . . . Villa Colomba unbearable to us now . . . we trust you will understand, and accept our deepest apologies and regrets . . . we know Mr. Browning would not probably desire to visit us in Florence, though of course . . ."

Sarianna wrote to Mrs. Bronson. "Terrible accident . . . we trust, with his Maker . . . Robert not at his best . . . weather unsettled . . . hope to make our way now to Venice, since Florence is out of the question . . ."

The sky was like slate. The poet was trapped in the pleasant room. Sheets of water ran down his windows and collected on his balcony. He thought of other deaths. Five years ago he had been planning to ascend another mountain with another woman; going to rouse her, after his morning swim, full of life, he had come round her balcony and looked through her window to see her kneeling, composed and unnatural, head bowed to the ground. She had been still warm when he went in and released her from this posture. Remembering this, he went through the shock of her dead warmth again, and shuddered. He had gone up the mountain, all the same, alone, and had made a poem of it, a poem which clambered with difficulty around the topic of what if anything survived, of which hands, if any, moulded or received us. He had been half-ashamed of his assertion of his own liveliness and vigour, half-exalted by height and oxygen and achievement, as he had meant to be. This dead young man was unknown to him. For a moment his imagination reached after him, and imagined him, in his turn, as it was his nature to imagine, reaching after the unattainable, up there. Man's reach must exceed his grasp. Or what's a Heaven for? Perhaps the young man was a very conventional and unambitious young man: he did not know: it was his idea, that height went with reaching, even if defeated, as we all are, and must be. Over dinner, Mrs. Miller asked him if he would write a poem on the tragedy; this might, she suggested, bring comfort to the bereaved parents. No, he said. No, he would not. And elaborated, for good manners' sake. Even the greatest tragedies in his life had rarely stirred him directly to composition. They left him mute. He should hate any mechanical attempt to do what would only acquire worth from being a spontaneous outflow. Poems arose like birds setting off from stray twigs of facts to flights of more or less distance, unpredictably and often after many years. This was not to say that this tragedy, any tragedy, did not affect his whole mind and have its influence, more or less remarkably, on what he wrote. As he explained, his attention elsewhere, what he had explained before and would explain again, say, when Miss Teena Rochfort set fire to her skirts with a spark in her sewing basket, in 1883, he thought of the young painter, now dead, and of his son, whose nude sculptures had been objects of moral opprobrium to ladies like Mrs. Miller, and of Mrs. Miller's hat. There was a poem in that, in her stolid and disagreeable presence, bedizened with murdered innocents, and the naked life of art and love. Lines came into his head.

What
(Excuse the interruption) clings
Half-savage-like around your hat?
Ah, do they please you? Wild-bird wings . . .

Yes. "Clothed with murder." That would do. A black irritability was assuaged. He smiled with polite enthusiasm.

The lady sits in the window. The scholar, turning the browned pages, discovers the letter that she will receive. At first, in the story that he is reading and constructing this letter appears to be hopeful. The poet and his sister will not go further south. They will set their steps towards Venice. But it is not to be. Further letters are exchanged. Torrential rain in Bologna . . . Robert's pains worse . . . medical opinion advisable . . . roads impassable . . . deeply regret disappointing you and even more our own disappointment . . . return to London. An opportunity has been missed. A tentative love has not flowered. Next year, however, is better. The poet returns to Venice, meets in the lady's drawing room the Pretender to the French and Spanish thrones, discusses with him the identity of the Man in the Iron Mask, exposes himself, undaunted, on the Lido, to sea-fret and Adriatic gust, reads tombstones, kisses hands, and remarks on the seagulls.

Aunt Juliana kept, pressed in the family Bible, a curious portrait of a young girl, who looked out of one live eye and one blank, unseeing one, oval like those of angels on monumental sculpture.

RACINE AND THE TABLECLOTH

When was it clear that Martha Crichton-Walker was the antagonist? Emily found this word for her much later, when she was a grown woman. How can a child, undersized and fearful, have enough of a self to recognise an antagonist? She might imagine the malice of a cruel stepmother or a jealous sister, but not the clash of principle, the essential denial of an antagonist. She was too young to have thought-out beliefs. It was Miss Crichton-Walker's task, after all, to form and guide the unformed personality of Emily Bray. Emily Bray's ideas might have been thought to have been imparted by Martha Crichton-Walker, and this was in part the case, which made the recognition of antagonism peculiarly difficult, certainly for Emily, possibly for both of them.

The first time Emily saw Miss Crichton-Walker in action was the first evening of her time at the school. The class was gathered together, in firelight and lamplight, round Miss Crichton-Walker's hearth, in her private sitting room. Emily was the only new girl: she had arrived in mid-year, in exceptional circumstances (a family illness). The class were thirteen years old. There were twenty-eight of them, twenty-nine with Emily, a fact whose significance had not yet struck Emily. The fireside evening was Miss Crichton-Walker's way of noticing the death of a girl who had been in the class last term and had been struck by peritonitis after an operation on a burst appendix. This girl had been called Jan but had been known to the other girls as Hodgie. Did you hear about Hodgie, they all said to each other, rushing in with the news, mixing a kind of fear with a kind of glee, an undinted assurance of their own perpetuity. This was unfortunate for Emily; she felt like a substitute for Hodgie, although she was not. Miss Crichton-Walker gave them all pale cocoa and sugar-topped buns, and told them to sit on the floor round her. She spoke gently about their friend Hodgie whom they must all remember as she had been, full of life, sharing everything, a happy girl. She knew they were shocked; if at any later time they were to wish to bring any anxieties or regrets to her, she would be glad to share them. Regrets was an odd word, Emily perhaps noticed, though at that stage she was already willing enough to share Martha Crichton-Walker's tacit assumption that the girls would be bound to have regrets. Thirteen-year-old girls are unkind and in groups they are cruel. There would have been regrets, however full of life and happy the lost Hodgie had been.

Miss Crichton-Walker told the girls a story. It made a peaceful scene, with the young faces turned up to the central storyteller, or down to the carpet. Emily Bray studied Miss Crichton-Walker's appearance, which was firmly benign and breastless. Rolled silver curls, almost like a barrister's wig, were aligned round a sweet face, very soft-skinned but nowhere slack, set mild. The eyes were wide and very blue, and the mouth had no droop, but was firm and even, straight-set. Lines led finely to it but did not carve any cavity or depression: they lay lightly, like a hairnet. Miss Crichton-Walker wore, on this occasion and almost always, a very fine woollen dress, nun's veiling with a pleated chest, long fitted sleeves, and a plain white Peter Pan collar. At her neck was a simple oval silver brooch. There was something essentially girlish—not skittish, or sullen, or liquid, but unmarked, about this face and body, which were also those of a neat, elderly woman.

The story was allegorical. It was about a caddis grub which scuttled about on the floor of a pond, making itself a makeshift tube house of bits of gravel, twigs, and weed to cover its vulnerable and ugly little grub body. Its movements were awkward and painful, its world dank and dimly lit. One day it was seized with an urge to climb which it could not ignore. Painfully it drew its squashy length out of its abandoned house and made its way, bursting and anguished, up a tall bulrush. In the bright outer air it hardened, cased in, and then most painfully burst and split, issuing forth with fine iridescent wings and darting movements, a creature of light and air. Miss Crichton-Walker enjoyed this tale of contrasts. Emily Bray could not make out—she was never much to make out, it was her failing—what the other girls thought or felt. Always afterwards she imagined the dead Hodgie as grublike and squashy. During the telling she imagined the others as little girls, although she herself was the smallest in size, puny and stick-like. They all sat in their dressing gowns and pyjamas, washed and shapeless. Later in the dormitory they would chatter agitatedly, full of opinions and feelings, pointing fingers, jutting chins. Here they were secret and docile. Miss Crichton-Walker told them they had had a peaceful evening together and that had been good. Emily Bray saw that there were two outsiders in the room. There was herself, set aside from the emotion that was swimming around, and there was Miss Crichton-Walker who wanted them all to be sharing something.

Every Wednesday and every Sunday the school walked into the centre of the cathedral city to go to church. On Wednesday they had their own service, shared with their brother school, Holy Communion and Morning Prayer. On Sunday they made part—a large part—of the general congregation. There were rules about walking through the city; they did not go in a crocodile, but were strictly forbidden to walk more than two abreast through the narrow streets. Three laughing girls, horseplaying perhaps, had once swept over an old lady outside Boot's, had fractured frail bones and been cautioned by the Police. A result of this reasonable ruling was that it was important for each girl to have a partner, someone to walk with, a best friend. Girls of that age choose best friends naturally, or so Emily had observed, who had not had a best friend since her days in the junior school, before her unfortunate habits became pronounced. The church-walking added forms and rituals to the selection and rejection of best friends. Everyone knew if a couple split up, or a new couple was formed. Emily discovered quickly enough that there was a floating population of rejects, rag, tag, bobtail, who formed feebler ties, ad hoc partnerships, with half an eye on the chance of a rift between a more acceptable pairing. She assumed she would belong with these. She had no illusions about her chances of popularity in the class. The best she could hope for was decent anonymity. She also knew that decent anonymity was unlikely. When the exam results came, she would be found out. In the interim, she realised quickly enough the significance of the size of the class, twenty-nine girls. There would always be a final reject, one running round when all the musical chairs were occupied. That one would be Emily Bray.

You might suppose that grown-up, intelligent schoolmistresses would be capable of seeing the significance of twenty-nine, or that it might be possible for Emily to point it out, or recall it to them, if they did not. You also almost certainly know enough about conventional institutional rigours to be unsurprised that it was quite impossible for Emily to say anything coherent when, as happened regularly, she was caught up in the street and reprimanded for tagging along in a threesome. (Walking anywhere alone was an unthinkable and serious offence.) She dreaded Wednesdays and Sundays, working herself up on Tuesdays and Saturdays to beg, with mortified mock-casual misery, to be allowed to come along. After she began to get exam results, the situation, as she had foreseen, worsened. With appalling regularity, with unnatural ease and insulting catholicity, Emily Bray came first in almost everything except maths and domestic science. She came first in the theoretical paper of the domestic science, but her handiwork let her down. She was a simply intellectual creature. She was physically undeveloped, no good at sport, no one to chatter to about sex, or *schwärmerei,* delicious shoes or pony club confrontations. She had an image of herself in their minds as a kind of abacus in its limited frame, clicking mnemonics, solving problems, recording transactions. She waited to be disliked and they duly disliked her. There were clever girls, Flora Marsh, for example, who were not so disliked: Flora was peaceably beautiful, big and slender and athletic and wholesome, genuinely modest, wanting to be mother of six and live in the country. Flora had a horse and a church partner, Catherine, she had known since she was five. Flora's handwriting was even and generous, flowing on in blue running curves and rhythmic spaces. Emily Bray wrote hunched over the page, jabbing at it with a weak-nibbed fountain pen. There was never a misspelled word, but the whole was blotted and a little smeared and grimy, the lines uneven, the characters without settled forms. In Emily's second year Miss Crichton-Walker addressed their class on its work and said in front of all of them that it was her habit always to read the best set of exam papers. In this case that was, as they all knew, Emily Bray's but she was afraid that she had had to return these unfinished since she was distressed by the aggressive handwriting. The papers were a disgrace in other ways too, nastily presented, and dirty. If Emily would be kind enough to make a fair copy she would be delighted to read them. She delivered this judgment, as was her habit, with a slight smile, not deprecating, not mitigating, but pleased and admiring. Admiring the accuracy of her own expressions, or pleased with the placing of the barb? It did not occur to young Emily to ask herself that question, though she noted and remembered the smile accurately enough to answer it, when she was ready, when her account was made up. But the child did not know what judgment the woman would make, or indeed that the woman would judge. The child believed she was shrugging off the judgment of herself. Of course the paper was dirty: schools thought dirt mattered; she believed it did not. She opposed herself like a shut sea anemone, a wall of muscle, a tight sphincter. It is also true, changing the metaphor, that the judgment dropped in heavily and fast, like a stone into a pond, to rest unshifted on the bottom.

She noted the word, aggressive, as on that earlier occasion she had noted "regrets." She remembered writing those speedy, spattered pages—an essay on Hamlet's delays, a character analysis of Emma Woodhouse. She had written for pleasure. She had written for an imaginary ideal Reader, perfectly aware of her own strengths and failings, her approximations to proper judgments, her flashes of understanding. If she had thought for ten minutes she would have known that no such Reader existed, there was only Miss Harvey and beyond Miss Harvey Miss Crichton-Walker. But she never yielded those ten minutes. If the real Reader did not exist it was necessary to invent Him, and Emily did so. The pronoun is an accurate rendering of Emily's vaguest intimation of his nature. In a female institution where justice, or judgment, was Miss Crichton-Walker, benign impartiality seemed to be male. Emily did not associate the Reader with the gods worshipped in the cathedral on Sundays. God the Judge and God the Friend and God the rushing wind of the Spirit were familiars of Miss Crichton-Walker invoked with an effort of ecstasy in evening prayers in the school, put together with music and branched stone and beautiful words and a sighing sentiment in the choir stalls. Emily could not reasonably see why the propensity to believe this myth should have any primary guarantee of touching at truth, any more than the propensity to believe Apollo, or Odin, or Gautama Buddha, or Mithras. She was not aware that she believed in the Reader, though as she got older she became more precise and firm about his attributes. He was dry and clear, he was all-knowing but not messily infinite. He kept his proportion and his place. He had no face and no imaginary arms to enfold or heart to beat: his nature was not love, but understanding. Invoked, as the black ink spattered in the smell of chalk dust and dirty fingers, he brought with him a foreign air, sunbaked on sand, sterile, heady, tolerably hot. It is not too much to say that in those seemingly endless years in that place Emily was enabled to continue because she was able to go on believing in the Reader.

She did not make a fair copy of her papers for Miss Crichton-Walker. She believed that it was not really expected of her, that the point to be made had been made. Here she may have been doing Miss Crichton-Walker an injustice, though this is doubtful. Miss Crichton-Walker was expert in morals, not in *Hamlet* or *Emma*.

When she was fifteen Emily devised a way of dealing with the church walk. The city was mediaeval still in many parts, and, more particularly, was surrounded with long stretches of city wall, with honey-pale stone battlements, inside which two people could walk side by side, looking out over the cathedral close and the twisting lanes, away down to the surrounding plain. She discovered that if she ducked back behind the church, under an arched gateway, she could, if she went briskly, walk back along the ramparts almost all the way, outflanking the mainstream of female pairs, descending only for the last few hundred yards, where it was possible to dodge through back streets to where the school stood, in its pleasant gardens, inside its own lesser barbed wall. No one who has not been an inmate can know exactly how powerful is the hunger for solitude which grows in the constant company, day and night, feeding, washing, learning, sleeping, almost even, with partition walls on tubular metal stems, excreting. It is said women make bad prisoners because they are not by nature communal creatures. Emily thought about these things in the snatched breathing spaces she had made on the high walls, but thought of the need for solitude as hers only, over against the crushing others, though they must all also, she later recognised, have had their inner lives, their reticences, their inexpressive needs. She thought things out on that wall, French grammar and Euclid, the existence of males, somewhere else, the purpose of her life. She grew bold and regular—there was a particular tree, a self-planted willow, whose catkins she returned to each week, tight dark reddish buds, bursting silvery grey, a week damp and glossy grey fur and then the full pussy willow, softly bristling, powdered with bright yellow in the blue. One day when she was standing looking at these vegetable lights Miss Crichton-Walker and another figure appeared to materialise in front of her, side by stiff side. They must have come up one of the flights of steps from the grass bank inside the wall, now bright with daffodils and crocus; Emily remembered them appearing headfirst, as though rising from the ground, rather than walking towards her. Miss Crichton-Walker had a grey woollen coat with a curly lambskin collar in a darker pewter; on her head was a matching hat, a cylinder of curly fur. There were two rows of buttons on her chest; she wore grey kid gloves and sensible shoes, laced and rigorous. She stood there for a moment on the wall and saw Emily Bray by her willow tree. There was no question in Emily's mind that they had stared at each other, silently. Then Miss Crichton-Walker pointed over the parapet, indicating some cloud formation to her companion, of whose identity Emily formed no impression at all, and they passed on, in complete silence. She even wondered wildly, as she hurried away back towards the school, if she had not seen them at all.

She had, of course. Miss Crichton-Walker waited until evening prayers to announce, in front of the school, that she wanted to see Emily Bray, tomorrow after lunch, thus leaving Emily all night and half a day to wonder what would be said or done. It was a school without formal punishments. No one wrote lines, or sat through detentions, or penitently scrubbed washroom floors. And yet everyone, not only Emily Bray, was afraid of committing a fault before Miss Crichton-Walker. She could make you feel a real worm, the girls said, the lowest of the low, for having illegal runny honey instead of permitted hard honey, for running across the tennis lawns in heavy shoes, for smiling at boys. What she could do to those who cheated or stole or bullied was less clear and less urgent. On the whole they didn't. They were on the whole nice girls. They accepted Miss Crichton-Walker's judgment of them, and this was their heavy punishment.

Emily stood in front of Miss Crichton-Walker in her study. Between their faces was a silver rose bowl, full of spring flowers. Miss Crichton-Walker was small and straight in a large upright armchair. She asked Emily what she had been doing on the wall, and Emily said that she had no one to walk home from church with, so came that way. She thought of adding, most girls of my age, in reasonable day schools, can walk alone in a city in the middle of the morning, quite naturally, anybody might. Miss Crichton-Walker said that Emily was arrogant and unsociable, had made little or no effort to fit in with the community ever since she came, appeared to think that the world was made for her convenience. She set herself against everything, Miss Crichton-Walker said, she was positively depraved. Here was another word to add to those others, regrets, aggressive, depraved. Emily said afterwards to Flora Marsh, who asked what had happened, that Miss Crichton-Walker had told her that she was depraved. Surely not, said Flora, and, yes she did, said Emily, she did, that is what she *thinks*. You may have your own views about whether Miss Crichton-Walker could in sober fact have uttered the word depraved, in her soft, silvery voice, to an awkward girl who had tried to walk alone in mid-morning, to look at a pussy willow, to think. It may be that Emily invented the word herself, saying it for bravado to Flora Marsh after the event, though I would then argue, in defence of Emily, that the word must have been in the air during that dialogue for her to pick up, the feeling was there, Miss Crichton-Walker sensed her solitude as something corrupt, contaminating, depraved. What was to be done? For the next four weeks, Miss Crichton-Walker said, she would walk back from church with Emily herself. It was clear that she found this prospect as disagreeable as Emily possibly could. She was punishing both of them.

What could they say to each other, the awkward pair, one shuffling downcast, one with a regular inhibited stride? Emily did not regard it as her place to initiate any conversation: she believed any approach would have been unacceptable, and may well have been right. You will think that Miss Crichton-Walker might have taken the opportunity to draw Emily out, to find out why she was unhappy, or what she thought of her education. She did say some things that might have been thought to be part of such a conversation, though she said them reluctantly, in a repressed, husky voice, as though they were hard to bring out. She was content for much the larger part of their four weeks' perambulation to say nothing at all, pacing it out like prison exercise, a regular rhythmic pavement-tapping with which Emily was compelled to try to keep time. Occasionally spontaneous remarks broke from her, not in the strained, clutching voice of her confidential manner, but with a sharp, clear ring. These were remarks about Emily's personal appearance for which she felt—it is not too strong a word, though this time it is mine, or Emily's; Martha Crichton-Walker is innocent of uttering it—she felt disgust. "For the second week running you have a grey line round your neck, Emily, like the scum you deposit round the rim of the bath." "You have a poor skin, Emily. Ask Sister to give those blackheads some attention: you must have an abnormal concentration of grease in your nasal area, or else you are unusually skimpy in your attention to your personal hygiene. Have you tried medicated soap?" "Your hair is lank, Emily. I do not like to think of the probable state of your hatband." "May I see your hands? I have never understood how people can bring themselves to bite their nails. How unpleasant and profitless to chew away one's own flesh in this manner. I see you are imbued with ink as some people are dyed with nicotine: it is just as disagreeable. Perhaps the state of your hands goes some way to explain your very poor presentation of your work: you seem to *wallow* in ink to a quite unusual extent. Please purchase a pumice stone and a lemon and scour it away before we go out next week. Please borrow a knife from the kitchen and prise away the boot-polished mud from your shoe heels—that is a lazy way of going on that does not deceive the eye, and increases the impression of slovenliness."

None of these remarks was wholly unjust, though the number of them, the ingenuity with which they were elaborated and dilated on, were perhaps excessive? Emily imagined the little nose sniffing at the armpits of her discarded vests, at the stains on her pants. She sweated with anxiety inside her serge overcoat, waiting outside Miss Crichton-Walker's study, and imagined Miss Crichton-Walker could smell her fear rising out of the wool, running down her lisle stockings. Miss Crichton-Walker seemed to be without natural exudations. A whiff of lavender, a hint of mothball.

She talked to Emily about her family. Emily's family do not come into this story, though you may perhaps be wondering about them, you might need at least to know whether the authority they represented would be likely to reinforce that of Miss Crichton-Walker, or to present some counterbalance, some other form of moral priority. Emily Bray was a scholarship girl, from a large Potteries family of five children. Emily's father was a foreman in charge of a kiln which fired a curious mixture of teacups thick with lilies of the valley, dinner plates edged severely with gold dagger-shapes, and virulently green pottery dogs with gaping mouths to hold toothbrushes or rubber bands. Emily's mother had, until her marriage, been an elementary school teacher, trained at Homerton in Cambridge, where she had developed the aspiration to send her sons and daughters to that university. Emily was the eldest of the five children; the next one, Martin, was a mongol. Emily's mother considered Martin a condign punishment of her aspirations to betterment. She loved him extravagantly and best. The three younger ones were left to their own resources, much of the time. Emily felt for them, and their cramped, busy, noisy little life, some of the distaste Miss Crichton-Walker felt for her, perhaps for all the girls. There are two things to note in this brief summing-up—a hereditary propensity to feel guilty, handed down to Emily from her briefly ambitious mother, and the existence of Martin.

Miss Crichton-Walker knew about Martin, of course. He had been part of the argument for Emily's scholarship, awarded on grounds of social need, in line with the principles of the school, rather than academic merit. Miss Crichton-Walker, insofar as she wanted to talk to Emily at all, wanted to talk about Martin. Tell me about your brothers and sisters, dear, she said, and Emily listed them, Martin, thirteen, Loma, ten, Gareth, eight, Amanda, five. Did she miss them, said Miss Crichton-Walker, and Emily said no, not really, she saw them in the holidays, they were very noisy, if she was working. But you must love them, said Miss Crichton-Walker, in her choking voice, you must feel you are, hmm, not properly part of their lives? Emily did indeed feel excluded from the bustle of the kitchen, and more confusedly, more anxiously, from her mother's love, by Martin. But she sensed, rightly, that Miss Crichton-Walker wished her to feel cut off by the privilege of being at the school, guilty of not offering the help she might have done. She described teaching Amanda to read, in two weeks flat, and Miss Crichton-Walker said she noticed Emily did not mention Martin. Was that because she was embarrassed, or because she felt badly about him? She must never be embarrassed by Martin's misfortune, said Miss Crichton-Walker, who was embarrassed by Emily's inkstains and shoe mud most sincerely, she must acknowledge her own. I do love him, said Emily, who did, who had nursed and sung to him, when he was smaller, who suffered from his crashing forays into her half-bedroom, from scribbled-on exercises, bath-drowned books. She remembered his heavy amiable twinkle. We all love him, she said. You must try to do so, said Miss Crichton-Walker.

Miss Crichton-Walker had her lighter moments. Some of these were part of the school's traditional pattern, in which she had her traditional place, such as the telling of the school ghost story at Hallowe'en, a firelit occasion for everyone, in the stark dining room, by the light of two hundred candles inside the grinning orange skins of two hundred swedes. The girls sat for hours hollowing out these heads, at first nibbling the sweet vegetable, then revolted by it. For days afterwards the school smelled like a byre: during the storytelling the roasting smell of singed turnip overlay the persisting smell of the raw scrapings. For an hour before the storytelling they had their annual time of licence, running screaming through the dark garden, in sheets and knitted spiderwebs, jointed paper skeletons and floating batwings. The ghost story concerned an improbable encounter between a Roman centurion and a phantom cow in a venerable clump of trees in the centre of which stood an old and magnificent swing. Anyone meeting the white cow would vanish, the story ran, as in some other time the centurion had vanished, though imperfectly, leaving traces of his presence amongst the trees, the glimpsed sheen on a helmet, the flutter of his leather skirting. There was always a lot of suppressed giggling during Miss Crichton-Walker's rendering of this tale, which, to tell the truth, lacked narrative tension and a conclusive climax. The giggling was because of the proliferate embroidered legends which were in everyone's mind of Miss Crichton-Walker's secret, nocturnal, naked swinging in that clump of trees. She had once very determinedly, in Emily's presence, told a group of the girls that she enjoyed sitting naked in her room, on the hearth by the fire in the evening. It is very pleasant to feel the air on your skin, said Miss Crichton-Walker, holding her hands judicially before her chest, fingertips touching. It is natural and pleasant. Emily did not know what authority there was for the legend that she swung naked at night in the garden. She had perhaps once told such a group of girls that she would *like* to do so, that it would be good and pleasant to swoop unencumbered through the dark air, to touch the lowest branches of the thick trees with naked toes, to feel the cool rush along her body. There were in any case now several stories of her having been solidly seen doing just that, urging herself to and fro, milky-white in the dark. This image, with its moon face and rigid imperturbable curls was much more vivid in Emily's mind at Hallowe'en than any ghostly cow or centurion. The swing, in its wooden authority and weight, reminded Emily of a gibbet. The storytelling, more vaguely, reminded her of the first evening and the allegorizing of Hodgie's death.

Their first stirrings of appetite and anxiety, directed at the only vaguely differentiated mass of the brother school's congregation, aroused considerable efforts of repressive energy in Miss Crichton-Walker. It was said that under a previous, more liberal headmistress, the boys had been encouraged to walk the girls back from church. No one would even have dared to propose this to her. That there were girls who flouted this prohibition Emily knew, though only by remote hearsay. She could not tell one boy from another and was in love with Benedick, with Pierre, with Max Ravenscar, with Mr. Knightley. There was an annual school dance, to which the boys were brought in silent, damp-palmed, hunched clumps in two or three buses. Miss Crichton-Walker could not prevent this dance: it was an ancient tradition: the boys' headmaster and the governors liked it to exist as a sign of educational liberality. But she spoke against it. For weeks before the arrival of the boys she spent her little Saturday evening homilies on warning the girls. It was not clear, from what she said, exactly what she was warning against. She was famous in the Lower Sixth for having managed explicitly to say that if any boy pressed too close, held any girl too tightly, that girl must say composedly, "Shall we sit this one out?" Girls rolled on their dormitory beds gasping out this *mot* in bursts of wild laughter and tones of accomplished parody. (The school was full of accomplished parodists of Miss Crichton-Walker.) They polished their coloured court shoes, scarlet and peacock, and fingered the stiff taffeta folds of their huge skirts, which they wore with demure and provocative silk shirts, and tightly-pulled wide belts. In later years Emily remembered as the centre of Miss Crichton-Walker's attack on sexual promptings, on the possibilities of arousal, a curiously elaborate disquisition on the unpleasantness and unnatural function of the female razor. She could not bring herself to mention the armpits. She spoke at length, with an access of clarity and precision, about the evil effects on the skin of frequent shaving of the legs, which left "as I know very well, an unsightly dark stubble, which then has to be treated more and more frequently, once you have shaved away the first natural soft down. Any gardener will tell you that grass grows coarser after it has once been cut. I ask all the girls who have razors in the school to send them home, please, and all girls to ask their parents not to send such things through the post." It was also during the weeks preceding the dance that she spoke against deodorants, saying that they were unnecessary for young girls and that the effects of prolonged chemical treatment of delicate skin were not yet known. A little talcum powder would be quite sufficient if they feared becoming heated.

I am not going to describe the dance, which was sad for almost all of them, must have been, as they stood in their resolutely unmingled ranks on either side of the grey school hall. Nothing of interest really happened to Emily on that occasion, as she must, in her secret mind, have known it would not. It faded rapidly enough in her memory, whereas Miss Crichton-Walker's peculiar anxiety about it, even down to her curious analogy between razors and lawn mowers, remained stamped there, clear and pungent, an odd and significant trace of the days of her education. In due course this memory accrued to itself Emily's later reflections on the punning names of depilatories, all of which aroused in her mind a trace image of Miss Crichton-Walker's swinging, white, hairless body in the moonlight. Veet. Immac. Nair. Emily at the time of the static dance was beginning to sample the pleasures of being a linguist. Nair sounded like a Miltonic coinage for Satanic scaliness. Veet was a thick English version of French rapidity and discreet efficiency. Immac, in the connexion of Miss Crichton-Walker, was particularly satisfying, carrying with it the Latin, maculata, stained or spotted, immaculata, unstained, unspotted, and the Immaculate Conception, which, Emily was taught at this time, referred to the stainless or spotless begetting of the Virgin herself, not to the subsequent self-contained, unpunctured, manless begetting of the Son. The girls in the dormitories were roused by Miss Crichton-Walker to swap anecdotes about Veet, which according to them had "the—most—terrible—*smell*" and produced a stinking slop of hairy grease. No one sent her razor home. It was generally agreed that Miss Crichton-Walker had too little bodily hair to know what it was to worry about it.

Meanwhile, and at the same time, there was Racine. You may be amused that Miss Crichton-Walker should simultaneously ban ladies' razors and promote the study of *Phèdre*. It is amusing. It is amusing that the same girls should already have been exposed to the betrayed and betraying cries of Ophelia's madness. "Then up he rose, and doffed his clothes, and dupped the chamber door. Let in the maid that out a maid, never departed more." It is the word "dupped" that is so upsetting in that little song, perhaps because it recalls another

Shakespearean word that rhymes with it, Iago's black ram tupping the white ewe, Desdemona. Get thee to a nunnery, said Hamlet, and there was Emily, in a nunnery, never out of one, in a rustle of terrible words and delicate and gross suggestions, the stuff of her studies. But that is not what I wanted to say about Racine. Shakespeare came upon Emily gradually, she could accommodate him, he had always been there. Racine was sudden and new. That is not it, either, not what I wanted to say.

Think of it. Twenty girls or so—were there so many?—in the A-level French class, and in front of each a similar, if not identical small, slim greenish book, more or less used, more or less stained. When they riffled through the pages, the text did not look attractive. It proceeded in strict, soldierly columns of rhymed couplets, a form disliked by both the poetry lovers and the indifferent amongst them. Nothing seemed to be happening, it all seemed to be the same. The speeches were very long. There appeared to be no interchange, no battle of dialogue, no action. *Phèdre.* The French teacher told them that the play was based on the *Hippolytus* of Euripides, and that Racine had altered the plot by adding a character, a young girl, Aricie, whom Hippolytus should fall in love with. She neglected to describe the original play, which they did not know. They wrote down, Hippolytus, Euripides, Aricie. She told them that the play kept the unities of classical drama, and told them what these unities were, and they wrote them down. The Unity of Time = One Day. The Unity of Space = One Place. The Unity of Action = One Plot. She neglected to say what kind of effect these constrictions might have on an imagined world: she offered a half-hearted rationale she clearly despised a little herself, as though the Greeks and the French were children who made unnecessary rules for themselves, did not see wider horizons. The girls were embarrassed by having to read this passionate singsong verse aloud in French. Emily shared their initial reluctance, their near-apathy. She was later to believe that only she became a secret addict of Racine's convoluted world, tortuously lucid, savage, and controlled. As I said, the imagination of the other girls' thoughts was not Emily's strength. In Racine's world, all the inmates were gripped wholly by incompatible passions which swelled uncontrollably to fill their whole universe, brimming over and drowning its horizons. They were all creatures of excess, their secret blood burned and boiled and an unimaginably hot bright sun glared down in judgment. They were all horribly and beautifully interwoven, tearing each other apart in a perfectly choreographed dance, every move inevitable, lovely, destroying. In this world men and women had high and terrible fates which were themselves and yet greater than themselves. Phèdre's love for Hippolyte was wholly unnatural, dragging her world askew, wholly inevitable, a force like a flood, or a conflagration, or an eruption. This art described a world of monstrous disorder and excess and at the same time ordered it with iron control and constrictions, the closed world of the classical stage and the prescribed dialogue, the flexible, shining, inescapable steel mesh of that regular, regulated singing verse. It was a world in which the artist was in unusual collusion with the Reader, his art like a mapping trellis between the voyeur and the terrible writhing of the characters. It was an austere and adult art, Emily thought, who knew little about adults, only that they were unlike Miss Crichton-Walker, and had anxieties other than those of her tired and overstretched mother. The Reader was adult. The Reader saw with the pitiless clarity of Racine—and also with Racine's impersonal sympathy—just how far human beings could go, what they were capable of.

After the April foolery, Miss Crichton-Walker said she would not have believed the girls were capable of it. No one, no one Emily knew at least, knew how the folly had started. It was "passed on," in giggled injunctions, returning again embroidered to earlier tellers. It must have originated with some pair, or pairs, of boys and girls who had managed to make contact at the static dance, who had perhaps sat a few waltzes out together, as Miss Crichton-Walker had bidden. The instruction they all received was that on Sunday, April 1, the boys were to sit on the girls' side of the church and vice versa. Not to mingle, that is. To change places en bloc, from the bride's side to the bridegroom's. No rationale was given for this jape, which was immediately perceived by all the girls and boys involved as exquisitely funny, a kind of epitome of disorder and misrule. The bolder spirits took care to arrive early, and arrange themselves decorously in their contrary pews. The others followed like meek sheep. To show that they were not mocking God, the whole congregation then worshipped with almost unnatural fervour and devotion, chanting the responses, not wriggling or shifting in their seats. The Vicar raised his eyebrows, smiled benignly, and conducted the service with no reference to the change.

Miss Crichton-Walker was shocked, or hurt, to the quick. It was as though, Emily thought very much later, some kind of ritual travesty had happened, the Dionysiac preparing of Pentheus, in his women's skirts, for the maenads to feast on. Though this analogy is misleading: Miss Crichton-Walker's anguish was a kind of puritanical modesty. What outraged her was that, as she saw it, she, and the institution of which she was the head, had been irrevocably shamed in front of the enemy. In the icy little speech she made to the school at the next breakfast she did not mention any insult to the church, Emily was almost sure. Nor did she dart barbs of precise, disgusted speech at the assembled girls: she was too upset for that. Uncharacteristically she wavered, beginning, "Something has happened . . . something has taken place . . . you will all know what I am speaking of . . ." gathering strength only when she came to her proposed expiation of the sin. "Because of what you have done," she said, "I shall stand here, without food, during all today's meals. I shall eat nothing. You can watch me while you eat, and think about what you have done."

Did they? Emily's uncertainty about the thoughts of the others held for this extraordinary act of vicarious penance, too. Did they laugh about it? Were they shocked and anxious? Through all three meals of the day they ate in silence, forks clattering vigorously on plates, iron spoons scraping metal trays, amongst the smell of browned shepherd's pie and institutional custard, whilst that little figure stood, doll-like, absurd and compelling, her fine lips pursed, her judicial curls regular round her motionless cheeks. Emily herself, as always, she came to understand, reacted with a fatal doubleness. She *thought* Miss Crichton-Walker was behaving in an undignified and disproportionate manner. She *felt,* gloomily and heavily, that she had indeed greatly damaged Miss Crichton-Walker, had done her a great and now inexpiable wrong, for which Miss Crichton-Walker was busily heaping coals of fire on her uncomprehending but guilty head. Miss Crichton-Walker was atoning for Emily's sin, which Emily had not, until then, known to be a sin. Emily was trapped.

When the A-level exams came, Emily developed a personality, not perhaps, you will think, a very agreeable one. She was approaching a time when her skills would be publicly measured and valued, or so she thought, as she became increasingly aware that they were positively deplored, not only by the other girls, but by Miss Crichton-Walker. The school was academically sound but made it a matter of principle not to put much emphasis on these matters, to encourage leadership, community spirit, charity, usefulness, and other worthy undertakings. Girls went to university but were not excessively, not even much praised for this. Nevertheless, Emily knew it was there. At the end of the tunnel—which she visualised, since one must never allow a metaphor to lie dead and inert, as some kind of curving, tough, skinny tube in which she was confined and struggling, seeing the outside world dimly and distorted—at the end of the tunnel there was, there must be, light and a rational world full of aspiring Readers. She prepared for the A level with a desperate chastity of effort, as a nun might prepare for her vows. She learned to write neatly, overnight it seemed, so that no one recognised these new, confident, precisely black unblotted lines. She developed a pugnacious tilt to her chin. Someone in her form took her by the ears and banged her head repeatedly on the classroom wall, crying out "you don't even have to try, you smug little bitch . . ." but this was not true. She struggled secretly for perfection. She read four more of Racine's plays, feverishly sure that she would, when the time came, write something inadequate, ill-informed about his range, his beliefs, his wisdom. As I write, I can feel you judging her adversely, thinking, what a to-do, or even, smug little bitch. If I had set out to write a story about someone trying for perfection as a high diver, perhaps, or as a long distance runner, or even as a pianist, I should not so have lost your sympathy at this point. I could have been sure of exciting you with heavy muscles going up the concrete steps for the twentieth or thirtieth time, with the smooth sheet of aquamarine always waiting, the rush of white air, white air in water, the drum in the eardrums, the conversion of flesh and bone to a perfect parabola. You would have understood this in terms of some great effort of your own, at some time, as I now take pleasure in understanding the work of televised snooker players, thinking a series of curves and lines and then making these real, watching the balls dart and clatter and fall into beautiful shapes, as I also take pleasure in the skill of the cameramen, who can show my ignorant eye, picking out this detail and that, where the beautiful lines lie, where there are impossibilities in the way, where the danger is, and where success.

Maybe I am wrong in supposing that there is something inherently distasteful in the struggles of the solitary clever child. Or maybe the reason is not that cleverness—academic cleverness—is distasteful, but that writing about it is *déjà vu,* wearisome. That's what they all become, solitary clever children, complaining writers, misunderstood. Not Emily. She did not become a writer, about her misunderstood cleverness or anything else.

Maybe you are not unsympathetic at all, and I have now made you so. You can do without a paranoid narrator. Back to Miss Crichton-Walker, always in wait.

On the evening before the first exam, Miss Crichton-Walker addressed to the whole school one of her little homilies. It was summer, and she wore a silvery grey dress, with her small silver brooch.

In front of her was a plain silver bowl of flowers—pink roses, blue irises, something white and lacy and delicate surrounding them. The exams, she told the school, were due to begin tomorrow, and she hoped the junior girls would remember to keep quiet and not to shout under the hall windows whilst others were writing. There were girls in the school, she said, who appeared to attach a great deal of importance to exam results. Who seemed to think that there was some kind of exceptional merit in doing well. She hoped she had never allowed the school to suppose that her own values were wrapped up in this kind of achievement. Everything they did mattered, mattered very much, everything was of extreme importance in its own way. She herself, she said, had written books, and she had embroidered tablecloths. She would not say that there was not as much lasting value, as much pleasure for others, in a well-made tablecloth as in a well-written book.

While she talked, her eyes appeared to meet Emily's, steely and intimate. Any good speaker can do this, can appear to single out one or another of the listeners, can give the illusion that all are personally addressed. Miss Crichton-Walker was not a good speaker, normally: her voice was always choked with emotion, which she was not so much sharing as desperately offering to the stony, the uncaring of her imagination. She expected to be misunderstood, even in gaudier moments to be reviled, though persisting. Emily understood this without knowing how she knew it, or even that she knew it. But on this one occasion she knew with equal certainty that Miss Crichton-Walker's words were for her, that they were delivered with a sweet animus, an absolute antagonism into which Miss Crichton-Walker's whole cramped self was momentarily directed. At first she stared back angrily, her little chin grimly up, and thought that Miss Crichton-Walker was exceedingly vulgar, that what mattered was not exam results, God save the mark, but *Racine.* And then, in a spirit of almost academic justice, she tried to think of the virtue of tablecloths, and thought of her own auntie Florence, in fact a great-aunt. And, after a moment or two, twisted her head, broke the locked gaze, looked down at the parquet.

In the Potteries, she had many great-aunts. Auntie Annie, Auntie Ada, Auntie Miriam, Auntie Gertrude, Auntie Florence. Auntie Florence was the eldest and had been the most beautiful. She had always looked after her mother, in pinched circumstances, and had married late, having no children of her own, though always, Emily's mother said, much in demand to look after other people's. Her mother had died when Florrie was fifty-four, demented and senile. Her husband had had a stroke, that year, and had lain helplessly in bed for the next ten, fed and tended by Auntie Florrie. She had had, in her youth, long golden hair, so long she could sit on it. She had always wanted to travel abroad, Auntie Florrie, whose education had ceased formally at fourteen, who read Dickens and Trollope, Dumas and Harriet Beecher Stowe. When Uncle Ted died at last, Aunt Florrie had a little money and thought she might travel. But then Auntie Miriam sickened, went off her feet, trembled uncontrollably and Florrie was called in by her children, busy with their own children. She was the one who was available, like Emily's mother said. She had always been as strong as a horse, toiling up and down them stairs, fetching and carrying for Gran, for Uncle Ted, and then for poor Miriam. She always looked so wholesome and ready for anything. But she was seventy-two when Miriam died and arthritis got her. She couldn't go very far. She went on with the embroidery she'd always done, beautiful work of all kinds, bouquets and arabesques and trellises of flowers in jewelled colours on white linen, or in white silk on white pillowcases, or in rainbow colours and patterns from every century, Renaissance, Classical, Victorian, Art Nouveau, on satin cushion covers. If you went to see her you took her a present of white satin to work on. She liked heavy bridal satin best. She liked the creamy whites and could never take to the new glaring whites in the nylon satins. When she was eighty-five the local paper had an article in it about her marvellous work, and a photograph of Auntie Florrie in her little sitting room, sitting upright amongst all the white rectangles of her needlework, draped on all the furniture. Aunt Florrie still wore a woven crown of her own thinning hair. She had a good neighbour, Emily's mother said, who came in and did for her. She couldn't do much work, now, though. The arthritis had got her hands.

After Miss Crichton-Walker's little talk, Emily began to cry. For the first half hour of the crying she herself thought that it was just a nervous reaction, a kind of irritation, because she was so strung-up for the next day's examination, and that it would soon stop. She cried at first rather noisily in a subterranean locker room, swaying to and fro and gasping a little, squatting on a bench above a metal cage containing a knot of canvas hockey boots and greying gym shoes. When bedtime came, she thought she ought to stop crying now, she had had her time of release and respite. She must key herself up again. She crept sniffing out into the upper corridors, where Flora Marsh met her and remarked kindly that she looked to be in a bad way. At this Emily gave a great howl, like a wounded creature, and alarmed Flora by staggering from side to side of the corridor as though her sense of balance were gone. Flora could get no sense out of her: Emily was dumb: Flora said perhaps she should go to the nursery, which was what they called the sick bay, should see Sister. After all, they had A-level Latin the next day, she needed her strength. Emily allowed herself to be led through the already-darkened school corridors, moaning a little, thinking, inside her damp and sobbing head in a lucid tic-tac, that she was like an ox, no, like a heifer it would have to be, like Keats's white heifer in the Grecian urn . . . lowing at the skies . . . Dusty round white lamps hung cheerlessly from metal chains.

Sister was a small, wiry, sensible widow in a white coat and flat rubber-soled shoes. She made Emily a cup of Ovaltine, and put her into an uncomfortable but friendly cane armchair, where Emily went on crying. It became clear to all three of them that there was no prospect of Emily ceasing to cry. The salt tears flooded and filmed her eyes, brimmed over and ran in wet sheets down her face, flowing down her neck in cold streamlets, soaking her collar. The tic-tac in Emily's mind thought of the death of Seneca, the life simply running away, warm and wet, the giving-up. Sister sent Flora Marsh to fetch Emily's things, and Emily, moving her arms like a poor swimmer in thick water, put on her nightdress and climbed into a high hospital bed in the nursery, a hard, cast iron–headed bed, with white cotton blankets. The tears, now silent, darkened and gathered in the pillow. Emily put her knees up to her chin and turned her back on Sister, who pulled back some wet hair, out of her nightdress collar. What has upset her, Sister asked Flora Marsh. Flora didn't know, unless it was something the Headmistress had said. Emily heard them at a huge distance, minute in a waste of waters. Would she be fit to take her exams, Flora asked, and Sister replied, with a night's sleep.

Emily was double. The feeling part had given up, defeated, abandoned to the bliss of dissolution. The thinking part chattered away toughly, tapping out pentameters and alexandrines with and against the soothing flow of the tears. The next morning the feeling part, still watery, accepted tea and toast shakily from Sister; the thinking part looked out craftily from the cavern behind the glistening eyes and stood up, and dressed, and went wet-faced to the Latin exam. There Emily sat, and translated, and scanned, and constructed sentences and paragraphs busily, for a couple of hours. After, a kind of wild hiccup broke in her throat and the tears started again, as though a tap had been turned on, as though something, everything, must be washed away. Emily crept back to the nursery and lay on the iron bed, cold-cheeked and clammy, buffeted by a gale of tags from Horace, storm cries from *Lear,* domestic inanities from Mrs. Bennett, subjunctives and conditionals, sorting and sifting and arranging them, tic-tac, whilst the tears welled. In this way she wrote two German papers, and the English. She was always ready to write but could never remember what she had written, dissolved in tears, run away. She was like a runner at the end of a marathon, moving on will, not on blood and muscle, who might, if you put out a hand to touch him, fall and not rise again.

She received a visit. There was an empty day between the English and the final French, and Emily lay curled in the iron bed, weeping. Sister had drawn the blinds halfway down the windows, to close out the glare of the summer sun, and the cries of tennis players on the grass courts out in the light. In the room the air was thick and green like clouded glass, with pillars of shadow standing in it, shapes underwater. Miss Crichton-Walker advanced precisely towards the bedside, bringing her own shadow, and the creak of rubber footsteps. Her hair in the half-light glistened green on silver: her dress was mud-coloured, or seemed so, with a little, thickly-crocheted collar. She pulled out a tubular chair and sat down, facing Emily, her hands folded composed in her lap, her knees tightly together, her lips pursed. Crying had not thickened Emily's breathing but vacated its spaces: Miss Crichton-Walker smelled very thinly of mothballs, which, in the context, Emily interpreted as the sharp mustiness of ether or chloroform, a little dizzy. She lay still. Miss Crichton-Walker said, "I am sorry to hear that you are unwell, Emily, if that is the correct term. I am sorry that I was not informed earlier, or I should have come to see you earlier. I should like you to tell me, if you can, why you are so distressed?"

"I don't know," said Emily, untruthfully.

"You set high store by these examinations, I know," said the mild voice, accusing. "Perhaps you overreached yourself in some way, overextended yourself, were overambitious. It is a pity, I always think, to force young girls to undergo these arbitrary stresses of judgment when it should surely be possible more accurately to judge the whole tenor of their life and work. Naturally I shall write to the Board of Examiners if you feel—if I feel—you may not quite have done yourself justice. That would be a great disappointment but not a disaster, not by any means a disaster. There is much to be learned in life from temporary setbacks of this kind."

"I have sat all my papers," said Emily's drugged, defensive voice. Miss Crichton-Walker went on.

"I always think that one real failure is necessary to the formation of any really resolved character. You cannot expect to see it that way just now, but I think you will find it so later, if you allow yourself to experience it fully."

Emily knew she must fight, and did not know how. Half of her wanted to respond with a storm of loud crying, to drown this gentle concerned voice with rude noise. Half of her knew, without those words, that that way was disaster, was capitulation, was the acceptance of this last, premature judgment. She said, "If I don't talk, if I just go on, I think I may be all right, I think."

"You do not seem to be all right, Emily."

Emily began to feel faint and dizzy as though the mothballs were indeed anaesthetic. She concentrated on the area below the judging face: the little knots and gaps in the crochet work, which lay sluggish and inexact, as crochet, even the best, always will, asymmetrical daisies bordered with little twisted cords. Little twisted cords of the soft thick cotton were tied at Miss Crichton-Walker's neck, in a constricting little bow that gathered and flounced the work and then hung down in two limp strands, each nearly knotted at its end. Where was Racine, where was the saving thread of reasoned discourse, where the Reader's dry air? The blinds bellied and swayed slightly. A tapestry of lines of verse like musical notation ran through Emily's imagination as though on an endless rolling scroll, the orderly repetitious screen of the alexandrine somehow visually mapped by the patterning of Aunt Florrie's exquisite drawn-thread work, little cornsheaves of threads interspersed by cut openings, tied by minute stitches, a lattice, a trellis.

C'était pendant l'horreur d'une profonde nuit.
Ma mère Jézabel devant moi s'est montrée
Comme au jour de sa mort pompeusement parée . . .

Another bedside vision, highly inappropriate. The thinking Emily smiled in secret, hand under cheek.

"I think I just want to keep quiet, to concentrate . . ."

Miss Crichton-Walker gathered herself, inclining her silver-green coils slightly towards the recumbent girl.

"I am told that something I said may have upset you. If that is so, I am naturally very sorry. I do not need to tell you that what I said was well-meant, and, I hope, considered, said in the interest of the majority of the girls, I believe, and not intended to give offence to any. You are all equally my concern, with your varying interests and gifts. It may be that I felt the need of others more at that particular time than your need: perhaps I believed that you were better provided with self-esteem than most. I can assure you that there was no personal application intended. And that I said nothing I do not wholly believe."

"No. Of course not."

"I should like to know whether you did take exception to what I said."

"I don't want to—"

"I don't want to leave you without clearing up this uncomfortable matter. I would hate—I would be very distressed—to think I had caused even unintentional pain to any girl in my charge. Please tell me if you thought I spoke amiss."

"Oh no. No, I didn't. No."

How reluctant a judge, poor Emily, how ill-equipped, how hopeless, to the extent of downright lying, of betraying the principles of exactness. The denial felt like a recantation without there having been an affirmation to recant.

"So now we understand each other. I am very glad. I have brought you some flowers from my little garden: Sister is putting them in water. They should brighten your darkness a little. I hope you will soon feel able to return to the community. I shall keep myself informed of your well-being, naturally."

*

The French papers were written paragraph by slow paragraph. Emily's pen made dry, black, running little marks on the white paper: Emily's argument threaded itself, a fine line embellished by bright beads of quotations. She did not make it up; she knew it, and recognised it, and laid it out in its ordered pattern. Between paragraphs Emily saw, in the dark corners of the school hall, under dusty shields of honour, little hallucinatory scenes or tableaux, enacting in doorways and window embrasures a charade of the aimlessness of endeavour. She wrote a careful analysis of the clarity of the exposition of Phèdre's devious and confused passion and looked up to see creatures gesticulating on the fringed edge of her consciousness like the blown ghosts trying to pass over the Styx. She saw Miss Crichton-Walker, silvery-muddy, as she had been in the underwater blind-light of the nursery, gravely indicating that failure had its purpose for her. She saw Aunt Florrie, grey and faded and resigned amongst the light thrown off the white linen cloths and immaculate bridal satins of her work, another judge, upright in her chair. She saw Martin, of whom she thought infrequently, on an occasion when he had gleefully tossed and rumpled all the papers spread on her little table, mild, solid, uncomprehending flesh amongst falling sheets of white. She saw even the long racks of ghost-glazed, unbaked pots, their pattern hidden beneath the blurred film of watery clay, waiting to go into the furnace of her father's kiln and be cooked into pleasantly clean and shining transparency. Why go on, a soft voice said in her inner ear, what is all this fuss about? What do you know, it asked justly enough, of incestuous maternal passion or the anger of the gods? These are not our concerns: we must make tablecloths and endure. Emily knew about guilt, Miss Crichton-Walker had seen to that, but she did not know about desire, bridled or unbridled, the hooked claws of flame in the blood. She wrote a neat and eloquent paragraph about Phèdre's always-present guilt, arching from the first scene to the end, which led her to feel terror at facing Minos her father, judge of the Underworld, which led her ultimately to feel that the clarity of her vision dirtied the light air, the purity of daylight. From time to time, writing this, Emily touched nervously the puffed sacs under her swollen eyes: she was struggling through liquid, she could not help irrelevantly seeing Phèdre's soiled clarity of gaze in terms of her own overwept, sore vision, for which the light was too much.

In another place, the Reader walked in dry, golden air, in his separate desert, waiting to weigh her knowledge and her ignorance, to judge her order and her fallings-off. When Emily had finished her writing she made her bow to him, in her mind, and acknowledged that he was a mythical being, that it was not possible to live in his light.

Who won, you will ask, Emily or Miss Crichton-Walker, since the Reader is mythical and detached, and can neither win nor lose? Emily might be thought to have won, since she had held to her purpose successfully: what she had written was not gibberish but exactly what was required by the scrupulous, checked and counter-checked examiners, so that her marks, when they came, were the highest the school had ever seen. Miss Crichton-Walker might be thought to have won, since Emily was diagnosed as having broken down, was sent home under strict injunctions not to open a book, and was provided by her mother with a piece of petit-point to do through the long summer, a Victorian pattern of blown roses and blue columbine, stretched across a gripping wooden hoop, in which she made dutiful cross after cross blunt-needled, tiny and woollen, pink, buff, crimson, sky blue, royal blue, Prussian blue, creating on the underside a matted and uncouth weft of lumpy ends and trailing threads, since finishing off neatly was her weakest point. Emily might be thought to have won in the longer run, since she went to university indeed, from where she married young and hastily, having specialised safely in French language. If Emily herself thought that she had somehow lost, she thought this, as is the nature of things, in a fluctuating and intermittent way, feeling also a steady warmth towards her mild husband, a tax inspector, and her two clever daughters, and beyond that a certain limited satisfaction in the translation work she did part-time for various international legal bodies.

One day, however, she was called to see the deputy head of her eldest daughter's school, a shining steel and glass series of cubes and prisms, very different from her own dark, creeper-covered place of education. The deputy head was birdlike, insubstantial and thin in faded denim; his thin grey hair was wispy on his collar; his face was full of mild concern as he explained his anxieties about Emily's daughter. You must try to understand, he told Emily, that just because you are middle-class and university-educated, you need not expect your daughter to share your priorities. I have told Sarah myself that if she wants to be a gardener we shall do everything we can to help her, that her life is her own, that everything all the girls do here is of great importance to us, it all matters equally, all we want is for them to find themselves. Emily said in a small, dull voice that what Sarah wanted was to be able to do advanced French and advanced maths and that she could not really believe that the school had found this impossible to timetable and arrange. The deputy head's expression became extensively gentler and at the same time judicially set. You must allow, he told Emily, that parents are not always the best judge of their child's aptitudes. You may very well—with the best of intentions, naturally—be confusing Sarah's best interests with your own unfulfilled ambitions. Sarah may not be an academic child. Emily dared not ask him, as she should have done, as furious Sarah, frustrated and rebellious, was expecting her to do, if he *knew* Sarah, on what he was founding this judgment. Sarah's French, she said, is very good indeed; it is my subject, I know. She has a natural gift. He smiled his thin disbelief, his professional dismissal, and said that was her view, but not necessarily the school's. We are here to educate the whole human being, he told Emily, to educate her for life, for forming personal relations, running a home, finding her place in society, understanding her responsibilities. We are very much aware of Sarah's needs and problems—one of which, if I may speak frankly, is your expectations. Perhaps you should try to trust us? In any case, it is absolutely impossible to arrange the timetable so that Sarah may do both maths and French.

That old mild voice sounded through this new one: Emily walked away through the glassy-chill corridors thinking that if it had not been for that earlier authority she would have defied this one, wanting to stone the huge, silent panes of glass and let the dry light through, despising her own childishness.

At home, Sarah drew a neat double line under a geometric proof, laid out for the absent scanning of an unfalteringly accurate mind, to whose presence she required access. What Sarah made of herself, what Sarah saw, is Sarah's story. You can believe, I hope, you can afford to believe, that she made her way into its light.

MEDUSA'S ANKLES

She had walked in one day because she had seen the *Rosy Nude* through the plate glass. That was odd, she thought, to have that lavish and complex creature stretched voluptuously above the coat rack, where one might have expected the stare, silver and supercilious or jetty and frenzied, of the model girl. They were all girls now, not women. The rosy nude was pure flat colour, but suggested mass. She had huge haunches and a monumental knee, lazily propped high. She had round breasts, contemplations of the circle, reflections on flesh and its fall.

She had asked cautiously for a cut and blow-dry. He had done her himself, the owner, Lucian of "Lucian's," slender and soft-moving, resembling a balletic Hamlet with full white sleeves and tight black trousers. The first few times she came it was the trousers she remembered, better than his face, which she saw only in the mirror behind her own, and which she felt a middle-aged disinclination to study. A woman's relation with her hairdresser is anatomically odd. Her face meets his belt, his haunches skim her breathing, his face is far away, high and behind. His face had a closed and monkish look, rather fine, she thought, under soft, straight, dark hair, bright with health, not with added fats, or so it seemed.

"I like your Matisse," she said, the first time.

He looked blank.

"The pink nude. I love her."

"Oh, that. I saw it in a shop. I thought it went exactly with the colour scheme I was planning."

Their eyes met in the mirror.

"I thought she was wonderful," he said. "So calm, so damn sure of herself, such a lovely colour, I do think, don't you? I fell for her, absolutely. I saw her in this shop in the Charing Cross Road and I went home, and said to my wife, I might think of placing her in the salon, and she thought nothing to it, but the next day I went back and just got her. She gives the salon a bit of class. I like things to have class."

In those days the salon was like the interior of a rosy cloud, all pinks and creams, with creamy muslin curtains here and there, and ivory brushes and combs, and here and there—the mirror frames, the little trollies—a kind of sky blue, a dark sky blue, the colour of the couch or bed on which the rosy nude spread herself. Music played—Susannah hated piped music—but this music was tinkling and tripping and dropping, quiet seraglio music, like sherbet. He gave her coffee in pink cups, with a pink and white wafer biscuit in the saucer. He soothed her middle-aged hair into a cunningly blown and natural windswept sweep, with escaping strands and tendrils, softening brow and chin. She remembered the hairdressing shop of her wartime childhood, with its boarded wooden cubicles, its advertisements for Amami shampoo, depicting ladies with blond pageboys and red lips, in the forties bow which was wider than the thirties rosebud. Amami, she had always supposed, rhymed with smarmy and was somehow related to it. When she became a linguist, and could decline the verb "to love" in several languages, she saw suddenly one day that Amami was an erotic invitation, or command. Amami, love me, the blondes said, under their impeccably massed rolls of hair. Her mother had gone draggled under the chipped dome of the hairdryer, bristling with metal rollers, bobby pins, and pipe cleaners. And had come out under a rigidly bouncy "set," like a mountain of wax fruit, that made her seem artificial and embarrassing, drawing attention somehow to the unnatural whiteness of her false teeth.

They had seemed like some kind of electrically shocking initiation into womanhood, those clamped domes descending and engulfing. She remembered her own first "set," the heat and buzzing, and afterwards a slight torn tenderness of the scalp, a slight tindery dryness to the hair.

In the sixties and seventies she had kept a natural look, had grown her hair long and straight and heavy, a chestnut-glossy curtain, had avoided places like this. And in the years of her avoidance, the cubicles had gone, everything was open and shared and aboveboard, blow-dryers had largely replaced the hoods, plastic spikes the bristles.

She had had to come back because her hair began to grow old. The ends split, the weight of it broke, a kind of frizzed fur replaced the gloss. Lucian said that curls and waves—following the lines of the new unevenness—would dissimulate, would render natural-looking, that was, young, what was indeed natural, the death of the cells. Short and bouncy was best, Lucian said, and proved it, tactfully. He stood above her with his fine hands cupped lightly round her new bubbles and wisps, like the hands of a priest round a Grail. She looked, quickly, quickly, it was better than before, thanked him and averted her eyes.

She came to trust him with her disintegration.

He was always late to their appointment, to all appointments. The salon was full of whisking young things, male and female, and he stopped to speak to all of them, to all the patient sitters, with their questing, mirror-bound stares. The telephone rang perpetually. She sat on a rosy foamy pouffe and read in a glossy magazine, *Her Hair,* an article at once solemnly portentous and remorselessly jokey (such tones are common) about the hairdresser as the new healer, with his cure of souls. Once, the magazine informed her, the barber had been the local surgeon, had drawn teeth, set bones, and dealt with female problems. Now in the rush of modern alienated life, the hair-dresser performed the all-important function of listening. He elicited the tale of your troubles and calmed you.

Lucian did not. He had another way. He created his own psychia-trist and guru from his captive hearer. Or at least, so Susannah found, who may have been specially selected because she was plump, which could be read as motherly, and because, as a university teacher she was, as he detected, herself a professional listener. He asked her advice.

"I don't see myself shut in here for the next twenty years. I want more out of life. Life has to have a meaning. I tried Tantric Art and the School of Meditation. Do you know about that sort of thing, about the inner life?"

His fingers flicked and flicked in her hair, he compressed a ridge and scythed it.

"Not really. I'm an agnostic."

"I'd like to know about art. You know about art. You know about that pink nude, don't you? How do I find out?"

She told him to read Lawrence Gowing, and he clamped the tress he was attending to, put down his scissors, and wrote it all down in a little dove-grey leather book. She told him where to find good extramural classes and who was good amongst the gallery lecturers.

Next time she came it was not art, it was archaeology. There was no evidence that he had gone to the galleries or read the books.

"The past pulls you," he said. "Bones in the ground and gold coins in a hoard, all that. I went down to the City and saw them digging up the Mithraic temples. There's a religion, all that bull's blood, dark and light, fascinating."

She wished he would tidy her head and be quiet. She could recognise the flitting mind, she considered. It frightened her. What she knew, what she cared about, what was coherent, was separate shards for him to flit over, remaining separate. You wrote books and gave lectures, and these little ribbons of fact shone briefly and vanished.

"I don't want to put the best years of my life into making suburban old dears presentable," he said. "I want something more."

"What?" she said, meeting his brooding stare above the wet mat of her mop. He puffed foam into it and said, "Beauty, I want beauty. I must have beauty. I want to sail on a yacht amongst the Greek isles, with beautiful people." He caught her eye. "And see those temples and those sculptures." He pressed close, he pushed at the nape of her neck, her nose was near his discreet zip.

"You've been washing it without conditioner," he said. "You aren't doing yourself any good. I can tell."

She bent her head submissively, and he scraped the base of her skull.

"You could have highlights," he said in a tone of no enthusiasm. "Bronze or mixed autumnal."

"No thanks. I prefer it natural."

He sighed.

He began to tell her about his love life. She would have inclined, on the evidence before her eyes, to the view that he was homosexual. The salon was full of beautiful young men, who came, wielded the scissors briefly, giggled together in corners, and departed. Chinese, Indonesian, Glaswegian, South African. He shouted at them and giggled with them, they exchanged little gifts and paid off obscure little debts to each other. Once she came in late and found them sitting in a circle, playing poker. The girls were subordinate and brightly hopeless. None of them lasted long. They wore—in those days—pink overalls with cream silk bindings. She could tell he had a love life because of the amount of time he spent alternately pleasing and blustering on the telephone, his voice a blotting-paper hiss, his words inaudible, though she could hear the peppery rattle of the other voice, or voices, in the earpiece. Her sessions began to take a long time, what with these phone calls and with his lengthy explanations, which he would accompany with gestures, making her look at his mirrored excitement, like a boy riding a bicycle with hands off.

"Forgive me if I'm a bit distracted," he said. "My life is in crisis. Something I never believed could happen has happened. All my life I've been looking for something and now I've found it."

He wiped suds casually from her wet brow and scraped her eye-corner. She blinked.

"Love," he said. "Total affinity. Absolute compatibility. A miracle. My other half. A perfectly beautiful girl."

She could think of no sentence to answer this. She said, schoolmistressy—what other tone was there?—"And this has caused the crisis?"

"She loves me, I couldn't believe it but it is true. She loves me. She wants me to live with her."

"And your wife?"

There was a wife, who had thought nothing to the purchase of the *Rosy Nude.*

"She told me to get out of the house. So I got out. I went to her flat—my girlfriend's. She came and fetched me back—my wife. She said I must choose, but she thinks I'll choose her. I said it would be better for the moment just to let it evolve. I told her how do I know what I want, in this state of ecstasy, how do I know it'll last, how do I know she'll go on loving me?"

He frowned impatiently and waved the scissors dangerously near her temples.

"All she cares about is respectability. She says she loves me but all she cares about is what the neighbours say. I like my house, though. She keeps it nice, I have to say. It's not stylish, but it is in good taste."

Over the next few months, maybe a year, the story evolved, in bumps and jerks, not, it must be said, with any satisfactory narrative shape. He was a very bad storyteller, Susannah realised slowly. None of the characters acquired any roundness. She formed no image of the nature of the beauty of the girlfriend, or of the way she spent her time when not demonstrating her total affinity for Lucian. She did not know whether the wife was a shrew or a sufferer, nervous or patient or even ironically detached. All these wraith-personae were inventions of Susannah's own. About six months through the narrative Lucian said that his daughter was very upset about it all, the way he was forced to come and go, sometimes living at home, sometimes shut out.

"You have a daughter?"

"Fifteen. No, seventeen, I always get ages wrong!"

She watched him touch his own gleaming hair in the mirror, and smile apprehensively at himself.

"We were married very young," he said. "Very young, before we knew what was what."

"It's hard on young girls, when there are disputes at home."

"It is. It's hard on everyone. She says if I sell the house she'll have nowhere to live while she takes her exams. I have to sell the house if I'm to afford to keep up my half of my girlfriend's flat. I can't keep up the mortgages on both. My wife doesn't want to move. It's understandable, I suppose, but she has to see we can't go on like this. I can't be torn apart like this, I've got to decide."

"You seem to have decided for your girlfriend."

He took a deep breath and put down everything, comb, scissors, hairdryer.

"Ah, but I'm scared. I'm scared stiff if I take the plunge, I'll be left with nothing. If she's got me all the time, my girlfriend, perhaps she won't go on loving me like this. And I like my house, you know, it feels sort of comfortable to me, I'm used to it, all the old chairs. I don't quite like to think of it all sold and gone."

"Love isn't easy."

"You can say that again."

"Do you think I'm getting thinner on top?"

"What? Oh no, not really, I wouldn't worry. We'll just train this little bit to fall across there like that. Do you think she has a right to more than half the value of the house?"

"I'm not a lawyer. I'm a classicist."

"We're going on that Greek holiday. Me and my girlfriend. Sailing through the Greek Isles. I've bought scuba gear. The salon will be closed for a month."

"I'm glad you told me."

While he was away the salon was redecorated. He had not told her about this, also, as indeed, why should he have done? It was done very fashionably in the latest colours, battleship grey and maroon. Dried blood and instruments of slaughter, Susannah thought on her return. The colour scheme was one she particularly disliked. Everything was changed. The blue trollies had been replaced with hi-tech steely ones, the ceiling lowered, the faintly aquarial plate glass was replaced with storm-grey-one-way-see-through-no-glare which made even bright days dull ones. The music was now muted heavy metal. The young men and young women wore dark grey Japanese wrappers and what she thought of as the patients, which included herself, wore identical maroon ones. Her face in the mirror was grey, had lost the deceptive rosy haze of the earlier lighting.

The *Rosy Nude* was taken down. In her place were photographs of girls with grey faces, coal-black eyes, and spiky lashes, under bonfires of incandescent puce hair which matched their lips, rounded to suck, at microphones perhaps, or other things. The new teacups were black and hexagonal. The pink flowery biscuits were replaced by sugar-coated minty elliptical sweets, black and white like Go counters. She thought, after the first shock of this, that she would go elsewhere. But she was afraid of being made, accidentally, by anyone else, to look a fool. He understood her hair, Lucian, she told herself. It needed understanding, these days, it was not much anymore, its life was fading from it.

"Did you have a good holiday?"

"Oh idyllic. Oh yes, a dream. I wish I hadn't come back. She's been to a solicitor. Claiming the matrimonial home for all the work she's done on it, and because of my daughter. I say, what about when she grows up, she'll get a job, won't she? You can't assume she'll hang around Mummy forever, they don't."

"I need to look particularly good this time. I've won a prize. A Translator's Medal. I have to make a speech. On television."

"We'll have to make you look lovely, won't we? For the honour of the salon. How do you like our new look?"

"It's very smart."

"It is. It is. I'm not quite satisfied with the photos, though. I thought we could get something more intriguing. It has to be photos to go with the grey."

He worked above her head. He lifted her wet hair with his fingers and let the air run through it, as though there was twice as much as there was. He pulled a twist this way, and clamped it to her head, and screwed another that way, and put his head on one side and another, contemplating her uninspiring bust. When her head involuntarily followed his he said quite nastily, "Keep still, can you, I can't work if you keep bending from side to side like a swan."

"I'm sorry."

"No harm done, just keep still."

She kept still as a mouse, her head bowed under his repressing palm. She turned up her eyes and saw him look at his watch, then, with a kind of balletic movement of wrists, scissors, and finger points above her brow, drive the sharp steel into the ball of his thumb, so that blood spurted, so that some of his blood even fell onto her scalp.

"Oh dear. Will you excuse me? I've cut myself. Look."

He waved the bloody member before her nose.

"I saw," she said. "I saw you cut yourself."

He smiled at her in the mirror, a glittery smile, not meeting her eyes.

"It's a little trick we hairdressers have. When we've been driving ourselves and haven't had time for a bite or a breather, we get cut, and off we go, to the toilet, to take a bite of Mars Bar or a cheese roll if the receptionist's been considerate. Will you excuse me? I am faint for lack of food."

"Of course," she said.

He flashed his glass smile at her and slid away.

She waited. A little water dripped into her collar. A little more ran into her eyebrows. She looked at her poor face, under its dank cap and its two random corkscrews, aluminium clamped. She felt a gentle protective rage towards this stolid face. She remembered, not as a girl, as a young woman under all that chestnut fall, looking at her skin, and wondering how it could grow into the crêpe, the sag, the opulent soft bags. This was her face, she had thought then. And this, too, now, she wanted to accept for her face, trained in a respect for precision, and could not. What had left this greying skin, these flakes, these fragile stretches with no elasticity, was her, was her life, was herself. She had never been a beautiful woman, but she had been attractive, with the attraction of liveliness and warm energy, of the flow of quick blood and brightness of eye. No classic bones, which might endure, no fragile birdlike sharpness that might whitely go forward. Only the life of flesh, which began to die.

She was in a panic of fear about the television, which had come too late, when she had lost the desire to be seen or looked at. The cameras search jowl and eye-pocket, expose brushstroke and cracks in shadow and gloss. So interesting are their revelations that words, mere words, go for nothing, fly by whilst the memory of a chipped tooth, a strayed red dot, an inappropriate hair, persists and persists.

If he had not left her so long to contemplate her wet face, it might not have happened.

On either side of her mysteries were being enacted. On the left, a head was crammed into a pink nylon bag, something between a bank robber's stocking and a monstrous Dutch cap. A young Chinese man was peacefully teasing threads of hair through the meshes of this with a tug and a flick, a tug and a flick. The effect was one of startling hideous pink baldness, tufted here and there. On her right, an anxious plump girl was rolling another girl's thick locks into snaky sausages of aluminium foil. There was a thrum of distant drums through the loudspeakers, a clash and crash of what sounded like shaken chains. It is all nonsense, she thought, I should go home, I can't, I am wet. They stared transfixed at their respective ugliness.

He came back, and took up the scissors, listlessly enough.

"How much did you want off?" he said casually. "You've got a lot of broken ends. It's deteriorating, you haven't fed it while I've been away."

"Not too much off, I want to look natural, I . . ."

"I've been talking to my girlfriend. I've decided. I shan't go back anymore to my wife. I can't bear it."

"She's too angry?"

"She's let herself go. It's her own fault. She's let herself go altogether. She's let her ankles get fat, they swell over her shoes, it disgusts me, it's impossible for me."

"That happens to people. Fluid absorption . . ."

She did not look down at her own ankles. He had her by the short hairs at the nape of her neck.

"Lucian," said the plump girl, plaintively, "can you just take a look here at this perm, I can't seem to get the hang of this."

"You'd better be careful," said Lucian, "or Madam'll go green and fry and you'll be in deep trouble. Why don't you just come and finish off Madam here—you don't mind, do you, dear? Deirdre is very good with your sort of hair, very tactful, I'm training her myself—I'd better take a look at this perm. It's a new method we're just trying out, we've had a few problems, you see how it is . . ."

Deirdre was an elicitor, but Susannah would not speak. Vaguely, far away, she heard the anxious little voice. "Do you have children, dear, have you far to go home, how formal do you like it, do you want back-combing . . . ?" Susannah stared stony, thinking about Lucian's wife's ankles. Because her own ankles rubbed her shoes, her sympathies had to be with this unknown and ill-presented woman. She remembered with sudden total clarity a day when, Suzie then, not Susannah, she had made love all day to an Italian student on a course in Perugia. She remembered her own little round rosy breasts, her own long legs stretched over the side of the single bed, the hot, the wet, his shoulders, the clash of skulls as they tried to mix themselves completely. They had reached a point when neither of them could move, they had loved each other so much, they had tried to get up to get water, for they were dying of thirst, they were soaked with sweat and dry-mouthed, and they collapsed back upon the bed, naked skin on naked skin, unable to rise. What was this to anyone now? Rage rose in her, for the fat-ankled woman, like a red flood, up from her thighs across her chest, up her neck, it must flare like a flag in her face, but how to tell in this daft cruel grey light? Deirdre was rolling up curls, piling them up, who would have thought the old woman had so much hair on her head? Sausages and snail shells, grape clusters and twining coils. She could only see dimly, for the red flood was like a curtain at the back of her eyes, but she knew what she saw. The Japanese say demons of another world approach us through mirrors as fish rise through water, and, bubble-eyed and trailing fins, a fat demon swam towards her, turret-crowned, snake-crowned, her mother fresh from the dryer in all her embarrassing irreality.

"There," said Deirdre. "That's nice. I'll just get a mirror."

"It isn't nice," said Susannah. "It's hideous."

There was a hush in the salon. Deirdre turned a terrified gaze on Lucian.

"She did it better than I do, dear," he said. "She gave it a bit of lift. That's what they all want, these days. I think you look really nice."

"It's horrible," said Susannah. *"I look like a middle-aged woman with a hairdo."*

She could see them all looking at each other, sharing the knowledge that this was exactly what she was.

"Not natural," she said.

"I'll get Deirdre to tone it down," said Lucian.

Susannah picked up a bottle, full of gel. She brought it down, heavily, on the grey glass shelf, which cracked.

"I don't want it toned down, I want," she began, and stared mesmerised at the crack, which was smeared with gel.

"I want my real hair back," Susannah cried, and thumped harder, shattering both shelf and bottle.

"Now, dear, I'm sorry," said Lucian in a tone of sweet reason. She could see several of him, advancing on her; he was standing in a corner and was reflected from wall to wall, a cohort of slender, trousered swordsmen, waving the bright scissors like weapons.

"Keep away," she said. "Get off. Keep back."

"Calm yourself," said Lucian.

Susannah seized a small cylindrical pot and threw it at one of his emanations. It burst with a satisfying crash and one whole mirror became a spiderweb of cracks, from which fell, tinkling, a little heap of crystal nuggets. In front of Susannah was a whole row of such bombs or grenades. She lobbed them all around her. Some of the cracks made a kind of strained singing noise, some were explosive. She whirled a container of hairpins about her head and scattered it like a nailbomb. She tore dryers from their sockets and sprayed the puce punk with sweet-smelling foam. She broke basins with brushes and tripped the young Chinese male, who was the only one not apparently petrified, with a hissing trolley, swaying dangerously and scattering puffs of cotton wool and rattling trails of clips and tags. She silenced the blatter of the music with a well-aimed imitation alabaster pot of Juvenescence Emulsion, which dripped into the cassette which whirred more and more slowly in a thickening morass of blush-coloured cream.

When she had finished—and she went on, she kept going, until there was nothing else to hurl, for she was already afraid of what must happen when she had finished—there was complete human silence in the salon. There were strange, harshly musical sounds all round. A bowl rocking on a glass shelf. A pair of scissors, dancing on a hook, their frenzy diminishing. Uneven spasmodic falls of glass, like musical hailstones on shelves and floors. A susurration of hairpins on paper. A slow creaking of damaged panes. Her own hands were bleeding. Lucian advanced crunching over the shining silt, and dabbed at them with a towel. He too was bloodied—specks on his shirt, a fine dash on his brow, nothing substantial. It was a strange empty battlefield, full of glittering fragments and sweet-smelling rivulets and puddles of venous-blue and fuchsia-red unguents, patches of crimson-streaked foam and odd intense spills of orange henna or cobalt and copper.

"I'd better go," she said, turning blindly with her bleeding hands, still in her uncouth maroon drapery.

"Deirdre'll make you a cup of coffee," said Lucian. "You'd better sit down and take a breather."

He took a neck brush and swept a chair for her. She stared, irresolute.

"Go on. We all feel like that, sometimes. Most of us don't dare. Sit down."

They all gathered round, the young, making soothing, chirruping noises, putting out hands with vague patting, calming gestures.

"I'll send you a cheque."

"The insurance'll pay. Don't worry. It's insured. You've done me a good turn in a way. It wasn't quite right, the colours. I might do something different. Or collect the insurance and give up. Me and my girlfriend are thinking of setting up a stall in the Antique Hypermarket. Costume jewellery. Thirties and forties kitsch. She has sources. I can collect the insurance and have a go. I've had enough of this. I'll tell you something, I've often felt like smashing it all up myself, just to get out of it—like a great glass cage it is—and go out into the real world. So you mustn't worry, dear."

She sat at home and shook, her cheeks flushed, her eyes bright with tears. When she had pulled herself together, she would go and have a shower and soak out the fatal coils, reduce them to streaming rattails. Her husband came in, unexpected—she had long given up expecting or not expecting him, his movements were unpredictable and unexplained. He came in tentatively, a large, alert, ostentatiously work-wearied man. She looked up at him speechless. He saw her. (Usually he did not.)

"You look different. You've had your hair done. I like it. You look lovely. It takes twenty years off you. You should have it done more often."

And he came over and kissed her on the shorn nape of her neck, quite as he used to do.

THE CHINESE LOBSTER

The proprietors of the Orient Lotus alternate frenetic embellishment with periods of lassitude and letting go. Dr. Himmelblau knows this, because she has been coming here for quick lunches, usually solitary, for the last seven years or so. She chose it because it was convenient—it is near all her regular stopping places, the National Gallery, the Royal Academy, the British Museum—and because it seemed unpretentious and quietly comfortable. She likes its padded seats, even though the mock leather is split in places. She can stack her heavy book bags beside her and rest her bones.

The window on to the street has been framed in struggling cheese plants as long as she can remember. They grow denser, dustier, and still livelier as the years go by. They press their cut-out leaves against the glass, the old ones holly-dark, the new ones yellow and shining. The glass distorts and folds them, but they press on. Sometimes there is a tank of coloured fish in the window, and sometimes not. At the moment, there is not. You can see bottles of soy sauce, and glass containers which dispense toothpicks, one by one, and chrome-plated boxes full of paper napkins, also frugally dispensed one by one.

Inside the door, for the last year or so, there has been a low square shrine, made of bright jade-green pottery, inside which sits a little brass god, or sage, in the lotus position, his comfortable belly on his comfortable knees. Little lamps, and sticks of incense, burn before him in bright scarlet glass pots, and from time to time he is decorated with scarlet and gold shiny paper trappings. Dr. Himmelblau likes the colour mixture, the bright blue-green and the saturated scarlet, so nearly the same weight. But she is a little afraid of the god, because she does not know who he is, and because he is obviously *really* worshipped, not just a decoration.

Today there is a new object, further inside the door, but still before the tables or the coathangers. It is a display case, in black lacquered wood, standing about as high as Dr. Himmelblau's waist—she is a woman of medium height—shining with newness and sparkling with polish. It is on four legs, and its lid and side walls—about nine inches deep—are made of glass. It resembles cases in museums, in which you might see miniatures, or jewels, or small ceramic objects.

Dr. Himmelblau looks idly in. The display is brightly lit, and arranged on a carpet of that fierce emerald-green artificial grass used by greengrocers and undertakers.

Round the edges on opened shells is a border of raw scallops, the pearly flesh dulling, the repeating half-moons of the orange-pink roes playing against the fierce green.

In the middle, in the very middle, is a live lobster, flanked by two live crabs. All three, in parts of their bodies, are in feeble perpetual motion. The lobster, slowly in this unbreathable element, moves her long feelers and can be seen to move her little claws on the end of her legs, which cannot go forward or back. She is black, and holds out her heavy great pincers in front of her, shifting them slightly, too heavy to lift up. The great muscles of her tail crimp and contort and collapse. One of the crabs, the smaller, is able to rock itself from side to side, which it does. The crabs' mouths can be seen moving from side to side, like scissors; all three survey the world with mobile eyes still lively on little stalks. From their mouths comes a silent hissing and bubbling, a breath, a cry. The colours of the crabs are matt, brick, cream, a grape-dark sheen on the claw-ends, a dingy, earthy encrustation on the hairy legs. The lobster was, is, and will not be, blue-black and glossy. For a moment, in her bones, Dr. Himmelblau feels their painful life in the thin air. They stare, but do not, she supposes, see her. She turns on her heel and walks quickly into the body of the Orient Lotus. It occurs to her that the scallops, too, are still in some sense, probably, alive.

The middle-aged Chinese man—she knows them all well, but knows none of their names—meets her with a smile, and takes her coat. Dr. Himmelblau tells him she wants a table for two. He shows her to her usual table, and brings another bowl, china spoon, and chopsticks. The muzak starts up. Dr. Himmelblau listens with comfort and pleasure. The first time she heard the muzak, she was dismayed, she put her hand to her breast in alarm at the burst of sound, she told herself that this was not after all the peaceful retreat she had supposed. Her noodles tasted less succulent against the tin noise and then, the second or the third time, she began to notice the tunes, which were happy, banal, Western tunes, but jazzed up and sung in what she took to be Cantonese. "Oh what a beautiful *morning*. Oh what a beautiful *day*. I've got a kind of *feel*ing. Everything's *go*-ing my *way*." Only in the incomprehensible nasal syllables, against a zithery plink and plunk, a kind of gong, a sort of bell. It was not a song she had ever liked. But she has come to find it the epitome of restfulness and cheerfulness. Twang, tinkle, plink, *plink*. A cross-cultural object, an occidental Orient, an oriental Western. She associates it now with the promise of delicate savours, of warmth, of satisfaction. The middle-aged Chinese man brings her a pot of green tea, in the pot she likes, with the little transparent rice-grain flowers in the blue and white porcelain, delicate and elegant.

She is early. She is nervous about the forthcoming conversation. She has never met her guest personally, though she has of course seen him, in the flesh and on the television screen; she has heard him lecture, on Bellini, on Titian, on Mantegna, on Picasso, on Matisse. His style is orotund and idiosyncratic. Dr. Himmelblau's younger colleagues find him rambling and embarrassing. Dr. Himmelblau, personally, is not of this opinion. In her view, Perry Diss is always talking about something, not about nothing, and in her view, which she knows to be the possibly crabbed view of a solitary intellectual, nearing retirement, this is increasingly rare. Many of her colleagues, Gerda Himmelblau believes, do not *like* paintings. Perry Diss does. He loves them, like sound apples to bite into, like fair flesh, like sunlight. She is thinking in his style. It is a professional hazard, of her own generation. She has never had much style of her own, Gerda Himmelblau—only an acerbic accuracy, which is an *easy* style for a very clever woman who looks as though she ought to be dry. Not arid, she would not go so far, but dry. Used as a word of moderate approbation. She has long fine brown hair, caught into a serviceable knot in the nape of her neck. She wears suits in soft dark, not-quite-usual colours—damsons, soots, black tulips, dark mosses—with clean-cut cotton shirts, not masculine, but with no floppy bows or pretty ribbons—also in clear colours, palest lemon, deepest cream, periwinkle, faded flame. The suits are cut soft but the body inside them is, she knows, sharp and angular, as is her Roman nose and her judiciously tightened mouth.

She takes the document out of her handbag. It is not the original, but a photocopy, which does not reproduce all the idiosyncrasies of the original—a grease stain, maybe butter, here, what looks like a bloodstain, watered-down at the edges, there, a kind of Rorschach stag beetle made by folding an inkblot, somewhere else. There are also minute drawings, in the margins and in the text itself. The whole is contained in a border of what appear to be high-arched wishbones, executed with a fine brush, in India ink. It is addressed in large majuscules

TO THE DEAN OF WOMEN STUDENTS
DR. GERDA HIMMELBLAU

and continues in minute minuscules

from peggi nollett, woman and student.

It continues:

> I wish to lay a formal complaint against the DISTINGUISHED VISITING PROFESSOR the Department has seen fit to appoint as the supervisor of my disertation on *The Female Body and Matisse.*
>
> In my view, which I have already made plain to anyone who cared to listen, and specificly to Doug Marks, Tracey Avison,

Annie Manson, and also to you, Dr. Gerda Himmelblau, this person should never have been assigned to direct this work, as he is *completley out of sympathy* with its feminist project. He is a so-called EXPERT on the so-called MASTER of MODERNISM but what does he know about Woman or the internal conduct of the Female Body, which has always until now been MUTE and had no mouth to speak.

Here followed a series of tiny pencil drawings which, in the original, Dr. Himmelblau could make out to be lips, lips ambiguously oral or vaginal, she put it to herself precisely, sometimes parted, sometimes screwed shut, sometimes spattered with what might be hairs.

His criticisms of what I have written so far have always been null and extremely agressive and destructive. He does not understand that my project is ahistorical and *need not involve* any description of the so-called development of Matisse's so-called style or approach, since what I wish to state is esentially *critical,* and presented from a *theoretical* viewpoint with insights provided from contemporary critical methods to which the cronology of Matisse's life or the order in which he comitted his "paintings" is *totaly irelevant.*

However although I thought I should begin by stating my theoretical position yet again I wish at the present time to lay a spercific complaint of *sexual harasment* against the DVP. I can and will go into much more detail believe me Dr. Himmelblau but I will set out the gist of it so you can see there is something here *you must take up.*

I am writing while still under the effect of the shock I have had so please excuse any incoherence.

It began with my usual dispirting CRIT with the DVP. He asked me why I had not writen more of the disertation than I had and I said I had not been very well and also preocupied with getting on with my artwork, as you know, in the

Joint Honours Course, the creative work and the Art History get equal marks and I had reached a *very difficult stage* with the Work. But I had writen some notes on Matisse's *distortions* of the Female Body with respect especially to the spercificaly Female Organs, the Breasts the Cunt the Labia etc etc and also to his ways of acumulating Flesh on certain Parts of the Body which appeal to Men and tend to imobilise Women such as grotesquely swollen Thighs or protruding Stomachs. I mean to conect this in time to the whole tradition of the depiction of Female Slaves and Odalisques but I have not yet done the research I would need to write on this.

Also his Women tend to have no features on their faces, they are Blanks, like Dolls, I find this sinister.

Anyway I told the DVP what my line on this was going to be even if I had not writen very much and he argued with me and went so far as to say I was hostile and full of hatred to Matisse. I said this was not a relevant criticism of my work and that Matisse was hostile and full of hatred towards women. He said Matisse was full of love and desire towards women (!!!!!) and I said *"exactly"* but he did not take the point and was realy quite cutting and undermining and dismisive and unhelpful even if no worse had hapened. He even said in his view I ought to fail my degree which is no way for a supervisor to behave as you will agree. I was so tense and upset by his atitude that I began to cry and he pated me on my shoulders and tried to be a bit nicer. So I explained how busy I was with my art-work and how my artwork, which is a series of mixed-media pieces called Erasures and Undistortions was a part of my criticism of Matisse. So he *graciously* said he would like to see my artwork as it might help him to give me a better grade if it contributed to my ideas on Matisse. He said art students often had dificulty expresing themselves verbally although he himself found language "as sensuous as paint." [It is not my place to say anything about his prose style but I could.] [This sentence is heavily but legibly crossed out.]

Anyway he came—*kindly*—to my studio to see my Work. I could see immediately he did not like it, indeed was repeled by it which I supose was not a surprise. It does not try to be agreable or seductive. He tried to put a good face on it and admired one or two *minor* pieces and went so far as to say there was a great power of feeling in the room. I tried to explain my project of *revising* or *reviewing* or *rearranging* Matisse. I have a three-dimensional piece in wire and plaster-of-paris and plasticine called *The Resistance of Madame Matisse* which shows her and her daughter being *tortured* as they *were* by the Gestapo in the War whilst *he* sits like a Buddha cutting up pretty paper with scissors. They wouldn't tell him they were being tortured in case it disturbed his *work.* I felt sick when I found out that. The torturers have got identical scissors.

Then the DVP got personal. He put his arm about me and hugged me and said *I had got too many clothes on. He said they were a depressing colour* and he thought I ought to take them all off and *let the air get to me.* He said he would like to see me in bright colours and that I was really a *very pretty girl* if I would let myself go. I said my clothes were a statement about myself, and he said they were a *sad statement* and then he grabed me and began kissing me and fondling me and stroking intimate parts of me—it was disgusting—I will not write it down, but I can describe it clearly, believe me Dr. Himmelblau, if it becomes necesary, I can give chapter and verse of every detail, I am still shaking with shock. The more I strugled the more he insisted and pushed at me with his body until I said I would get the police the moment he let go of me, and then he came to his senses and said that in the *good old days* painters and models felt a bit of *human warmth and sensuality* towards each other in the studio, and I said, not in my studio, and he said, clearly not, and went off, saying it seemed to him *quite likely* that I should fail both parts of my Degree.

Gerda Himmelblau folds the photocopy again and puts it back into her handbag. She then reads the personal letter which came with it.

> Dear Dr. Himmelblau,
>
> I am sending you a complaint about a horible experience I have had. Please take it seriously and please help me. I am so unhapy, I have so little confidence in myself, I spend days and days just lying in bed wondering what is the point of geting up. I try to live for my work but I am very easily discouraged and sometimes everything seems so black and pointless it is almost hystericaly funny to think of twisting up bits of wire or modeling plasticine. Why bother I say to myself and realy there isn't any answer. I realy think I might be better off dead and after such an experience as I have just had I do slip back towards that way of thinking of thinking of puting an end to it all. The doctor at the Health Centre said just try to snap out of it what does *he* know? He ought to listen to people he can't realy know what individual people might do if they did *snap* as he puts it out of it, anyway out of what does he mean, snap out of what? The dead are snaped *into* black plastic sacks I have seen it on television body bags they are called. I realy think a lot about being a body in a black bag that is what I am good for. Please help me Dr. Himmelblau. I frighten myself and the contempt of others is the last straw snap snap snap snap.
>
> Yours sort of hopefully,
> Peggi Nollett.

Dr. Himmelblau sees Peregrine Diss walk past the window with the cheese plants. He is very tall and very erect—columnar, thinks Gerda Himmelblau—and has a great deal of well-brushed white hair remaining. He is wearing an olive-green cashmere coat with a black velvet collar. He carries a black lacquered walking stick, with a silver knob, which he does not lean on, but swings. Once inside the door, observed by but not observing Dr. Himmelblau, he studies the little god in his green shade, and then stands and looks gravely down on the lobster, the crabs, and the scallops. When he has taken them in he nods to them, in a kind of respectful acknowledgement, and proceeds into the body of the restaurant, where the younger Chinese woman takes his coat and stick and bears them away. He looks round and sees his host.

They are the only people in the restaurant; it is early.

"Dr. Himmelblau."

"Professor Diss. Please sit down. I should have asked whether you like Chinese food—I just thought this place might be convenient for both of us—"

"Chinese food—well-cooked, of course—is one of the great triumphs of the human species. Such delicacy, such intricacy, such simplicity, and so *peaceful* in the ageing stomach."

"I like the food here. It has certain subtleties one discovers as one goes on. I have noticed that the restaurant is frequented by large numbers of real Chinese people—families—which is always a good sign. And the fish and vegetables are always fresh, which is another."

"I shall ask you to be my guide through the plethora of the menu. I do not think I can face Fried Crispy Bowels, however much, in principle, I believe in venturing into the unknown. Are you partial to steamed oysters with ginger and spring onions? So intense, so *light* a flavour—"

"I have never had them—"

"Please try. They bear no relation to cold oysters, whatever you think of those. Which of the duck dishes do you think is the most succulent . . . ?"

They chat agreeably, composing a meal with elegant variations, a little hot flame of chilli here, a ghostly fragrant sweetness of lychee there, the slaty tang of black beans, the elemental earthy crispness of beansprouts. Gerda Himmelblau looks at her companion, imagining him willy-nilly engaging in the assault described by Peggi Nollett. His skin is tanned, and does not hang in pouches or folds, although it is engraved with crisscrossing lines of very fine wrinkles absolutely all over—brows, cheeks, neck, the armature of the mouth, the eye-corners, the nostrils, the lips themselves. His eyes are a bright cornflower blue, and must, Dr. Himmelblau thinks, have been quite extraordinarily beautiful when he was a young man in the 1930s. They are still surprising, though veiled now with jelly and liquid, though bloodshot in the corners. He wears a bright cornflower-blue tie, in rough silk, to go with them, as they must have been, but also as they still are. He wears a corduroy suit, the colour of dark slate. He wears a large signet ring, lapis lazuli, and his hands, like his face, are mapped with wrinkles but still handsome. He looks both fastidious, and marked by ancient indulgence and dissipation, Gerda Himmelblau thinks, fancifully, knowing something of his history, the bare gossip, what everyone knows.

She produces the document during the first course, which is glistening viridian seaweed, and prawn and sesame toasts. She says,

"I have had this rather unpleasant letter which I must talk to you about. It seemed to me important to discuss it informally and in an unofficial context, so to speak. I don't know if it will come as a surprise to you."

Perry Diss reads quickly, and empties his glass of Tiger beer, which is quickly replaced with another by the middle-aged Chinese man.

"Poor little bitch," says Perry Diss. "What a horrible state of mind to be in. Whoever gave her the idea that she had any artistic talent ought to be shot."

Don't say bitch, Gerda Himmelblau tells him in her head, wincing.

"Do you remember the occasion she complains of?" she asks carefully.

"Well, in a way I do, in a way. Her account isn't very recognisable. We did meet last week to discuss her complete lack of progress on her dissertation—she appears indeed to have *regressed* since she put in her proposal, which I am glad to say I was *not* responsible for accepting. She has forgotten several of the meagre facts she once knew, or appeared to know, about Matisse. I do not see how she can *possibly* be given a degree—she is ignorant and lazy and pigheadedly misdirected—and I felt it my duty to tell her so. In my experience, Dr. Himmelblau, a lot of harm has been done by misguided kindness to lazy and ignorant students who have been cosseted and *nurtured* and never told they are not up to scratch."

"That may well be the case. But she makes specific allegations—you went to her studio—"

"Oh yes. I went. I am not as brutal as I appear. I did try to give her the benefit of the doubt. That part of her account bears some resemblance to the truth—that is, to what I remember of those very disagreeable events. I did say something about the inarticulacy of painters and so on—you can't have worked in art schools as long as I have without knowing that some can use words and some can only use materials—it's interesting how you can't always predict *which.*

"Anyway, I went and looked at her so-called Work. The phraseology is catching. 'So-called.' A pantechnicon contemporary term of abuse."

"And?"

"The work is *horrible,* Dr. Himmelblau. It disgusts. It desecrates. Her studio—in which the poor creature also eats and sleeps—is papered with posters of Matisse's work. *La Rêve. Le Nu rose. Le Nu bleu. Grande Robe bleue. La Musique. L'Artiste et son modèle. Zorba sur la terrasse.* And they have all been smeared and defaced. With what looks like *organic matter*—blood, Dr. Himmelblau, beef stew or faeces—I incline towards the latter since I cannot imagine good daube finding its way into that miserable tenement. Some of the daubings are deliberate reworkings of bodies or faces—changes of outlines—some are like thrown tomatoes—probably *are* thrown tomatoes—and eggs, yes—and some are *great swastikas of shit.* It is appalling. It is pathetic."

"It is no doubt meant to disgust and desecrate," states Dr. Himmelblau, neutrally.

"And what does that matter? *How can that excuse it?*" roars Perry Diss, startling the younger Chinese woman, who is lighting the wax lamps under the plate warmer, so that she jumps back.

"In recent times," says Dr. Himmelblau, "art has traditionally had an element of protest."

"Traditional protest, hmph," shouts Perry Diss, his neck reddening. "Nobody minds protest, I've protested in my time, we all have, you aren't the real thing if you don't have a go at being shocking, protest is *de rigeur, I know.* But what I object to here, is the shoddiness, the laziness. It *seems to me*—forgive me, Dr. Himmelblau—but this—this *caca* offends something I do hold sacred, a word that would make that little bitch *snigger,* no doubt, but sacred, yes—it seems to me, that if she could have produced *worked copies* of those—those masterpieces—those shining—never mind—if she could have *done some work*—understood the blues, and the pinks, and the whites, and the oranges, yes, and the blacks too—and if she could still have brought herself to feel she must—must *savage* them—then I would have had to feel some respect."

"You have to be careful about the word masterpieces," murmurs Dr. Himmelblau.

"Oh, I know all that stuff, I know it well. But you have got to listen to me. It can have taken at the maximum *half an hour*—and there's no evidence anywhere in the silly girl's work that she's ever spent more than that actually *looking at* a Matisse—she has no accurate memory of one when we talk, *none,* she amalgamates them all in her mind into one monstrous female corpse bursting with male aggression—she can't *see,* can't you see? And for half an hour's shit-spreading we must give her a degree?"

"Matisse," says Gerda Himmelblau, "would sometimes make a mark, and consider, and put the canvas away for weeks or months until he *knew* where to put the next mark."

"I know."

"Well—the—the shit-spreading may have required the same consideration. As to location of daubs."

"Don't be silly. I *can see* paintings, you know. I did look to see if there was any wit in where all this detritus was applied. Any visual *wit,* you know, I know it's meant to be funny. There wasn't. It was just slapped on. It was horrible."

"It was meant to disturb you. It disturbed you."

"Look—Dr. Himmelblau—whose side are you on? I've read your Mantegna monograph. *Mes compliments,* it is a *chef-d'oeuvre*. Have you *seen* this stuff. Have you for that matter *seen* Peggi Nollett?"

"I am not on anyone's *side,* Professor Diss. I am the Dean of Women Students, and I have received a formal complaint against you, about which I have to take formal action. And that could be, in the present climate, very disturbing for me, for the Department, for the University, and for yourself. I may be exceeding my strict duty in letting you know of this in this informal way. I am very anxious to know what you have to say in answer to her specific charge.

"And yes, I have seen Peggi Nollett. Frequently. And her work, on one occasion."

"Well then. If you have seen her you will know that I can have made no such—no such *advances* as she describes. Her skin is like a *potato* and her body is like a *decaying potato,* in all that great bundle of smocks and vests and knitwear and penitential hangings. Have you seen her legs and arms, Dr. Himmelblau? They are bandaged like mummies, they are all swollen with strapping and strings and then they are contained in nasty black greaves and gauntlets of plastic with buckles. You expect some awful yellow ooze to seep out between the layers, ready to be smeared on *La Joie de vivre*. And her hair, I do not think her hair can have been washed for some years. It is like a carefully preserved old frying pan, grease undisturbed by water. You *cannot believe* I could have brought myself to touch her, Dr. Himmelblau?"

"It is difficult, certainly."

"It is impossible. I may have told her that she would be better if she wore fewer layers—I may even, imprudently—thinking, you understand, of potatoes—have said something about letting the air get to her. But I assure you that was as far as it went. I was trying against my instincts to converse with her as a human being. The rest is her horrible fantasy. I hope you will believe me, Dr. Himmelblau. You yourself are about the only almost-witness I can call in my defence."

"I do believe you," says Gerda Himmelblau, with a little sigh.

"Then let that be the end of the matter," says Perry Diss. "Let us enjoy these delicious morsels and talk about something more agreeable than Peggi Nollett. These prawns are as good as I have ever had."

"It isn't so simple, unfortunately. If she does not withdraw her complaint you will both be required to put your cases to the Senate of the University. And the University will be required—by a rule made in the days when university senates had authority and power and *money*—to retain QCs to represent both of you, should you so wish. And in the present climate I am very much afraid that whatever the truth of the matter, you will lose your job, and whether you do or don't lose it there will be disagreeable protests and demonstrations against you, your work, your continued presence in the University. And the Vice-Chancellor will fear the effect of the publicity on the funding of the College—and the course, which is the only Joint Honours Course of its kind in London—may have to close. It is *not* seen by our profit-oriented masters as an essential part of our new—'Thrust,' I think they call it. Our students do not contribute to the export drive—"

"I don't see why not. They can't *all* be Peggi Nolletts. I was about to say—have another spoonful of bamboo shoots and beansprouts—I was about to say, very well, I'll resign on the spot and save you any further bother. But I don't think I can do that. Because I won't give in to lies and blackmail. And because that woman *isn't an artist,* and *doesn't work,* and *can't see,* and should not have a degree. And because of Matisse."

"Thank you," says Gerda Himmelblau, accepting the vegetables. And, "Oh dear yes," in response to the declaration of intent. They eat in silence for a moment or two. The Cantonese voice asserts that it is a beautiful *morning.* Dr. Himmelblau says,

"Peggi Nollett is not well. She is neither physically nor mentally well. She suffers from anorexia. Those clothes are designed to obscure the fact that she has starved herself, apparently, almost to a skeleton."

"Not a potato. A fork. A pin. A coathanger. I see."

"And is in a very depressed state. There have been at least two suicide bids—to my knowledge."

"Serious bids?"

"How do you define serious? Bids that would perhaps have been effective if they had not been well enough signalled—for rescue—"

"I see. You do know that this does not alter the fact that she has no talent and doesn't work, and can't see—"

"She *might*—if she were well—"

"Do you think so?"

"No. On the evidence I have, no."

Perry Diss helps himself to a final small bowlful of rice. He says,

"When I was in China, I learned to end a meal with pure rice, quite plain, and to taste every grain. It is one of the most beautiful tastes in the world, freshly-boiled rice. I don't know if it would be if it was all you had every day, if you were starving. It would be differently delicious, differently haunting, don't you think? You can't describe this taste."

Gerda Himmelblau helps herself, manoeuvres delicately with her chopsticks, contemplates pure rice, says, "I see."

"Why Matisse?" Perry Diss bursts out again, leaning forward. "I can see she is ill, poor thing. You can *smell* it on her, that she is ill. That alone makes it unthinkable that anyone—that I—should *touch* her—"

"As Dean of Women Students," says Gerda Himmelblau thoughtfully, "one comes to learn a great deal about anorexia. It appears to stem from self-hatred and inordinate self-absorption. Especially with the body, and with that image of our own body we all carry around with us. One of my colleagues who is a psychiatrist collaborated with one of your colleagues in Fine Art to produce a series of drawings—clinical drawings in a sense—which I have found most instructive. They show an anorexic person before a mirror, and what *we* see—staring ribs, hanging skin—and what *she* sees—grotesque bulges, huge buttocks, puffed cheeks. I have found these most helpful."

"Ah. *We* see coathangers and forks, and *she* sees potatoes and vegetable marrows. There is a painting in that. You could make an interesting painting out of that."

"Please—the experience is terrible to her."

"Don't think I don't know. I am not being flippant, Dr. Himmelblau. I am, or was, a serious painter. It is not flippant to see a painting in a predicament. Especially a predicament which is essentially visual, as this is."

"I'm sorry. I am trying to think *what to do.* The poor child wishes to annihilate herself. *Not to be.*"

"So I understand. But *why Matisse*? If she is so obsessed with bodily horrors why does she not obtain employment as an emptier of bedpans or in a maternity ward or a hospice? And if she must take on Art, why does she not rework Giacometti into Maillol, or vice versa, or take on that old goat, Picasso, who did things to women's bodies out of genuine *malice*? Why *Matisse*?"

"Precisely for that reason, as you must know. Because he paints silent bliss. *Luxe, calme et volupté.* How can Peggi Nollett bear *luxe, calme et volupté*?"

"When I was a young man," says Perry Diss, "going through my own Sturm und Drang, I was a bit bored by all that. I remember telling someone—my wife—it all was *easy and flat.* What a fool. And then, one day I saw it. I saw how hard it is to see, and how full of pure power, once seen. Not *consolation,* Dr. Himmelblau, *life and power.*" He leans back, stares into space, and quotes,

> *"Mon enfant, ma soeur,*
> *Songe à la douceur*
> *D'aller là-bas vivre ensemble!*
> *Aimer à loisir*
> *Aimer et mourir*
> *Au pays qui te ressemble!—*
> *Là, tout n'est qu'ordre et beauté*
> *Luxe, calme et volupté."*

Dr. Himmelblau, whose own life has contained only a modicum of *luxe, calme et volupté,* is half-moved, half-exasperated by the vatic enthusiasm with which Perry Diss intones these words. She says drily,

"There has always been a resistance to these qualities in Matisse, of course. Feminist critics and artists don't like him because of the way in which he expands male eroticism into whole placid panoramas of well-being. Marxists don't like him because he himself said he wanted to paint to please businessmen."

"Businessmen and intellectuals," says Perry Diss.

"Intellectuals don't make it any more acceptable to Marxists."

"Look," says Perry Diss. "Your Miss Nollett wants to shock. She shocks with simple daubings. Matisse was cunning and complex and violent and controlled and *he knew he had to know exactly what he was doing.* He knew the most shocking thing he could tell people about the purpose of his art was that it was designed *to please and to be comfortable.* That sentence of his about the armchair is one of the most wickedly provocative things that has ever been said about painting. You can daub the whole of the Centre Pompidou with manure from top to bottom and you will *never* shock as many people as Matisse did by saying art was like an armchair. People remember that with horror who know nothing about the context—"

"Remind me," says Gerda Himmelblau.

"'What I dream of, is an art of balance, of purity, of quietness, without any disturbing subjects, without worry, which may be, for everyone who works with the mind, for the businessman as much as for the literary artist, something soothing, something to calm the brain, something analogous to a good armchair which relaxes him from his bodily weariness . . .'"

"It would be perfectly honourable to argue that that was a very *limited* view—" says Gerda Himmelblau.

"Honourable but impercipient. Who is it that understands *pleasure,* Dr. Himmelblau? Old men like me, who can only just remember their bones not hurting, who remember walking up a hill with a spring in their step like the red of the Red Studio.

Blind men who have had their sight restored and get giddy with the colours of trees and plastic mugs and the *terrible blue* of the sky. Pleasure is *life,* Dr. Himmelblau, and most of us don't have it, or not much, or mess it up, and when we see it in those blues, those roses, those oranges, that vermilion, we should fall down and worship—for it is *the thing itself.* Who knows a good armchair? A man who has bone cancer, or a man who has been tortured, he can recognise a good armchair . . ."

"And poor Peggi Nollett," says Dr. Himmelblau. "How can she see that, when she mostly wants to die?"

"Someone intent on bringing an action for rape, or whatever she calls it, can't be all that keen on death. She will want to savour her triumph over her doddering male victim."

"She is *confused,* Professor Diss. She puts out messages of all kinds, cries for help, threats . . ."

"Disgusting artworks—"

"It is truly not beyond her capacities to—to take an overdose and leave a letter accusing you—or me—of horrors, of insensitivity, of persecution—"

"Vengefulness can be seen for what it is. Spite and malice can be seen for what they are."

"You have a robust confidence in human nature. And you simplify. The despair is as real as the spite. They are part of each other."

"They are failures of imagination."

"Of course," says Gerda Himmelblau. "Of course they are. Anyone who could imagine the terror—the pain—of those who survive a suicide—against whom a suicide is *committed*—could not carry it through."

Her voice has changed. She knows it has. Perry Diss does not speak but looks at her, frowning slightly. Gerda Himmelblau, driven by some pact she made long ago with accuracy, with truthfulness, says,

"Of course, when one is at that point, imagining others becomes unimaginable. Everything seems clear, and simple, and *single;* there is only one possible thing to be done—"

Perry Diss says,

"That is true. You look around you and everything is bleached, and clear, as you say. You are in a white box, a white room, with no doors or windows. You are looking through clear water with no movement—perhaps it is more like being inside ice, inside the white room. There is only one thing possible. It is all perfectly clear and simple and plain. As you say."

They look at each other. The flood of red has subsided under Perry Diss's skin. He is thinking. He is quiet.

Any two people may be talking to each other, at any moment, in a civilised way about something trivial, or something, even, complex and delicate. And inside each of the two there runs a kind of dark river of unconnected thought, of secret fear, or violence, or bliss, hoped-for or lost, which keeps pace with the flow of talk and is neither seen nor heard. And at times, one or both of the two will catch sight or sound of this movement, in himself, or herself, or, more rarely, in the other. And it is like the quick slip of a waterfall into a pool, like a drop into darkness. The pace changes, the weight of the air, though the talk may run smoothly onwards without a ripple or quiver.

Gerda Himmelblau is back in the knot of quiet terror which has grown in her private self like a cancer over the last few years. She remembers, which she would rather not do, but cannot now control, her friend Kay, sitting in a heavy hospital armchair covered with mock-hide, wearing a long white hospital gown, fastened at the back, and a striped towelling dressing gown. Kay is not looking at Gerda. Her mouth is set, her eyes are sleepy with drugs. On the white gown are scarlet spots of fresh blood, where needles have injected calm into Kay. Gerda says, "Do you remember, we are going to the concert on Thursday?" and Kay says, in a voice full of stumbling ill-will, "No, I don't, what concert?" Her eyes flicker, she looks at Gerda and away, there is something malign and furtive in her look. Gerda has loved only one person in her life, her schoolfriend,

Kay. Gerda has not married, but Kay has—Gerda was bridesmaid—and Kay has brought up three children. Kay was peaceful and kindly and interested in plants, books, cakes, her husband, her children, Gerda. She was Gerda's anchor of sanity in a harsh world. As a young woman Gerda was usually described as "nervous" and also as "lucky to have Kay Leverett to keep her steady." Then one day Kay's eldest daughter was found hanging in her father's shed. A note had been left, accusing her schoolfellows of bullying. This death was not immediately the death of Kay—these things are crueller and slower. But over the years, Kay's daughter's pain became Kay's, and killed Kay. She said to Gerda once, who did not hear, who remembered only later, "I turned on the gas and lay in front of the fire all afternoon, but nothing happened." She "fell" from a window, watering a window box. She was struck a glancing blow by a bus in the street. "I just step out now and close my eyes," she told Gerda, who said don't be silly, don't be unfair to bus drivers. Then there was the codeine overdose. Then the sleeping pills, hoarded with careful secrecy. And a week after Gerda saw her in the hospital chair, the success, that is to say, the real death.

The old Chinese woman clears the meal, the plates veiled with syrupy black-bean sauce, the unwanted cold rice grains, the uneaten *mange touts*.

Gerda remembers Kay saying, earlier, when her pain seemed worse and more natural, and must have been so much less, must have been bearable in a way:

"I never understood how anyone *could*. And now it seems so clear, almost the only possible thing to do, do you know?"

"No, I don't," Gerda had said, robust. "You *can't do that* to other people. You have no right." "I suppose not," Kay had said, "but it doesn't feel like that." "I shan't listen to you," Gerda had said. "Suicide can't be handed on."

But it can. She knows now. She is next in line. She has flirted with lumbering lorries, a neat dark figure launching herself blindly into the road. Once, she took a handful of pills, and waited to see if she would wake up, which she did, so on that day she continued, drowsily nauseated, to work as usual. She believes the impulse is wrong, to be resisted. But at the time it is white, and clear, and simple. The colour goes from the world, so that the only stain on it is her own watching mind. Which it would be easy to wipe away. And then there would be no more pain.

She looks at Perry Diss who is looking at her. His eyes are half-closed, his expression is canny and watchful. He has used her secret image, the white room, accurately; they have shared it. *He knows that she knows,* and what is more, she knows that he knows. How he knows, or when he discovered, does not matter. He has had a long life. His young wife was killed in an air raid. He caused scandals, in his painting days, with his relations with models, with young respectable girls who had not previously been models. He was the co-respondent in a divorce case full of dirt and hatred and anguish. He was almost an important painter, but probably not quite. At the moment his work is out of fashion. He is hardly treated seriously. Like Gerda Himmelblau he carries inside himself some chamber of ice inside which sits his figure of pain, his version of kind Kay thick-spoken and malevolent in a hospital hospitality chair.

The middle-aged Chinese man brings a plate of orange segments. They are bright, they are glistening with juice, they are packed with little teardrop sacs full of sweetness. When Perry Diss offers her the oranges she sees the old scars, well-made *efficient* scars, on his wrists. He says,

"Oranges are the real fruit of Paradise, I always think. Matisse was the first to understand orange, don't you agree? Orange in light, orange in shade, orange on blue, orange on green, orange in black—

"I went to see him once, you know, after the war, when he was living in that apartment in Nice. I was full of hope in those days, I loved him and was enraged by him and meant to outdo him, some time soon, when I had just learned this and that—which I never did. He was ill then, he had come through this terrible operation, the nuns who looked after him called him *'le ressuscite.'*

"The rooms in that apartment were shrouded in darkness. The shutters were closed, the curtains were drawn. I was terribly shocked—I thought he *lived in the light,* you know, that was the idea I had of him. I blurted it out, the shock, I said, 'Oh, how can you bear to shut out the light?' And he said, quite mildly, quite courteously, that there had been some question of him going blind. He thought he had better acquaint himself with the dark. And then he added, 'and anyway, you know, black is the colour of light.' Do you know the painting *La Porte noire*? It has a young woman in an armchair quite at ease in a peignoir striped in lemon and cadmium and . . . over a white dress with touches of cardinal red—her hair is yellow ochre and scarlet—and at the side is the window and the coloured light and behind—above—is the black door. Almost no one could paint the colour black as he could. Almost no one."

Gerda Himmelblau bites into her orange and tastes its sweetness. She says,

"He wrote, 'I believe in God when I work.'"

"I think he also said, 'I am God when I work.' Perhaps he is—not my God, but where—where I find that. I was brought up in the hope that I would be a priest, you know. Only I could not bear a religion which had a tortured human body hanging from the hands over its altars. No, I would rather have *The Dance.*"

Gerda Himmelblau is gathering her things together. He continues,

"That is why I meant what I said, when I said that young woman's—muck-spreading—offended what I called sacred. What are we to do? I don't want her to—to punish us by self-slaughter—nor do I wish to be seen to condone the violence—the absence of *work*—"

Gerda Himmelblau sees, in her mind's eye, the face of Peggi Nollett, potato-pale, peering out of a white box with cunning, angry eyes in the slit between puffed eyelids. She sees golden oranges, rosy limbs, a voluptuously curved dark blue violin case, in a black room. One or the other must be betrayed. Whatever she does, the bright forms will go on shining in the dark. She says,

"There is a simple solution. What she wants, what she has always wanted, what the Department has resisted, is a sympathetic supervisor—Tracey Avison, for instance—who shares her way of looking at things—whose beliefs—who cares about political ideologies of that kind—who will—"

"Who will give her a degree and let her go on in the way she is going on. It is a defeat."

"Oh yes. It is a question of how much it matters. To you. To me. To the Department. To Peggi Nollett, too."

"It matters very much and not at all," says Perry Diss. "She may see the light. Who knows?"

They leave the restaurant together. Perry Diss thanks Dr. Himmelblau for his food and for her company. She is inwardly troubled. Something has happened to her white space, to her inner ice, which she does not quite understand. Perry Diss stops at the glass box containing the lobster, the crabs, the scallops—these last now decidedly dead, filmed with an iridescent haze of imminent putrescence. The lobster and the crabs are all still alive, all, more slowly, hissing their difficult air, bubbling, moving feet, feelers, glazing eyes. Inside Gerda Himmelblau's ribs and cranium she experiences, in a way, the pain of alien fish-flesh contracting inside an exoskeleton. She looks at the lobster and the crabs, taking accurate distant note of the loss of gloss, the attenuation of colour.

"I find that *absolutely appalling,* you know," says Perry Diss. "And at the same time, exactly at the same time, I don't give a damn? D'you know?"

"I know," says Gerda Himmelblau. She does know. Cruelly, imperfectly, voluptuously, clearly. The muzak begins again. "*Oh* what a *beautiful morning. Oh* what a *beautiful day.*" She reaches up, in a completely uncharacteristic gesture, and kisses Perry Diss's soft cheek.

"Thank you," she says. "For everything."

"Look after yourself," says Perry Diss.

"Oh," says Gerda Himmelblau, "I will. I will."

DRAGONS' BREATH

Once upon a time, in a village in a valley surrounded by high mountains, lived a family with two sons and a daughter, whose names were Harry, Jack, and Eva. The village was on the lower slopes of the mountains, and in the deep bowl of the valley was a lake, clear as crystal on its shores, and black as ink in its unplumbed centre. Thick pine forests grew in the shadow of the mountain ridges, but the village stood amongst flowery meadows and orchards, and cornfields, not luscious, but sufficient for the needs of the villagers. The peaks of the mountains were inaccessible, with blue ice shadows and glittering snowfields. The sides of the mountain were scored with long descending channels, like the furrows of some monstrous plough. In England the circular impressions around certain hills are ascribed to the coiling grip of ancient dragons, and in that country there was a tale that in some primeval time the channels had been cut by the descent of giant worms from the peaks. In the night, by the fire, parents frightened children pleasurably with tales of the flaming, cavorting descent of the dragons.

Harry, Jack, and Eva were not afraid of dragons, but they were, in their different ways, afraid of boredom. Life in that village repeated itself, generation after generation. They were born, they became lovers, they became parents and grandparents, they died. They were somewhat inbred, to tell the truth, for the outside world was far away, and hard to reach, and only a few traders came and went, in the summer months, irregularly. The villagers made a certain traditional kind of rug, on handlooms, with a certain limited range of colours from vegetable dyes they made themselves—a blood-red, a dark blue with a hint of green, a sandy yellow, a charcoal black. There were a few traditional designs, which hardly varied: a branching tree, with fruit like pomegranates, and roosting birds, somewhat like pheasants, or a more abstract geometrical design, with disks of one colour threaded on a crisscrossing web of another on the ground of a third. The rugs were on the whole made by the women, who also cooked and washed. The men looked after the livestock, worked the fields and made music. They had their own musical instrument, a wailing pipe, not found anywhere else, though most of them had not travelled far enough to know that.

Harry was a swineherd and Jack dug in the fields, sowed and harvested. Harry had a particular friend amongst the pigs, a young boar called Boris, a sagacious creature who made cunning escapes and dug up unexpected truffles. But Boris's playfulness was not enough to mitigate Harry's prevailing boredom. He dreamed of great cities beyond the mountain, with streaming crowds of urgent people, all different, all busy. Jack liked to see the corn come up, green spikes in the black earth, and he knew where to find ceps and wild honey, but these treats did little to mitigate his prevailing boredom. He dreamed of ornamental gardens inside high walls surrounding huge palaces. He dreamed of subtle tastes, spices and fiery spirits unknown in the valley. He dreamed also of wilder dances, bodies flung about freely, to music on instruments he knew only by hearsay: the zither, the bongo drum, the grand piano, tubular bells.

Eva made the rugs. She could have woven in her sleep, she thought, and often did, waking to find her mind buzzing with repeats and variations, twisting threads and shifting warp and weft. She dreamed of unknown colours, purple, vermilion, turquoise, and orange, colours of flowers and feathers, soft silks, sturdy cottons. She dreamed of an older Eva, robed in crimson and silver. She dreamed of the sea, which she could not imagine, she dreamed of salt water and tasted her own impatient tears. She was not good at weaving, she made her tension too tight, and her patterns bunched, but this was her task. She was a weaver. She wanted to be a traveller, a sailor, a learned doctor, an opera singer in front of flaring footlights and the roar of the crowd.

The first sign may have been the hunters' reports of unusual snow slides in the high mountains. Or maybe it was, as some of them later claimed, dawns that were hectically rosy, sunsets that flared too crimson. They began to hear strange rumblings and crackings up there, above the snowline, which they discussed, as they discussed every strange and every accustomed sound, with their repetitious measuring commentary that made Jack and Harry grind their teeth with rage at the sameness of it all. After a time it became quite clear that the rim of the mountains directly above the village, both by day and by night, was flickering and dancing with a kind of fiery haze, a smoky salmon-pink, a burst here and there of crimson and gold. The colours were rather beautiful, they agreed as they watched from their doorsteps, the bright ribbons of colour flashing through the grey-blue smokiness of the air, and then subsiding. Below this flaming rim the white of the snow was giving way to the gaunt grey of wet rock, and the shimmer—and yes, steam—of new water.

They must have been afraid from the beginning: they could see well enough that large changes were taking place, that everything was on the move, earth and air, fire and water. But the fear was mixed with a great deal of excited *interest,* and with even a certain pleasure in novelty, and with aesthetic pleasure, of which many of them were later ashamed. Hunting parties went out in the direction of the phenomenon and came back to report that the hillside seemed to be on the move, and was boiling and burning, so that it was hard to see through the very thick clouds of ash and smoke and steam that hung over the movement. The mountains were not, as far as anyone knew, volcanic, but the lives of men are short beside the history of rocks and stones, so they wondered and debated.

After some time they saw on the skyline lumps like the knuckles of a giant fist, six lumps, where nothing had been, lumps that might represent objects the size of large sheds or small houses, at that distance. And over the next few weeks the lumps advanced, in smoke and spitting sparks, regularly and slowly, side by side, without hesitation or deviation, down the mountainside. Behind each tump trailed a long, unbending tube, as it were, or furrow ridge, or earthwork, coming over the crest of the mountain, over the rim of their world, pouring slowly on and down.

Some brave men went out to prospect but were forced back by clouds of scalding steam and showers of burning grit. Two friends, bold hunters both, went out and never returned.

One day a woman in her garden said: "It is almost as though it was not landslides but creatures, great worms with fat heads creeping down on us. Great fat, nodding bald heads, with knobs and spouts and whelks and whorls on them, and nasty hot wet eyes in great caverns in their muddy flesh, that glint blood-red, twelve eyes, can you see them, and twelve hairy nostrils on blunt snouts made of grey mud." And after conversations and comparisons and pointings and descriptions they could all see them, and they were just as she said, six fat, lolling, loathsome heads, trailing heavy bodies as long as the road from their village to the next, trailing them with difficulty, even with pain, it seemed, but unrelenting and deadly slow.

When they were nearer—and the slowness of their progress was dreamlike, unreal—their great jaws could be seen, jaws wide as whales and armed with a scythelike horny or flinty edge like a terrible beak, with which they excavated and swallowed a layer of the earth and whatever was on it—bushes, fences, haystacks, fruit trees, a couple of goats, a black and white cow, a duck pond and the life in it. They sucked and scythed, with a soughing noise, and they spat out fine ash, or dribbled it from the lips of the terrible jaws, and it settled on everything. As they approached, the cloud of ash came before them, and settled on everything in the houses and gardens, coated the windows, filmed the wells. It stank, the ash, it was unspeakably foul. At first they grumbled and dusted, and then they gave up dusting, for it was no use, and began to be afraid. It was all so slow that there was a period of unreal, half-titillating fear, before the real, sick, paralysing fear took hold, which was when the creatures were close enough for men and women to see their eyes, which were rimmed with a gummy discharge, like melting rubber, and their tongues of flame. The tongues of flame were nothing like the brave red banners of painted dragons in churches, and nothing like the flaming swords of archangels. They were molten and lolling, covered with a leathery transparent skin thick with crimson warts and taste buds glowing like coals, the size of cabbages, slavering with some sulphurous glue and stinking of despair and endless decay that would never be clean again in the whole life of the world. Their bodies were repulsive, as they humped and slithered and crushed, slow and grey and indiscriminate. Their faces were too big to be seen as faces—only identified in parts, successively. But the stench was the worst thing, and the stench induced fear, then panic, then a fatalistic tremor of paralysis, like rabbits before stoats, or mice before vipers.

The villagers discussed for far too long the chances of the village being destroyed. They discussed also expedients for diverting or damaging the worms, but these were futile, and came to nothing. They discussed also the line of the creatures' advance; whether it crossed the village, or whether it might be projected to pass by it on one side or another. Afterwards it might have been easy to agree that it was always clear that the village stood squarely in the path of that terrible descent, but hope misleads, and inertia misleads, and it is hard to imagine the vanishing of what has seemed as stable as stone. So the villagers left it very late to make a plan to evacuate their village, and in the end left hurriedly and messily, running here and there in the stink and smoke of that bad breath, snatching up their belongings, putting them down and snatching up others, seething like an ants' nest. They ran into the forest with sacks of corn and cooking pots, with featherbeds and sides of bacon, completely bewildered by the presence of the loathsome creatures. It was not clear that the worms exactly saw the human beings. The human beings were not on their scale, as small creatures that inhabit our scalps, or burrow in the salad leaves we eat are not visible to us, and we take no account of them.

The villagers' life in the forest became monotonous, boring even, since boredom is possible for human beings in patches of tedium between exertion and terror. They were very cold, especially at night, they were hungry and their stomachs were constantly queasy, both with fear and with their ramshackle diet. They knew they were beyond the perimeter of the worms' breath, and yet they smelled its foul odour, in their dreams, in the curl of smoke from their campfires, in rotting leaves. They had watchers posted, who were placed to be able to see in the distance the outline of the village, who saw the line of gross heads advancing imperceptibly, who saw bursts of sudden flame and spurts of dense smoke that must have been the kindling of houses. They were watching the destruction of their world, and yet they felt a kind of ennui which was part of all the other distress they felt. You might ask—where were the knights, where were the warriors who would at least ride out and try to put an arrow or a bullet through those drooling eyes. There was talk of this round the campfires, but no heroes sprang up, and it is probable that this was wise, that the things were invulnerable to the pinprick of human weapons. The elders said it was best to let things go by, for those huge bodies would be almost as noisome dead as alive in the village midst. The old women said that old tales told that dragons' breath paralysed the will, but when they were asked for practical advice, *now,* they had none to offer. You could want to kill yourself, Eva found out, because you were sleeping on a tree-root, on the hard ground, which pressed into your flesh and became an excruciating pain, boring in both senses.

Harry and Jack finally went with some other young men, out in the direction of the village, to see from close quarters the nature and extent of the devastation. They found they were walking towards a whole wall of evil-smelling smoke and flame, extending across acres of pastureland and cornfield, behind which the great craglike protuberances of the heads could be seen, further apart now, moving on like the heads of water at the mouth of a flooding delta. Jack said to Harry that this fanning out of the paths left little chance that anything in the village might be left standing, and Harry replied distractedly that there were figures of some sort moving in the smoke, and then said that they were the pigs, running here and there, squealing. A pig shot out of the smoke, panting and squeaking, and Harry called out, "Boris!" and began to run after his pig, which snorted wildly and charged back into the darkness, followed by Harry, and Jack saw pig and human in sooty silhouette before he heard a monstrous sucking sound, and an exhalation of hot vapours and thick, choking fiery breath which sent him staggering and fainting back. When he came to, his skin was thick with adhesive ash and he could hear, it seemed to him, the liquids boiling and burning in the worm's belly.

For a moment he thought he would simply lie there, in the path of that jaw, and be scooped up with the cornfield and the hedgerow. Then he found he had decided to roll away, and little by little, rolling, crawling and scrambling, he put patches of space between himself and the worm. He lay for several hours, then, winded and sick, under a thornbush, before picking himself painfully up, and returning to the camp in the forest. He hoped that Harry too would return, but was not surprised, not really surprised, when he did not.

And so it dragged on, for weeks and months, with the air full of ash and falling cinders, with their clothes and flesh permeated by that terrible smell, until little by little the long loathsome bodies dragged past, across the fields and the meadows, leaving behind those same furrows of rocky surface, scooped clean of life and growth. And from a hilly point they saw the creatures, side by side, cross the sandy shore of the lake, and without changing pace or hesitating, advance across the shallows, as though driven by mechanical necessity, or by some organic need like the periodic return of toads or turtles to a watery world to breed. And the great heads dipped to meet the lake surface, and where they met it, it boiled, and steamed and spat like a great cauldron. And then the heads went under the surface, which still boiled, puckered and bubbling, as the slow lengths of the long bodies humped and slithered, day after day, over the sand and down through the water to the depths, until finally only blunt, ugly butts could be seen, under the shallows, and then one day, as uncertainly as their coming had been established, it became clear that their going was over, that the worms had plunged into, through, under the lake, leaving only the harsh marks of their bodies' weight and burning breath in the soil, the rock, the vegetable world crushed and withered.

When the villagers returned to look on their village from a distance, the devastation seemed uniform: the houses flattened, the trees uprooted, the earth scored, channelled, ashy, and smoking. They wandered in the ruins, turning over bricks and boards, some people finding, as some people always will, lost treasures and trivia in the ashes, a coin, half a book, a dented cooking pot. And some people who had vanished in the early chaos returned, with singed eyebrows or seared faces, and others did not. Jack and Eva came back together, and for a moment could not work out in what direction to look for the ruins of what had been their house. And then, coming round a heap of fallen rubble, they saw it there, untouched. One of the dragon troughs passed at a distance, parallel to the garden fence, but the fence stood, and inside the fence the garden, the veranda, the doors and windows were as they had always been, apart from the drifting ash. And Jack lifted the stone under which the key was always kept, and there was the key, where it had always been. And Jack and Eva went into the house, and there were tables and chairs, fireplace and bookcase, and Eva's loom, standing in the window, at the back of the house, where you looked out on the slopes and then up at the peaks of the mountains. And there was a heavy humping sound against the back door, which Jack opened. And when he opened it, there was Boris the pig, hanging his head a little, and giving off an odour of roast pork, with not a bristle on his charred rind, but with pleasure and recognition in his deep-set little eyes.

When they saw that the pig had by some miracle, or kindness of luck, escaped the dragon breath and the fiery tongues, they hoped, of course, that Harry too would return. They hoped he would return for days and months, and against their reasonable judgment, for years. But he did not.

*

Eva dusted her rug, which was lightly filmed with ash, since it was at the back of the house, and the windows were well made. She saw the colours—red, blue, yellow, black—as though she had never seen colour before, and yet with disturbed pleasure at their familiarity. An archaeologist, finding this room, and this rug on this loom in it, say two thousand years later, might have felt intense excitement that these things were improbably intact, and intense curiosity about the workmanship, and even about the daily life that could be partly imagined around the found artefacts. Eva felt such amazement now, about her own work, the stubborn persistence of wood and wool and bone shuttle, or the unfinished tree with its squatting pheasants and fat pomegranates. She felt inwardly moved and shaken, also, by this form of her own past, and the past of her mother and grand-mother, and by the traces of her moments of flowing competence, and of her periods of bunching, tension, anxiety, fumbling. Jack too felt delight and amazement, walking repeatedly across the house from the windows which opened on smouldering devastation to those from which you could see the unchanging mountains. Both embraced Boris, restored and rescued, feeling his wet snout and warm flanks. Such wonder, such amazement, are the opposite, the exact opposite, of boredom, and many people only know them after fear and loss. Once known, I believe, they cannot be completely forgotten; they cast flashes and floods of paradisal light in odd places and at odd times.

The villagers rebuilt their village, and the rescued things in the rescued house stood amongst new houses in whose gardens new flowers and vegetables sprouted, and new saplings were planted. The people began to tell tales about the coming of the worms down the mountain, and the tales too were the opposite of boredom. They made ash and bad breath, crushing and swallowing, interesting, exciting, almost beautiful. Some things they made into tales, and some things they did not speak. Jack told of Harry's impetuous bravery, rushing into the billowing smoke to save his pig, and nobody told the day-to-day misery of the slowly diminishing hope of his return. The resourcefulness and restoration of the pig were celebrated, but not his inevitable fate, in these hard days. And these tales, made from those people's wonder at their own survival, became, in time, charms against boredom for their children and grandchildren, riddling hints of the true relations between peace and beauty and terror.

THE DJINN IN THE NIGHTINGALE'S EYE

Once upon a time, when men and women hurtled through the air on metal wings, when they wore webbed feet and walked on the bottom of the sea, learning the speech of whales and the songs of the dolphins, when pearly-fleshed and jewelled apparitions of Texan herdsmen and houris shimmered in the dusk on Nicaraguan hillsides, when folk in Norway and Tasmania in dead of winter could dream of fresh strawberries, dates, guavas, and passion fruits and find them spread next morning on their tables, there was a woman who was largely irrelevant, and therefore happy.

Her business was storytelling, but she was no ingenious queen in fear of the shroud brought in with the dawn, nor was she a naquibolmalek to usher a shah through the gates of sleep, nor an ashik, a lover-minstrel singing songs of Mehmet the Conqueror and the sack of Byzantium, nor yet a holy dervish in short skin trousers and skin skullcap, brandishing axe or club and making its shadow terrible. She was no meddah, telling incredible tales in the Ottoman court or the coffeehouses by the market. She was merely a narratologist, a being of secondary order, whose days were spent hunched in great libraries scrying, interpreting, decoding the fairy tales of childhood and the vodka posters of the grown-up world, the unending romances of golden coffee drinkers, and the impeded couplings of doctors and nurses, dukes and poor maidens, horsewomen and musicians. Sometimes also, she flew. In her impoverished youth she had supposed that scholarship was dry, dusty and static, but now she knew better. Two or three times a year she flew to strange cities, to China, Mexico, and Japan, to Transylvania, Bogotá, and the South Seas, where narratologists gathered like starlings, parliaments of wise fowls, telling stories about stories.

At the time when my story begins the green sea was black, sleek as the skins of killer whales, and the sluggish waves were on fire, with dancing flames and a great curtain of stinking smoke. The empty deserts were seeded with skulls, and with iron canisters, containing death. Pestilence crept invisibly from dune to dune. In those days men and women, including narratologists, were afraid to fly east, and their gatherings were diminished. Nevertheless our narratologist, whose name was Gillian Perholt, found herself in the air, between London and Ankara. Who can tell if she travelled because she was English and stolid and could not quite imagine being blasted out of the sky, or because, although she was indeed an imaginative being, and felt an appropriate measure of fear, she could not resist the idea of the journey above the clouds, above the minarets of Istanbul, and the lure of seeing the Golden Horn, the Bosphorus, and the shores of Europe and Asia face to face? Flying is statistically safer than any other travel, Gillian Perholt told herself, and surely at this time, only slightly less safe, statistically only a little less.

She had a phrase for the subtle pleasures of solitary air travel. She spoke it to herself like a charm as the great silver craft detached itself from its umbilical tube at Heathrow, waddled like an albatross across the tarmac and went up, up, through grey curtains of English rain, a carpet of woolly iron-grey English cloud, a world of swirling vapour, trailing its long limbs and scarves past her tiny porthole, in the blue and gold world that was always there, above the grey, always. "Floating redundant" she said to herself, sipping champagne, nibbling salted almonds, whilst all round her spread the fields of heaven, white and rippling, glistening and gleaming, rosy and blue in the shadows, touched by the sun with steady brightness. "Floating redundant," she murmured blissfully as the vessel banked and turned and a disembodied male voice spoke in the cabin, announcing that there was a veil of water vapour over France but that that would burn off, and then they would see the Alps, when the time came. "Burn off" was a powerful term, she thought, rhetorically interesting, for water does not burn and yet the sun's heat reduces this water to nothing; I am in the midst of fierce forces. I am nearer the sun than any woman of my kind, any ancestress of mine, can ever have dreamed of being, I can look in his direction and stay steadily here, floating redundant.

The phrase was, of course, not her own; she was, as I have said, a being of a secondary order. The phrase was John Milton's, plucked from the air, or the circumambient language, at the height of his powers, to describe the beauty of the primordial coils of the insinuating serpent in the Paradise garden. Gillian Perholt remembered the very day these words had first coiled into shape and risen in beauty from the page, and struck at her, unsuspecting as Eve. There she was, sixteen years old, a golden-haired white virgin with vague blue eyes (she pictured herself so) and there on the ink-stained desk in the dust was the battered emerald-green book, ink-stained too, and secondhand, scribbled across and across by dutiful or impatient female fingers, and everywhere was a smell, still drily pungent, of hot ink and linoleum and dust if not ashes, and there he was, the creature, insolent and lovely before her.

> not with indented wave,
> Prone on the ground, as since, but on his rear,
> Circular base of rising folds, that towered
> Fold above fold a surging maze, his head
> Crested aloft and carbuncle his eyes;
> With burnished neck of verdant gold, erect
> Amidst his circling spires, that on the grass
> Floated redundant: pleasing was his shape,
> And lovely.

And for an instant Gillian Perholt had *seen,* brilliant and swaying, not the snake Eve had seen in the garden, nor yet the snake that had risen in the dark cave inside the skull of blind John Milton, but a snake, the snake, the same snake, in some sense, made of words and visible to the eye. So, as a child, from time to time, she had *seen* wolves, bears, and small grey men, standing between her and the safety of the door, or her father's sleeping Sunday form in an armchair. But I digress, or am about to digress. I called up the snake (I saw him too, in my time) to explain Dr. Perholt's summing-up of her own state.

In those days she had been taught to explain "floating redundant" as one of Milton's magical fusings of two languages—"floating," which was Teutonic and to do with floods, and "redundant," which was involved and Latinate, and to do with overflowings. Now she brought to it her own wit, a knowledge of the modern sense of "redundant," which was to say, superfluous, unwanted, unnecessary, let go. "I'm afraid we shall have to let you go," employers said, everywhere, offering freedom to reluctant Ariels, as though the employees were captive sprites, only too anxious to rush uncontrolled into the elements. Dr. Perholt's wit was only secondarily to do with employment, however. It was primarily to do with her sex and age, for she was a woman in her fifties, past childbearing, whose two children were adults now, had left home and had left England, one for Saskatchewan and one for São Paulo, from where they communicated little, for they were occupied with children of their own. Dr. Perholt's husband also had left home, had left Dr. Perholt, had removed himself after two years of soul-searching, two years of scurrying in and out of his/their home, self-accusation, irritability, involuntary impotence, rejection of lovingly cooked food, ostentatious display of concealed messages, breathed phone calls when Dr. Perholt appeared to be sleeping, missed dinner engagements, mysterious dips in the balance at the bank, bouts of evil-smelling breath full of brandy and stale smoke, also of odd-smelling skin, with touches of alien sweat, hyacinths, and stephanotis. He had gone to Majorca with Emmeline Porter and from there had sent a fax message to Gillian Perholt, saying he was a coward for doing it this way, but it was also done to save her, and that he was never coming home.

Gillian Perholt happened to be in her study when the fax began to manifest itself, announced by a twangling bell and a whirring sound. It rose limp and white in the air and flopped exhausted over the edge of the desk—it was long and self-exculpatory, but there is no need for me to recount it to you, you can imagine it very well for yourself. Equally, you can imagine Emmeline Porter for yourself, she has no more to do with this story. She was twenty-six, that is all you need to know, and more or less what you supposed, probably, anyway. Gillian watched the jerky progress and flopping of the fax with admiration, not for Mr. Perholt's fluency, but for the way in which agitated black scribbling could be fed into a machine slit in Majorca and appear simultaneously in Primrose Hill. The fax had been bought for Mr. Perholt, an editorial consultant, to work from home when he was let go or made redundant in the banal sense, but its main user was Gillian Perholt, who received email and story variants from narratologists in Cairo and Auckland, Osaka and Port of Spain. Now the fax was hers, since he was gone. And although she was now redundant as a woman, being neither wife, mother, nor mistress, she was by no means redundant as a narratologist but on the contrary, in demand everywhere. For this was a time when women were privileged, when female narratologists had skills greatly revered, when there were pythonesses, abbesses, and sibyls in the world of narratology, who revealed mysteries and kept watch at the boundaries of correctness.

On receiving the fax, Gillian Perholt stood in the empty study and imagined herself grieving over betrayal, the loss of love, the loss of companionship perhaps, of respect in the world, maybe, as an ageing woman rejected for one more youthful. It was a sunny day in Primrose Hill, and the walls of the study were a cheerful golden colour, and she saw the room fill up with golden light and felt full of lightness, happiness, and purpose. She felt, she poetically put it to herself, like a prisoner bursting chains and coming blinking out of a dungeon. She felt like a bird confined in a box, like a gas confined in a bottle, that found an opening, and rushed out. She felt herself expand in the space of her own life. No more waiting for meals. No more grumbling and jousting, no more exhausted anticipation of alien feelings, no more snoring, no more farts, no more trace of stubble in the washbasin.

She considered her reply. She wrote:

> OK. Agreed. Clothes in bales in store. Books in chests ditto. Will change locks. Have a good time. G.

She knew she was lucky. Her ancestresses, about whom she thought increasingly often, would probably have been dead by the age she had reached. Dead in childbed, dead of influenza, or tuberculosis, or puerperal fever, or simple exhaustion, dead, as she travelled back in time, from worn-out unavailing teeth, from cracked kneecaps, from hunger, from lions, tigers, sabre-toothed tigers, invading aliens, floods, fires, religious persecution, human sacrifice, why not? Certain female narratologists talked with pleasurable awe about wise Crones but she was no crone, she was an unprecedented being, a woman with porcelain-crowned teeth, laser-corrected vision, her own store of money, her own life and field of power, who flew, who slept in luxurious sheets around the world, who gazed out at the white fields under the sun by day and the brightly turning stars by night as she floated redundant.

The conference in Ankara was called "Stories of Women's Lives." This was a pantechnicon title to make space for everyone, from every country, from every genre, from every time. Dr. Perholt was met at the airport by an imposing bearded Turkish professor, dark and smiling, into whose arms she rushed with decorous cries of joy, for he was an old friend, they had been students together amongst mediaeval towers and slow, willow-bordered rivers, they had a story of their own, a very minor subplot, a thread now tenuous, now stronger, but never broken, in the tapestry of both lives. Dr. Perholt was angry at the blond Lufthansa hostess who bowed gravely to the grey businessmen as they disembarked, goodbye, sir, and thank you, goodbye, sir, and thank you, but gave Dr. Perholt a condescending "Bye-bye, dear." But Orhan Rifat, beyond the airport threshold, was as always alive with projects, new ideas, new poems, new discoveries. They would visit Izmir with a group of Turkish friends. Gillian would then visit Istanbul, his city.

The conference, like most conferences, resembled a bazaar, where stories and ideas were exchanged and changed. It took place in a cavernous theatre with no windows on the outside world but well provided with screens where transparencies flickered fitfully in the dark. The best narratologists work by telling and retelling tales. This holds the hearer from sleep and allows the teller to insert him- or herself into the tale. Thus a fierce Swiss writer told the horrid story of Typhoid Mary, an innocent polluter, an unwitting killer. Thus the elegant Leyla Doruk added passion and flamboyance to her version of the story of the meek Fanny Price, trembling and sickly in the deepest English wooded countryside. Orhan Rifat was to speak last: his title was "Powers and Powerlessness: Djinns and Women in *The Arabian Nights*." Gillian Perholt spoke before him. She had chosen to analyse the Clerk's Tale from *The Canterbury Tales,* which is the story of Patient Griselda. No one has ever much liked this story, although it is told by one of Chaucer's most sympathetic pilgrims, the book-loving, unworldly Clerk of Oxford, who took it from Petrarch's Latin, which was a rendering of Boccaccio's Italian. Gillian Perholt did not like this story; that was why she had chosen to tell it, amongst the stories of women's lives. What do I think of, she had asked herself, on receiving the invitation, when I think of "Stories of Women's Lives," and had answered herself with a thrill and a shudder, "Patient Griselda."

So now she told it, in Ankara, to a mixed audience of scholars and students. Most of the Turkish students were like students everywhere, in jeans and tee shirts, but conspicuous in the front row were three young women with their heads wrapped in grey scarves, and dotted amongst the young men in jeans were soldiers—young officers—in uniform. In the secular Turkish republic the scarves were a sign of religious defiance, an act of independence with which liberal-minded Turkish professors felt they should feel sympathy, though in a Muslim state much of what they themselves taught and cared about would be as objectionable, as forbidden, as the covered heads were here. The young soldiers, Gillian Perholt observed, listened intently and took assiduous notes. The three scarved women, on the other hand, stared proudly ahead, never meeting the speakers' eyes, as though completely preoccupied with their own conspicuous self-assertion. They came to hear all the speakers. Orhan had asked one of them, he told Gillian, why she dressed as she did. "My father and my fiancé say it is right," she had said. "And I agree."

The story of Patient Griselda, as told by Gillian Perholt, is this.

There was once a young marquis, in Lombardy, whose name was Walter. He enjoyed his life, and his sports—hunting and hawking—as young men do, and had no desire to marry, perhaps because marriage appeared to him to be a form of confinement, or possibly because marriage is the end of youth, and its freedom from care, if youth is free from care. However his people came and urged him to take a wife, perhaps, as they told him, because he should think of begetting an heir, perhaps because they felt marriage would steady him. He professed himself moved by their arguments and invited them to his wedding, on a certain day he fixed on—with the condition that they swore to accept this bride, whoever she might be.

It was one of Walter's peculiarities that he liked to make people swear in advance to accept unconditionally and without repining whatever he himself might choose to do.

So the people agreed and made ready for the wedding on the chosen day. They made a feast and prepared rich clothes, jewels, and bed linen for the unknown bride. And on the chosen day the priest was waiting, and the bridal procession mounted, and still no one knew who the bride was to be.

Now Griseldis, or Grisilde, or Grisildis or Grissel or Griselda was the daughter of a poor peasant. She was both beautiful and virtuous. On the day fixed for the wedding she set out to fetch water from the well; she had all the domestic virtues and meant to finish her housework before standing in the lane with the other peasants to cheer as the bridal procession wound past. Weddings make spectators—participating spectators—of us all. Griselda wanted to be part of the wedding, and to look at the bride, as we all do. We all like to look at brides. Brides and princesses, those inside the story, imagined from the outside. Who knows but Griselda was looking forward to imagining the feelings of this unknown woman as she rode past.

Only the young Lord rode up, and did not ride past, but stopped, and made her put down her pitcher, and wait. And he spoke to her father, and said that it was his intention to make Griselda his wife, if her father would give his consent to her will. So the young Lord spoke to the young woman and said he wanted to make her his bride, and that his only requirement was that she should promise to obey him in everything, to do whatever he desired, without hesitating or repining, at every moment of the day or night. And Griselda, "quakynge for drede" as Chaucer tells us, swore that never willingly, in act or thought, would she disobey him, on pain of death—though she would fear to die, she told the young Lord.

And then young Walter commanded immediately that her clothes should be taken off and that she should be clothed in the rich new garments he had prepared, with her hair dressed and her head crowned with a jewelled coronet. And so she went away to be married, and to live in the castle, and Chaucer tells us, he takes care to tell us, that she showed great qualities of judgment, reconciliation of disputes, bounty, and courtesy in her new position, and was much loved by the people.

But the story goes inexorably on, past the wedding, into the ominous future foreshadowed by the pledge exacted and vouchsafed. And consider this, said Gillian Perholt at this point in the story: in almost all stories of promises and prohibitions, the promises and prohibitions carry with them the inevitability of failure, of their own breaking. Orhan Rifat smiled into his beard, and the soldiers wrote rapidly, presumably about promises and prohibitions, and the grey-scarved women stared fixedly ahead.

After a time, Chaucer says, Griselda gave birth to a daughter, although she would rather have borne a son; but everyone rejoiced, for once it is seen that a woman is not barren, a son may well come next. And at this point it came into Walter's head that he must test his wife. It is interesting, said Gillian, that here the Clerk of Oxford dissociates himself as narrator from his protagonist, and says he cannot see why this testing seemed to be necessary. But he goes on to tell how Walter informed his wife gravely that the people grumbled at having a peasant's daughter set over them, and did not want such a person's child to be set above them. He therefore proposed, he said, to put her daughter to death. And Griselda answered that she and her child were his to do with as he thought best. So Walter sent a rough sergeant to take the child, from the breast. And Griselda kissed it goodbye, asking only that the baby should be buried where wild creatures could not tear it.

And after a further time, Griselda gave birth to a son, and the husband, still intent on testing, had this child too taken from the breast and carried away to be killed. And Griselda kept steadily to her pact, assuring him that she was not grieved or hurt; that her two children had brought her only sickness at first "and after, woe and pain."

And then there was a lull in the narrative, said Gillian, a lull long enough for the young children who were secretly being brought up in Bologna to reach puberty, adolescence, a marriageable age. A lull as long as the space between Acts III and IV of *A Winter's Tale* during which Hermione the Queen is hidden away and thought to be dead, and her daughter, Perdita, abandoned and exposed, is brought up by shepherds, wooed by a Prince, and forced to flee to Sicily, where she is happily reunited with her repentant father and her lost mother who appears on a pedestal as a statue and is miraculously given her life and happiness again by art. In the *Winter's Tale,* said Gillian, the lovely daughter is the renewal of the mother, as the restoration of Persephone was the renewal of the fields in Spring, laid waste by the rage of Demeter, the mother-goddess. Here Gillian's voice faltered. She looked out at the audience and told them how Paulina, Hermione's friend and servant, had taken on the powers of witch, artist, storyteller, and had restored the lost queen to life. Personally, said Gillian, I have never been able to stomach—to bear—that plotted dénouement, which is the opposite of the restoration of Persephone in Spring. For human beings do not die and spring up again like the grass and the corn, they live one life and get older. And from Hermione—and as you may know already, from Patient Griselda—most of that life has been taken by plotting, has been made into a grey void of forced inactivity.

What did Griselda do whilst her son, and more particularly her daughter, were growing up? The story gallops. A woman's life runs from wedding to childbirth to nothing in a twinkling of an eye. Chaucer gives no hint of subsequent children, though he insists that Griselda remained true in love and patience and submission. But her husband had to excess Paulina's desire to narrate, to orchestrate, to direct. He busied himself, he gained a dispensation from the Pope to put away his wife, Griselda, and to marry a young bride. The people muttered about the murdered children. But Walter, if we are to believe the story, went to his patient wife and told her that he intended to replace her with a younger and more acceptable bride, and that she must return to her father, leaving behind the rich clothes and jewels and other things which had been his gift. And still Griselda was patient, though Chaucer here gives her words of power in her patience which keep the reader's sympathy, and fend off the reader's impatience which might sever that sympathy.

Naked, Griselda tells her husband, she came from her father, and naked she will return. But since he has taken all her old clothes she asks him for a smock to cover her nakedness, since "the womb in which your children lay, should not, as I walk, be seen bare before the people. Let me not," says Griselda, "go by the way like a worm. In exchange for my maidenhead which I brought with me and cannot take away, give me a smock." And Walter graciously allows her the shift she stands in, to cover her nakedness.

But Walter thought of other twists to the intrigue, since every twist made his plotted dénouement more splendid and satisfactory. No sooner, it seemed, was Griselda back at home, than her husband was there, asking her to return to the castle and prepare the rooms and the feast for his new young bride. No one could do it better, he told her. You might think that the pact was over on her return to her father's house, but this was not Griselda's idea: patiently she returned, patiently she cooked, cleaned, prepared, made up the marriage bed.

And the bridal procession arrived at the castle, with the beautiful girl in the midst, and Griselda worked away in the hall in her poor clothes, and the feast was set, and the lords and ladies sat down to eat. Now indeed, apparently, Griselda was a belated spectator at the wedding. Walter called Griselda to him and asked her what she thought of his wife and her beauty. And Griselda did not curse her, or indeed him, but answered always patiently, that she had never seen a fairer woman, and that she both beseeched and warned him "never to prick this tender maiden with tormenting" as he had done her, for the young bride was softly brought up and would not endure it.

And now Walter had his dénouement, the end of his story, and revealed to Griselda that his bride was not his bride, but her daughter, and the squire her son, and that all would now be well and she would be happy, for he had done all this neither in malice nor in cruelty, but to test her good faith, which he had not found wanting. So now they could be reconciled.

And what did Griselda do? asked Gillian Perholt? And what did she say, and what did she do? repeated Dr. Perholt. Her audience was interested. It was not a story most of them knew beyond the title and its idea, Patient Griselda. Would the worm turn? one or two asked themselves, moved by Griselda's image of her own naked flesh. They looked up to Dr. Perholt for an answer, and she was silent, as if frozen. She stood on the stage, her mouth open to speak, and her hand out, in a rhetorical gesture, with the lights glittering on her eyeballs. She was am ample woman, a stout woman, with a soft clear skin, clothed in the kind of draped linen dress and jacket that is best for stout women, a stone-coloured dress and jacket, enlivened by blue glass beads.

And Gillian Perholt stared out of glassy eyes and heard her voice fail. She was far away and long ago—she was a pillar of salt, her voice echoed inside a glass box, a sad piping like a lost grasshopper in winter. She could move neither fingers nor lips, and in the body of the hall, behind the grey-scarved women, she saw a cavernous form, a huge, female form, with a veiled head bowed above emptiness and long slack-sinewed arms, hanging loosely around emptiness, and a draped, cowled garment ruffling over the windy vacuum of nothing, a thing banal in its conventional awfulness, and for that very reason appalling because it was there, to be seen, her eyes could distinguish each fold, could measure the red rims of those swollen eyes, could see the cracks in the stretched lips of that toothless, mirthless mouth, could see that it was many colours, and all of them grey, grey. The creature was flat-breasted and its withered skin was exposed above the emptiness, the windy hole that was its belly and womb.

This is what I am afraid of, thought Gillian Perholt, whose intelligence continued to work away, to think of ways to ascertain whether or not the thing was a product of hallucination or somehow out there on an unexpected wavelength.

And just as Orhan rose to come to her help, seeing her stare like Macbeth at the feast, she began to speak again, as though nothing had happened, and the audience sighed and sat back, ill at ease but courteous.

And what did Griselda do? asked Gillian Perholt. And what did

Griselda say and what did she do? repeated Dr. Perholt. First, all mazed, uncomprehending, she swooned. When she revived, she thanked her husband for having saved her children, and told her children that her father had cared for them tenderly—and she embraced both son and daughter, tightly, tightly, and still gripping them fell again into terrible unconsciousness, gripping so tightly that it was almost impossible for the bystanders to tear the children from her grasp. Chaucer does not say, the Clerk of Oxford does not say, that she was strangling them, but there is fear in his words, and in the power of her grip, all her stoppered and stunted energy forcing all three into unconsciousness, unknowing, absence from the finale so splendidly brought about by their lord and master.

But of course, she was revived, and again stripped of her old clothes, and dressed in cloth of gold and crowned with jewels and restored to her place at the feast. To begin again.

And I wish to say a few words, said Gillian Perholt, about the discomfort of this terrible tale. You might suppose it was one of that group of tales in which the father or king or lord tries to marry his daughter, after his wife's death, as the original Leontes tried to marry Perdita in the tale that precedes the *Winter's Tale,* the tale of a man seeking the return of spring and youth and fertility in ways inappropriate for human beings as opposed to grass and the flowers of the field. This pattern is painful but natural, this human error which tales hasten to punish and correct. But the peculiar horror of Patient Griselda does not lie in the psychological terror of incest or even of age. It lies in the narration of the story and Walter's relation to it. The story is terrible because Walter has assumed too many positions in the narration; he is hero, villain, destiny, God, and narrator—there is no *play* in this tale, though the Clerk and Chaucer behind him try to vary its tone with reports of the people's contradictory feelings, and with the wry final comment on the happy marriage of Griselda's son, who

fortunat was eek in mariage,
Al putte he nat his wyf in greet assay.
This world is nat so strong, it is no nay,
As it hath been in olde tymes yoore.

And the commentator goes on to remark that the moral is *not* that wives should follow Griselda in humility, for this would be impossible, unattainable, even if desired. The moral is that of Job, says the Clerk, according to Petrarch, that human beings must patiently bear what comes to them. And yet our own response is surely outrage—at what was done to Griselda—at what was taken from her, the best part of her life, what could not be restored—at the energy stopped off. For the stories of women's lives in fiction are the stories of stopped energies—the stories of Fanny Price, Lucy Snowe, even Gwendolen Harleth, are the stories of Griselda, and all come to that moment of strangling, willed oblivion.

Gillian Perholt looked up. The creature, the ghoul, was gone. There was applause. She stepped down. Orhan, who was forthright and kind, asked if she felt unwell and she said that she had had a dizzy turn. She thought it was nothing to worry about. A momentary mild seizure. She would have liked to tell him about the apparition too, but was prevented. Her tongue lay like lead in her mouth, and the thing would not be spoken. What cannot be spoken continues its vigorous life in the veins, in the brain cells, in the nerves. As a child she had known that if she could describe the grey men on the stairs, or the hag in the lavatory, they would vanish. But she could not. She imagined them lusciously and in terror and occasionally saw them, which was different.

Orhan's paper was the last in the conference. He was a born performer, and always had been, at least in Gillian's experience. She remembered a student production of *Hamlet* in which they had both taken part. Orhan had been Hamlet's father's ghost and had curdled everyone's blood with his deep-voiced rhetoric. His beard was now, as it had not been then, "a sable silvered," and had now, as it had had then, an Elizabethan cut—though his face had sharpened from its youthful thoughtfulness and he now bore a resemblance, Gillian thought, to Bellini's portrait of Mehmet the Conqueror. She herself had been Gertrude, although she had wanted to be Ophelia, she had wanted to be beautiful and go passionately mad. She had been the Queen who could not see the spirit stalking her bedchamber: this came into her mind, with a renewed, now purely imaginary vision of the Hermione-Griselda ghoul, as she saw Orhan, tall, imposing, smiling in his beard, begin to speak of Scheherazade and the djinniyah.

"It has to be admitted," said Orhan, "that misogyny is a driving force of pre-modern story collections—perhaps especially of the frame stories—from *Katha Sarit Sagara, The Ocean of Story,* to the *Thousand and One Nights, Alf Layla wa-Layla.* Why this should be so has not, as far as I know, been fully explained, though there are reasons that could be put forward from social structures to depth psychology—the sad fact remains that women in these stories for the most part are portrayed as deceitful, unreliable, greedy, inordinate in their desires, unprincipled, and simply dangerous, operating powerfully (apart from sorceresses and female ghouls and ogres) through the structures of powerlessness. What is peculiarly interesting about the *Thousand and One Nights* in terms of the subject of our conference, is the frame story, which begins with two kings driven to murderous despair by the treachery of women, yet has a powerful heroine-narrator, Scheherazade, who must daily save her own life from a blanket vicarious vengeance on all women by telling tales in the night, tales in the bed, in the bedchamber, to her innocent little sister—Scheherazade whose art is an endless beginning and delaying and ending and beginning and delaying and ending—a woman of infinite resource and sagacity," said Orhan smiling, "who is nevertheless using cunning and manipulation from a position of total powerlessness with the sword of her fate more or less in her bedchamber hanging like the sword of Damocles by a metaphorical thread, the thread of her narrative, with her shroud daily prepared for her the next morning. For King Shahriyar, like Count Walter, has taken upon himself to be husband and destiny, leaving only the storytelling element, the plotting, to his wife, which is enough. Enough to save her, enough to provide space for the engendering and birth of her children, whom she hides from her husband as Walter hid his from Griselda, enough to spin out her life until it becomes love and happy-ever-after, so to speak, as Griselda's does. For these tales are not psychological novels, are not concerned with states of mind or development of character, but bluntly with Fate, with Destiny, with what is prepared for human beings. And it has been excellently said by Pasolini the filmmaker that the tales in the *Thousand and One Nights* all end with the disappearance of destiny which 'sinks back into the somnolence of daily life.' But Scheherazade's own life could not sink back into somnolence until all the tales were told. So the dailiness of daily life is her end as it is Cinderella's and Snow White's but not Mme Bovary's or Julien Sorel's who die but do not vanish into the afterlife of stories. But I am anticipating my argument, which, like my friend and colleague Dr. Perholt's argument, is about character and destiny and sex in the folktale, where character is *not* destiny as Novalis said it was, but something else is.

"And first I shall speak of the lives of women in the frame story, and then I shall briefly discuss the story of Camaralzaman and Princess Budoor, which is only half-told in the manuscripts of the *Nights* . . ."

Gillian Perholt sat behind the grey-scarved women and watched Orhan's dark hooked face as he told of the two kings and brothers Shahriyar and Shahzaman, and of how Shahzaman, setting out on a journey to his brother went back home to bid his wife farewell, found her in the arms of a kitchen boy, slew them both immediately, and set out on his journey consumed by despair and disgust. These emotions were only relieved when he saw from his brother's palace window the arrival in a secret garden of his brother's wife and twenty slave girls. Of these ten were white and ten black, and the black cast off their robes revealing themselves to be young males, who busily tupped the white females, whilst the queen's black lover Mas'ud came out of a tree and did the same for her. This amused and relieved Shahzaman, who saw that his own fate was the universal fate, and was able to demonstrate to his brother, at first incredulous and then desperate with shame and wrath, that this was so. So the two kings, in disgust and despondency, left the court and their life at the same moment and set out on a pilgrimage in search of someone more unfortunate than themselves, poor cuckolds as they were.

Note, said Orhan, that at this time no one had attempted the lives of the queen and her black lover and the twenty lascivious slaves.

And what the two kings met was a djinn, who burst out of the sea like a swaying black pillar that touched the clouds, carrying on his head a great glass chest with four steel locks. And the two kings (like Mas'ud before them) took refuge in a tree. And the djinn laid himself down to sleep, as luck, or chance, or fate would have it, under that very tree, and opened the chest to release a beautiful woman—one he had carried away on her wedding night—on whose lap he laid his head and immediately began to snore. Whereupon the woman indicated to the two kings that she knew where they were, and would scream and reveal their presence to the djinn unless they immediately came down and satisfied her burning sexual need. The two kings found this difficult, in the circumstances, but were persuaded by threats of immediate betrayal and death to do their best. And when they had both made love to the djinn's stolen wife, as she lay with opened legs on the desert sand under the tree, she took from both of them their rings, which she put away in a small purse on her person, which already contained ninety-eight rings of varying fashions and materials. And she told the two kings with some complacency that they were all the rings of men with whom she had been able to deceive the djinn, despite being locked in a glass case with four steel locks, kept in the depths of the raging roaring sea. And the djinn, she explained, had tried in vain to keep her pure and chaste, not realising that nothing can prevent or alter what is predestined, and that when a woman desires something, nothing can stop her.

And the two kings concluded, after they were well escaped, that the djinn was more unfortunate than they were, so they returned to the palace, put Shahriyar's wife and the twenty slaves to the sword, replaced the female slaves in the harem, and instituted the search for virgin brides who should all be put to death after one night "to save King Shahriyar from the wickedness and cunning of women." And this led to Scheherazade's resourceful plan to save countless other girls by substituting narrative attractions for those of inexperienced virginity, said Orhan, smiling in his beard, which took her a thousand and one nights. And in these frame stories, said Orhan, destiny for men is to lose dignity because of female rapacity and duplicity, and destiny for women is to be put to the sword on that account.

What interests me about the story of Prince Camaralzaman, said Orhan, is the activity of the djinn in bringing about a satisfactory adjustment to the normal human destiny in the recalcitrant prince. Camaralzaman was the beloved only son of Sultan Shahriman of Khalidan. He was the child of his father's old age, born of a virgin concubine with ample proportions, and he was very beautiful, like the moon, like new anemones in spring, like the children of angels. He was amiable but full of himself, and when his father urged him to marry to perpetuate his line, he cited the books of the wise, and their accounts of the wickedness and perfidy of women, as a reason for refraining. "I would rather die than allow a woman to come near me," said Prince Camaralzaman. "Indeed," he said grandly, "I would not hesitate to kill myself if you wished to force me into marriage." So his father left the topic for a year, during which Camaralzaman grew even more beautiful, and then asked again, and was told that the boy had done even more reading, which had simply convinced him that women were immoral, foolish, and disgusting, and that death was preferable to dealing with them. And after another year, on the advice of his vizir, the king approached the prince formally in front of his court and was answered with insolence. So, on the advice of the vizir, the king confined his son to a ruined Roman tower, where he left him to fend for himself until he became more amenable.

Now, in the water tank of the tower lived a djinniyah, a female djinn, who was a Believer, a servant of Suleyman, and full of energy. Djinns, as you may or may not know, are one of the three orders of created intelligences under Allah—the angels, formed of light, the djinns, formed of subtle fire, and man, created from the dust of the earth. There are three orders of djinns—fliers, walkers, and divers; they are shape-shifters, and like human beings, divided into servants of God and servants of Iblis, the demon lord. The Koran often exhorts the djinns and men equally to repentance and belief, and there do exist legal structures governing the marriage and sexual relations of humans and djinns. They are creatures of this world, sometimes visible, sometimes invisible; they haunt bathrooms and lavatories, and they fly through the heavens. They have their own complex social system and hierarchies, into which I will not divagate. The djinniyah in question, Maimunah, was a flier, and flew past the window of Camaralzaman's tower, where she saw the young man, beautiful as ever in his sleep, flew in, and spent some time admiring him. Out again in the night sky she met another flying afrit, a lewd unbeliever called Dahnash who told her excitedly of a beautiful Chinese Princess, the lady Budoor, confined to her quarters by her old women, for fear she should stab herself, as she had sworn to do when threatened with a husband, asking, "How shall my body, which can hardly bear the touch of silks, tolerate the rough approaches of a man?" And the two djinns began to dispute, circling on leathery wings in the middle air, as to which human creature, the male or the female, was the most beautiful. And the djinniyah commanded Dahnash to fetch the sleeping princess from China and lay her beside Prince Camaralzaman for comparison, which was performed, within an hour. The two genies, male and female, disputed hotly—and in formal verse—without coming to any conclusions as to the prize for beauty. So they summoned up a third being—a huge earth spirit, with six horns, three forked tails, a hump, a limp, one immense and one pygmy arm, with claws and hooves, and monstrously lengthy masculinity. And this being performed a triumphal dance about the bed, and announced that the only way to test the relative power of these perfect beauties was to wake each in turn and see which showed the greater passion for the other, and the one who aroused the greatest lust would be the winner. So this was done; the prince was woken, swooning with desire and respect, and put to sleep with his desire unconsummated, and the princess was then woken, whose consuming need aroused power and reciprocating desire in the sleeping prince, and "that happened which did happen." And before I go on to recount and analyse the separation and madness of Camaralzaman and Budoor, the prince's long search, disguised as a geomancer, for his lost love, their marriage, their subsequent separation, owing to the theft of a talisman from the princess's drawers by a hawk, Princess Budoor's resourceful disguise as her husband, her wooing of a princess, her wooing of her own husband to what he thought were unnatural acts—before I tell all this I would like to comment on the presence of the djinns at this defloration of Budoor by Camaralzaman, their unseen delight in the human bodies, the strangeness of the apprehension of the secret consummation of first love as in fact the narrative contrivance of a group of bizarre and deeply involved onlookers, somewhere between gentlemen betting at a horse race, *entremetteurs, metteurs-en-scène,* or storytellers, and gentlemen and ladies of the bedchamber. This moment of narrative, said Orhan, has always puzzled and pleased me because it is told from the point of view of these three magical beings, the prime instigator female, the subordinate ones male. What is the most private moment of choice in a human life—the loss of virginity, the mutual loss of virginity indeed, in total mutual satisfaction and bliss—takes place as a function of the desire and curiosity and competitive urgings of fire creatures from sky and earth and cistern. Camaralzaman and Budoor—here also like Count Walter—have tried to preserve their freedom and their will, have rejected the opposite sex as ugly and disgusting and oppressive—

and here in deepest dream they give way to their destiny which is conducted somewhere between comedy and sentimentality by this bizarre unseen trio—of whom the most redundant, from the point of view of the narrative, is also the largest, the most obtrusive, the most memorable, the horned, fork-tailed appallingly disproportioned solid earth-troll who capers in glee over the perfectly proportioned shapes of the two sleeping beauties. It is as though our dreams were watching us and directing our lives with external vigour whilst we simply enact their pleasures passively, in a swoon. Except that the djinns are more solid than dreams and have all sorts of other interests and preoccupations besides the young prince and princess . . .

The soldiers were writing busily; the scarved women stared ahead motionlessly, holding their heads high and proud. Gillian Perholt listened with pleasure to Orhan Rifat, who had gone on to talk more technically about the narrative imagination and its construction of reality in tales within tales within tales. She was tired; she had a slight temperature; the air of Ankara was full of fumes from brown coal, calling up her childhood days in a Yorkshire industrial city, where sulphur took her breath from her and kept her in bed with asthma, day after long day, reading fairy tales and seeing the stories pass before her eyes. And they had gone to see *The Thief of Baghdad* when she was little; they had snuffed the sulphur as the enchanted horse swooped across the screen and the genie swelled from a speck to a cloud filling the whole seashore. There had been an air raid whilst they were in the cinema: the screen had flickered and jumped, and electric flashes had disturbed the magician's dark glare; small distant explosions had accompanied the princess's wanderings in the garden; they had all had to file out and hide in the cellars, she remembered, and she had wheezed, and imagined wings and fire in the evening air. What did I think my life was to be, then? Gillian Perholt asked herself, no longer listening to Orhan Rifat as he tried to define some boundary of credulity between fictive persons in the fictions of fictive persons in the fiction of real persons, in the reader and the writer. I had this idea of a woman I was going to be, and I think it was before I knew what sex was (she had been thinking with her body about the swooning delight of Camaralzaman and Princess Budoor) but I imagined I would be married, a married woman, I would have a veil and a wedding and a house and Someone—someone devoted, like the thief of Baghdad, and a dog. I wanted—but not by any stretch of the imagination to be a narratologist in Ankara, which is so much more interesting and surprising, she told herself, trying to listen to what Orhan Rifat was saying about thresholds and veils.

The next day she had half a day to herself and went to the Museum of Anatolian Civilisations, which all her Turkish friends assured her she should not miss, and met an Ancient Mariner. The British Council car left her at the entrance to the museum, which is a modern building, cut into the hillside, made unobtrusively of wood and glass, a quiet, reflective, thoughtful, elegant place, in which she had looked forward to being alone for an hour or two, and savouring her delightful redundancy. The ancient person in question emerged soundlessly from behind a pillar or statue and took her by the elbow. American? he said, and she replied indignantly, No, English, thus embarking willy-nilly on a conversation. I am the official guide, this person claimed. I fought with the English soldiers in Korea, good soldiers, the Turks and the English are both good soldiers. He was a heavy, squat, hairless man, with rolling folds between his cranium and his shoulders, and a polished gleam to his broad naked head, like marble. He wore a sheepskin jacket, a military medal, and a homemade-looking badge that said GUIDE. His forehead was low over his eye sockets—he had neither brows nor lashes—and his wide mouth opened on a whitely gleaming row of large false teeth. I can show you everything, he said to Gillian Perholt, gripping her elbow, I know things you will never find out for yourself. She said neither yes nor no, but went down into the hall of the museum, with the muscular body of the ex-soldier shambling after her. Look, he said, as she stared into a reconstructed earth-dwelling, look how they lived in those days the first people, they dug holes like the animals, but they made them comfortable for themselves. Look here at the goddess. One day, think, they found themselves turning the bits of clay in their hands, and they saw a head and a body, see, in the clay, they saw a leg and an arm, they pushed a bit and pinched a bit here and there and there she was, look at her, the little fat woman. They loved fat, it meant strength and good prospects of children and living through the winter, to those naked people, they were probably thin and half-starved with hunting and hiding in holes, so they made her fat, fat, fat was life to them. And who knows why they made the first little woman, a doll, an image, a little offering to the goddess, to propitiate her—what came first, the doll or the goddess we cannot know—but we *think* they worshipped her, the fat woman, we think they thought everything came out of her hole, as they came out of their underground houses, as the plants and trees come out in the spring after the dark. Look at her here, here she is very old, eight thousand years, nine thousand years before your Christian time counting, here she is only the essential, a head, and arms, and legs and lovely fat belly, breasts to feed, no need even for hands or feet, here, see no face. Look at her, made out of the dust of the earth by human fingers so old, so old you can't really imagine.

And Gillian Perholt looked at the little fat dolls with their bellies and breasts, and pulled in her stomach muscles, and felt the fear of death in the muscles of her heart, thinking of these centuries-old fingers fashioning flesh of clay.

And later, he said, guiding her from figure to figure, she became powerful, she became the goddess in the lion throne, see here she sits, she is the ruler of the world now, she sits in her throne with her arms on the lion heads, and see there, the head of the child coming out between her legs, see how well those old people knew how to show the little skull of the baby as it turns to be born.

There were rows of the little baked figurines; all generically related, all different also. The woman in rolls of fat on the squat throne, crowned with a circlet of clay, and the arms of the throne were standing lions and her buttocks protruded behind her, and her breasts fell heavy and splayed, and her emptying belly sagged realistically between her huge fat knees. She was one with her throne, the power of the flesh. Her hands were lion heads, her head bald as the ancient soldier's and square down the back of the fat neck as his was.

We don't like our girls fat now, said the ancient one, regretfully. We like them to look like young boys, the boys out of the Greek gymnasium round the corner. Look at her, though, you can see how powerful she was, how they touched her power, scratching the shape into her breasts there, full of goodness they thought and hoped.

Gillian Perholt did not look at the old soldier whose voice was full of passion; she had not exactly consented to his accompanying narrative, and the upper layer of her consciousness was full of embarrassed calculations about how much Turkish cash she was carrying and how that would convert into pounds sterling, and how much such a guide might require at the end of his tale, if she could not shed him. So they trod on, one behind the other, she never turning her head or meeting his eye, and he never ceasing to speak into her ear, into the back of her studious head, as he darted from glass case to glass case, manoeuvring his bulk lightly and silently, as though shod with felt. And in the cases the clay women were replaced by metal stags and sun disks, and the tales behind her were tales of kings and armies, of sacrifice and slaughter, of bride sacrifice and sun offerings, and she was helplessly complicit, for here was the best, the most assured raconteur she could hope to meet. She knew nothing of the Hittites or the Mesopotamians or the Babylonians or the Sumerians, and not much of the Egyptians and the Romans in this context, but the soldier did, and made a whole wedding from a two-spouted wine jar in the form of ducks, or from a necklace of silver and turquoise, and a centuries-old pot of kohl he made a nervous bride, looking in a bronze mirror—his whisper called up her black hair, her huge eyes, her hand steadying the brush, her maid, her dress of pleated linen. He talked too, between centuries and between cases, of the efficiency of the British and

Turkish soldiers fighting side by side on the Korean hillsides, and Gillian remembered her husband saying that the Turks' punishments for pilfering and desertion had been so dreadful that they were bothered by neither. And she thought of Orhan, saying, "People who think of Turks think of killing and lasciviousness, which is sad, for we are complicated and have many natures. Including a certain ferocity. And a certain pleasure in good living."

The lions of the desert were death to the peoples of Anatolia, said the old guide, as they neared the end of their journey, which had begun with the earth dwellers and moved through the civilisations that built the sun-baked ziggurats, towards the lion gates of Nineveh and Assyria. That old goddess, she sat on the lion throne, the lions were a part of her power, she was the earth and the lions. And later the kings and the warriors tamed the lions and took on their strength, wore their skins and made statues of them as guardians against the wild. Here are the Persian lions, the word is Aslan, they are strength and death, you can walk through that carved lion-gate into the world of the dead, as Gilgamesh did in search of Enkidu, his friend who was dead. Do you know the story of Gilgamesh, the old man asked the woman, as they went through the lion gates together, she always in front and with averted eyes. The museum had arranged various real carved walls and gates into imaginary passages and courtyards, like a minor maze in a cool light. They were now, in the late afternoon, the only two people in the museum, and the old soldier's voice was hushed, out of awe perhaps, of the works of the dead, out of respect perhaps, for the silence of the place, where the glass cases gleamed in the shadows.

See here, he said, with momentary excitement, see here is the story of Gilgamesh carved in stone if you know how to read it. See here is the hero clothed in skins and here is his friend the wild man with his club—here is their meeting, here they wrestle and make friends on the threshold of the king's palace. Do you know Enkidu? He was huge and hairy, he lived with the beasts in the woods and fields, he helped them escape the trappers and hunters. But the trappers asked Gilgamesh the king to send a woman, a whore, who tempted Enkidu to leave the world of the gazelles and the herds and come to the king, who fought him and loved him. And they were inseparable, and together they killed the giant Humbaba—tricked and killed him in the forest. They trick and kill him, they are young and strong, there is nothing they cannot do. But then Gilgamesh's youth and strength attract the attention of the goddess Ishtar—she was the goddess of Love, and also of War—she is the same goddess you know, ma'am, as Cybele and Astarte—and when the Romans came with their Diana she was the same goddess—terrible and beautiful—whose temples were surrounded by whores—holy whores—whose desires could not be denied. And Ishtar wanted to marry Gilgamesh but he repelled her—he thought she would trick him and destroy him, and he made the mistake of telling her so, telling her he didn't want her, he wanted to remain free—for she had destroyed Tammuz, he said, whom the women wailed for, and she had turned shepherds into wolves and rejected lovers into blind moles, and she had destroyed the lions in pits and the horses in battle, although she loved their fierceness. And this made Ishtar angry—and she sent a great bull from heaven to destroy the kingdom, but the heroes killed the bull—see here in the stone they drive their sword behind his horns—and Enkidu ripped off the bull's thigh and threw it in the face of Ishtar. And she called the temple whores to weep for the bull and decided Enkidu must die. See here, he lies sick on his bed and dreams of death. For young men, you know, they do not know death, or they think of it as a lion or a bull to be wrestled and conquered. But sick men know death, and Enkidu dreamed of His coming—a birdman with a ghoul face and claws and feathers—for the loathsome picture of death, you see, is from the vulture—and Enkidu dreamed that this Death was smothering him and turning him into the bird man and that he was going to the Palace of the gods of the underworld—and there, Enkidu saw in his dream, there was no light at all and no joy and the people ate dust and fed on clay. There is a goddess down there too—here she is—Ereshkigal the Queen of the underworld. And both Gilgamesh and Enkidu wept at this dream—it terrified them—it took away all their strength—and then Enkidu died, in terrible pain, and Gilgamesh could not be comforted. He would not accept that his friend was gone and would never come back. He was young and strong, he would not accept that there was death walking in the world. Young men are like that, you know, it's a truth—they think they can defy what's coming because their blood is hot and their bodies are strong.

And Gilgamesh remembered his ancestor, Uta-Napishtim, who was the only man who had survived when the earth was flooded; they said he lived in the underworld and had the secret of living forever. So Gilgamesh travelled on and travelled on, and came to a mountain called Mashu, and at the mountain's gate were the man-scorpions, demons you know, like dragons. We can pretend that this gate is the gate of the underworld—the Sumerian people, the Babylonian people, they made great solid gates to their buildings and built guardians into the gates. See here are lions, and here, at this gate, are genies—you say genies?—yes, genies—there were good genies and bad genies in Babylon, they were called *utukku* and some were good and some were evil—the good ones were like these guardians here who are bulls with wings and wise faces of men—they are called *shedu* or *lamassu*—they stand here as guardians, but they could take other shapes, they walked invisibly behind men in the streets; every one had his genie, some people say, and they protected them—there is an old saying: "He who has no genie when he walks in the streets wears a headache like a garment." That's interesting, don't you think?

Gillian Perholt nodded. She had a headache herself—she had had a kind of penumbral headache, accompanied by occasional stabs from invisible stilettos or ice splinters since she had seen the Griselda-ghoul, and everything shimmered a little, with a grey shimmer, in the space between the gate and the narratives carved in relief on the stone tablets. The old soldier had become more and more animated, and now began to act out Gilgamesh's arrival at the gates of Mount Meshu, almost dancing like a bear, approaching, stepping back, staring up, skipping briskly from the courtyard to the space between the gateposts, raising his fingers to his bald skull for horns and answering himself in the person of the scorpion-men. (These are *good* genies, ma'am, said the old soldier parenthetically. The scorpion-men might have been dangerous ones, *edimmu* or worse, *arallu*, who came out of the underworld and caused pestilence, they sprang from the goddess's bile, you must imagine terrifying scorpion-men in the place of these bulls with wings.) They say, Why have you come? And Gilgamesh says, "For Enkidu my friend. And to see my father, Uta-Napishtim, amongst the gods." And they say, "No man born of woman has gone into the mountain; it is very deep; there is no light and the heart is oppressed with darkness. Oppressed with darkness." He skipped out again and strode resolutely in, as Gilgamesh. She thought, he is a descendant of the ashiks of whom I have read, who dressed in a uniform of skins, and wore a skin hat and carried a club or a sword as a professional prop. They made shadows with their clubs on café walls and in market squares. The old soldier's shadow mopped and mowed amongst the carved *utukku:* he was Gilgamesh annihilated in the dark; he came out into the light and became Siduri, the woman of the vine, in the garden at the edge of the sea with golden bowl and golden vats of wind; he became Urshanabi the ferryman of the Ocean, disturbed at the presence of one who wore skins and ate flesh, in the other world. He was, Gillian Perholt thought suddenly, related to Karagöz and Hacivat, the comic heroes and animators of the Turkish shadow puppets, who fought both demons from the underworld and fat capitalists. Orhan Rifat was a skilled puppeteer: he had a leather case full of the little figures whom he could bring to life against a sheet hung on a frame, against a white wall.

"And Uta-Napishtim," said the Ancient Mariner, sitting down suddenly on a stone lion, and fixing Gillian Perholt with his eye, Uta-Napishtim told Gilgamesh that there was a plant, a flower, that grew under the water. It was a flower with a sharp thorn that would wound his hands—but if he could win it he would have his lost youth again. So Gilgamesh tied heavy stones to his feet and sank into the deep water and walked in the seabed, and came to the plant, which did prick him, but he grasped it and brought it up again into the light. And Gilgamesh set out again with Urshanabi the ferryman to take the flower back to the old men of his city, Uruk, to bring back their lost youths. And when they had travelled on and on, said the Ancient Mariner, weaving his way between the ancient monuments in his shuffling dance, he came to a deep well of cool water, and he bathed in it, and refreshed himself. But deep in the pool there was a snake, and this snake sensed the sweetness of the flower. So it rose up through the water, and snatched the flower, and ate it. And then it cast off its skin, in the water, and swam down again, out of sight. And Gilgamesh sat down and wept, his tears ran down his face, and he said to Urshanabi the ferryman, "Was it for this that I worked so hard, is it for this that I forced out my heart's blood? For myself I have gained nothing—I don't have it, a beast out of the earth has it now. I found a sign and I have lost it."

The heavy bald head turned towards Gillian Perholt and the lashless eyelids slid blindly down over the eyeballs for a moment in what seemed to be exhaustion. The thick hands fumbled at the pockets of the fleece-lined jacket for a moment, as though the fingers were those of Gilgamesh, searching for what he had lost. And Gillian's inner eye was full of the empty snakeskin, a papery shadowy form of a snake which she saw floating at the rim of the well into which the muscular snake had vigorously vanished.

"What does it mean, my lady?" asked the old man. "It means that Gilgamesh must die now—he has seen that he could grasp the thorn and the flower and live forever—but the snake took it just by chance, not to hurt him, but because it liked the sweetness. It is so sad to hold the sign and lose it, it is a sad story—because in most stories where you go to find something you bring it back after your struggles, I think, but here the beast, the creature, just took it, just by chance, after all the effort. They were a sad people, ma'am, very sad. Death hung over them."

⋆

When they came out into the light of day she gave him what Turkish money she had, which he looked over, counted, and put in his pocket. She could not tell if he thought it too little or too much: the folds of his bald head wrinkled as he considered it. The British Council driver was waiting with the car; she walked towards him. When she turned to say goodbye to the Mariner, he was no longer to be seen.

Turks are good at parties. The party in Izmir was made up of Orhan's friends—scholars and writers, journalists and students. "Smyrna," said Orhan, as they drove into the town, holding their noses as they went along the harbour front with its stench of excrement, "Smyrna of the merchants," as they looked up at the quiet town on its conical hill. "Smyrna where we like to think Homer was born, the place most people agree he was probably born."

It was spring, the air was light and full of new sunshine. They ate stuffed peppers and vine leaves, kebabs and smoky aubergines in little restaurants; they made excursions and ate roasted fishes at a trestle table set by a tiny harbour, looking at fishing boats that seemed timeless, named for the stars and the moon. They told each other stories. Orhan told of his tragicomic battle with the official powers over his beard, which he had been required to shave before he was allowed to teach. A beard in modern Turkey is symbolic of religion or Marxism, neither acceptable. He had shaved his beard temporarily but now it flourished anew, like mown grass, Orhan said, even thicker and more luxuriant. The conversation moved to poets and politics: the exile of Halicarnassus, the imprisonment of the great Nazim Hikmet. Orhan recited Hikmet's poem "Weeping Willow," with its fallen rider and the drumming beat of the hooves of the red horsemen, vanishing at the gallop. And Leyla Serin recited Faruk Nafiz Çamlibel's *Göksu,* with its own weeping willow.

> Whenever my heart would wander in Göksu
> The garden in my dreams falls on the wood.

At dusk the roses seem a distant veil
The phantom willow boughs a cloak and hood.

Bulbuls and hoopoes of a bygone age
Retell their time-old ballads in the dark
The blue reflecting waters hear and show
The passing of Nedim with six-oared barque . . .

And Gillian told the story of her encounter with the old soldier in the Anatolian museum. "Maybe he was a djinn," said Orhan. "A djinn in Turkish is spelled C-I-N and you can tell one, if you meet it, in its human form, because it is naked and hairless. They can take many forms but their human form is hairless."

"He had a hairy coat," said Gillian, "but he was hairless. His skin was ivory-yellow, beeswax colour, and he had no hair anywhere."

"Certainly a djinn," said Orhan.

"In that case," said the young Attila, who had spoken on "Bajazet in the Harem," "how do you explain the Queen of Sheba?"

"What should I explain about her?" said Orhan.

"Well," said Attila, "in Islamic tradition, Solomon travelled from Mecca to Sheba to see this queen, who was said to have hairy legs like a donkey because she was the daughter of a djinn. So Solomon asked her to marry him, and to please him she used various unguents and herbs to render her legs as smooth as a baby's skin . . ."

"Autres pays, autres moeurs," said Leyla Doruk. "You can't pin down djinns. As for Dr. Perholt's *naqqual,* he seems to be related to the earth spirit in the story of Camaralzaman, don't you think so?"

They went also on an excursion to Ephesus. This is a white city risen, in part, from the dead: you can walk along a marble street where Saint Paul must have walked; columns and porticoes, the shell of an elegant library, temples and caryatids are again upright in the spring sun. The young Attila frowned as they paced past the temple façades and said they made him shiver: Gillian thought he was thinking of the death of nations, but it turned out that he was thinking of something more primitive and more immediate, of earthquakes. And when he said that, Gillian looked at the broken stones with fear too.

In the museum are two statues of the Artemis of Ephesus, whose temple, the Artemision, was one of the Seven Wonders of the Ancient World, rediscovered in the nineteenth century by a dogged and inspired English engineer, John Turtle Wood. The colossal Artemis is more austere, and like Cybele, the Magna Mater, turret-crowned, with a temple on her head, under whose arches sit winged sphinxes. Her body is a rising pillar: her haunches can be seen within its form but she wears like a skirt the beasts of the field, the wood, the heavens, all geometrically arranged in quadrangles between carved stone ropes, in twos and threes: bulls, rams, antelopes, winged bulls, flying sphinxes with women's breasts and lion heads, winged men and huge hieratic bees, for the bee is her symbol, and the symbol of Ephesus. She is garlanded with flowers and fruit, all part of the stone of which she is made: lions crouch in the crook of her arm (her hands are lost) and her headdress or veil is made of ranks of winged bulls, like the genies at the gates in the Ankara museum. And before her she carries, as a date palm carries dates, her triple row of full breasts, seven, eight, eight, fecundity in stone. The lesser Artemis, whom the Turks call Güzel Artemis and the French La Belle Artémis, stands in front of a brick wall and has a less Egyptian, more oriental, faintly smiling face. She too wears the beasts of earth and air like a garment, bulls and antelopes, winged bulls and sphinxes, with the lions couched below the rows of pendent breasts in their shadow. Her headdress too is woven of winged bulls, though her temple crown is lost. But she has her feet, which are side by side inside a reptilian frill or scallop or serpent tail, and at these feet are honeycombed beehives. Her eyes are wide, and heavy-lidded: she looks out of the stone.

The party admired the goddess. Orhan bowed to her, and Leyla Doruk and Leyla Serin explained her cult to Gillian Perholt, how she was certainly really a much older goddess than the Greek Artemis or the Roman Diana, an Asian earth goddess, Cybele, Astarte, Ishtar, whose temple was served by virgins and temple prostitutes, who combined extremes of abundant life and fierce slaughter, whose male priests castrated themselves in a frenzy of devotion, like those dying gods, Tammuz, Attis, Adonis, with whose blood the rivers ran red to the sea. The women wept for these dying divinities, said Leyla Serin. It was believed that Coleridge found his wonderful phrase "woman wailing for her demon lover" in descriptions of these ritual mournings.

There was a priest, said Leyla Doruk, the Megabyxus; that is a Persian word, and it means set free by God. He was probably a foreign eunuch. There were three priestesses—the Virgin Priestess, the Novice, the Future Priestess, and the Old Priestess who taught the young ones. The priestesses were called Melissae, which is bees. And there were priests called the Acrobatae who walked on tiptoe, and priests called the Essenes, another non-Greek word, Essen means king bee—the Greeks didn't know that the queen bee is a queen, but we know now . . .

"Her breasts are frightening," said Gillian Perholt. "Like Medusa's snakes, too much, but an orderly too much."

"Some people now say the breasts are not breasts but eggs," said Attila. "Symbols of rebirth."

"They *have* to be breasts," said Gillian Perholt. "You cannot see this figure and not read those forms as breasts."

"Some say," said Leyla Doruk, smiling, "that they were bulls' testicles, sacrificed to her, you know, hung round her in her honour, as the—the castrated priests'—parts—once were."

They were ripe and full and stony.

"They are metaphors," said Orhan. "They are many things at once, as the sphinxes and winged bulls are many things at once."

"You admire her, our goddess," said Leyla Doruk.

She is not yours, thought Gillian. You are latecomers. She is older and stronger. Then she thought: but she is more yours than mine, all the same. The brick wall behind the Güzel Artemis, the beautiful Artemis, was hung with plastic ivy, fading creamy in the sunlight.

The two Leylas stood with Gillian Perholt in front of the Güzel Artemis and each took her by one arm, laughing.

"Now, Dr. Perholt," said Leyla Osman, "you must make a wish. For here, if you stand between two people with the same name, and wish, it will come true."

Leyla Doruk was large and flowing; Leyla Serin was small and birdlike. Both had large dark eyes and lovely skins. They made Gillian Perholt feel hot, Anglo-Saxon, padded and clumsy. She was used to ignoring these feelings. She said, laughing,

"I am enough of a narratologist to know that no good ever comes of making wishes. They have a habit of twisting the wishers to their own ends."

"Only foolish wishes," said Leyla Serin. "Only the uninstructed, who don't think."

"Like the peasant who saved a magic bird which gave him three wishes, and he wished for a string of sausages in his pan, and they were there, and his wife said that that was a foolish wish, a stupid wish, a string of sausages with the whole world to wish for, and he was so mad at her, he wished the sausages would stick to her nose, and they did, and that was two wishes, and he had to use the third on detaching them."

For a moment this fictive Nordic peasant's wife, decorated with sausage strings, was imaginatively present also before the goddess with her rows of dangling breasts. Everyone laughed. Wish, Gillian, said Orhan. You are quite intelligent enough not to wish for anything silly.

"In England," said Gillian, "when we wish, when we cut our birthday cakes, we scream out loud, to turn away the knife, I suppose."

"You may scream if you want to," said Leyla Serin.

"I am not in England," said Gillian Perholt. "And it is not my birthday. So I shall not scream, I shall concentrate on being intelligent, as Orhan has commanded."

She closed her eyes, and concentrated, and wished, seeing the red light inside her eyelids, as so often before, hearing a faint drumming of blood in her ears. She made a precise and careful wish to be asked to give the keynote address at the Toronto Conference of narratologists in the fall and added a wish for a first-class airfare and a hotel with a swimming pool, as a kind of wishing package, she explained to the blood thrumming in her eyes and ears, and opened the eyes again, and shook her head before the smiling Artemis. Everyone laughed. You looked so serious, they said, squeezing her arms before they let go, and laughing.

They walked through old-new Ephesus and came to the theatre. Orhan stood against the ruined stage and said something incantatory in Turkish which he then explained to Gillian was Dionysus's first speech, his terrible, smiling, threatening speech at the beginning of *The Bacchae.* He then threw one arm over his shoulder and became cloaked and tall and stiffly striding where he had been supple and smiling and Eastern. "Listen, Gillian," he said:

> "I could a tale unfold whose lightest word
> Would harrow up thy soul, freeze thy young blood
> Make thy two eyes like stars, start from their spheres,
> Thy knotted and combined locks to part.
> And each particular hair to stand on end
> Like quills upon the fretful porpentine.
> But this eternal blazon must not be
> To ears of flesh and blood."

"Angels and ministers of grace defend us," said Gillian, laughing, remembering the young Orhan stalking the English student stage; thinking too of Mehmet the Conqueror, as Bellini saw him, eloquent, watchful, and dangerous.

"I was good," said Orhan, "in those days. It was his part. Shakespeare himself played the Ghost. Did you know that, Attila? When you speak these words you speak the words he spoke."

"Not on this stage," said Attila.

"Now," said Orhan. "Now it is here."

Angels had made Gillian think of Saint Paul. Angels had sprung open St. Paul's prison in Ephesus. She had sat in Sunday school, hearing a fly buzzing against a smeared high window in the vestry and had hated the stories of Saint Paul and the other apostles because they were true, they were told to her as true stories, and this somehow stopped off some essential imaginative involvement with them, probably because she didn't believe them, if required to believe they were true. She was Hamlet and his father and Shakespeare: she saw Milton's snake and the miraculous flying horse of the Thief of Baghdad, but Saint Paul's angels rested under suspicion of being made-up because she had been told they were special because *true*. Saint Paul had come here to Ephesus to tell the people here that Artemis was not true, was not real, because she was a god made with hands. He had stood here, precisely here, in this theatre, she understood slowly; this real man, a provincial interloper with a message, had stood here, where she now stood. She found this hard to believe because Saint Paul had always seemed to her so cardboard, compared, when she met them later, to Dionysus, to Achilles, to Priam. But he had come here with his wrath against handmade gods. He had changed the world. He had been a persecutor and had been blinded by light on the road to Damascus (for that moment he was not cardboard, he was consumed by light) and had set out to preach the new god, whom he had not, in his human form, known. In Ephesus he had caused "no small stir." His preaching had angered Demetrius, a silversmith, who made silver shrines for the goddess. And Demetrius stirred up the people of Ephesus against the saint, who claimed "they be no gods which are made with hands" and told them that the foreign preacher would not only set their craft at naught but also "the temple of the great goddess Diana should be despised, and her magnificence should be destroyed, whom all Asia and the world worshippeth."

"And when they heard these sayings, they were full of wrath, and cried out, saying, Great is Diana of the Ephesians.

"And the whole city was filled with confusion: and having caught Gaius and Artistarchus, men of Macedonia, Paul's companions in travel, they rushed with one accord into the theatre.

"And there for two hours they continued to cry Great is Diana of the Ephesians."

And because of the uproar, which was calmed by the town clerk, Paul left the city of Ephesus and set off for Macedonia.

So the bristling apostle was beaten by commerce and the power of the goddess.

"You know," said Leyla Doruk, "that your Virgin Mary came and died here. It is not certain, as it is not certain that Homer was born in Izmir, but it is said to be so, and her house was discovered because of a sick German lady in the nineteenth century who saw it in visions, the house and the hills, and when they came to look it was there, or so they say. We call it Panaya Kapulu, there is a Christian church too. She came with John, they say, and died here."

At a nightclub in Istanbul once, Gillian had been shocked, without quite knowing why, to find one of those vacant, sweetly pink and blue church Virgins, life-size, standing as part of the decorations, part hat stand, part dumbwaitress, as you might find a many-handed Hindu deity or a plaster Venus in an equivalent occidental club. Now suddenly, she saw a real bewildered old woman, a woman with a shrivelled womb and empty eyes, a woman whose son had been cruelly and very slowly slaughtered before her eyes, shuffling through the streets of Ephesus, waiting quietly for death until it came. And then, afterwards, this old woman, this real dead old woman had in part become the mother goddess, the Syria Dea, the crowned Queen. She was suddenly aware of every inch of her own slack and dying skin. She thought of the stone eyes of the goddess, of her dangerous dignity, of her ambiguous plump breasts, dead balls, intact eggs, wreathed round her in triumph and understood that real-unreal was not the point, that the goddess was still, and always had been, and in the foreseeable future would be more alive, more energetic, infinitely more powerful than she herself, Gillian Perholt, that she would stand here before her children, and Orhan's children, and their children's children and smile, when they themselves were scattered atomies.

And when she thought this, standing amongst a group of smiling friends in the centre of the theatre at Ephesus, she experienced again the strange stoppage of her own life that had come with the vision of Patient Griselda. She put out a hand to Orhan and could move no more; and it seemed that she was in a huge buzzing dark cloud, sparking with flashes of fire, and she could smell flowers, and her own blood, and she could hear rushing and humming in her veins, but she could not move a nerve or a muscle. And after a moment, a kind of liquid sob rose in her throat, and Orhan saw the state she was in, and put an arm round her shoulder, and steadied her, until she came to herself.

In the aeroplane on the way back to Istanbul, Orhan said to Gillian:

"Forgive me, are you quite well?"

"Never better," said Gillian, which was in many senses true. But she knew she must answer him. "I do truly mean, I feel more alive now than ever before. But lately I've had a sense of my fate—my death, that is—waiting for me, manifesting itself from time to time, to remind me it's there. It isn't a battle. I don't fight it off. It takes charge for a moment or two, and then lets go again, and steps back. The more alive I am, the more suddenly it comes."

"Should you see a doctor?"

"When I am so *well,* Orhan?"

"I am delighted to see you so well," said Orhan. The plane came down into Istanbul and the passengers began a decorous and delightful clapping, applause perhaps for the pilot's skill, applause perhaps for another successful evasion of fate.

In Istanbul Orhan Rifat, a very happily married man, returned to his family, and Gillian Perholt settled in for a few days in the Peri Palas Hotel, which was not the famous Pera Palas, in the old European city across the Golden Horn, but a new hotel, of the kind Gillian liked best, combining large hard beds, elegant mirrored bathrooms, lifts, and a swimming pool with local forms and patterns—tiled fountains, Turkish tiles with pinks and cornflowers in the bathrooms, carpets woven with abundant silky flowers in the small sitting rooms and writing rooms. It was constructed around a beehive of inner courtyards, with balconies rising one above the other, and silky translucent white-gold curtains behind functional double-glazed balcony doors. Gillian had developed a late passion for swimming. Flying distorts the human body—the middle-aged female body perhaps particularly—the belly balloons, the ankles become cushions of flesh and air, the knees round into puffballs, toes and fingers are swollen and shiny. Gillian had learned never to look in the mirror on arrival, for what stared out at her was a fleshy monster. She had learned to hurry to the pool, however little she felt inclined to exert herself, for what air pressure inflates, water pressure delicately makes weightless and vanishing. The pool at the Peri Palas was empty on the day of Gillian's arrival, and very satisfactory, if small. It was underground, a large tank, tiled in a dark emerald green, lit from within by gold-rimmed lamps, and the walls of its cavern were tiled with blue and green tiles covered with chrysanthemums and carnations, edged with gold mosaic, glinting and gleaming in the golden light. Oh the bliss, said Gillian to herself as she extended her sad body along the green rolls of swaying liquid and felt it vanish, felt her blood and nerves become pure energy, moved forward with a ripple like a swimming serpent. Little waves of her own making lapped her chin in this secret cistern; her ears were full of the soft whisper and plash of water, her eyes were wide upon green and green, woven with networks of swaying golden light. She basked, she rolled, she flickered ankles and wrists, she turned on her back and let her hair fan on the glassy curves. The nerves unknotted, the heart and lungs settled and pumped, the body was alive and joyful.

When Orhan took her to Topkapi her body was still comfortable from the swimming, which her skin remembered as the two of them looked down from the Sultan's upper window on the great dark tank under cedars where once the women of the harem swam together in the sun. In the harem too was the Sultan's bath, a quite different affair, a central box inside a series of carved boxes and cupboards inside the quarters of the Valide Sultan, his mother, where his nakedness could be guarded by many watchful eyes from assassin's knives. Here too, as in Ephesus, Gillian Perholt struggled with the passions of real stories. Here in the cages the sons of the sultans had waited for the eunuchs with the silken cords that would end their lives and make the throne safe for the chosen one. Here intriguing or unsatisfactory women had been caught and tied in sacks and drowned; here captives, or unsatisfactory servants, had been beheaded for a whim of an absolute ruler. How did they live with such fear? She said to Orhan:

"It is as you said of Shahriyar and I said of Walter—there must be a wonderful pleasure for some people in being other people's fates and destinies. Perhaps it gave them the illusion that their own fates too were in their own hands—"

"Perhaps," said Orhan. "Perhaps life mattered less to them, their own or anyone else's."

"Do you really think they thought that?"

"No," said Orhan, looking round the empty maze of hidden rooms and secret places. "No, not really. We like to say that. They believed in a future life. We can't imagine that."

★

Showing her round Istanbul, nevertheless, Orhan became more Turkish. Before the great gold throne of Murat III studded with emeralds, and cushioned in gold and white silk, he said,

"We were a nomadic people. We came over the steppes from Mongolia, from China. Our thrones are portable treasures, our throne rooms resemble tents, we put our skill into small things, daggers and bowls and cups." She remembered the rhythms of his recitation of the poem of the red horsemen.

In the Haghia Sophia she had her third encounter with Fate, or with something. Haghia Sophia is a confusing place, echoing and empty, hugely domed and architecturally uncertain, despite its vast and imposing space: it has been church and mosque and modern museum; it has minarets and patches, ghosts, of ruined gold mosaics of Byzantine emperors and the Christian mother and child. The emperor Justinian built it from eclectic materials, collecting pillars and ornaments from temples in Greece and Egypt, including pillars from the temple of the goddess in Ephesus. It could feel—Gillian had expected it to feel—like a meeting place of cultures, of East and West, the Christian Church and Islam, but it did not. It felt like an empty exhausted barn, exhausted by battle and pillage and religious rage. Whatever had been there had gone, had fled long ago, Gillian felt, and Orhan too showed no emotion, but returned to his European academic self, pointing out the meanings of the mosaics and talking of his own new thoughts about the absurdities of the theories of Marcuse which had been all the rage in the sixties, when they began to teach. "There is a curious pillar here," he said vaguely, "somewhere or other, with a hole of some sort, where people wish, you might like to see that, if I can find it. The stone is worn away by people touching it, I forget what it does, but you might like to see it."

"It doesn't matter," said Gillian.

"They put a brass casing round the magic stone to preserve it," said Orhan. "But the pilgrims have worn it away, they have eaten into the pillar just with touching, through the brass and the stone. Now where is it, I should be able to find it. It is like wearing away with waterdrops, wearing away with faith, I find that quite interesting, I wish I could remember what it *does*."

When they came to it, there was a family already clustered round it, a Pakistani father and his wife and two daughters, richly beautiful in saris, one pink and gold, one peacock and flame, one blue and silver. They had found the pillar with the hole and its brass casing, and the three women were clustered round it, stroking, putting their hands in and out, chattering like subdued birds. The father, dignified in his black coat, approached Orhan, and asked if he spoke English. Orhan said yes, and was asked to help translate an account of the pillar from a French-Turkish guidebook.

Whilst he did this, the three women, in their fluttering silk, turned laughing to Gillian Perholt, and stretched out three soft hands with gold bangles on their wrists, pulling her by her sleeve, by her hand, towards the pillar, laughing softly. They patted Dr. Perholt's shoulders, they put arms around her and pushed and pulled, smiling and laughing, they took her hand in theirs with strong, wiry grips and inserted it into the hole, showing her in mime what she must do, turn her hand in the hole, touching the inside rim, round, round, round, three times. She pulled back instinctively, out of an English hygienic horror of something so much touched by so many, and out of a more primitive fear, of something clammy, and moist, and nasty in the dark inside. But the women insisted; they were surprisingly forceful. There was liquid of some kind in there, some pool of something in the stem of the pillar. Dr. Perholt's skin crawled and the women laughed, and Orhan recited the story of the pillar in English to the other man. Apparently, he said, it had been touched by Saint Gregory Thaumaturge, the Miracle Worker, he had put his power into it. The water inside the pillar was efficacious for diseases of vision and for fertility. The women laughed more loudly, clustering round Dr. Perholt. The father told Orhan how he had made pilgrimage to all the holy shrines of Islam; he had travelled far and seen much. He supposed Orhan too had made pilgrimages. Orhan nodded, grave and noncommittal; he was interested. The West was evil, said the respectable black-coated pilgrim. Evil, decadent, and sliding into darkness. But power was arising. There would be a jihad. True religion would bring the cleansing sword and destroy the filth and greed and corruption of the dying West, and a religious world would be established in its ashes; these things were not only possible, they were already happening. The seeds were sown, the sparks were set, the field of spears would spring up, the fire would consume. This was what he said, this paterfamilias, standing in Haghia Sophia, whose stones had run with blood, whose cavernous spaces had been piled high with corpses, whose spirit had died, Gillian Perholt felt, but maybe felt because she could not feel the new spirit, which spoke to this family, and in them filled her with fear. Orhan, she saw, was in some way enjoying himself. He prolonged the conversation, nodding gravely, inserting mild questions—"you have seen signs, mn?"—making no move to change his interlocutor's impression that he was a good Muslim, in a mosque.

His family came everywhere with him, said the pilgrim. They like to see new places. And she, does she speak English?

It was clear that Gillian had been taken for a quiet Muslim wife. She had been standing two paces behind Orhan as he cast about for the magic pillar. Orhan replied gravely:

"She *is* English. She is a visiting professor. An eminent visiting professor."

Orhan, a child of Atatürk's new world, was enjoying himself. Atatürk had emancipated women. Leyla Serin and Leyla Doruk were also his children, powerful people, thinking teachers. Orhan liked drama, and he had made a nice little revelatory clash. The Pakistani gentleman was not happy. He and Gillian looked at each other, both, she thought, remembering things he had said a moment ago about London being a sewer of decay and the Commonwealth a dead body, putrefying and shrivelling away to nothing. She could not meet the Pakistani's eye; she was English and embarrassed for him. He could not meet her eye. She was a woman, and should not have been there, with a man who was not her husband, in a museum that was also a mosque. He gathered his flock—who still smiled at Gillian, fluttering their elegant fingers in farewell. "Hrmph," said Orhan. "Istanbul is a meeting place for many cultures. You didn't like the pillar, Gillian? Your face was very funny, very ladylike."

"I don't like Haghia Sophia," said Gillian. "I expected to. I like the idea of Sophia, of Wisdom, I like it that she is wise and female, I expected to feel—something—in her church. And there is a wet hole for fertility wishes. In a pillar that might have come from the Temple of Artemis."

"Not that pillar, I think," said Orhan.

"If I was a postmodernist punster," said Gillian, "I would make something of Haghia Sophia. She has got old, she has turned into a Hag. But I can't, because I respect etymologies, it means holy. Hag is my word, a northern word, nothing to do with here."

"You have said it now," said Orhan. "Even if you repudiate it. Lots of American students here do think Hag is Hag. They get excited about Crones."

"I don't," said Gillian.

"No," said Orhan, not revealing what he himself thought about hags and crones. "We shall go to the Bazaar. Shopping is good for the souls of Western women. And Eastern. And men like it too."

It was true that the Grand Bazaar was livelier and brighter than the vast cavern of Haghia Sophia. Here was a warren of arcades, of Aladdin's caves full of lamps and magical carpets, of silver and brass and gold and pottery and tiles. Here and there behind a shop front, seated in an armchair at a bench surrounded by dangling lamps and water shakers from the baths, or sitting cross-legged on a bale of carpets amongst a tent of carpets, Orhan had ex-students who brought cups of Turkish coffee, tulip-shaped glasses of rose tea to Gillian, and displayed their wares. The carpet seller had written a Ph.D. on *Tristram Shandy,* and now travelled into Iraq, Iran, Afghanistan, bringing back carpets on journeys made by camel, by jeep, into the mountains. He showed Gillian pallid kilims in that year's timid Habitat colours, pale 1930s eau-de-nil and bois-de-rose with a sad null grey. No, said Gillian, no, she wanted richness, the dark bright blues, the crimsons and scarlets, the golds and rusts of the old carpets with their creamy blossoms, their trees full of strange birds and flowers. The West is fickle, said Bulent the carpet seller, they say they want these insipid colours this year, and the women in India and Iran buy the wool and the silk, and the next year, when the carpets are made, they want something else, black and purple and orange, and the women are ruined, their profit is lost, heaps of carpets lie round and rot. I think you will like this carpet, said Bulent, pouring coffee; it is a wedding carpet, a dowry carpet, to hang on the wall of a nomad's tent. Here is the tree of life, crimson and black on midnight blue. This you like. Oh yes, said Gillian, seeing the dark woven tree against the yellows and whites of her Primrose Hill room, now hers alone. The woman, whoever she was, had made it strong and complex, flaunting and subtle. I can't haggle, said Gillian to Orhan, I'm English. You would be surprised, said Orhan, at some English people's skill in that art. But Bulent is my student, and he will give you a fair price, for love of *Tristram Shandy*. And suddenly Gillian felt well again, full of life and singing with joy, away from the puddle in the pillar and the brooding Hag, hidden away in an Aladdin's cave made of magic carpets with small delightful human artefacts, an unknown woman's wedding carpet, sentimental Sterne's monumental fantasia on life before birth, black-brown coffee poured from a bright copper pan, tasting rich and almost, but not quite, unbearably strong and sweet.

Another of Orhan's students had a little shop in the central square of the market maze, Iç Bedesten, a shop whose narrow walls were entirely hung with pots, pans, lamps, bottles, leather objects, old tools whose purpose was unguessable, chased daggers and hunting knives, shadow puppets made of camel skin, perfume flasks, curling tongs.

"I will give you a present," said Orhan. "A present to say goodbye."

(He was leaving the next day for Texas, where a colloquium of narratologists was studying family sagas in Dallas. Gillian had a talk to give at the British Council and three more days in Istanbul.)

"I will give you the shadow puppets, Karagoz and Hacivat, and here is the magic bird, the Simurgh, and here is a woman involved with a dragon, I think she may be a djinee, with a little winged demon on her shoulders, you might like her."

The small figures were wrapped carefully in scarlet tissue. Whilst this was happening Gillian poked about on a bench and found a bottle, a very dusty bottle amongst an apparently unsorted pile of new/old things. It was a flask with a high neck, that fitted comfortably into the palms of her hands, and had a glass stopper like a miniature dome. The whole was dark, with a regular whirling pattern of white stripes moving round it. Gillian collected glass paperweights: she liked glass in general, for its paradoxical nature, translucent as water, heavy as stone, invisible as air, solid as earth. Blown with human breath in a furnace of fire. As a child she had loved to read of glass balls containing castles and snowstorms, though in reality she had always found these disappointing and had transferred her magical attachment to the weights in which coloured forms and carpets of geometric flowers shone perpetually and could be made to expand and contract as the sphere of glass turned in her fingers in the light. She liked to take a weight back from every journey, if one could be found, and had already bought a Turkish weight, a cone of glass like a witch's hat, rough to touch, greenish-transparent like ice, with the concentric circles, blue, yellow, white, blue, of the eye which repels the evil eye, at the base.

"What is this?" she asked Orhan's student, Feyyaz.

He took the flask from her, and rubbed at the dust with a finger.

"I'm not an expert in glass," he said. "It could be *çesm-i bülbül,* nightingale's eye. Or it could be fairly recent Venetian glass. *Çesm-i bülbül* means nightingale's eye. There was a famous Turkish glass workshop at Incirköy—round about 1845 I think—made this famous Turkish glass, with this spiral pattern of opaque blue and white stripes, or red sometimes, I think. I don't know why it is called eye of the nightingale. Perhaps nightingales have eyes that are transparent and opaque. In this country we were obsessed with nightingales. Our poetry is full of nightingales."

"Before pollution," said Orhan, "before television, everyone came out and walked along the Bosphorus and in all the gardens, to hear the first nightingales of the year. It was very beautiful. Like the Japanese and the cherry blossom. A whole people, walking quietly in the spring weather, listening."

Feyyaz recited a verse in Turkish and Orhan translated.

> "In the woods full of evening the nightingales are silent
> The river absorbs the sky and its fountains
> Birds return to the indigo shores from the shadows
> A scarlet bead of sunshine in their beaks."

Gillian said, "I must have this. Because the word and the thing don't quite match, and I love both of them. But if it is *çesm-i bülbül* it will be valuable . . ."

"It probably isn't," said Feyyaz. "It's probably recent Venetian. Our glassmakers went to Venice in the eighteenth century to learn, and the Venetians helped us to develop the techniques of the nineteenth century. I will sell it to you as if it were Venetian, because you like it, and you may imagine it is *çesm-i bülbül* and perhaps it will be, is, that is."

"Feyyaz wrote his doctoral thesis on Yeats and Byzantium," said Orhan.

Gillian gave the stopper an experimental twist, but it would not come away, and she was afraid of breaking it. So the nightingale's-eye bottle too was wrapped in scarlet tissue, and more rose tea was sipped, and Gillian returned to her hotel. That evening there was a farewell dinner in Orhan's house, with music, and raki, and generous beautiful food. And the next day, Gillian was alone in her hotel room.

★

Time passes differently in the solitude of hotel rooms. The mind expands, but lazily, and the body contracts in its bright box of space. Because one may think of anything at all, one thinks for a long time of nothing. Gillian in hotel rooms was always initially tempted by channel-surfing on the television; she lay amongst crimson and creamy roses on her great bed and pointed the black lozenge with its bright buttons imperiously at the screen. Transparent life flickered and danced across it: Gillian could make it boom with sound, the rush of traffic and violins, voices prophesying war and voices dripping with the promise of delectable yogurt/Orangina/tutti-frutti/Mars Bars frozen stiff. Or she could leave it, which she preferred, a capering shadow theatre. Ronald Reagan, smiling and mouthing, glassy in the glass box between the glassy wings of his speech, or an aeroplane falling in flames on a mountain, fact or stunt? a priest driving a racing car round a corniche, narrative or advertisement? Turks discussing the fullness and fatness of tomatoes in a field, more new cars, in cornfields, up mountains, falling from skyscrapers, a houri applying a tongue tip to raspberry fudge and sighing, an enormous tsetse fly expending enormous energy in puncturing a whole screenful of cowflesh, jeeps full of dirty soldiers in helmets brandishing machine guns, trundling through dusty streets, fact or drama, which? Tennis.

Tennis in French, from courts like red deserts, tennis from Monte Carlo where it was high noon, under the sun past which Istanbul had begun to roll two hours ago, tennis male and it appeared, live, on a channel where nothing ever happened but the human body (and mind, indeed, also) stretched, extended, driven, triumphant, defeated, in one endless, beautifully designed narrative. Dr. Perholt was accustomed to say, in her introductory talks on narratology, that whoever designed the rules and the scoring system of tennis was a narrative genius of the first order, comparable to those ancient storytellers who arranged animal helpers in threes and thought up punishments for disregarded prohibitions. For the more even the combat, said Dr. Perholt, the more difficult the scoring makes it for one combatant to succeed. At deuce, at six-all, the stakes are raised, not one but two points are needed to assure victory, not one but two games, thus ensuring the maximum tension and the maximum pleasure to the watchers. Tennis in the glass box she loved as she had loved bedtime stories as a child. She loved the skill of the cameramen—the quick shot of a sweating face in a rictus of strain, the balletic shot of the impossibly precise turning feet, the slow lazy repeat of the lung-bursting leap, taken at the speed with which a leaf falls slowly through the air, slowly, slowly, resting on air, as the camera can make these heavy muscled men hang at rest in their billowing shirts. She had only come to love tennis so much when she was beyond being expected to take part in it; when her proper function was only as audience. Now she delighted in its geometry, the white lines of increasing difficulty, of hope and despair, the acid gold sphere of the ball, the red dust flying, the woven chequered barrier of the net. She had her narrative snobbisms. A live match was always more enticing than a recorded one, even if it was impossible for her to find out first the score of the latter, for someone, somewhere, *knew* who had won, the tense was past, and thus the wonderful open-endedness of a story which is most beautifully designed towards satisfactory closure but is still undecided, would be lost, would be a cheat. For darkness might descend on a live match, or the earth open. A live match was live, was a story in progress towards an end which had not yet come but which must, *almost certainly* come. And in the fact of the *almost* was the delight.

A live match (Becker-Leconte) was promised within an hour. She had time for a shower, she judged, a good hot shower, and then she could sit and dry slowly and watch the two men run. So she turned on the shower, which was large and brassy, behind a glass screen at one end of the bath, an enclosing screen of pleasing engraved climbing roses with little birds sitting amongst their thorny stems. It had a pleasant brass frame, the glass box. The water was a little cloudy, and a little brassy itself in colour, but it was hot, and Gillian disported herself in its jets, soaped her breasts, shampooed her hair, looked ruefully down at what it was better not to look at, the rolls of her midriff, the sagging muscles of her stomach. She remembered, as she reached for her towel, how perhaps ten years ago she had looked complacently at her skin on her throat, at her solid enough breasts and had thought herself well-preserved, unexceptionable. She had tried to imagine how this nice, taut, flexible skin would crimp and wrinkle and fall and had not been able to. It was her skin, it was herself, and there was no visible reason why it should not persist. She had known intellectually that it must, it must give way, but its liveliness then had given her the lie. And now it was all going, the eyelids had soft little folds, the edges of the lips were fuzzed, if she put on lipstick it ran in little threads into the surrounding skin.

She advanced naked towards the bathroom mirror in room 49 in the Peri Palas Hotel. The mirror was covered with shifting veils of steam, amongst which, vaguely, Gillian saw her death advancing towards her, its hair streaming dark and liquid, its eyeholes dark smudges, its mouth open in its liquescent face in fear of their convergence. She dropped her head sadly, turned aside from the encounter, and took out the hanging towelling robe from its transparent sheath of plastic. There were white towelling slippers in the cupboard with "Peri Palas" written on them in gold letters. She made herself a loose turban of a towel and thus solidly enveloped she remembered the *çesm-i bülbül* bottle and decided to run it under the tap, to bring the glass to life. She took it out of its wrappings—it was really *very* dusty, almost clay-encrusted—and carried it into the bathroom, where she turned on the mixer-tap in the basin, made the water warm, blood-heat, and held the bottle under the jet, turning it round and round. The glass became blue, threaded with opaque white canes, cobalt-blue, darkly bright, gleaming and wonderful. She turned it and turned it, rubbing the tenacious dust spots with thumbs and fingers, and suddenly it gave a kind of warm leap in her hand, like a frog, like a still-beating heart in the hands of a surgeon. She gripped and clasped and steadied, and her own heart took a fierce, fast beat of apprehension, imagining blue glass splinters everywhere. But all that happened was that the stopper, with a faint glassy grinding, suddenly flew out of the neck of the flask and fell, tinkling but unbroken, into the basin. And out of the bottle in her hands came a swarming, an exhalation, a fast-moving dark stain which made a high-pitched buzzing sound and smelled of woodsmoke, of cinnamon, of sulphur, of something that might have been incense, of something that was not leather, but was? The dark cloud gathered and turned and flew in a great paisley or comma out of the bathroom. I am seeing things, thought Dr. Perholt, following, and found she could not follow, for the bathroom door was blocked by what she slowly made out to be an enormous foot, a foot with five toes as high as she was, surmounted by yellow horny toenails, a foot encased in skin that was olive-coloured, laced with gold, like snakeskin, not scaly but somehow mailed. It was between transparent and solid. Gillian put out a hand. It was palpable, and very hot to the touch, not hot as a coal but considerably hotter than the water in which she had been washing the bottle. It was dry and slightly electric. A vein beat inside the ankle, a green-gold tube encasing an almost emerald liquid.

Gillian stood and considered the foot. Anything with a foot that size, if at all proportionate, could not be contained in one hotel room. Where was the rest? As she thought this, she heard sounds, which seemed to be speech of some kind, deep, harsh, but musical, expletives perhaps, in a language she couldn't identify. She put the stopper back in the bottle, clutching it firmly, and waited.

The foot began to change shape. At first it swelled and then it diminished a little, so that Gillian could have squeezed round it, but thought it more prudent not to try. It was now the size of a large armchair, and was drawn back, still diminishing, so that Gillian felt able to follow. The strange voice was still muttering, in its incomprehensible speech. Gillian came out and saw the djinn, who now took up half her large room, curled round on himself like a snake, with his huge head and shoulders pushing against the ceiling, his arms stretched round inside two walls, and his feet and body wound over her bed and trailing into the room. He seemed to be wearing a green silk tunic, not too clean, and not long enough, for she could see the complex heap of his private parts in the very centre of her rosy bed. Behind him was a great expanse of shimmering many-coloured feathers, peacock feathers, parrot feathers, feathers from birds of paradise, which appeared to be part of a cloak that appeared to be part of him, but was not wings that sprouted in any conventional way from shoulder blade or spine. Gillian identified the last ingredient of his smell, as he moved his cramped members to look down on her. It was a male smell, a strong horripilant male smell.

His face was huge, oval, and completely hairless. He had huge bruised-green oval eyelids over eyes sea-green flecked with malachite. He had high cheekbones and an imperious hooked nose, and his mouth was wide and sculpted like Egyptian pharaohs'.

In one of his huge hands was the television, on whose pearly screen, on the red dust, Boris Becker and Henri Leconte rushed forward, jumped back, danced, plunged. The smack of the tennis ball could be heard, and the djinn had turned one of his large, elegantly carved ears, to listen.

He spoke to Gillian. She said,

"I don't suppose you speak English."

He repeated his original remark. Gillian said,

"Français? Deutsch? Español? Português?" She hesitated. She could not remember the Latin for Latin, and was not at all sure she could converse in that language. "Latin," she said finally.

"Je sçais le Français," said the djinn. *"Italiano anche. Era in Venezia."*

"Je préfère le français," said Gillian. "I am more fluent in that language."

"Good," said the djinn in French. He said, "I can learn quickly, what is your language?"

"Anglais."

"Smaller would be better," he said, changing tack. "It was agreeable to expand. I have been inside that bottle since 1850 by your reckoning."

"You look cramped," said Gillian, reaching for the French words, "in here."

The djinn considered the tennis players.

"Everything is relative. These people are extremely small. I shall diminish somewhat."

He did so, not all at once, so that for a moment the now only slightly larger-than-life being was almost hidden behind the mound of his private parts, which he then shrank and tucked away. It was almost a form of boasting. He was now curled on Gillian's bed, only one and a half times as large as she was.

"I am beholden to you," said the djinn, "for this release. I am empowered, indeed required, to grant you three wishes on that account. If there is anything you desire."

"Are there limits," asked the narratologist, "to what I may wish for?"

"An unusual question," said the djinn. He was still somewhat distracted by the insect-like drama of Boris Becker and Henri Leconte. "In fact different djinns have different powers. Some can only grant small things—"

"Like sausages—"

"A believer—a believing djinn—would find it repugnant to grant anyone of your religion pork sausages. But they are possible. There are laws of the preternatural within which we work, all of us, which cannot be broken. You may not, for instance, wish to have all your wishes granted in perpetuity. Three is three, a number of power. You may not wish for eternal life, for it is your nature to be mortal, as it is mine to be immortal. I cannot by magic hold together your atomies, which will dissolve—"

He said,

"It is good to speak again, even in this unaccustomed tongue. Can you tell me what these small men are made of, and what they are at? It resembles royal tennis as it was played in the days of Suleiman the Magnificent—"

"It is called 'lawn tennis' in my language. *Tennis sur gazon.* As you can see, this is being played on clay. I like to watch it. The men," she found herself saying, "are very beautiful."

"Indeed," agreed the djinn. "How have you enclosed them? The atmosphere here is full of presences I do not understand—it is all bustling and crowded with—I cannot find a word in my language or your own, that is, your second tongue—electrical emanations of living beings, and not only living beings but fruits and flowers and distant places—and some high mathematical game with travelling figures I can barely seize, like motes in the invisible air—something terrible has been done to my space—to exterior space since my incarceration—I have trouble in holding this exterior body together, for all the currents of power are so picked at and intruded upon . . . Are these men magicians, or are you a witch, that you have them in a box?"

"No, it is science. It is natural science. It is television. It is done with light waves and sound waves and cathode rays—I don't know *how* it is done, I am only a literary scholar, we don't know much, I'm afraid—we use it for information and amusement. Most people in the world now see these boxes, I suppose."

"Six-all, première manche," said the television. *"Jeu décisif. Service Becker."*

The djinn frowned.

"I am a djinn of some power," he said. "I begin to find out how these emanations travel. Would you like a homunculus of your own?"

"I have three wishes," said Dr. Perholt cautiously. "I do not want to expend one of them on the possession of a tennis player."

"Entendu," said the djinn. "You are an intelligent and cautious woman. You may wish when you will and the praeternatural laws require me to remain at your service until all three wishes have been made. Lesser djinns would tempt you into making your wishes rapidly and foolishly, for their own ends, but I am God-fearing and honourable (despite which I have spent much of my long life shut up in bottles), and I will not do that. All the same, I shall attempt to catch one of these travelling butterflies. They are spread along the waves of the atmosphere—not as we are when we travel—*in* the waves—I should be able to *concentrate* one—to move the matter as well as the emanation—the pleasure is to use the laws of its appearance here and intensify—I could easily *wish* him here—but I will, I will have him along his own trajectory—so—and so—"

A small Boris Becker, sandy-browed, every gold hair on his golden body gleaming sweat, was standing on the chest of drawers, perhaps twice the size of his television image, which was frozen in mid-stroke on the screen. He blinked his sandy lashes over his blue eyes and looked around, obviously unable to see more than a blur around him.

"Scheiss," said the tiny Becker. *"Scheiss und Scheiss. Was ist mit mir?"*

"I could manifest us to him," said the djinn. "He would be afeard."

"Put him back. He will lose the set."

"I could expand him. Life-size. We could speak to him."

"Put him back. It isn't *fair.*"

"You don't want him?"

"Scheiss. Warum kannich nicht . . ."

"No. I don't."

The Becker on the screen was frozen into an attitude, his racket raised, his head back, one foot lifting. Henri Leconte advanced towards the net. The commentator announced that Becker had had a seizure, which delighted the djinn, who had indeed seized him. *"Scheiss,"* said the forlorn small Becker in the bedroom. "Return him," said Dr. Perholt imperiously, adding quickly, "That is not one of my three wishes, you must do what seems to you best, but you must understand that you are disappointing millions of people, all round the world, interrupting this story—I'm sorry, *déformation professionelle,* I should say, this game—"

"Why are your homunculi not three-dimensional?" asked the djinn.

"I don't know. We can't do that. We may learn. You seem to understand it better than I do, however long you have been in that bottle. Please put him back."

"To please you," said the djinn with grave gallantry. He picked up the mannikin-Becker, twisted him rapidly like a top, murmured something, and the Becker on the screen collapsed on the court in a heap.

"You have hurt him," said Gillian accusingly.

"It is to be hoped not," said the djinn with an uncertain note.

Becker in Monte Carlo got up unsteadily and was escorted off the court, his hands to his head.

"They will not be able to continue," said Gillian crossly, and then put her hand to her mouth in amazement, that a woman with a live djinn on her bed should still be interested in the outcome of a tennis match, only part of which she had seen.

"You could wish him well," said the djinn, "but he will probably be well anyway. More than probably, almost certainly. You must wish for your heart's desire."

"I wish," said Gillian, "for my body to be as it was when I last really *liked* it, if you can do that."

The great green eyes settled on her stout figure in its white robe and turban.

"I can do that," he said. "I can do that. If you are quite sure that that is what you most desire. I can make your cells as they were, but I cannot delay your Fate."

"It is courteous of you to tell me that. And yes, it is what I desire. It is what I have desired hopelessly every day these last ten years, whatever else I may have desired."

"And yet," said the djinn, "you are well enough as you are, in my opinion. Amplitude, madame, is desirable."

"Not in my culture. And moreover, there is the question of temporal decay."

"That I suppose, but do not wholly understand sympathetically. We are made of fire, and do not decay. You are made of dust, and return to it."

He raised his hand and pointed at her, one finger lazily extended, a little like Michelangelo's Adam.

She felt a fierce contraction in the walls of her belly, in her loose womb.

"I am glad to see you prefer ripe women to green girls," said the djinn. "I too am of that opinion. But your ideal is a little meagre. Would you not care to be rounder?"

"Excuse me," said Gillian, suddenly modest, and retreated into the bathroom, where she opened her robe and saw in the demisted mirror a solid and unexceptionable thirty-five-year-old woman, whose breasts were full but not softened, whose stomach was taut, whose thighs were smooth, whose nipples were round and rosy. Indeed the whole of this serviceable and agreeable body was flushed deep rose, as though she had been through a fire, or a steam bath. Her appendix scar was still there, and the mark on her knee where she had fallen on a broken bottle hiding under the stairs from an air raid in 1944. She studied her face in the mirror; it was not beautiful but it was healthy and lively and unexceptionable; her neck was a clean column and her teeth, she was happy to see and feel, more numerous, more securely planted. She undid the coiled towel and her hair sprang out, damp, floppy, long, and unfaded. I can go in the streets, she said to herself, and still be recognisably who I am, in my free and happy life; only I shall *feel* better, I shall like myself more. That was an *intelligent* wish, I shall not regret it. She brushed out her hair, and went back to the djinn, who was lolling on the bedspread, watching Boris Becker, who had lost the first set, and was ranging the court like a tiger in the beginning of the second. The djinn had also helped himself to the glossy shopping magazines which lay in the drawer of the bedside table, and to the Gideon Bible which, with the Koran, was also there. From these he appeared to have absorbed the English language by some kind of cerebral osmosis.

"Hmn," he said in that language. "Who is she that looketh forth as the morning, fair as the moon, clear as the sun, and terrible as an army with banners? This is your language, I can learn its rules quickly, I find. Are you pleased, madame, with the outcome of your wish? We have a little sister and she hath no breasts: what shall we do for our sister in the day when she shall be spoken for? I see from these images that in this time you prefer your ladies without breasts, like boys. A curious form of asceticism, if that is what it is, or perversity possibly, it may be. I am not a djinn who ever needed to lurk in bath-houses to catch young boys from behind. I have consorted with ladies of all kinds, with the Queen of Sheba herself, with the Shulamite whose breasts were like clusters of grapes and ripe pomegranates, whose neck was a tower of ivory and the smell of whose nose was like apples. A boy is a boy and a woman is a woman, my lady. But these images have lovely eyes, they are skilful with the kohl."

"If you consorted with the Queen of Sheba," said the scholar, "how did you come to be shut in what I believe is at the earliest a *nineteenth-century* bottle, *çesm-i bülbül,* if not Venetian?"

"Certainly *çesm-i bülbül,*" said the djinn. "Freshly made and much prized by its owner, the beautiful Zefir, wife of Mustafa Emin Bey, in Smyrna. I came into that bottle through a foolish accident and a too-great fondness for the conversation of women. That was my third incarceration: I shall be more careful in the future. I am happy to tell you my history, whilst you decide upon your two remaining wishes, but I am also curious to know your own—are you wife, or widow, and how do you come to be inhabiting this splendid apartment with flowing waters in the Peri Palas as your shining books tell me this place is called? What I know of England is little and unfriendly. I know the tale of the pale slaves from the island in the north of whom a Roman bishop said *'Non Angli sed angeli.'* And I know about Bisnismen, from the conversation in the caravanserai in Smyrna. You are rumoured to be thick red people who cannot bend or smile, but I have learned never to trust rumours and I find you graceful."

"My name is Gillian Perholt," said Dr. Perholt. "I am an independent woman, a scholar, I study tale-telling and narratology." (She thought he could learn this useful word; his green eyes glittered.) "I am in Turkey for a conference, and return to my island in a week's time. I do not think my history will interest you, much."

"On the contrary. I am temporarily in your power, and it is always wise to understand the history of those who hold power over you. I have lived much of my life in harems, and in harems the study of apparently uneventful personal histories is a matter of extreme personal importance. The only truly independent woman I have known was the Queen of Sheba, my half cousin, but I see that things have changed since her day. What does an independent woman wish for, Djil-yan Peri-han?"

"Not much," said Gillian, "that I haven't got. I need to think. I need to be intelligent. Tell me the story of your three incarcerations. If that would not bore you."

She was later to wonder how she could be so matter-of-fact about the presence of the gracefully lounging oriental daimon in a hotel room. At the time, she unquestioningly accepted his reality and his remarks as she would have done if she had met him in a dream—that is to say, with a certain difference, a certain knowledge that the reality in which she was was not everyday, was not the reality in which Dr. Johnson refuted Bishop Berkeley's solipsism with a robust kick at a trundling stone. She was accustomed also to say in lectures that it was possible that the human need to tell tales about things that were unreal originated in dreams, and that memory had certain things also in common with dreams; it rearranged, it made clear, simple narratives, certainly it invented as well as recalling. Hobbes, she told her students, had described imagination as decayed memory. She had at no point the idea that she might "wake up" from the presence of the djinn and find him gone as though he had never been; but she did feel she might move suddenly—or he might—into some world where they no longer shared a mutual existence. But he persisted, his fingernails and toenails solid and glistening, his flesh with its slightly simmering quality, his huge considering eyes, his cloak of wings, his scent, with its perfumes and smokiness, its pheromones, if djinns have pheromones, a question she was not ready to put to him. She suggested ordering a meal from Room Service, and together they chose charred vegetable salad, smoked turkey, melons and passion fruit sorbet; the djinn made himself scarce whilst this repast was wheeled in, and added to it, upon his reappearance, a bowl of fresh figs and pomegranates and some intensely rose-perfumed *loukoum*. Gillian said that she need not have ordered anything if he could do that, and he said that she did not allow for the effects of curiosity on one who had been cramped in a bottle since 1850 (your reckoning, he said in French)—he desired greatly to see the people and way of life of this late time.

"Your slaves," he said, "are healthy and smiling. That is good."

"There are no slaves, we no longer have slaves—at least not in the West and not in Turkey—we are all free," said Gillian, regretting this simplification as soon as it was uttered.

"No slaves," said the djinn thoughtfully. "No sultans, maybe, either?"

"No sultans. A republic. Here. In my country we have a Queen. She has no power. She is—a representative figure."

"The Queen of Sheba had power," said the djinn, folding his brow in thought, and adding dates, sherbet, quails, *marrons glacés,* and two slices of *tarte aux pommes* to the feast spread before them. "She would say to me, as her spies brought her news of his triumphal progress across the desert, the great Suleiman, blessed be his memory, she would say, 'How can I, a great Queen, submit to the prison house of marriage, to the invisible chains which bind me to the bed of a man?' I advised her against it. I told her her wisdom was hers and she was free as an eagle floating on the waves of the air and seeing the cities and palaces and mountains below her with an even eye. I told her her body was rich and lovely but her mind was richer and lovelier and more durable—for although she was partly of our kind, she was a mortal being, like you—djinns and mortals cannot produce an immortal scion, you know, as donkeys and horses can only produce a seedless mule. And she said she knew I was in the right: she sat amongst the cushions in her inner room, where no one came, and twisted her dark hair in her hand, and knit her brow in thought, and I looked at the great globes of her breasts and the narrowness of her waist and her huge soft fundament like two great heaps of silky sand, and was sick with desire for her, though I said nothing of that, for she liked to play with me a little, she had known me since she was born, I had come invisibly in and out of her sleeping chamber and kissed her soft mouth and stroked her back as she grew, and I knew as well as any of her female slaves the little touches that made her shiver with bliss, but all was in play only, and she liked to consult me on serious matters, on the intentions of the kings of Persia and Bessarabia, on the structure of a ghazal, on medicines for choler and despair, on the disposition of the stars. And she said she knew I was right, and that her freedom was her true good, not to be surrendered, and that only I—an immortal djinn—and a few women, advised her so, but that most of her court, men and women, and her human family were in favour of marriage with this Suleiman (blessed be his memory), who advanced across the desert day by day, growing in her mind as I could grow and shrink before her eyes. And when he came, I saw that I was lost, for she desired him. It is true to say that he was desirable, his loins and his buttocks in his silk trousers were of a perfect beauty, and his fingers were long and wonderfuly quick—he could play on a woman as well as he could play on a lute or a flute—but at first she did not know that she desired him, and I, like a fool, went on telling her to think of her proud autonomy, of her power to go in and out as she pleased. And she agreed with all I said, she nodded gravely and once dropped a hot tear, which I licked up—never have I desired any creature so, woman or djinn or peri or boy like a fresh-peeled chestnut. And then she began to set him tasks which seemed impossible—to find a particular thread of red silk in the whole palace, to guess the secret Name of the djinn her mother, to tell her what women most desire—and I knew even more surely that I was lost, for he could speak to the beasts of the earth and the birds of the air, and djinns from the kingdom of fire, and he found ants to discover the thread, and an Ifrit from the kingdom of fire to tell him the Name, and he looked into her eyes and told her what women most desire, and she lowered her eyes and said he was right, and granted him what *he* desired, which was to wed her and take her to his bed, with her lovely curtain of flesh still unparted and her breath coming in little pants of desire that I had never heard, never, and never should again. And when I saw him tear her maidenhead and the ribbon of red blood flow onto the silk sheets, I gave a kind of groan, and he became aware of my presence. He was a great magician, blessed be his name, and could see me well enough, though I was invisible. And he lay there, bathed in her sweat and his, and took account of certain little love bites—most artistically placed, and unfortunately not invisible—in the soft hollows of her collar-bone, and—elsewhere, you may imagine. And he could see the virgin blood well enough, or I imagine my fate might have been worse, but he imprisoned me with a word of power in a great metal flask there was in the room, and sealed me in with his own seal, and she said nothing, she made no plea for me—though I am a believer, and not a follower of Iblis—only lay back and sighed, and I saw her tongue caress her pearly teeth, and her soft hand reach out to touch those parts of him which had given her such pleasure, and I was nothing to her, a breath in a bottle. And so I was cast into the Red Sea, with many others of my kind, and languished there for two and a half thousand years until a fisherman drew me up in his net and sold the bottle to a travelling pedlar, who took me to the bazaar in Istanbul where I was bought by a handmaid of Princess Mihrimah, daughter of Suleiman the Magnificent, and taken to the Abode of Bliss, the Eski Saray, the harem in the palace."

"Tell me," said Gillian Perholt, interrupting his story, "what do women most desire?"

"Do you not know?" said the djinn. "If you do not know already, I cannot tell you."

"Maybe they do not all desire the same thing."

"Maybe you do not. Your own desires, Djil-yan Peri-han, are not clear to me. I cannot read your thoughts, and that intrigues me. Will you not tell me your life?"

"It is of no interest. Tell me what happened when you were bought by Princess Mihrimah."

"This lady was the daughter of the Sultan, Suleiman the Magnificent and his concubine Roxelana, la Rossa, the woman out of Galicia, daughter of a Ukrainian priest and known in Turkish as Hurrem, the laughing one. She was terrible as an army with the banners, Roxelana. She defeated the Sultan's early love, Gülbahar, the Rose of Spring, whom he adored, and when she bore him a son, she laughed him fiercely into marrying her, which no concubine, no Christian, had ever achieved. And when the kitchens burned—in your year 1540 it must be—she marched her household into the Seraglio—a hundred ladies-in-waiting and the eunuchs, all quaking in their shoes for fear of being disembowelled on the spot—but they were more afraid of her laughter—and so she settled in the palace itself. And Mihrimah's husband, Rüstem Pasha, was the grand vizir after Ibrahim was strangled. I remember Suleiman the Magnificent—his face was round with blue eyes, the nose of a ram, the body of a lion, a full beard, a long neck—he was a big man, a king of men, a man without fear or compromise, a glorious man . . . Those who came after were fools and boys. That was her fault, Roxelana's fault. She intrigued against his son Mustafa, Gülbahar's son, who was like his father and would have been a wise ruler—she persuaded Suleiman he was treacherous, and so when he came boldly into his father's presence they were waiting for him, the mutes with the silk strangling cords, and he tried to cry to the janissaries who loved him, but the stranglers beat him down and stopped his breath. I saw it all, for I had been sent to see it by my new young mistress, a slave girl who belonged to Mihrimah and opened my bottle, believing it contained perfume for her mistress's bath. She was a Christian and a Circassian, Gülten, pale for my tastes, and tremulous and given to weeping and wringing her hands. And when I appeared to her in that secret bathroom she could only faint and I had great trouble in rousing her and explaining to her that she had three wishes, because she had released me, and that I meant her no harm and could do her no harm, for I was the slave of the bottle until the wishes were performed. And the poor silly thing was distractedly in love with Prince Mustafa and wished immediately that she could find favour in his eyes. Which came about—he sent for her—I spoke to him—I escorted her to his bedchamber, I told her how to please him—he was very much like his father and loved poems, and singing, and good manners. And then the silly girl wished she could become pregnant—"

"That was only natural."

"Natural but very stupid. Better to use the wish *against* pregnancy, my lady, and also foolish to waste the wish in such a hurry, for they were both young and lusty and hot-blooded, and what did happen would have happened without my interference, and I could have helped her in more important ways. For of course when Roxelana heard that Gülten was to bear Mustafa's child, she ordered her eunuchs to sew her up in a sack and throw her from the Seraglio Point into the Bosphorus. And I thought to myself, having flown back from Mustafa's execution, that at any moment she would bethink herself of me, and wish—I don't know exactly what—but wish to be far away—or out of the sack—or back in Circassia—I waited for her to formulate the wish, because once she had made it we would both be free, I to fly where I pleased and she to live, and bear her child. But her limbs were frozen cold, and her lips were blue as lapis with terror, and her great blue eyes were starting out of her head—and the gardeners—the executioners were also the gardeners, you know—bundled her into the sack like a dead rosebush—and carried her away to the cliff over the Bosphorus. And I thought of rescuing her at every moment—but I calculated that she *must,* even involuntarily, wish for her life, and that if I delayed, and went invisibly through the garden in the evening—the roses were in full bloom, the perfume was intense to swooning—and over she went, and drowned, before I could quite make up my mind to the fact that she was in no state to make any wish.

"So there was I," said the djinn, "half-emancipated, you could say, but still tied to the bottle by the third unperformed task. I found I was free to wander during the day within a certain range of the enchanted flask, but I was compelled to return at night and shrink myself to its compass and sleep there. I was a prisoner of the harem, and likely to remain so, for my bottle was securely hidden under a tile in the floor of a bathroom, a secretly loosened tile, known only to the drowned Circassian. For women closed into those places find many secret places to hide things, for they like to have one or two possessions of their own—or a place to hide letters—that no one else, they fondly think, knows of. And I found I was unable to attract anyone's attention to the tile and the bottle; these things were out of my power.

"And so I haunted the Topkapi Sarayi for just under a hundred years, attached by a silken cord, you might say poetically, to the flask hidden in the bathroom floor. I saw Roxelana persuade Suleiman the Magnificent to write to the Shah Tahmasp of Persia, with whom their youngest son, Bayezid, had taken refuge, and command the Shah to execute the young Prince—which he would not do for hospitality's sake, but allowed it to be done by Turkish mutes, as was customary, and Bayezid was put to death, with his four sons and a fifth, three years of age, hidden in Bursa. He would have made an excellent ruler, too, I think—and so it was generally thought."

"Why?" asked Gillian Perholt.

"It was customary, my lady, and Roxelana wished to assure a safe succession for her eldest son, Selim, Selim the Sot, Selim the drunkard, Selim the poet, who died in a bathhouse after too many flasks of wine. Roxelana was long dead, buried beside the Süleymaniye, and Mihrimah her daughter built a new mosque to commemorate Suleiman, with the help of the great architect, Sinan, who made the Süleymaniye in holy rivalry with Haghia Sophia. And I watched sultans come and go—Murad III who was ruled by women, and strangled five of his brothers, Mehmed III who strangled nineteen of his, and then gave them sumptuous burials—he died when a dervish predicted he would live another fifty-five days—on the fifty-fifth, in fear and trembling. I watched Mustafa, the holy madman, who was brought from the cages of the princes, deposed, brought back after the slaughter of the boy Osman, and deposed by Murad IV who was the most cruel. Can you imagine a man, my lady, who could see a circle of lovely girls dancing in a meadow, and order them all to be drowned because they sang too loudly? No one spoke in those days, in the palace, for fear of attracting his attention. He could have a man killed because his teeth chattered involuntarily for fear of being put to death. And when he was dying he ordered the death of his only surviving brother, Ibrahim. But his mother, Kösem, the Greek, the Valide Sultan, lied to him and said it was done, when it was not. I saw him smile and try to get up to see the corpse, and fall back in his death throes.

"As for Ibrahim. He was a fool, a cruel fool, who loved things of the harem where he had grown up. He listened to an old storyteller in the harem—a woman from north of the Ukraine, who told him of northern kings who made love to their concubines in rooms entirely lined with sables, and with sables on their couches and sables on their bodies. So he made himself a great robe, sable without, sable within, with great jewels for buttons, which he wore whilst he satisfied his lust—the smell was not good, after a time. And he believed that the pleasures of the flesh would be more intense the larger the expanse of flesh with which he coped, so he sent out janissaries over all his lands to seek out the fleshiest, the hugest women, and bring them to his couch, where he scrambled all over them dragging the edges of his dark furs like a beast. And that is how I came to return to my bottle, for the fattest of all, the most voluptuous, the most like a sweet-breathed cow, whose anklets were twice your present waist, madame—she was an Armenian Christian, she was docile and short of breath—it was she who was so heavy that she dislodged the tile under which my bottle lay concealed—and so I stood before her in the bathroom and she wheezed with anxiety. I told her that the Valide Sultan planned to have her strangled that night at the banquet she was dressing for, and I thought she would utter a wish—wish herself a thousand miles away, or wish that someone would strangle the Valide Sultan—or even wish a small wish, such as 'I wish I knew what to do,' and I would have told her what to do, and rushed on wide wings to the ends of the earth afterwards.

"But this globular lady was self-satisfied and slow-witted, and all she could think of to say was 'I wish you were sealed up in your bottle again, infidel Ifrit, for I want nothing to do with dirty djinns. You smell bad,' she added, as I coiled myself back into atomies of smoke and sighed myself into the flask and replaced the stopper. And she carried my flask through the rose garden where my white Circassian had been carried, and threw me over the Seraglio Point into the Bosphorus. She undertook this herself; I could feel the voluptuous rippling and juddering of her flesh as she progressed along the paths. I was about to say she had not taken so much exercise in years, but that would be unjust—she had to use her musculature very vigorously in certain ways to cope with the more extreme projects of Sultan Ibrahim. And Kösem did have her strangled that night, just as I had told her. It would have been more interesting to have been released by those doughty Sultanas, by Roxelana or Kösem, but my luck was femininity.

"And so I tossed about in the Bosphorus for another two hundred and fifty years and was then fished up by another fisherman and sold as an antique to a merchant of Smyrna, who gave me—or my flask—as a love token to his young wife Zefir, who had a collection of curious-shaped bottles and jars in her quarters in the harem. And Zefir saw the seal on the bottle and knew what it was, for she was a great reader of tales and histories. She told me later she spent all night in fear, wondering whether to open the flask, in case I might be angry, like the djinn who threatened to kill his rescuer because he had become enraged over the centuries, that the poor man had taken so long to come to his aid. But she was a brave creature, Zefir, and ardent for knowledge, and mortally bored, so one day, alone in her chamber she pushed away the seal . . ."

"What was she like?" said Gillian, since the djinn appeared to have floated off into a reminiscent reverie.

His eyelids were half-closed and the edges of his huge nostrils fluttered.

"Ah," he said, "Zefir. She had been married at fourteen to the merchant who was older than she was, and was kind enough to her, kind enough, if you call treating someone like a toy dog or a spoiled baby or a fluffy fat bird in a cage being kind. She was good-looking enough, a sharp, dark person, with secret black-brown eyes and an angry line of a mouth that pulled in at the corners. She was wayward and angry, Zefir, and she had nothing at all to do. There was an older wife who didn't like her and didn't talk to her, and servants, who seemed to her to be mocking her. She spent her time sewing huge pictures in silk—pictures of stories—the stories from the Shahnama, of Rüstem and the Shah Kaykavus who tried to emulate the djinns and fly, and devised a method of some ingenuity—he tied four strong yet hungry eagles to a throne, and four juicy legs of mutton to the rising posts of the canopy of the throne—and then he seated himself, and the eagles strove to reach the meat, and lifted the throne—and the shah—towards the heavens. But the eagles tired, and the throne and its occupant fell to earth—she had embroidered him coming down headlong and head-first, and she had sewed him a rich carpet of flowers to fall on, for she thought him aspiring, and not a fool. You should have seen the beauty of her silk legs of mutton, like the life—or rather, death. She was a great artist, Zefir, but no one saw her art. And she was angry because she knew she was capable of many things she couldn't even define to herself, so they seemed like bad dreams—that is what she told me. She told me she was eaten up with unused power and thought she might be a witch—except, she said, if she were a man, these things she thought about would be ordinarily acceptable. If she had been a man, and a Westerner, she would have rivalled the great Leonardo whose flying machines were the talk of the court of Suleiman one summer—

"So I taught her mathematics, which was bliss to her, and astronomy, and many languages, she studied secretly with me, and poetry—we wrote an epic poem about the travels of the Queen of Sheba—and history, I taught her the history of Turkey and the history of the Roman Empire, and the history of the Holy Roman Empire—I bought her novels in many languages, and philosophical treatises, Kant and Descartes and Leibnitz—"

"Wait," said Gillian. "Was this her wish, that you should teach her these things?"

"Not exactly," said the djinn. "She wished to be wise and learned, and I had known the Queen of Sheba, and what it was to be a wise woman . . ."

"Why did she not wish to *get out of there*?" asked Gillian.

"I advised against it. I said the wish was bound to go wrong, unless she was better informed about the possible places or times she might wish herself into—I said there was no hurry—"

"You enjoyed teaching her."

"Rarely among humankind can there have been a more intelligent being," said the djinn. "And not only intelligent." He brooded.

"I taught her other things also," he said. "Not at first. At first I flew in and out with bags of books and papers and writing things that I then hid by temporarily vanishing them into her bottle collection—so she could always call on Aristotle from the red glass perfume bottle, or Euclid from the green tear bottle, without needing me to reembody them—"

"And did that count as a wish?" asked Gillian severely.

"Not really." The djinn was evasive. "I taught her a few magical skills—to help her—because I loved her—"

"You loved her—"

"I loved her anger. I loved my own power to change her frowns to smiles. I taught her what her husband had not taught her, to enjoy her own body, without all the gestures of submission and non-disturbance of his own activities the silly man seemed to require."

"You were in no hurry for her to escape—to exercise her new powers somewhere else—"

"No. We were happy. I like being a teacher. It is unusual in djinns—we have a natural propensity to trick and mislead your kind. But your kind is rarely as greedy for knowledge as Zefir. I had all the time in the world—"

"*She* didn't," said Gillian who was trying to feel her way into this story, occluded by the djinn's own feelings, it appeared. She felt a certain automatic resentment of this long-dead Turkish prodigy, the thought of whom produced the dreaming smile on the lips of what she had come to think of—so quickly—as *her* djinn. But she also felt troubled on Zefir's behalf, by the djinn's desire to be both liberator and imprisoner in one.

"I know," said the djinn. "She was mortal, I know. What year is it now?"

"It is 1991."

"She would be one hundred and sixty-four years old, if she lived. And our child would be one hundred and forty, which is not possible for such a being."

"A child?"

"Of fire and dust. I planned to fly with him round the earth, and show him the cities and the forests and the shores. He would have been a great genius—maybe. I don't know if he was ever born."

"Or she."

"Or she. Indeed."

"What happened? Did she wish for *anything at all*? Or did you prevent her to keep her prisoner? How did you come to be in my *çesm-i bülbül* bottle? I do not understand."

"She was a very clever woman, like you, Djil-yan, and she knew it was wise to wait. And then—I think—I know—she began to wish—to desire—that I should stay with her. We had a whole world in her little room. I brought things from all over the world—silks and satins, sugarcane and pawpaw, sheets of green ice, Donatello's Perseus, aviaries full of parrots, waterfalls, rivers. One day, unguardedly, she wished she could fly with me when I went to the Americas, and then she could have bitten off her tongue, and almost wasted a second wish undoing the first, but I put a finger on her lip—she was so quick, she understood in a flash—and I kissed her, and we flew to Brazil, and to Paraguay, and saw the Amazon River which is as great as a sea, and the beasts in the forests there, where no man treads, and she was blissfully warm against my heart inside the feathered cloak—there are spirits with feathered cloaks out there, we found, whom we met in the air above the forest canopy—and then I brought her back to her room, and she fainted with joy and disappointment."

He came to another halt, and Dr. Perholt, savouring *loukoum,* had to encourage him.

"So she had two wishes. And became pregnant. Was she happy to be pregnant?"

"Naturally, in a way, she was happy, to be carrying a magic child. And naturally, in another, she was afraid: she said perhaps she should ask for a magic palace where she could bring up the child in safety in a hidden place—but that was not what she wanted—she said also she was not sure she wanted a child at all, and came near wishing him out of existence—"

"But you saved him."

"I loved her. He was mine. He was a small seed, like a curved comma of smoke in a bottle; he grew and I watched him. She loved me, I think, she could not wish him undone."

"Or her. Or perhaps you could see which it was?"

He considered.

"No. I did not see. I supposed, a son."

"But you never saw him born."

"We quarrelled. Often. I told you she was angry. By nature. She was like a squall of sudden shower, thunder, and lightning. She berated me. She said I had ruined her life. Often. And then we played again. I would make myself small, and hide. One day, to amuse her, I hid in the new *çesm-i bülbül* bottle that her husband had given her: I flowed in gracefully and curled myself; and she began suddenly to weep and rail and said, 'I wish I could forget I had ever seen you.' And so she did. On the instant."

"But—" said Dr. Perholt.

"But?" said the genie.

"But why did you not just flow out of the bottle again? Solomon had not sealed that bottle—"

"I had taught her a few sealing spells, for pleasure. For my pleasure, in being in her power, and hers, in having power. There are humans who play such games of power with manacles and ropes. Being inside a bottle has certain things—a *few* things—in common with being inside a woman—a certain pain that at times is indistinguishable from pleasure. We cannot die, but at the moment of becoming infinitesimal inside the neck of a flask, or a jar, or a bottle—we can shiver with the apprehension of extinction—as humans speak of dying when they reach the height of bliss, in love. To be nothing, in the bottle—to pour my seed into her—it was a little the same. And I taught her the words of power as a kind of wager—a form of gambling. Russian roulette," said the djinn, appearing to pluck these unlikely words from the air.

"So I was in, and she was out, and had forgotten me," he concluded.

"And now," said the djinn, "I have told you the history of my incarcerations, and you must tell me your history."

"I am a teacher. In a university. I was married and now I am free. I travel the world in aeroplanes and talk about storytelling."

"Tell me your story."

A kind of panic overcame Dr. Perholt. It seemed to her that she had no story, none that would interest this hot person with his searching look and his restless intelligence. She could not tell him the history of the Western world since Zefir had mistakenly wished him forgotten in a bottle of *çesm-i bülbül* glass, and without that string of wonders, how could he understand her?

He put a great hand on her towelled shoulder. Through the towel, even, his hand was hot and dry.

"Tell me anything," said the djinn.

She found herself telling him how she had been a girl at a boarding-school in Cumberland, a school full of girls, a school with nowhere to hide from gaggles and klatsches of girls. It may be she told him this because of her imagined vision of Zefir, in the women's quarters in Smyrna in 1850. She told him about the horror of dormitories full of other people's sleeping breath. I am a naturally *solitary* creature, the doctor told the djinn. She had written a secret book, her first book, she told him, during this imprisonment, a book about a young man called Julian who was in hiding, disguised as a girl called Julienne, in a similar place. In hiding from an assassin or a kidnapper, she could barely remember, at this distance, she told the djinn. Her voice faded. The djinn was impatient. Was she a lover of women in those days? No, said Dr. Perholt, she believed she had written the story out of an emptiness, a need to imagine a boy, a man, the Other. And how did the story progress, asked the djinn, and could you not find a real boy or man, how did you resolve it? I could not, said Dr. Perholt. It seemed silly, in writing, I could see it was silly. I filled it with details, realistic details, his underwear, his problems with gymnastics, and the more realism I tried to insert into what was really a cry of desire—desire for nothing specific—the more silly my story. It should have been farce or fable, I see that now, and I was writing passion and tragedy and buttons done with verisimilitude. I burned it in the school furnace. My imagination failed. I got all enmeshed in what was realism and what was reality and what was true—my need not to be in that place—and my imagination failed. Indeed it may be because Julian/Julienne was such a ludicrous figure that I am a narratologist and not a maker of fictions. I tried to conjure him up—he had long black hair in the days when all Englishmen had short back-and-sides—but he remained resolutely absent, or almost absent. Not quite. From time to time, he had a sort of being, he was a sort of wraith. "Do you understand this?"

"Not entirely," said the djinn. "He was an emanation, like this Becker you would not let me give you."

"Only the emanation of an absence." She paused. "When I was younger there was a boy who was real."

"Your first lover."

"No. No. Not flesh and blood. A golden boy who walked beside me wherever I went. Who sat beside me at table, who lay beside me at night, who sang with me, who walked in my dreams. Who disappeared when I had a headache or was sick, but was always there when I couldn't move for asthma. His name was Tadzio, I don't know where I got that from, he came with it, one day, I just looked up and I saw him. He told me stories. In a language only we two spoke. One day I found a poem which said how it was, to live in his company. I did not know anyone else knew, until I read that poem."

"I know those beings—" said the djinn. "Zefir had known one. She said he was always a little transparent but moved with his own will, not hers. Tell me your poem."

When I was but thirteen or so
I went into a golden land,
Chimborazo, Cotopaxi
Took me by the hand.

My father died, my brother too,
They passed like fleeting dreams,
I stood where Popocatapetl
In the sunlight gleams.

I dimly heard the Master's voice,
And boys' far-off at play,
Chimborazo, Cotopaxi
Had stolen me away.

I walked in a great golden dream
To and fro from school—
Shining Popocatapetl
The dusty streets did rule.

I walked home with a gold dark boy
And never a word I'd say
Chimborazo, Cotopaxi
Had taken my speech away:

I gazed entranced upon his face
Fairer than any flower—
O shining Popocatapetl
It was thy magic hour:

The houses, people, traffic seemed
Thin fading dreams by day,
Chimborazo, Cotopaxi
They had stolen my soul away.

"I love that poem," said Dr. Perholt. "It has two things: names and the golden boy. The names are not the names of the boy, they are the romance of language, and *he* is the romance of language—he is more real than—reality—as the goddess of Ephesus is more real than I am—"

"And I am here," said the djinn.

"Indeed," said Dr. Perholt. "Incontrovertibly."

There was a silence. The djinn returned to the topic of Dr. Perholt's husband, her children, her house, her parents, all of which she answered without—in her mind or his—investing any of these now truly insignificant people with any life or colour. My husband went to Majorca with Emmeline Porter, she said to the djinn, and decided not to come back, and I was glad. The djinn asked about the complexion of Mr. Perholt and the nature of the beauty of Emmeline Porter and received null and unsatisfactory answers. They are wax images, your people, said the djinn indignantly.

"I do not want to think about them."

"That is apparent. Tell me something about yourself—something you have never told anyone—something you have never trusted to any lover in the depth of any night, to any friend, in the warmth of a long evening. Something you have kept for me."

And the image sprang in her mind, and she rejected it as insignificant.

"Tell me," said the djinn.

"It is insignificant."

"Tell me."

"Once, I was a bridesmaid. To a good friend from my college who wanted a white wedding, with veils and flowers and organ music, though she was happily settled with her man already, they slept together, she said she was blissfully happy, and I believe she was. At college, she seemed very poised and formidable—a woman of power, a woman of sexual experience, which was unusual in my day—"

"Women have always found ways—"

"Don't sound like the *Arabian Nights.* I am telling you something. She was full of bodily grace, and capable of being happy, which most of us were not, it was fashionable to be disturbed and anguished, for young women in those days—probably young men too. We were a generation when there was something shameful about being an unmarried woman, a spinster—though we were all clever, like Zefir, my friends and I, we all had this greed for knowledge—we were scholars—"

"Zefir would have been happy as a teacher of philosophy, it is true," said the djinn. "Neither of us could quite think what she could be—in those days—"

"And my friend—whom I shall call Susannah, it wasn't her name, but I can't go on without one—my friend had always seemed to me to come from somewhere rather grand, a beautiful house with beautiful things. But when I arrived for the wedding her house was much like mine, small, like a box, in a row of similar houses, and there was a settee, there was a three-piece suite in moquette—"

"A three-piece suite in moquette?" enquired the djinn. "What horrid thing is this to make you frown so?"

"I knew it was no good telling you anything out of my world. It is too big for those rooms, it is too heavy, it *weighs everything down,* it is chairs and a sofa that sat on a beige carpet with splashy flowers on—"

"A sofa—" said the djinn, recognising a word. "A carpet."

"You don't know what I'm talking about. I should never have started on this. All English stories get bogged down in whether or not the furniture is socially and aesthetically acceptable. This wasn't. That is, I thought so then. Now I find everything interesting, because I live my own life."

"Do not heat yourself. You did not like the house. The house was small and the three-piece suite in moquette was big, I comprehend. Tell me about the marriage. The story is presumably about the marriage and not about the chairs and sofa."

"Not really. The marriage went off beautifully. She had a lovely dress, like a princess out of a story—those were the days of the princess-line in dresses—I had a princess-line dress too, in shot taffeta, turquoise and silver, with a heart-shaped neck, and she was wearing several net skirts, and over those silk, and over that white lace—and a *mass* of veiling—and real flowers in her hair—little rosebuds—there wasn't room for all those billows of wonderful stuff in her tiny bedroom. She had a bedside lamp with Peter Rabbit eating a carrot. And all this shimmering silk and stuff. On the day, she looked so lovely, out of another world. I had a big hat with a brim, it suited me. You can imagine the dresses, I expect, but you can't imagine the house, the place."

"If you say I cannot," replied the djinn, obligingly. "Why do you tell me this tale? I cannot believe this is what you have not told."

"The night before the wedding," said Gillian Perholt, "we bathed together, in her parents' little bathroom. It had tiles with fishes with trailing fins and big soulful cartoon eyes—"

"Cartoon?"

"Disney. It doesn't matter. *Comic* eyes."

"Comic tiles?"

"It doesn't matter. We didn't share the bath, but we washed together."

"And—" said the djinn. "She made love to you."

"No," said Dr. Perholt. "She didn't. I saw myself. First in the mirror, and then I looked down at myself. And then I looked across at her—she was pearly-white and I was more golden. And she was soft and sweet—"

"And you were not?"

"I was perfect. Just at that moment, just at the very end of being a girl, and before I was a woman, really, I was perfect."

She remembered seeing her own small, beautifully rising breasts, her warm, flat, tight belly, her long slender legs and ankles, her waist—her waist—

"She said, 'Some man is going to go mad with desire for you,'" said Gillian Perholt. "And I was all proud inside my skin, as never before or since. All golden." She thought. "Two girls in a suburban bathroom," she said, in an English deprecating voice.

The djinn said, "But when I changed you, that was not what you became. You are very nice now, very acceptable, very desirable now, but not perfect."

"It was terrifying. I was terrified. It was like"—she found a completely unexpected phrase—"like having a weapon, a sharp sword, I couldn't handle."

"Ah yes," said the djinn. "Terrible as an army with banners."

"But it didn't belong to me. I was tempted to—to love it—myself. It was lovely. But unreal. I mean, it was *there,* it was real enough, but I knew in my head it wouldn't stay—something would happen to it. I owed it"—she went on, searching for feelings she had never interrogated—"I owed it—some sort of adequate act. And I wasn't going to live up to it." She caught her breath on a sigh. "I am a creature of the mind, not the body, Djinn. I can look after my mind. I took care of that, despite everything."

"Is that the end of the story?" said the djinn after another silence. "Your stories are strange, glancing things. They peter out, they have no shape."

"It is what my culture likes, or liked. But no, it is not the end. There is a little bit more. In the morning Susannah's father brought my breakfast in bed. A boiled egg in a woolly cosy, a little silver-plated pot of tea, in a cosy knitted to look like a cottage, toast in a toast rack, butter in a butter dish, all on a little tray with unfolding legs, like the trays old ladies have in Homes."

"You didn't like the—the whatever was on the teapot? Your aesthetic sense, which is so violent, was in revolt again?"

"He suddenly leaned forwards and pulled my nightdress off my shoulders. He put his hands round my perfect breasts," said Dr. Perholt who was fifty-five and now looked thirty-two, "and he put his sad face down between them—he had glasses, they were all steamed up and knocked sideways, he had a little bristly moustache that crept over my flesh like a centipede, he *snuffled* amongst my breasts, and all he said was 'I can't bear it' and he rubbed his body against my counterpane—I only half-understood, the counterpane was artificial silk, eau-de-nil colour—he snuffled and jerked and twisted my breasts in his hands—and then he unfolded the little legs of the tray and put it over my legs and went away—to give away his daughter, which he did with great dignity and charm. And I felt sick, and felt my body was to blame. As though out of *that,*" she said lucidly, "was spun snuffling and sweat and three-piece suites and artificial silk and tea cozies—"

"And that is the end of the story?" said the djinn.

"That is where a storyteller would end it, in my country."

"Odd. And you met *me* and asked for the body of a thirty-two-year-old woman."

"I didn't. I asked for it to be as it was when I last *liked* it. I didn't like it then. I half-worshipped it, but it scared me—This is *my* body, I find it pleasant, I don't mind looking at it—"

"Like the potter who puts a deliberate flaw in the perfect pot."

"Maybe. If having lived a little is a flaw. Which it is. That girl's ignorance was a burden to her."

"Do you know now what other things you will wish for?"

"Ah, you are anxious to be free."

"On the contrary, I am comfortable, I am curious, I have all the time in the world."

"And I have everything I wish for, at present. I have been thinking about the story of the Queen of Sheba and what the answer might be to the question of what all women desire. I shall tell you the story of the Ethiopian woman whom I saw on the television box."

"I am all ears," said the djinn, extending himself on the bedspread and shrinking himself a little, in order to be able to accommodate himself at full length. "Tell me, this box, you can turn it to spy anywhere you desire in the world, you can see Manaus or Khartoum as you please?"

"Not exactly, though partly. For instance the tennis was coming live—we call it 'live' when we see it simultaneously with its happening—from Monte Carlo. But also we can make images—

stories—which we can replay to ourselves. The Ethiopian woman was part of a story—a film—made for the Save the Children Fund—which is a charitable body—which had given some food to a village in Ethiopia where there had been drought and famine, food specifically to give to the children, to keep them alive through the winter. And when they brought the food, they filmed the people of the village, the headmen and the elders, the children playing, and then they came back, the research workers came back, half a year later, to see the children and weigh them, to see how the food they had given had helped them."

"Ethiopia is a fierce country of fierce people," said the djinn. "Beautiful and terrible. What did you see in your box?"

"The aid workers were very angry—distressed and angry. The headman had promised to give the food only to the families with the small children the project was helping and studying—'project' is—"

"I know. I have known projectors in my time."

"But the headman had not done as he was asked. It was against his beliefs to feed some families and not others, and it was against everyone's beliefs to feed small children and not grown men, who could work in the fields, if anything could be grown there. So the food had been shared out too sparsely—and everyone was thinner—and some of the children were dead—many, I think—and others were very ill because the food had not been given to them.

"And the workers—the relief workers—the charitable people from America and Europe—were angry and upset—and the cameramen (the people who make the films) went out into the fields with the men who had had the food, and had sowed their crops in hope of rain—and had even had a little rain—and the men lifted the seedlings and showed the cameramen and the officials that the roots had been eaten away by a plague of sawfly, and there would be no harvest. And those men, standing in those fields, holding those dying, stunted seedlings, were in complete despair. They had no hope and no idea what to do. We had seen the starving in great gatherings on our boxes, you must understand—we knew where they were heading, and had sent the food because we were moved because of what we had seen.

"And then, the cameras went into a little hut, and there in the dark were four generations of women, the grandmother, the mother, and the young girl with her baby. The mother was stirring something in a pot over a fire—it looked like a watery soup—with a wooden stick—and the grandmother was sitting on a kind of bed against the wall, where the hut roof—which seemed conical—met it. They were terribly thin, but they weren't dying—they hadn't given up yet, they hadn't got those eyes looking out at nothing, or those slack muscles just waiting. They were beautiful people still, people with long faces and extraordinary cheekbones, and a kind of dignity in their movement—or what Westerners like me read as dignity, they are upright, they carry their heads up—

"And they interviewed the old woman. I remember it partly because of her beauty, and partly because of the skill of the cameraman—or woman—she was angular but not awkward, and she had one long arm at an angle over her head, and her legs extended on this bench—and the photographer had made them squared, as it were *framed* in her own limbs—she spoke out of an enclosure made by her own body, and her eyes were dark holes and her face was long, long. She made the edges of the box out of her body. They wrote in English letters across the screen a translation of what she was saying. She said there was no food, no food anymore and the little girl would starve, and there would be no milk, there would be no more food. And then she said, 'It is because I am a woman, I cannot get out of here, I must sit here and wait for my fate, if only I were not a woman I could go out and do something'—all in a monotone. With the men stomping about in the furrows outside kicking up dry dust and stunted seedlings in perfect despair.

"I don't know why I tell you this. I will tell you something else. I was told to wish on a pillar in Haghia Sophia—and before I could stop myself—it was—not a good pillar—I wished what I used to wish as a child."

"You wished you were not a woman."

"There were three veiled women laughing at me, pushing my hand into that hole.

"I thought, perhaps, that was what the Queen of Sheba told Solomon that all women desired."

The genie smiled.

"It was not. That was not what she told him. Not exactly."

"Will you tell me what she told him?"

"If you wish me to."

"I wish—Oh, no. No, that isn't what I wish."

Gillian Perholt looked at the djinn on her bed. The evening had come, whilst they sat there, telling each other stories. A kind of light played over his green-gold skin, and a kind of glitter, like the glitter from the Byzantine mosaics, where a stone here or there will be set at a slight angle to catch the light. His plumes rose and fell as though they were breathing, silver and crimson, chrysanthemum-bronze and lemon, sapphire-blue and emerald. There was an edge of sulphur to his scent, and sandalwood, she thought, and something bitter—myrrh, she wondered, having never smelled myrrh, but remembering the king in the Christmas carol:

> Myrrh is mine, its bitter perfume
> Breathes a life of gathering gloom,
> Sorrowing, sighing, bleeding, dying
> Sealed in a stone-cold tomb.

The outsides of his thighs were greener and the insides softer and more golden. He had pulled down his tunic, not entirely adequately: she could see his sex coiled like a folded snake and stirring.

"I wish," said Dr. Perholt to the djinn, "I wish you would love me."

"You honour me," said the djinn, "and maybe you have wasted

your wish, for it may well be that love would have happened anyway, since we are together, and sharing our life stories, as lovers do."

"Love," said Gillian Perholt, "requires generosity. I found I was jealous of Zefir and I have never been jealous of anyone. I wanted—it was more that I wanted to give *you* something—to give you my wish—" she said, incoherently. The great eyes, stones of many greens, considered her and the carved mouth lifted in a smile.

"You give and you bind," said the djinn, "like all lovers. You give yourself, which is brave, and which I think you have never done before—and I find you eminently lovable. Come."

And without moving a muscle Dr. Perholt found herself naked on the bed, in the arms of the djinn.

Of their lovemaking she retained a memory at once precise, mapped on to every nerve ending, and indescribable. There was, in any case, no one to whom she could have wished to describe the lovemaking of a djinn. All lovemaking is shape-shifting—the male expands like a tree, like a pillar, the female has intimations of infinity in the spaces which narrow inside her. But the djinn could prolong everything, both in space and in time, so that Gillian seemed to swim across his body forever like a dolphin in an endless green sea, so that she became arching tunnels under mountains through which he pierced and rushed, or caverns in which he lay curled like dragons. He could become a concentrated point of delight at the pleasure points of her arched and delighted body; he could travel her like some wonderful butterfly, brushing her here and there with a hot, dry, almost burning kiss, and then become again a folding landscape in which she rested and was lost, lost herself for him to find her again, holding her in the palm of his great hand, contracting himself with a sigh and holding her breast to breast, belly to belly, male to female. His sweat was like a smoke and he murmured like a cloud of bees in many languages—she felt her skin was on fire and was not consumed, and tried once to tell him about Marvell's lovers who had not "world enough and time" but could only murmur one couplet in the green cave of his ear. "My vegetable love should grow /

Vaster than empires and more slow." Which the djinn smilingly repeated, using the rhythm for a particularly delectable movement of his body.

And afterwards she slept. And woke alone in her pretty nightdress, amongst her pillows. And rose sadly and went to the bathroom, where the *çesm-i bülbül* bottle still stood, with her own finger traces on its moist sides. She touched it sadly, running her fingers down the spirals of white—I have had a dream, she thought—and there was the djinn, bent into the bathroom like the Ethiopian woman in the television box, making an effort to adjust his size.

"I thought—"

"I know. But as you see, I am here."

"Will you come to England with me?"

"I must, if you ask me. But also I should like to do that, I should like to see how things are now, in the world, I should like to see where you live, though you cannot describe it as interesting."

"It will be, if you are there."

But she was afraid.

And they went back to England, the narratologist, the glass bottle, and the djinn; they went back by British Airways, with the bottle cushioned in bubble plastic in a bag at Gillian Perholt's feet.

And when they got back, Dr. Perholt found that the wish she had made before Artemis between the two Leylas was also granted: there was a letter asking her to give the keynote paper in Toronto in the fall, and offering her a Club-class fare and a stay in the Xanadu Hotel, which did indeed have a swimming pool, a blue pool under a glass dome, sixty-four floors above Lake Ontario's shores. And it was cold and clear in Toronto, and Dr. Perholt settled herself into the hotel room, which was tastefully done in warm colours for cold winters, in chestnuts, browns, and ambers, with touches of flame. Hotel rooms have often the illusory presence of a magician's stage set—their walls are bare concrete boxes, covered with whipped-up white plaster, like icing on a cake, and then the soft things are hung from screwed-in poles and hooks, damask and voile, gilt-edged mirror and branching candelabra, to give the illusion of richness. But all could be swept away in a twinkling and replaced by quite other colours and textures—chrome for brass, purple for amber, white-spotted muslin for gold damask, and this spick-and-span temporariness is part of the charm. Dr. Perholt unpacked the nightingale's-eye bottle and opened the stopper, and the djinn came out, human-size, and waved his wing-cloak to uncramp it. He then shot out of the window to look at the lake and the city, and returned, saying that she must come with him over the water, which was huge and cold, and that the sky, the atmosphere, was so full of rushing faces and figures that he had had to thread his way between them. The filling of the airwaves with politicians and pop-stars, TV evangelists and vacuum cleaners, moving forests and travelling deserts, pornographic bottoms and mouths and navels, purple felt dinosaurs and insane white puppies—all this had deeply saddened the djinn, almost to the point of depression. He was like someone who had had the habit of riding alone across deserts on a camel, or rushing off across savannah on an Arab horse, and now found himself negotiating an endless traffic jam of film stars, tennis players, and comedians, amongst the Boeings circling to find landing slots. The Koran and the Old Testament, he told Dr. Perholt, forbade the making of graven images, and whilst these were not graven, they were images, and he felt they were infestations. The atmosphere, he told her, had always been full of unseen beings—unseen by her kind—and still was. But it now needed to be negotiated. It is as bad, said the djinn, in the upper air as in bottles. I cannot spread my wings.

"And if you were entirely free," said Dr. Perholt, "where would you go?"

"There is a land of fire—where my kind play in the flames—"

They looked at each other.

"But I do not want to go," said the djinn gently. "I love you, and I have all the time in the world. And all this chatter and all these flying faces, they are also interesting. I learn many languages. I speak many tongues. Listen."

And he made a perfect imitation of Donald Duck, followed by a perfect imitation of Chancellor Kohl's orotund German, followed by the voices of the Muppets, followed by a surprising rendition of Kiri Te Kanawa which had Dr. Perholt's neighbours banging on the partition wall.

The conference was in Toronto University, ivy-hung in Victorian Gothic. It was a prestigious conference, to use an adjective that at this precise moment is shifting its meaning from magical, from conjuring tricks, to "full of renown," "respectable in the highest," "most honourable." The French narratologists were there, Todorov and Genette, and there were various orientalists too, on the watch for Western sentiment and distortion. Gillian Perholt's title was "Wish-fulfilment and Narrative Fate: Some Aspects of Wish-Fulfilment as a Narrative Device." She had sat up late writing it. She had never learned not to put her lectures together under pressure and at the last minute. It was not that she had not thought the subject matter out in advance. She had. She had thought long and carefully, with the *çesm-i bülbül* bottle set before her like a holy image, with its blue and white stripes enfolding each other and circling and diminishing to its mouth. She had looked at her own strong pretty newish fingers travelling across the page, and flexed the comfortable stomach muscles. She had tried to be precise. Yet she felt, as she stood up to speak, that her subject had taken a great twist in her hands, like a magic flounder trying to return to the sea, like a divining rod pointing with its own energy into the earth, like a conducting rod shivering with the electrical forces in the air.

As usual, she had tried to incorporate the telling of a story, and it was this story that had somehow twisted the paper away from its subject. It would be tedious to recount all her arguments. Their tenor can be guessed from their beginning.

★

"Characters in fairy tales," said Gillian, "are subject to Fate and enact their fates. Characteristically they attempt to change this fate by magical intervention in its workings, and characteristically too, such magical intervention only reinforces the control of the Fate which waited for them, which is perhaps simply the fact that they are mortal and return to dust. The most clear and absolute version of this narrative form is the story of the appointment in Samarra—of the man who meets Death, who tells him that he is coming for him that evening, and flees to Samarra to avoid him. And Death remarks to an acquaintance that their first meeting was odd 'since I was to meet him in Samarra tonight.'

"Novels in recent time, have been about choice and motivation. Something of the ineluctable consequentiality of Samarra still clings to Raskolnikov's 'free' act of murder, for it calls down a wholly predictable and conventional vengeance. In the case of George Eliot's Lydgate, on the other hand, we do not feel that the 'spots of commonness' in his nature are instruments of inevitable fate in the same way: it was possible for him *not* to choose to marry Rosamund and destroy his fortune and his ambition. We feel that when Proust decides to diagnose sexual inversion in *all* his characters he is substituting the novelist's desires for the Fate of the real world; and yet that when Swann wastes years of his life for a woman who was not even his type, he made a choice, in time, that was possible but not inevitable.

"The emotion we feel in fairy tales when the characters are granted their wishes is a strange one. We feel the possible leap of freedom—I can have what I want—and the perverse certainty that this will change nothing; that Fate is fixed.

"I should like to tell you a story told to me by a friend I met in Turkey—where stories are introduced *bir var mis, bir yok mis,* perhaps it happened, perhaps it didn't, and have paradox as their inception."

She looked up, and there, sitting next to the handsome figure of

Todorov, was a heavy-headed person in a sheepskin jacket, with a huge head of white hair. This person had not been there before, and the white mane had the look of an extravagant toupee, which, with blue-tinted glasses, gave the newcomer a look of being cruelly in disguise. Gillian thought she recognised the lift of his upper lip, which immediately changed shape under her eyes as soon as she had this thought, becoming defiantly thin and pursed. She could not see into the eyes: when she tried, the glasses became almost sapphire in their rebarbative glitter.

"In the days when camels flew from roof to roof," she began, "and fish roosted in cherry trees, and peacocks were as huge as haystacks, there was a fisherman who had nothing, and who moreover had no luck fishing, for he caught nothing, though he cast his net over and over in a great lake full of weeds and good water. And he said, one more cast, and if that brings up nothing, I shall give up this métier, which is starving me, and take to begging at the roadside. So he cast, and his net was heavy, and he pulled in something wet and rolling and malodorous, which turned out to be a dead ape. So he said to himself, that is not nothing, nevertheless, and he dug a hole in the sand and buried the ape, and cast his net again, for a second last time. And this time too, it was full, and this time it struggled under the water, with a life of its own. So he pulled it up, full of hope, and what he had caught was a second ape, a moribund toothless ape, with great sores and scabs on its body, and a smell almost as disagreeable as its predecessor. Well, said the fisherman, I could tidy up this beast, and sell him to some street musician. He did not like the prospect. The ape then said to him—If you let me go, and cast again, you will catch my brother. And if you do not listen to his pleas, or make any more casts, he will stay with you and grant you anything you may wish for. There is a snag, of course, there is always a snag, but I am not about to tell you what it is.

"This limited honesty appealed to the fisherman, who disentangled the thin ape without much more ado, and cast again, and the net struggled away with satisfactory violence and it took all his force to bring it to shore. And indeed it contained an ape, a very large, glossy, *gleaming* ape, with, so my friend particularly told me, a most beautiful bottom, a mixture of very bright subtle blue, and a hot rose colour, suffused with poppy-coloured veins."

She looked at the sapphire-coloured dark glasses to see if she had done well and their owner nodded tersely.

"So the new ape said that if the fisherman would release him, and cast again, he would draw up a huge treasure, and a palace, and a company of slaves, and never want again. But the fisherman remembered the saying of the thin ape, and said to the new one, 'I wish for a new house, on the shore of this lake, and I wish for a camel, and I wish for a feast—of moderate proportions—to be ready-cooked in this house.'

"And immediately all these things appeared, and the fisherman offered a share of the delicious feast to the two apes, and they accepted.

"And he was a fisherman who had heard a great many tales in his time, and had an analytic bent, and he thought he understood that the danger of wishes lay in being overweening or hasty. He had no wish to find himself in a world where everything was made of gold and was quite inedible, and he had a strong intuition that the perpetual company of houris or the perpetual imbibing of sherbet and sparkling wine would be curiously wearisome. So he wished quietly for this and that: a shop full of tiles to sell and an assistant who understood them and was honest, a garden full of cedars and fountains, a little house with a servant girl for his old mother, and finally a little wife, such as his mother would have chosen for him, who was not to be beautiful as the sun and moon but kind and comfortable and loving. And so he went on, very peacefully, creating a world much more like the peaceful world of 'happy-ever-after' outside tales than the hectic one of the wishes granted by Grimm's flounder, or even Aladdin's djinn. And no one noticed his good fortune, much, and no one envied him or tried to steal it, since he was so discreet. And if he fell ill, or his little wife fell ill, he wished the illness away, and if someone spoke harshly to him he wished to forget it, and forgot.

"And the snag, you ask?

"This was the snag. He began to notice, slowly at first, and then quicker and quicker, that every time he made a wish, the great gleaming ape became a little smaller. At first just a centimetre there, and a centimetre here, and then more and more, so that he had to be raised on many cushions to eat his meals, and finally became so small that he sat on a little stool on top of the dining table and toyed with a tiny junket in a saltcellar. The thin ape had long gone his way, and returned again from time to time, now looking quite restored, in an ordinary sort of hairy way, with an ordinary blue bottom, nothing to be excited about. And the fisherman said to the thin ape:

" 'What will happen if I wish him larger again?'

" 'I cannot say,' said the ape. 'That is to say, I won't say.'

"And at night the fisherman heard the two apes talking. The thin one held the shining one in his hand and said sadly:

" 'It goes ill with you, my poor brother. You will vanish away soon; there will be nothing left of you. It is sad to see you in this state.'

" 'It is my Fate,' said the once-larger ape. 'It is my Fate to lose power and to diminish. One day I shall be so small, I shall be invisible, and the man will not be able to see me anymore to make any more wishes, and there I shall be, a slave ape the size of a pepper grain or a grain of sand.'

" 'We all come to dust,' said the thin ape sententiously.

" 'But not with this terrible speed,' said the wishing ape. 'I do my best, but still I am used and used. It is hard. I wish I were dead but none of my own wishes may be granted. Oh, it is hard, it is hard, it is hard.'

"And at this, the fisherman, who was a good man, rose out of his bed and went into the room where the two apes were talking, and said,

" 'I could not help hearing you and my heart is wrung for you. What can I do, O apes, to help you?'

"And they looked at him sullenly and would not answer.

"'I wish,' said the fisherman then, 'that you would take the next wish, if that is possible, and wish for your heart's desire.'

"And then he waited to see what would happen.

"And both apes vanished as if they had never been.

"But the house, and the wife, and the prosperous business did not vanish. And the fisherman continued to live as well as he could—though subject now to ordinary human ailments with the rest of us—until the day he died."

"In fairy tales," said Gillian, "those wishes that are granted and are not malign, or twisted towards destruction, tend to lead to a condition of beautiful stasis, more like a work of art than the drama of Fate. It is as though the fortunate had stepped off the hard road into an unchanging landscape where it is always spring and no winds blow. Aladdin's genie gives him a beautiful palace, and as long as this palace is subject to Fate, various magicians move it violently around the landscape, build it up and cause it to vanish. But at the end, it goes into stasis: into the pseudo-eternity of happy-ever-after. When we imagine happy-ever-after we imagine works of art: a family photograph on a sunny day, a Gainsborough lady and her children in an English meadow under a tree, an enchanted castle in a snowstorm of feathers in a glass dome. It was Oscar Wilde's genius to make the human being and the work of art change places. Dorian Gray smiles unchangingly in his eternal youth and his portrait undergoes his Fate, which is a terrible one, a fate of accelerating deterioration. The tale of Dorian Gray and also Balzac's tale of *La Peau de Chagrin,* the diminishing piece of wild ass's skin that for a time keeps Fate at bay, are related to other tales of the desire for eternal youth. Indeed we have methods now of granting a kind of false stasis, we have prostheses and growth hormone, we have plastic surgery and implanted hair, we can make humans into works of some kind of art or artifice. The grim and gallant fixed stares of Joan Collins and Barbara Cartland are icons of our wish for this kind of eternity.

"The tale of the apes, I think, relates to the observations of Sigmund Freud on the goal of all life. Freud was, whatever else he was, the great student of our desire, our will to live happily ever after. He studied our wishes, our fulfilment of our wishes, in the narrative of our dreams. He believed we rearranged our stories in our dream life to give ourselves happy endings, each according to his or her secret needs. (He claimed not to know what women really wanted, and this ignorance colours and changes his stories.) Then, in the repeated death dreams of the soldiers of the First World War he discovered a narrative that contradicted this desire for happiness, for wish fulfilment. He discovered, he thought, a desire for annihilation. He rethought the whole history of organic life under the sun, and came to the conclusion that what he called the 'organic instincts' were essentially *conservative*—that they reacted to stimuli by adapting in order to preserve, as far as possible, their original state. 'It would be in contradiction to the conservative nature of the instincts,' said Freud, 'if the goal of life were a state of things which had never been attained.' No, he said, what we desire must necessarily be an *old* state of things. Organisms strive, circuitously, to return to the inorganic—the dust, the stone, the earth—from which they came. *'The aim of all life is death,'* said Freud, telling his creation story in which the creation strives to return to the state before life was breathed into it, in which the shrinking of the *peau de chagrin,* the diminishing of the ape, is not the terrible concomitant of the life force, but its secret desire."

This was not all she said, but this was the second point at which she caught a flash of the sapphire glasses.

There were many questions, and Gillian's paper was judged a success, if somewhat confused.

Back in her hotel bedroom that night she confronted the djinn.

"You made my paper incoherent," she said. "It was a paper about fate and death and desire, and you introduced the freedom of wishing apes."

"I do not see what is incoherent," said the djinn. "Entropy rules us all. Power gets less, whether it derives from the magic arts or is made by nerves and muscle."

Gillian said, "I am ready now to make my third wish."

"I am all ears," said the djinn, momentarily expanding those organs to the size of elephants' ears. "Do not look doleful, Djil-yan, it may not happen."

"And where did you learn that catchphrase? Never mind. I shall almost believe you are trying to prevent my wish."

"No, no. I am your slave."

"I wish," said Gillian, "I wish you could have whatever you wish for—that this last wish may be your wish."

And she waited for the sound of thunder, or worse, the silence of absence. But what she heard was the sound of breaking glass. And she saw her bottle, the nightingale's-eye bottle, which stood on a glass sheet on the dressing table, dissolve like tears, not into sharp splinters, but into a conical heap of tiny cobalt-blue glass marbles, each with a white spiral coiled inside it.

"Thank you," said the djinn.

"Will you go?" asked the narratologist.

"Soon," said the djinn. "Not now, not immediately. You wished also, remember, that I would love you, and so I do. I shall give you something to remember me by—until I return—which, from time to time, I shall do—"

"If you remember to return in my lifetime," said Gillian Perholt.

"If I do," said the djinn, whose body now seemed to be clothed in a garment of liquid blue flame.

That night he made love to her, so beautifully that she wondered simultaneously how she could ever have let him go, and how she could ever have dared to keep such a being in Primrose Hill, or in hotel bedrooms in Istanbul or Toronto.

And the next morning he appeared in jeans and a sheepskin jacket, and said they were going out together, to find a gift. This time his hair—still fairly improbable—was a mass of dreadlocks, and his skin inclined to the Ethiopian.

In a small shop, in a side street, he showed her the most beautiful collection of modern weights she had ever seen. It is a modern Canadian art; they have artists who can trap a meshed and rolling geometrical sea, only visible at certain angles, and when visible glitters transparently with a rainbow of particles dusted with gold; they have artists who can enclose a red and blue flame forever in a cool glass sphere, or a dizzy cone of cobalt and emerald, reaching to infinity and meeting its own reflection. Glass is made of dust, of silica, of the sand of the desert, melted in a fiery furnace and blown into its solid form by human breath. It is fire and ice, it is liquid and solid, it is there and not there.

The djinn put into Dr. Perholt's hands a huge, slightly domed sphere inside which were suspended like commas, like fishing hooks, like fireworks, like sleeping embryos, like spurts of coloured smoke, like uncurling serpents, a host of coloured ribbons of glass amongst a host of breathed bubbles. They were all colours—gold and yellow, bright blue and dark blue, a delectable clear pink, a crimson, a velvet green, a whole host of busy movement. "Like rushing seed," said the djinn poetically. "Full of forever possibilities. And impossibilities, of course. It is a work of art, a great work of craft, it is a joyful thing, you like it?"

"Oh, yes," said Dr. Perholt. "I have never seen so many colours in one."

"It is called 'The Dance of the Elements,'" said the djinn. "I think that it is not your sort of title, but it suits it, I think. No?"

"Yes," said Dr. Perholt, who was sorrowful and yet full of a sense of things being as they should be.

The djinn watched the wrapping of the weight in shocking-pink tissue, and paid for it with a rainbow-coloured credit card with a hologram of the Venus de Milo, which caused an almost excessive fizzing amongst the terminals in the card machine. On the pavement he said,

"Goodbye. For the present."

" 'Now to the elements,' " said Dr. Perholt, " 'Be free and fare thou well.' "

She had thought of saying that some day, ever since she had first seen his monstrous foot from her bathroom door. She stood there, holding her glass weight. And the djinn kissed her hand, and vanished towards Lake Ontario like a huge cloud of bees, leaving behind on the pavement a sheepskin jacket that shrank slowly, to child size, to doll size, to matchbox size, to a few fizzing atoms, and was gone. He left also a moving heap of dreadlocks, like some strange hedgehog, which stirred a little, ran along a few feet, and vanished down a drain.

And did she ever see him again, you may ask? Or that may not be the question uppermost in your mind, but it is the only one to which you get an answer.

Two years ago, still looking thirty-five and comfortable, she was walking along Madison Avenue in New York, during a stop on the way to a narratological gathering in British Columbia, when she saw a shopwindow full of paperweights. These were not the work of artists like the Toronto artists who play with pure colour and texture, ribbons and threads and veils, stains and illusory movement. These were pure, old-fashioned, skilful representations: millefiori, latticework, crowns, canes, containing roses and violets, lizards and butterflies. Dr. Perholt went in, her eyes gleaming like the glass, and there in the dark shop were two elderly and charming men, happy men in a cavern bright with jewels, who for half an hour and with exquisite patience fetched out for Dr. Perholt sphere after sphere from the glass shelves in which they were reflected, and admired with her basketwork of fine white containing cornflower-blue posies, multicoloured cushions of geometric flowers, lovely as Paradise must have been in its glistening newness, bright with a brightness that would never fade, never come out into the dull air from its brilliant element.

Oh *glass,* said Dr. Perholt to the two gentlemen, it is not possible, it is only a solid metaphor, it is a medium for seeing and a thing seen at once. It is what art is, said Dr. Perholt to the two men, as they moved the balls of light, red, blue, green, on the visible and the invisible shelves.

"I like the geometrically patterned flowers best," said Dr. Perholt. "More than the ones that aim at realism, at looking real, don't you agree?"

"On the whole," said one of the two. "On the whole, the whole effect is better with the patterning, with the geometry of the glass and the geometry of the canes. But have you seen these? These are American."

And he gave her a weight in which a small snake lay curled on a watery surface of floating duckweed—a snake with a glass thread of a flickering tongue and an almost microscopic red-brown eye in its watchful but relaxed olive head. And he gave her a weight in which, in the solidity of the glass as though it were the deep water of a well, floated a flower, a flower with a rosy lip and a white hood, a green stem, long leaves trailing in the water, and a root specked and stained with its brown juices and the earth it had come from, a root trailing fine hair roots and threads and tendrils into the glassy medium. It was perfect because the illusion was near-perfect, and the attention to the living original had been so perfect that the undying artificial flower also seemed perfect. And Gillian thought of Gilgamesh, and the lost flower, and the snake. Here they were side by side, held in suspension.

She turned the weight over, and put it down, for its price was prohibitive.

She noticed, almost abstractedly, that there was a new dark age-stain on the back of the hand that held the weight. It was a pretty soft dried-leaf colour.

"I wish—" she said to the man behind the glass cage of shelves.

"You would like the flower," said a voice behind her. "And the snake with it, why not? I will give them to you."

And there he was behind her, this time in a dark overcoat and a white scarf, with a rather large wide-brimmed black velvet hat, and the sapphire glasses.

"What a nice surprise to see you again, sir," said the shopowner, holding out his hand for the rainbow credit card with the Venus de Milo. "Always unexpected, always welcome, most welcome."

And Dr. Perholt walked out into Madison Avenue with a gold-dark man and two weights, a snake and a flower. There are things in the earth, things made with hands and beings not made with hands that live a life different from ours, that live longer than we do, and cross our lives in stories, in dreams, at certain times when we are floating redundant. And Gillian Perholt was happy, for she had moved back into their world, or at least had access to it, as she had had as a child. She said to the djinn,

"Will you stay?"

And he said, "No. But I shall probably return again."

And she said, "If you remember to return in my lifetime."

"If I do," said the djinn.

A LAMIA IN THE CÉVENNES

In the mid-1980s Bernard Lycett-Kean decided that Thatcher's Britain was uninhabitable, a land of dog-eat-dog, lung-corroding ozone and floating money, of which there was at once far too much and far too little. He sold his West Hampstead flat and bought a small stone house on a Cévenol hillside. He had three rooms, and a large barn, which he weatherproofed, using it as a studio in winter and a storehouse in summer. He did not know how he would take to solitude, and laid in a large quantity of red wine, of which he drank a good deal at first, and afterwards much less. He discovered that the effect of the air and the light and the extremes of heat and cold were enough, indeed too much, without alcohol. He stood on the terrace in front of his house and battled with these things, with mistral and tramontane and thunderbolts and howling clouds. The Cévennes is a place of extreme weather. There were also days of white heat, and days of yellow heat, and days of burning blue heat. He produced some paintings of heat and light, with very little else in them, and some other paintings of the small river which ran along the foot of the steep, terraced hill on which his house stood; these were dark green and dotted with the bright blue of the kingfisher and the electric blue of the dragonflies.

These paintings he packed in his van and took to London and sold for largish sums of the despised money. He went to his own Private View and found he had lost the habit of conversation. He stared and snorted. He was a big man, a burly man, his stare seemed aggressive when it was largely baffled. His old friends were annoyed. He himself found London just as rushing and evil-smelling and unreal as he had been imagining it. He hurried back to the Cévennes. With his earnings, he built himself a swimming pool, where once there had been a patch of baked mud and a few bushes.

It is not quite right to say he built it. It was built by the Jardinerie Émeraude, two enterprising young men, who dug and lined and carried mud and monstrous stones, and built a humming powerhouse full of taps and pipes and a swirling cauldron of filter sand. The pool was blue, a swimming-pool blue, lined with a glittering tile mosaic, and with a mosaic dolphin cavorting amiably in its depths, a dark blue dolphin with a pale blue eye. It was not a boring rectangular pool, but an irregular oval triangle, hugging the contour of the terrace on which it lay. It had a white stone rim, moulded to the hand, delightful to touch when it was hot in the sun.

The two young men were surprised that Bernard wanted it blue. Blue was a little *moche,* they thought. People now were making pools steel grey or emerald green, or even dark wine red. But Bernard's mind was full of blue dots now visible across the southern mountains when you travelled from Paris to Montpellier by air. It was a recalcitrant blue, a blue that asked to be painted by David Hockney and only by David Hockney. He felt something else could and must be done with that blue. It was a blue he needed to know and fight. His painting was combative painting. That blue, that amiable, non-natural aquamarine, was different in the uncompromising mountains from what it was in Hollywood. There were no naked male backsides by his pool, no umbrellas, no tennis courts. The river water was sombre and weedy, full of little shoals of needlefishes and their shadows, of curling water snakes and the triangular divisions of flow around pebbles and boulders. This mild blue, here, was to be seen in *that* terrain.

He swam more and more, trying to understand the blue, which was different when it was under the nose, ahead of the eyes, over and around the sweeping hands and the flickering toes and the groin and the armpits and the hairs of his chest, which held bubbles of air for a time. His shadow in the blue moved over a pale eggshell mosaic, a darker blue, with huge paddle-shaped hands. The light changed, and with it, everything. The best days were under racing cloud, when the aquamarine took on a cool grey tone, which was then chased back, or rolled away, by the flickering gold-in-blue of yellow light in liquid. In front of his prow or chin in the brightest lights moved a mesh of hexagonal threads, flashing rainbow colours, flashing liquid silver-gilt, with a hint of molten glass; on such days liquid fire, rosy and yellow and clear, ran across the dolphin, who lent it a thread of intense blue. But the surface could be a reflective plane, with the trees hanging in it, with two white diagonals where the aluminium steps entered. The shadows of the sides were a deeper blue but not a deep blue, a blue not reflective and yet lying flatly *under* reflections. The pool was deep, for the Émeraude young men envisaged much diving. The wind changed the surface, frilled and furred it, flecked it with diamond drops, shirred it and made a witless patchwork of its plane. His own motion changed the surface—the longer he swam, the faster he swam, the more the glassy hills and valleys chopped and changed and ran back on each other.

Swimming was *volupté*—he used the French word, because of Matisse. *Luxe, calme et volupté.* Swimming was a strenuous battle with immense problems, of geometry, of chemistry, of apprehension, of style, of other colours. He put pots of petunias and geraniums near the pool. The bright hot pinks and purples were dangerous. They did something to that blue.

The stone was easy. Almost too blandly easy. He could paint chalky white and creamy sand and cool grey and paradoxical hot grey; he could understand the shadows in the high rough wall of monstrous cobblestones that bounded his land.

The problem was the sky. Swimming in one direction, he was headed towards a great rounded green mountain, thick with the bright yellow-green of dense chestnut trees, making a slightly innocent, simple arc against the sky. Whereas the other way, he swam towards crags, towards a bowl of bald crags, with a few pines and lines of dark shale. And against the green hump the blue sky was one blue, and against the bald stone another, even when for a brief few hours it was uniformly blue overhead, that rich blue, that cobalt, deep-washed blue of the south, which fought all the blues of the pool, all the green-tinged, duck-egg-tinged blues of the shifting water. But the sky had also its greenish days, and its powdery-hazed days, and its theatrical louring days, and none of these blues and whites and golds and ultramarines and faded washes harmonised in any way with the pool blues, though they all went through their changes and splendours in the same world, in which he and his shadow swam, in which he and his shadow stood in the sun and struggled to record them.

He muttered to himself. Why bother. Why does this *matter* so much. *What difference does it make to anything if I solve this blue* and just start again. I could just sit down and drink wine. I could go and be useful in a cholera camp in Colombia or Ethiopia. *Why bother to render the transparency in solid paint or air on a bit of board?* I could *just stop.*

He could not.

He tried oil paint and acrylic, watercolour and gouache, large designs and small plain planes and complicated juxtaposed planes. He tried trapping light on thick impasto and tried also glazing his surfaces flat and glossy, like seventeenth-century Dutch or Spanish paintings of silk. One of these almost pleased him, done at night, with the lights under the water and the dark round the stone, on an oval bit of board. But then he thought it was sentimental. He tried veils of watery blues on white in watercolour, he tried Matisse-like patches of blue and petunia—pool blue, sky blue, petunia—he tried Bonnard's mixtures of pastel and gouache.

His brain hurt, and his eyes stared, and he felt whipped by winds and dried by suns.

He was happy, in one of the ways human beings have found in which to be happy.

One day he got up as usual and as usual flung himself naked into the water to watch the dawn in the sky and the blue come out of the black and grey in the water.

There was a hissing in his ears, and a stench in his nostrils, perhaps a sulphurous stench, he was not sure; his eyes were sharp but his profession, with spirits and turpentine, had dulled his nostrils. As he moved through the sluggish surface he stirred up bubbles, which broke, foamed, frothed, and crusted. He began to leave a trail of white, which reminded him of polluted rivers, of the waste pipes of tanneries, of deserted mines. He came out rapidly and showered. He sent a fax to the Jardinerie Émeraude. What was Paradise is become the Infernal Pit. Where once I smelled lavender and salt, now I have a mephitic stench. What have you done to my water? Undo it, undo it. I cannot coexist with these exhalations. His French was more florid than his English. I am polluted, my work is polluted, *I cannot go on*. How could the two young men be brought to recognise the extent of the insult? He paced the terrace like an angry panther. The sickly smell crept like marsh grass over the flower pots, through the lavender bushes. An emerald-green van drew up, with a painted swimming pool and a painted palm tree. Every time he saw the van, he was pleased and irritated that this commercial emerald-and-blue had found an exact balance for the difficult aquamarine without admitting any difficulty.

The young men ran along the edge of the pool, peering in, their muscular legs brown under their shorts, their plimsolls padding. The sun came up over the green hill and showed the plague-stricken water-skin, ashy and suppurating. It is all OK, said the young men, this is a product we put in to fight algae, not because you *have* algae, M. Bernard, but in case algae might appear, as a precaution. It will all be exhaled in a week or two, the mousse will go, the water will clear.

"Empty the pool," said Bernard. "*Now*. Empty it now. I will not coexist for two weeks with this vapour. Give me back my clean salty water. *This water is my lifework*. Empty it *now*."

"It will takes days to fill," said one young man, with a French acceptance of Bernard's desperation. "Also there is the question of the allocation of water, of how much you are permitted to take."

"We could fetch it up from the river," said the other. In French this is literally, we could draw it *in* the river, *puiser dans le ruisseau*, like fishing. "It will be cold, ice-cold from the Source, up the mountain," said the Émeraude young men.

"Do it," said Bernard. "Fill it from the river. I am an Englishman, I swim in the North Sea, I like cold water. Do it. *Now.*"

The young men ran up and down. They turned huge taps in the grey plastic pipes that debouched in the side of the mountain. The swimming pool soughed and sighed and began, still sighing, to sink, whilst down below, on the hillside, a frothing flood spread and laughed and pranced and curled and divided and swept into the river. Bernard stalked behind the young men, admonishing them. "Look at that froth. We are polluting the river."

"It is only two litres. It is perfectly safe. Everyone has it in his pool, M. Bernard. It is tried and tested, it is a product for *purifying water.*" It is only you, his pleasant voice implied, who is pigheaded enough to insist on voiding it.

The pool became a pit. The mosaic sparkled a little in the sun, but it was a sad sight. It was a deep blue pit of an entirely unproblematic dull texture. Almost like a bathroom floor. The dolphin lost his movement and his fire, and his curvetting ripples, and became a stolid fish in two dimensions. Bernard peered in from the deep end and from the shallow end, and looked over the terrace wall at the hillside where froth was expiring on nettles and brambles. It took almost all day to empty and began to make sounds like a gigantic version of the bath-plug terrors of Bernard's infant dreams.

The two young men appeared carrying an immense boa constrictor of heavy black plastic pipe, and an implement that looked like a torpedo, or a diver's oxygen pack. The mountainside was steep, and the river ran green and chuckling at its foot. Bernard stood and watched. The coil of pipe was uncoiled, the electricity was connected in his humming pumphouse, and a strange sound began, a regular boum-boum, like the beat of a giant heart, echoing off the green mountain. Water began to gush from the mouth of the pipe into the sad dry depths of his pool pit. Where it trickled upwards, the mosaic took on a little life again, like crystals glinting.

"It will take all night to fill," said the young men. "But do not be afraid, even if the pool overflows, it will not come in your house, the slope is too steep, it will run away back to the river. And tomorrow we will come and regulate it and filter it and you may swim. But it will be very cold."

"Tant pis," said Bernard.

All night the black tube on the hillside wailed like a monstrous bullfrog, boum-boum, boum-boum. All night the water rose, silent and powerful. Bernard could not sleep; he paced his terrace and watched the silver line creep up the sides of the pit, watched the greenish water sway. Finally he slept, and in the morning his world was awash with river water, and the heart-beat machine was still howling on the riverbank, boum-boum, boum-boum. He watched a small fish skid and slide across his terrace, flow over the edge and slip in a stream of water down the hillside and back into the river. Everything smelled wet and lively, with no hint of sulphur and no clear smell of purified water. His friend Raymond Potter telephoned from London to say he might come on a visit; Bernard, who could not cope with visitors, was noncommittal and tried to describe his delicious flood as a minor disaster.

"You don't want river water," said Raymond Potter. "What about liver flukes and things, and bilharzia?"

"They don't have bilharzia in the Cévennes," said Bernard.

The Émeraude young men came and turned off the machine, which groaned, made a sipping sound and relapsed into silence. The water in the pool had a grassy depth it hadn't had. It was a lovely colour, a natural colour, a colour that harmonised with the hills, and it was not the problem Bernard was preoccupied with. It would clear, the young men assured him, once the filtration was working again.

Bernard went swimming in the green water. His body slipped into its usual movements. He looked down for his shadow and thought he saw out of the corner of his eye a swirling movement in the depths, a shadowy coiling. It would be strange, he said to himself, if there were a big snake down there, moving around. The dolphin was blue in green gloom. Bernard spread his arms and legs and floated. He heard a rippling sound of movement, turned his head, and found he was swimming alongside a yellow-green frog with a salmon patch on its cheek and another on its butt, the colour of the roes of scallops. It made vigorous thrusts with its hind legs, and vanished into the skimmer, from the mouth of which it peered out at Bernard. The underside of its throat beat, beat, cream-coloured. When it emerged, Bernard cupped his hands under its cool wet body and lifted it over the edge: it clung to his fingers with its own tiny fingers, and then went away, in long hops. Bernard went on swimming. There was still a kind of movement in the depths that was not his own.

This persisted for some days, although the young men set the filter in motion, tipped in sacks of white salt, and did indeed restore the aquamarine transparency, as promised. Now and then he saw a shadow that was not his, now and then something moved behind him; he felt the water swirl and tug. This did not alarm him, because he both believed and disbelieved his senses. He liked to imagine a snake. Bernard liked snakes. He liked the darting river snakes, and the long silver-brown grass snakes who travelled the grasses beside the river.

Sometimes he swam at night, and it was at night that he first definitely saw the snake, only for a few moments, after he had switched on the underwater lights, which made the water look like turquoise milk. And there under the milk was something very large, something coiled in two intertwined figures of eight and like no snake he had ever seen, a velvety black, it seemed, with long bars of crimson and peacock-eyed spots, gold, green, blue, mixed with silver moon-shapes, all of which appeared to dim and brighten and breathe under the deep water. Bernard did not try to touch; he sat down cautiously and stared. He could see neither head nor tail; the form appeared to be a continuous coil like a Möbius strip. And the colours changed as he watched them: the gold and silver lit up and went out, like lamps, the eyes expanded and contracted, the bars and stripes flamed with electric vermilion and crimson and then changed to purple, to blue, to green, moving through the rainbow. He tried professionally to commit the forms and the colours to memory. He looked up for a moment at the night sky. The Plough hung very low, and the stars glittered white-gold in Orion's belt on thick midnight velvet. When he looked back, there was the pearly water, vacant.

Many men might have run roaring in terror; the courageous might have prodded with a pool net, the extravagant might have reached for a shotgun. What Bernard saw was a solution to his professional problem, at least a nocturnal solution. Between the night sky and the breathing, dissolving eyes and moons in the depths, the colour of the water was solved, dissolved, it became a medium to contain a darkness spangled with living colours. He went in and took notes in watercolour and gouache. He went out and stared and the pool was empty.

For several days he neither saw nor felt the snake. He tried to remember it, and to trace its markings into his pool paintings, which became very tentative and watery. He swam even more than usual, invoking the creature from time to time. "Come back," he said to the pleasant blue depths, to the twisting coiling lines of rainbow light. "Come back, I need you."

And then, one day, when a thunderstorm was gathering behind the crest of the mountains, when the sky loured and the pool was unreflective, he felt the alien tug of the other current again, and looked round quick, quick, to catch it. And there was a head, urging itself sinuously through the water beside his own, and there below his body coiled the miraculous black velvet rope or tube with its shimmering moons and stars, its peacock eyes, its crimson bands.

The head was a snake head, diamond-shaped, half the size of his own head, swarthy and scaled, with a strange little crown of pale lights hanging above it like its own rainbow. He turned cautiously to look at it and saw that it had large eyes with fringed eyelashes, human eyes, very lustrous, very liquid, very black. He opened his mouth, swallowed water by accident, coughed. The creature watched him, and then opened its mouth, in turn, which was full of small, even, pearly human teeth. Between these protruded a flickering dark forked tongue, entirely serpentine. Bernard felt a prick of recognition. The creature sighed. It spoke. It spoke in Cévenol French, very sibilant, but comprehensible.

"I am so unhappy," it said.

"I am sorry," said Bernard stupidly, treading water. He felt the black coils slide against his naked legs, a tail tip across his private parts.

"You are a very beautiful man," said the snake in a languishing voice.

"You are a very beautiful snake," replied Bernard courteously, watching the absurd eyelashes dip and lift.

"I am not entirely a snake. I am an enchanted spirit, a Lamia. If you will kiss my mouth, I will become a most beautiful woman, and if you will marry me, I will be eternally faithful and gain an immortal soul. I will also bring you power, and riches, and knowledge you never dreamed of. But you must have faith in me."

Bernard turned over on his side, and floated, disentangling his brown legs from the twining coloured coils. The snake sighed.

"You do not believe me. You find my present form too loathsome to touch. I love you. I have watched you for months and I love and worship your every movement, your powerful body, your formidable brow, the movements of your hands when you paint. Never in all my thousands of years have I seen so perfect a male being. I will do anything for you—"

"Anything?"

"Oh, *anything.* Ask. Do not reject me."

"What I want," said Bernard, swimming towards the craggy end of the pool, with the snake stretched out behind him, "what I want, is to be able to paint your portrait, *as you are,* for certain reasons of my own, and because I find you very beautiful—if you would consent to remain here for a little time, as a snake—with all these amazing colours and lights—if I could paint you *in my pool*—just for a little time—"

"And then you will kiss me, and we will be married, and I shall have an immortal soul."

"Nobody nowadays believes in immortal souls," said Bernard.

"It does not matter if you believe in them or not," said the snake. "You have one and it will be horribly tormented if you break your pact with me."

Bernard did not point out that he had not made a pact, not having answered her request yes or no. He wanted quite desperately that she should remain in his pool, in her present form, until he had solved the colours, and was almost prepared for a Faustian damnation.

There followed a few weeks of hectic activity. The Lamia lingered agreeably in the pool, disposing herself wherever she was asked, under or on the water, in figures of three or six or eight or O, in spirals and tight coils. Bernard painted and swam and painted and swam. He swam less since he found the Lamia's wreathing flirtatiousness oppressive, though occasionally to encourage her, he stroked her sleek sides, or wound her tail round his arm or his arm round her tail. He never painted her head, which he found hideous and repulsive. Bernard liked snakes but he did not like women. The Lamia with female intuition began to sense his lack of enthusiasm for this aspect of her. "My teeth," she told him, "will be lovely in rosy lips, my eyes will be melting and mysterious in a human face. Kiss me, Bernard, and you will see."

"Not yet, not yet," said Bernard.

"I will not wait forever," said the Lamia.

Bernard remembered where he had, so to speak, seen her before. He looked her up one evening in Keats, and there she was, teeth, eyelashes, frecklings, streaks and bars, sapphires, greens, amethyst, and rubious-argent. He had always found the teeth and eyelashes repulsive and had supposed Keats was as usual piling excess on excess. Now he decided Keats must have seen one himself, or read someone who had, and felt the same mixture of aesthetic frenzy and repulsion. Mary Douglas, the anthropologist, says that *mixed* things, neither flesh nor fowl, so to speak, always excite repulsion and prohibition. The poor Lamia was a mess, as far as her head went. Her beseeching eyes were horrible. He looked up from his reading and saw her snake face peering sadly in at the window, her halo shimmering, her teeth shining like pearls. He saw to his locks: he was not about to be accidentally kissed in his sleep. They were each other's prisoners, he and she. He would paint his painting and think how to escape.

The painting was getting somewhere. The snake colours were a fourth term in the equation pool>sky>mountains-trees>paint. Their movement in the aquamarines linked and divided delectably, firing the neurones in Bernard's brain to greater and greater activity, and thus causing the Lamia to become sulkier and eventually duller and less brilliant.

"I am *so sad,* Bernard. I want to be a woman."

"You've had thousands of years already. Give me a few more days."

"You see how kind I am, when I am in pain."

What would have happened if Raymond Potter had not kept his word will never be known. Bernard had quite forgotten the liver-fluke conversation and Raymond's promised, or threatened, visit. But one day he heard wheels on his track, and saw Potter's dark red BMW creeping up its slope.

"Hide," he said to the Lamia. "Keep still. It's a dreadful Englishman of the fee-fi-fo-fum sort; he has a shouting voice, he *makes jokes,* he smokes cigars, he's bad news, *hide.*"

The Lamia slipped underwater in a flurry of bubbles like the Milky Way.

Raymond Potter came out of the car smiling and carried in a leg of wild boar and the ingredients of a ratatouille, a crate of red wine, and several bottles of eau-de-vie Poire William.

"Brought my own provisions. Show me the stove."

He cooked. They ate on the terrace, in the evening. Bernard did not switch on the lights in the pool and did not suggest that Raymond might swim. Raymond in fact did not like swimming; he was too fat to wish to be seen, and preferred eating and smoking. Both men drank rather a lot of red wine and then rather a lot of eau-de-vie. The smell of the mountains was laced with the smells of pork crackling and cigar smoke. Raymond peered drunkenly at Bernard's current painting. He pronounced it rather sinister, very striking, a bit weird, not quite usual, funny-coloured, a bit over the top? Looking at Bernard each time for a response and getting none, as Bernard, exhausted and a little drunk, was largely asleep. They went to bed, and Bernard woke in the night to realise he had not shut his bedroom window as he usually did; a shutter was banging. But he was unkissed and solitary; he slid back into unconsciousness.

The next morning Bernard was up first. He made coffee, he cycled to the village and bought croissants, bread, and peaches, he laid the table on the terrace and poured heated milk into a blue and white jug. The pool lay flat and still, quietly and incompatibly shining at the quiet sky.

Raymond made rather a noise coming downstairs. This was because his arm was round a young woman with a great deal of hennaed black hair, who wore a garment of that see-through cheesecloth from India which is sold in every southern French market. The garment was calf-length, clinging, with little shoulder straps and dyed in a rather musty brownish-black, scattered with little round green spots like peas. It could have been a sundress or a nightdress; it was only too easy to see that the woman wore nothing at all underneath. The black triangle of her pubic hair swayed with her hips. Her breasts were large and thrusting, that was the word that sprang to Bernard's mind. The nipples stood out in the cheesecloth.

"This is Melanie," Raymond said, pulling out a chair for her. She flung back her hair with an actressy gesture of her hands and sat down gracefully, pulling the cheesecloth round her knees and staring down at her ankles. She had long pale hairless legs with very pretty feet. Her toenails were varnished with a pink pearly varnish. She turned them this way and that, admiring them. She wore rather a lot of very pink lipstick and smiled in a satisfied way at her own toes.

"Do you want coffee?" said Bernard to Melanie.

"She doesn't speak English," said Raymond. He leaned over and made a guzzling, kissing noise in the hollow of her collarbone. "Do you, darling?"

He was obviously going to make no attempt to explain her presence. It was not even quite clear that he knew that Bernard had a right to an explanation, or that he had himself any idea where she had come from. He was simply obsessed. His fingers were pulled towards her hair like needles to a magnet: he kept standing up and kissing her breasts, her shoulders, her ears. Bernard watched Raymond's fat tongue explore the coil of Melanie's ear with considerable distaste.

"Will you have coffee?" he said to Melanie in French. He indicated the coffee pot. She bent her head towards it with a quick curving movement, sniffed it, and then hovered briefly over the milk jug.

"This," she said, indicating the hot milk. "I will drink this."

She looked at Bernard with huge black eyes under long lashes.

"I wish you joy," said Bernard in Cévenol French, "of your immortal soul."

"Hey," said Raymond, "don't flirt with my girl in foreign languages."

"I don't flirt," said Bernard. "I paint."

"And we'll be off after breakfast and leave you to your painting," said Raymond. "Won't we, my sweet darling? Melanie wants—Melanie hasn't got—she didn't exactly bring—you understand—all her clothes and things. We're going to go to Cannes and buy some real clothes. Melanie wants to see the film festival and the stars. You won't mind, old friend, you didn't want me in the first place. I don't want to interrupt your *painting. Chacun à sa boue,* as we used to say in the army, I know that much French."

Melanie held out her pretty fat hands and turned them over and over with considerable satisfaction. They were pinkly pale and also ornamented with pearly nail varnish. She did not look at Raymond, simply twisted her head about with what could have been pleasure at his little sallies of physical attention, or could have been irritation. She did not speak. She smiled a little, over her milk, like a satisfied cat, displaying two rows of sweet little pearly teeth between her glossy pink lips.

Raymond's packing did not take long. Melanie turned out to have one piece of luggage—a large green leather bag full of rattling coins, by the sound. Raymond saw her into the car like a princess, and came back to say goodbye to his friend.

"Have a good time," said Bernard. "Beware of philosophers."

"Where would I find any philosophers?" asked Raymond, who had done theatre design at art school with Bernard and now designed sets for a successful children's TV programme called *The A-Mazing Maze of Monsters*. "Philosophers are extinct. I think your wits are turning, old friend, with stomping around on your own. You need a girlfriend."

"I don't," said Bernard. "Have a good holiday."

"We're going to be married," said Raymond, looking surprised, as though he himself had not known this until he said it. The face of Melanie swam at the car window, the pearly teeth visible inside the soft lips, the dark eyes staring. "I must go," said Raymond. "Melanie's waiting."

Left to himself, Bernard settled back into the bliss of solitude. He looked at his latest work and saw that it was good. Encouraged, he looked at his earlier work and saw that that was good, too. All those blues, all those curious questions, all those almost-answers. The only problem was, where to go now. He walked up and down, he remembered the philosopher and laughed. He got out his Keats.

He reread the dreadful moment in *Lamia* where the bride vanished away under the coldly malevolent eye of the sage.

> Do not all charms fly
> At the mere touch of cold philosophy?
> There was an awful rainbow once in heaven:
> We know her woof, her texture; she is given
> In the dull catalogue of common things.
> Philosophy will clip an Angel's wings,
> Conquer all mysteries by rule and line,
> Empty the haunted air and gnomed mine—
> Unweave a rainbow, as it erewhile made
> The tender-personed Lamia melt into a shade.

Personally, Bernard said to himself, he had never gone along with Keats about all that stuff. By philosophy Keats seems to mean natural science, and personally he, Bernard, would rather have the optical mysteries of waves and particles in the water and light of the rainbow than any old gnome or fay. He had been at least as interested in the problems of reflection and refraction when he had had the lovely snake in his pool as he had been in its oddity—in its *otherness*—as snakes went. He hoped that no natural scientist would come along and find Melanie's blood group to be that of some sort of herpes, or do an X-ray and see something odd in her spine. She made a very good blowzy sort of a woman, just right for Raymond. He wondered what sort of a woman she would have become for him, and dismissed the problem. He didn't want a woman. He wanted another visual idea. A mystery to be explained by rule and line. He looked around his breakfast table. A rather nondescript orange-brown butterfly was sipping the juice of the rejected peaches. It had a golden eye at the base of its wings and a rather lovely white streak, shaped like a tiny dragon wing. It stood on the glistening rich yellow peach flesh and manoeuvred its body to sip the sugary juices and suddenly it was not orange-brown at all, it was a rich, gleaming intense purple.

And then it was both at once, orange-gold and purple-veiled, and then it was purple again, and then it folded its wings and the undersides had a purple eye and a soft green streak, and tan, and white edged with charcoal . . .

When he came back with his paintbox it was still turning and sipping. He mixed purple, he mixed orange, he made browns. It was done with a dusting of scales, with refractions of rays. The pigments were discovered and measured, the scales on the wings were noted and *seen,* everything was a mystery, serpents and water and light. He was off again. Exact study would not clip this creature's wings, it would dazzle his eyes with its brightness. Don't go, he begged it, watching and learning, don't go. Purple and orange is a terrible and violent fate. There is months of work in it. Bernard attacked it. He was happy, in one of the ways in which human beings are happy.

CHRIST IN THE HOUSE OF MARTHA AND MARY

Cooks are notoriously irascible. The new young woman, Dolores, was worse than most, Concepción thought. Worse and better, that was. She had an extraordinary fine nose for savours and spices, and a light hand with pastries and batters, despite her stalwart build and her solid arms. She could become a true artist, if she chose, she could go far. But she didn't know her place. She sulked, she grumbled, she complained. She appeared to think it was by some sort of unfortunate accident that she had been born a daughter of servants, and not a delicate lady like Doña Conchita who went to church in sweeping silks and a lace veil. Concepción told Dolores, not without an edge of unkindness, that she wouldn't look so good in those clothes, anyway. You are a mare built for hard work, not an Arab filly, said Concepción. You are no beauty. You are all brawn, and you should thank God for your good health in the station to which he has called you. Envy is a deadly sin.

It isn't envy, said Dolores. I want to live. I want time to think. Not to be pushed around. She studied her face in a shining copper pan, which exaggerated the heavy cheeks, the angry pout. It was true she was no beauty, but no woman likes being told so. God had made her heavy, and she hated him for it.

The young artist was a friend of Concepción's. He borrowed things, a pitcher, a bowl, a ladle, to sketch them over and over. He borrowed Concepción, too, sitting quietly in a corner, under the hooked hams and the plaits of onions and garlic, and drawing her face. He made Concepción look, if not ideally beautiful, then wise and graceful. She had good bones, a fine mouth, a wonderful pattern of lines on her brow, and etched beside her nose, which Dolores had not been interested in until she saw the shapes he made from them. His sketches of Concepción increased her own knowledge that she was not beautiful. She never spoke to him, but worked away in a kind of fury in his presence, grinding the garlic in the mortar, filleting the fish with concentrated skill, slapping dough, making a tattoo of sounds with the chopper, like hailstones, reducing onions to fine specks of translucent light. She felt herself to be a heavy space of unregarded darkness, a weight of miserable shadow in the corners of the room he was abstractedly recording. He had given Concepción an oil painting he had made, of shining fish and white solid eggs, on a chipped earthenware dish. Dolores did not know why this painting moved her. It was silly that oil paint on board should make eggs and fish more real, when they were less so. But it did. She never spoke to him, though she partly knew that if she did, he might in the end give her some small similar patch of light in darkness to treasure.

Sunday was the worst day. On Sunday, after Mass, the family entertained. They entertained family and friends, the priest and sometimes the bishop and his secretary, they sat and conversed, and Doña Conchita turned her dark eyes and her pale, long face to listen to the Fathers, as they made kindly jokes and severe pronouncements on the state of the nation, and of Christendom. There were not enough servants to keep up the flow of sweetmeats and pasties, syllabubs and jellies, quails and tartlets, so that Dolores was sometimes needed to fetch and carry as well as serve, which she did with an ill grace. She did not cast her eyes modestly down, as was expected, but stared around her angrily, watching the convolutions of Doña Conchita's neck with its pretty necklace, the tapping of her pretty foot, directed not at the padre whose words she was demurely attending to, but at young Don José on the other side of the room. Dolores put a hot dish of peppers in oil down on the table with such force that the pottery burst apart, and oil and spices ran into the damask cloth. Doña Ana, Doña Conchita's governess, berated Dolores for a whole minute, threatening dismissal, docking of wages, not only for clumsiness but for insolence. Dolores strode back into the kitchen, not slinking, but moving her large legs like walking oak trees, and began to shout. There was no need to dismiss her, she was off. This was no life for a human being. She was no worse than *they* were, and more use. She was off.

The painter was in his corner, eating her dish of elvers and *alioli*. He addressed her directly for the first time, remarking that he was much in her debt, over these last weeks, for her good nose for herbs, for her tact with sugar and spice, for her command of sweet and sour, rich and delicate. You are a true artist, said the painter, gesturing with his fork.

Dolores turned on him. He had no right to mock her, she said. He was a true artist, he could reveal light and beauty in eggs and fishes that no one had seen, and which they would then always see. She made pastries and dishes that went out of the kitchen beautiful and came back mangled and mashed—they don't notice what they're eating, they're so busy talking, and they don't eat most of it, in case they grow fat, apart from the priests, who have no other pleasures. They order it all for show, for show, and it lasts a minute only until they put the knife to it, or push it around their plate elegantly with a fork.

The painter put his head on one side, and considered her red face as he considered the copper jugs, or the glassware, narrowing his eyes to a slit. He asked her if she knew the story Saint Luke told, of Christ in the house of Martha and Mary. No, she said, she did not. She knew her catechism, and what would happen to sinners at the Last Judgment, which was on the wall of the church. And about butchered martyrs, who were also on the walls of the church.

They were sisters, the painter told her, who lived in Bethany. Jesus visited them, from time to time, and rested there. And Mary sat at his feet and listened to his words, and Martha was cumbered with much serving, as Saint Luke put it, and complained. She said to the Lord, "Dost thou not care that my sister hath left me to serve alone? Bid her therefore that she help me." And Jesus said to her, "Martha, Martha, thou art careful and troubled about many things:

but one thing is needful, and Mary hath chosen that good part, which shall not be taken away from her."

Dolores considered this, drawing her brows together in an angry frown. She said, "There speaks a man, for certain. There will always be serving, and someone will always be doomed to serving, and will have no choice or chance about the *better part*. Our Lord could make loaves and fishes from the air for the listeners, but mere mortals cannot. So we—Concepción and I—serve them whilst they have the *better part* they have chosen."

And Concepción said that Dolores should be careful, or she would be in danger of blaspheming. She should learn to accept the station the Lord had given her. And she appealed to the painter, should Dolores not learn to be content, to be patient? Hot tears sprang in Dolores's eyes. The painter said:

"By no means. It is not a question of accepting our station in the world as men have ordered it, but of learning not to be careful and troubled. Dolores here has her way to that better part, even as I have, and, like mine, it begins in attention to loaves and fishes. What matters is not that silly girls push her work about their plates with a fork, but that the work is good, that she understands what the wise understand, the nature of garlic and onions, butter and oil, eggs and fish, peppers, aubergines, pumpkins and corn. The cook, as much as the painter, looks into the essence of the creation, not, as I do, in light and on surfaces, but with all the other senses, with taste, and smell, and touch, which God also made in us for purposes. You may come at the *better part* by understanding emulsions, Dolores, by studying freshness and the edges of decay in leaves and flesh, by mixing wine and blood and sugar into sauces, as well as I may, and likely better than fine ladies twisting their pretty necks so that the light may catch their pretty pearls. You are very young, Dolores, and very strong, and very angry. You must learn *now,* that the important lesson—as long as you have your health—is that the divide is not between the servants and the served, between the leisured and the workers, but between those who are *interested* in the world and its multiplicity of forms and forces, and those who merely subsist, worrying or yawning. When I paint eggs and fishes and onions, I am painting the godhead—not only because eggs have been taken as an emblem of the Resurrection, as have dormant roots with green shoots, not only because the letters of Christ's name make up the Greek word for fish, but because the world is full of light and life, and the true crime is not to be interested in it. You have a way in. Take it. It may incidentally be a way out, too, as all skills are. The Church teaches that Mary is the contemplative life, which is higher than Martha's way, which is the active way. But any painter must question, which is which? And a cook also contemplates mysteries."

"I don't know," said Dolores, frowning. He tilted his head the other way. Her head was briefly full of images of the skeletons of fishes, of the whirlpool of golden egg-and-oil in the bowl, of the pattern of muscles in the shoulder of a goat. She said, "It is nothing, what I know. It is past in a flash. It is cooked and eaten, or it is gone bad and fed to the dogs, or thrown out."

"Like life," said the painter. "We eat and are eaten, and we are very lucky if we reach our three score years and ten, which is less than a flash in the eyes of an angel. The understanding persists, for a time. In your craft and mine."

He said, "Your frown is a powerful force in itself. I have an idea for a painting of Christ in the house of Martha and Mary. Would you let me draw you? I have noticed that you were unwilling."

"I am not beautiful."

"No. But you have power. Your anger has power, and you have power yourself, beyond that."

She had the idea, then, over the weeks and months when he visited from time to time and sketched her, and Concepción, or ate the *alioli* and supped her red peppers and raisins, praising the flavours, that he would make her heroic, a kind of goddess wielding spit and carving knife instead of spear and sword. She found herself posing, saw him noting the posing, and tried to desist. His interest in the materials of her art did indeed fire her own interest in them. She excelled herself, trying new combinations for him, offering new juices, frothing new possets. Concepción was afraid that the girl would fall in love with the artist, but in some unobtrusively clever way he avoided that. His slit stare, his compressed look of concentration, were the opposite of erotic. He talked to the girl as though she were a colleague, a partner in the mystery of his trade, and this, Concepción saw without wholly knowing that she saw it, gave Dolores a dignity, a presence, that amorous attentions would not have done. He did not show the women the sketches of themselves, though he gave them small drawings of heads of garlic and long capsicum to take to their rooms. And when, finally, the painting of *Christ in the House of Mary and Martha* was finished, he invited both women to come and look at it in his studio. He seemed, for the first time, worried about their reaction.

When they saw the painting, Concepción drew in her breath. There they both were, in the foreground at the left. She herself was admonishing the girl, pointing with a raised finger to the small scene at the top right-hand corner of the painting—was it through a window, or over a sill, or was it an image of an image on a wall? it was not clear—where Christ addressed the holy staring woman crouched at his feet whilst her sister stood stolidly behind, looking also like Concepción, who had perhaps modelled for her from another angle. But the light hit four things—the silvery fish, so recently dead that they were still bright-eyed, the solid white gleam of the eggs, emitting light, the heads of garlic, half-peeled and life-like, and the sulky, fleshy, furiously frowning face of the girl, above her fat red arms in their brown stuff sleeves. He had immortalised her ugliness, Concepción thought, she would never forgive him. She was used to paintings of patient and ethereal Madonnas. This was living flesh, in a turmoil of watchful discontent. She said, "Look how real the eyes of the fishes are," and her voice trailed foolishly away, as she and the painter watched the live Dolores watch her image.

She stood and stared. She stared. The painter shifted from foot to foot. Then she said, "Oh yes, I see what you saw, how very strange." She said, "How very strange, to have been looked at so intently." And then she began to laugh. When she laughed, all the down-drooping lines of cheek and lip moved up and apart. The knit brows sprang apart, the eyes shone with amusement, the young voice pealed out. The momentary coincidence between image and woman vanished, as though the rage was still and eternal in the painting and the woman was released into time. The laughter was infectious, as laughter is; after a moment Concepción, and then the painter, joined in. He produced wine, and the women uncovered the offering they had brought, spicy tortilla and salad greens. They sat down and ate together.

COLD

In a temperate kingdom, in the midst of a landmass, with great meandering rivers but no seashores, with deciduous forests, and grassy plains, a princess was born on a blue summer day. She was eagerly awaited, although she was the thirteenth child, for the first twelve royal children were all princes, and her mother longed for gentleness and softness, whilst her powerful father longed for delicacy and beauty. She was born after a long labour, which lasted a day and a night, just as the sun began to colour the sky, but before it had warmed the earth. She was born, like most babies, squashed and livid, with a slicked cap of thick black hair. She was slight enough, but perfectly shaped, and when the nurses had washed off her protective waxy crust the blood began to run red and rapid, to the tips of her fine fingers and under the blue of her lips. She had a fine, transparent skin, so the blush of blood was fiery and rosy; when her hair was washed, it sprang into a soft, black fur. She was pronounced—and was—beautiful. Her exhausted mother, whose own blood began to stir faster again as the child was laid on her breast, said she should be named Fiammarosa, a name that just came into her head at that moment, as a perfect description. Her father came in, and picked her up in her new rosy shawl, holding the tiny creature clasped in his two huge hands, with her little red legs waving, and her composed pink face yawning perfectly above his thumbs. He was, like his father before him, like all the kings of that country, a large, strong, golden-bearded, deep-voiced, smiling man, a good soldier who avoided conflict, a good huntsman who never killed heaps and droves of creatures, but enjoyed the difficulty of the chase, the dark of the forests, the rush of the rivers. When he saw his daughter, he fell in love with her vulnerable fragility, as fathers do. No one shall ever hurt you, he said to the little creature, whose wavering hand brushed against the soft curls of his beard, whose fingers touched his warm lips. No one. He kissed his wife's damp brow, and she smiled.

When Fiammarosa was a few months old, the sooty first hair, as it does, came out in wisps and strands, collecting on her white lawn pillows. In its place, slowly and strongly, grew pale golden hair, so pale it shone silver when the light was in it, though it could be sunny yellow seen against scalp, or brow, or, as it grew, on her narrow neck. As she drank in her mother's milk, she became milky; the flush faded as though it had never been, and the child's skin became softly pale, like white rose petals. Her bones were very fine, and the baby chubbiness all children assume before they move was only fleeting in her; she had sharp cheekbones, and a fine nose and chin, long, fine, sharp fingers and toes, even as an infant. Her eyes, under white brows and pearly eyelids, retained that dark, deep colour that is no colour, that in the newborn we call blue. The baby, said the nurse, was like fine bone china. She looked breakable. She behaved as though she herself thought she was fragile, moving little, and with a cautious carefulness. As she grew, and learned to crawl, and to walk, she grew thinner and whiter. The doctors pronounced her "delicate." She must be kept warm, they said, and rest frequently. She must be fed well, on nourishing things, things that would fill her out—she must drink concentrated soups, full of meat juices and rich with vegetables, she must have creams and zabagliones, fresh fruits and nourishing custards. This regime had a certain success. The white limbs filled out, the child's cheeks rounded over those edged bones, she acquired a pretty pout and faint dimples on her little fists. But with the milky flesh came languor. Her pale head dropped on its pale stalk. The gold hair lay flat and gleaming, unmoving like the surface of a still liquid. She walked at the right age, spoke at the right age, was docile and learned good manners without fuss. She had a habit of yawning, opening her shell-pink lips to show a row of perfect, gleaming, tiny white teeth, and a rosy tongue and gullet. She learned to put out a limp hand in front of this involuntary grimace, which had an aspect of intense laziness, and another aspect, her mother once thought, of a perfectly silent howl or cry.

Never was a young girl more loved. Her parents loved her, her nurses loved her, her twelve brothers, from the young men to the little boys, loved her, and tried to think of ways to please her, and to bring roses to the pale cheeks and a smile to the soft mouth. In spring weather, well wrapped in lambswool shawls and fur bonnets, she was driven out in a little carriage, in which she lolled amongst soft cushions, staring indifferently at the trees and the sky. She had her own little rose garden, with a pool full of rosy fish in green deeps, and a swing on which, in the warmest, brightest weather, her brothers pushed her gently to and fro, whilst she leaned her face on the cool chains and looked down at the grass. Picnics were brought out to this garden, and Fiammarosa reclined on a grassy slope, swathed in soft muslins, with a wide straw hat tied under her chin with pink ribbons, to protect her from sunburn. It was discovered that she had a taste for water ices, flavoured with blackberry and raspberry, and for chilled slices of watermelon. These delicacies brought a fleeting smile to her normally expressionless face. She liked to lie on the grassy bank and watch her brothers play badminton, but any suggestion, as she grew older, that she might join in brought on an attack of yawning, a drooping, a retreat to the darkened rooms of the palace. Her brothers brought her presents; she was unimpressed by parakeets and kittens, but became curiously attached to a little silver hand mirror, engraved with twining roses, from her eldest brother.

Her tutor loved her, too. He was a brilliant young man, destined to be a professor, who was writing a great history of the kingdom from its remotest beginnings, and had not wanted the court appointment at all. He loved her not despite, but because of, her lethargy. He was sorry for her. There were days when, for no reason he could discern, she was able to sit upright and concentrate, infrequent days when she suddenly surprised him with a page of elegant calculations, or an opinion as piercingly clever as it was unexpected, on a poem or a drawing he was discussing with her. She was no fool, Fiammarosa, but there was no life in her, most of the time. She yawned. She drooped. He would leave their study to fetch a book, and return to find the white head dropped onto the circle of the milky arms on the table, a picture of lassitude and boredom, or, just possibly, of despair. He asked her, on one of these days, if she felt ill, and she said, no, why should she?, directing at him a blank, gentle, questioning look. I feel much as usual, she said. Much as I always feel. She spoke, he thought, with a desperate patience. He closed the window, to keep out the draught.

During her early years, the earth went through one of its periodic coolings. Autumn came earlier and earlier, the rose leaves were blown about the enclosed garden, there was a nip in the air in late summer, and snow on the ground before the turn of the year. The palace people redoubled their efforts to protect the Princess, installing velvet curtains and bed-hangings. On very cold nights, they lit a fire in the pretty fireplace in her bedroom, so that the coloured streamers of reflected flames chased each other across the carved ceiling, and moved in the soft hangings on the walls. Fiammarosa was now at the edge of girlhood, almost a woman, and her dreams troubled her. She dreamed of dark blue spaces, in which she travelled, without moving a muscle, at high speeds above black and white fields and forests. In her dreams she heard the wind coil, howling, round the outside walls, and its shriek woke her, so that she heard with her ears what she had dreamed in her skull. The wind spoke with many voices, soft and shrill, rushing and eddying. Fiammarosa wanted to see it. She felt stifled in her soft blankets, in her lambswool gown. She went to the window, and dragged open the curtain. Behind it, her breath, the breath of the room, had frozen into white and glistening feathers and flowers on the glass, into illusory, disproportionate rivers with tributaries and frozen falls. Through these transparent, watery forms she could see the lawns and bushes, under snow, and the long tips of icicles poured down from the eaves above her. She put her cheek against the frozen tracery, and felt a bite, a burn, that was both painful and intensely pleasurable. Her soft skin adhered, ever so slightly, to the ice. Her eyes took in the rounded forms of the lawns under snow, the dark blue shadows across it, the glitter where the light from her window sliced it, and the paler glitter where the moonlight touched the surface. And her body came alive with the desire to lie out there, on that whiteness, face-to-face with it, fingertips and toes pushing into the soft crystals. The whole of her short, cosseted history was against her; she drew back from the glass, telling herself that although the snow blanket looked soft and pretty it was dangerous and threatening; its attraction was an illusion of the glass.

But all the next day, she was possessed by this image of her own naked body, stretched on a couch of snow. And the next night, when the palace was dark and silent, she put on a flowered silk wrap, covered with summer poppies, and crept down the stairs, to see if there was a way out into the garden. But all the doors she could find were locked, and barred, and she was discovered by a patrolling guardsman, to whom she said with a tentative smile that she had come down because she was hungry. He was not to know that she always had sweet biscuits by her bed. So he took her to the kitchen, and poured a glass of milk for her in the larder, and found her some white bread and jam, which she nibbled, still smiling at him, as she questioned him about his work, the places where the keys were kept, the times of his patrols. When she followed him into the larder, as he ladled milk from a great stone jar in the light of a candle, she felt cold rise from the stone floor, and pour from the thick walls, and sing outside the open grated window. The guard begged her to go into the kitchen—"You will catch your death in this draught," he said—but the Princess was stretching her fingers to touch the eddying air.

She thanked him prettily, and went back to her hot little room where, after a moment's thought, she took her wrought-iron poker and broke up the banked coals of her fire, feeling faint as she hung over it, with the smoke and the bright sparks, but happy, as the life went out of the coals, the reds burned darker, and were replaced by fine white ash, like the snow. Then she took off her gown, and rolled open the nest of bedclothes, and pulled back the great curtains—it was not possible to open the window—and lay back, feeling the sweat of her efforts cool delectably in the crevices of her skin.

The next night she reconnoitred the corridors and cupboards, and the night after that she went down in the small hours, and took a small key from a hook, a key that unlocked a minor side door, that led to the kitchen garden, which was now, like everywhere else, under deep snow, the taller herbs stiffly draggled, the tufted ones humped under white, the black branches brittle with the white coating frozen along their upper edges. It was full moon. Everything was black and white and silver. The Princess crept in her slippers between the beds of herbs, and then bent down impulsively and pulled off the slippers. The cold snow on the soles of her feet gave her the sense of bliss that most humans associate with warm frills of water at the edge of summer seas, with sifted sand, with sunny stone. She ran faster. Her blood hummed. Her pale hair floated in the wind of her own movement in the still night. She went under an arch and out through a long ride, running lightly under dark, white-encrusted boughs, into what in summer was a meadow. She did not know why she did what she did next. She had always been decorous and docile. Her body was full of an electric charge, a thrill, from an intense cold. She threw off her silk wrap, and her creamy woollen nightgown, and lay for a moment, as she had imagined lying, with her naked skin on the cold white sheet. She did not sink; the crust was icy and solid. All along her body, in her knees, her thighs, her small round belly, her pointed breasts, the soft inner skin of her arms, she felt an intense version of that paradoxical burn she had received from the touch of the frosted window. The snow did not numb Fiammarosa; it pricked and hummed and brought her, intensely, to life. When her front was quite chilled, she turned over on her back, and lay there, safe inside the form of her own faint impression on the untouched surface. She stared up, at the great moon with its slaty shadows on its white-gold disk, and the huge fields of scattered, clustered, far-flung glittering wheeling stars in the deep darkness, white on midnight, and she was, for the first time in her life, happy. This is who I am, the cold Princess thought to herself, wriggling for sheer pleasure in the snow-dust, this is what I want. And when she was quite cold, and completely alive and crackling with energy, she rose to her feet, and began a strange, leaping dance, pointing sharp fingers at the moon, tossing her long mane of silver hair, sparkling with ice crystals, circling and bending and finally turning cartwheels under the wheeling sky. She could feel the cold penetrating her surfaces, all over, insistent and relentless. She even thought that some people might have thought that this was painful. But for her, it was bliss. She went in with the dawn, and lived through the day in an alert, suspended, dreaming state, waiting for the deep dark, and another excursion into the cold.

Night after night, now, she went and danced in the snowfield. The deep frost held and she began to be able to carry some of her cold energy back into her daily work. At the same time, she began to notice changes in her body. She was growing thinner, rapidly—the milky softness induced by her early regime was replaced with a slender, sharp, bony beauty. And one night, as she moved, she found that her whole body was encased in a transparent, crackling skin of ice, that broke into spiderweb-fine veined sheets as she danced, and then reformed. The sensation of this double skin was delicious. She had frozen eyelashes and saw the world through an ice-lens; her tossing hair made a brittle and musical sound, for each hair was coated and frozen. The faint sounds of shivering and splintering and clashing made a kind of whispered music as she danced on. In the daytime now, she could barely keep awake, and her nighttime skin persisted patchily in odd places, at the nape of her neck, around her wrists, like bracelets. She tried to sit by the window, in her lessons, and also tried surreptitiously to open it, to let in the cold wind, when Hugh, her tutor, was briefly out of the room. And then, one day, she came down, rubbing frost out of her eyelashes with rustling knuckles, and found the window wide open, Hugh wrapped in a furred jacket, and a great book open on the table.

"Today," said Hugh, "we are going to read the history of your ancestor, King Beriman, who made an expedition to the kingdoms beyond the mountains, in the frozen North, and came back with an icewoman."

Fiammarosa considered Hugh.

"Why?" she said, putting her white head on one side, and looking at him with sharp, pale blue eyes between the stiff lashes.

"I'll show you," said Hugh, taking her to the open window. "Look at the snow on the lawns, in the rose garden."

And there, lightly imprinted, preserved by the frost, were the tracks of fine bare feet, running lightly, skipping, eddying, dancing.

Fiammarosa did not blush; her whiteness became whiter, the ice-skin thicker. She was alive in the cold air of the window.

"Have you been watching me?"

"Only from the window," said Hugh, "to see that you came to no harm. You can see that the only footprints are fine, and elegant, and naked. If I had followed you I should have left tracks."

"I see," said Fiammarosa.

"And," said Hugh, "I have been watching you since you were a little girl, and I recognise happiness and health when I see it."

"Tell me about the icewoman."

"Her name was Fror. She was given by her father, as a pledge for a truce between the ice-people and King Beriman. The chronicles describe her as wondrously fair and slender, and they say also that King Beriman loved her distractedly, and that she did not return his love. They say she showed an ill will, liked to haunt caverns and rivers and refused to learn the language of this kingdom. They say she danced by moonlight, on the longest night, and that there were those in the kingdom who believed she was a witch, who had enchanted the King. She was seen, dancing naked, with three white hares, which were thought to be creatures of witchcraft, under the moon, and was imprisoned in the cells under the palace. There she gave birth to a son, who was taken from her, and given to his father. And the priests wanted to burn the icewoman, 'to melt her stubbornness and punish her stiffness,' but the King would not allow it.

"Then one day, three northmen came riding to the gate of the castle, tall men with axes on white horses, and said they had come 'to take back our woman to her own air.' No one knew how they had been summoned: the priests said that it was by witchcraft that she had called to them from her stone cell. It may have been. It seems clear that there was a threat of war if the woman was not relinquished. So she was fetched out, and 'wrapped in a cloak to cover her thinness and decay' and told she could ride away with her kinsmen. The chronicler says she did not ask to see her husband or her tiny son, but 'cold and unfeeling as she had come' mounted behind one of the northmen and they turned and rode away together.

"And King Beriman died not long after, of a broken heart or of witchcraft, and his brother reigned until Leonin was old enough to be crowned. The chronicler says that Leonin made a 'warm-blooded and warm-hearted' ruler, as though the blood of his forefathers ran true in him, and the 'frozen lymph' of his maternal stock was melted away to nothing.

"But I believe that after generations, a lost face, a lost being, can find a form again."

"You think I am an icewoman."

"I think you carry the inheritance of that northern princess. I think also that her nature was much misunderstood, and that what appeared to be kindness was extreme cruelty—paradoxically, probably her life was preserved by what appeared to be the cruellest act of those who held her here, the imprisonment in cold stone walls, the thin prison dress, the bare diet."

"I felt that in my bones, listening to your story."

"It is *your* story, Princess. And you too are framed for cold. You must live—when the thaw comes—in cool places. There are ice-houses in the palace gardens—we must build more, and stock them with blocks of ice, before the snow melts."

Fiammarosa smiled at Hugh with her sharp mouth. She said:

"You have read my desires. All through my childhood I was barely alive. I felt constantly that I must collapse, vanish, fall into a faint, stifle. Out there, in the cold, I am a living being."

"I know."

"You choose your words very tactfully, Hugh. You told me I was 'framed for cold.' That is a statement of natural philosophy, and time. It may be that I have ice in my veins, like the icewoman, or something that boils and steams at normal temperatures, and flows busily in deep frost. But you did not tell me I had a cold nature. The icewoman did not look back at her husband and son. Perhaps she was cold in her soul, as well as in her veins?"

"That is for you to say. It is so long ago, the tale of the icewoman. Maybe she saw King Beriman only as a captor and conqueror? Maybe she loved someone else, in the North, in the snow? Maybe she felt as you feel, on a summer's day, barely there, yawning for faintness, moving in shadows."

"How do you know how I feel, Hugh?"

"I watch you. I study you. I love you."

Fiammarosa noticed, in her cool mind, that she did not love Hugh, whatever love was.

She wondered whether this was a loss, or a gain. She was inclined to think, on balance, that it was a gain. She had been so much loved, as a little child, and all that heaping of anxious love had simply made her feel ill and exhausted. There was more life in coldness. In solitude. Inside a crackling skin of protective ice that was also a sensuous delight.

After this clarification, even when the thaw came, and the snow ran away, and fell in damp, crashing masses from the roof and the branches, Fiammarosa's life was better. Hugh convinced the King and Queen that their daughter needed to be cold to survive, and the ingenuity that had been put into keeping her warm and muffled was diverted, on his suggestion, into the construction of ice-houses, and cool bedrooms with stone walls on the north side of the palace. The new Fiammarosa was full of spiky life. She made little gardens of mountain snow-plants around her ice-retreats, which stood like so many summerhouses in the woods and the gardens. No one accused her of witchcraft—this was a later age—but there was perhaps a little less love for this coldly shining, fiercely energetic, sharp being than there had been for the milky girl in her rosy cushions. She studied snow crystals and ice formations under a magnifying glass, in the winter, and studied the forms of her wintry flowers and mosses in the summer. She became an artist—all princesses are compelled to be artists, they must spin, or draw, or embroider, and she had always dutifully done so, producing heaps of cushions and walls of good-enough drawings. She hated "good enough" but had had to be content with it. Now she began to weave tapestries, with silver threads and ice-blue threads, with night violets and cool primroses, which mixed the geometric forms of the snow crystals with the delicate forms of the moss and rosettes of petals, and produced shimmering, intricate tapestries that were much more than "good enough," that were unlike anything seen before in that land. She became an assiduous correspondent, writing to gardeners and natural philosophers, to spinners of threads and weavers all over the world. She was happy, and in the winter, when the world froze again under an iron-grey sky, she was ecstatic.

Princesses, also, are expected to marry. They are expected to marry for dynastic reasons, to cement an alliance, to placate a powerful rival, to bear royal heirs. They are, in the old stories, gifts and rewards, handed over by their loving fathers to heroes and adventurers who must undergo trials, or save people. It would appear, Fiammarosa had thought as a young girl, reading both histories and wonder tales, that princesses are commodities. But also, in the same histories and tales, it can be seen that this is not so. Princesses are captious and clever choosers. They tempt and test their suitors, they sit like spiders inside walls adorned with the skulls of the unsuccessful, they require superhuman feats of strength and cunning from their suitors, and are not above helping out, or weeping over, those who appeal to their hearts. They follow their chosen lovers through rough deserts, and ocean tempests, they ride on the wings of the north wind and enlist the help of ants and eagles, trout and mice, hares and ducks, to rescue these suddenly helpless husbands from the clutches of scheming witches, or ogre-kings. They do have, in real life, the power to reject and some power to choose. They are wooed. She had considered her own cold heart in this context and had thought that she would do better, ideally, to remain unmarried. She was too happy alone to make a good bride. She could not think out a course of action entirely but had vaguely decided upon a course of prevarication and intimidation, if suitors presented themselves. For their own sakes, as much as for her own. She was sorry, in the abstract—she thought a great deal in the abstract, it suited her—for anyone who should love her, or think it a good idea to love her. She did not believe she was truly lovable. Beside her parents, and her brothers, whose love was automatic and unseeing, the only person who truly loved her was Hugh. And her cold eye, and her cold mind, had measured the gulf between what Hugh felt for her and what she felt for him. She tried never to let it show; she was grateful, his company was comfortable to her. But both he and she were intelligent beings, and both knew how things stood.

The King had his own ideas, which he believed were wise and subtle, about all this. He believed his daughter needed to marry more than most women. He believed she needed to be softened and opened to the world, that she had inherited from the unsatisfactory icewoman a dangerous, brittle edge which would hurt her more than anyone else. He believed it would be good for his daughter to be melted smooth, though he did not, in his thinking, push this metaphor too far. He had a mental image of an icicle running with water, not of an absent icicle and a warm, formless pool. He thought the sensible thing would be to marry this cold creature to a prince from the ice lands from which the original Fror had been snatched by King Beriman, and he sent letters to Prince Boris, beyond the mountains, with a sample of his daughter's weaving, and a painting of her white beauty, her fine bones, blue eyes, and cool gold hair. He was a great believer in protocol, and protocol had always, at these times, meant that the picture and the invitation must go to many princes, and not only one. There must be a feast, and something of a competition. What happened customarily was that the Princess's portrait would go simultaneously (allowing for the vagaries of horses and camels, galleons and mule trains) to many eligible princes. The princes, in turn, on receiving the portrait, would return gifts, sumptuous gifts, striking gifts, to the King, to be given to the Princess. And if she found them acceptable (or if her father did), then the princes would make the journey in person, and the Princess, in person, would make her choice. In this way, the King offended none of his proud neighbours, leaving the choice to the whim, or the aesthetic inclination, of the young woman herself. Of course, if there were any pressing reason why one alliance was more desirable than another, most fathers would enlighten their daughters, and some would exhort or threaten. In the case of Fiammarosa none of this applied. Her father wished her to marry for her own good, and he wished her to marry Prince Boris simply because his kingdom was cold and full of icebergs and glaciers, where she would be at home. But he did not say this, for he knew that women are perverse.

The portraits, the letters, dispersed through the known world. After a time, the presents began to return. A small golden envoy from the East brought a silken robe, flame-coloured, embroidered with peacocks, light as air. A rope of pearls, black, rose, and luminous pale ones, the size of larks' eggs, came from an island kingdom, and a three-dimensional carved chess game, all in different jades, with little staircases and turrets edged with gold, came from a tiny country between two deserts. There were heaps of gold and silver plates, a leopard in a cage, which sickened and died, a harp, a miniature pony, and an illuminated treatise on necromancy. The King and

Queen watched Fiammarosa as she gravely thanked the messengers. She appeared to be interested in the mechanism of an Orcalian musical box, but only *scientifically* interested, so to speak. Then Prince Boris's envoy arrived, a tall fair man with a gold beard and two gold plaits, riding a hairy, flea-bitten warhorse, and followed by packhorses with great pine chests. He opened these with a flourish, and brought out a robe of silver fox fur, an extraordinary bonnet, hung with the black-tipped tails of ermine stoats, and a whalebone box, polished like a new tooth, containing a necklace of bears' claws threaded on a silver chain. The Princess put her thin hands, involuntarily, to her slender throat. The envoy said that the necklace had been worn by Prince Boris's mother, and by her mother before her. He was clad in fleeces and wore a huge circular fur hat coming down over his ears. Fiammarosa said that the gifts were magnificent. She said this so gracefully that her mother looked to see if some ancestral inkling in her responded to bears' claws. There was no colour at all in her lips, or in her cheeks, but with her that could be a sign of pleasure—she whitened, where other women blushed. The King thought to himself that a man and his gifts were not the same thing. He thought that the narrow neck would have a barbaric beauty, circled by the polished sharp claws, but he did not wish to see it.

The last envoy declared that he was not the last envoy, having been parted from his fellows on their dangerous voyage. They had travelled separately, so that one at least of them might arrive with his gift. Prince Sasan, he said, had been much moved by the Princess's portrait. She was the woman he had seen in his dreams, said the envoy, lyrically. The Princess, whose dreams entertained no visitors, only white spaces, wheeling birds and snowflakes, smiled composedly, without warmth. The envoy's gift took a long time to unwrap. It was packed in straw, and fine leather, and silk. When it was revealed, it appeared at first sight to be a rough block of ice. Then, slowly, it was seen to be a glass palace, within the ice, so to speak, as hallucinatory turrets and chambers, fantastic carvings and pillars, reveal themselves in the ice and snow of mountain peaks. But once the eye had learned to read the irregularities of the surface, the magnifications and the tunnels within the block, it was seen to be a most cunningly wrought and regularly shaped transparent castle, within whose shining walls corridors ran into fretted chambers, staircases (with carved balustrades) mounted and descended in spirals and curves, in which thrones and pompous curtained beds stood in glistening cubicles, in which miraculous fine curtains of translucent glass floated between archways in still space. The glass castle was large enough for the centre to be hidden from the eye, though all the wide landings, the narrow passages, the doors and gangways, directed the eye to where the thickness of the transparent glass itself resisted penetration. Fiammarosa touched its cool surface with a cool finger. She was entranced by the skill of the layering. It was all done in a crystal-clear glass, with a green-blue tinge to it in places, and a different green-blue conferred simply by thickness itself. The eye looked through, and through, and in. Light went through, and through, and in. Solid walls of light glittered and, seen through their substance, trapped light hung in bright rooms like bubbles. There was one other colour, in all the perspectives of blue, green, and clear. From the dense, invisible centre little tongues of rosy flame (made of glass) ran along the corridors, mounted, gleaming, in the stairwells and hallways, threaded like ribbons round galleries, separated, and joined again as flames do, round pillars and gates. Behind a curtain of blue, a thread of rose and flame shone and twisted. The Princess walked round, and back, looking in. "It is an image of my master's heart," said the lyrical envoy. "It is a poetic image of his empty life, which awaits the delicate warmth of the Princess Fiammarosa in every chamber. He has been set on fire by his vision of the portrait of the Princess."

The envoy was a sallow young man, with liquid brown eyes. The bluff King and the careful Queen were not impressed by his rhetoric. The Princess went on walking round the glass block, staring in. It was not clear that she had heard his latest remarks.

★

The second envoy from Prince Sasan arrived a few days later, dusty and travel-worn, another sallow man with brown eyes. His gift was dome-shaped. He too, as he unwrapped it, spoke lyrically of the contents. He did not appear to be speaking to a script; lyricism appeared to spring naturally to the lips of the Sasanians. His gift, he said, was an image, a metaphor, a symbol, for the sweetness and light, the summer world which the thought of the Princess had created in the mind of his master.

The second gift was also made of glass. It was a beehive, a transparent, shining form constructed of layers of hexagonal cells, full of white glass grubs, and amber-coloured glass honey. Over the surface of the cells crawled, and in the solid atmosphere hung and floated, wonderfully wrought insects, with furry bodies, veined wings, huge eyes, and fine antennae. They even carried bags of golden pollen on their black, thread-glass legs. Around the hive were glass flowers with petals of crumpled and gleaming yellow glass, with crowns of fine stamens, with bluebells and fine-throated purple hoods. A fat bee was half-buried in the heart of a spotted snapdragon. Another uncoiled a proboscis and sipped the heart of a campanula. So, said the lyrical envoy, was the heart of his master touched by the warm thought of the Princess, so was love seeded, and sweetness garnered, in the garden of his heart. Hugh thought that this might be too much for his austere pupil, but she was not listening. She had laid her cool cheek against the cool glass dome, as if to catch the soundless hum of the immobile spun-glass wings.

The third envoy arrived bloodied and incoherent. He had been set upon by bandits and had been forced to hide his package in a hollow tree, from which he had retrieved it, late at night. He unpacked it before the court, murmuring incoherently, "So delicate, I shall be tortured, never forgiven, has harm come to it?" His package was in two parts, tall and cylindrical, fat and spherical. Out of the cylindrical part came a tall glass stem, and a series of fine, fine, glass rods, olive green, amber, white, which he built, breathing heavily, into an extraordinarily complex web of branches and twigs. It was large—the height, maybe, of a two-year-old child. Folded into his inner garments he had a plan of the intervals of the sprouting of the branches. The assembly took a long time—the Queen suggested that they go and take refreshment and leave the poor, anxious man to complete his labour unobserved and in peace, but Fiammarosa was entranced. She watched each slender stem find its place, breathing quietly, staring intently. The spherical parcel proved to contain a pleroma of small spherical parcels, all nestling together, from which the envoy took a whole world of flowers, fruit, twining creepers, little birds, frost-forms and ice-forms. Part of the tree he hung with buds, tight and bursting, mossy and glistening, rosy and sooty-black. Then he hung blossoms of every kind, apple and cherry, magnolia and catkins, hypericum and chestnut candles. Then he added, radiating between all these, the fruits, oranges and lemons, silver pears and golden apples, rich plums and damsons, ruddy pomegranates and clustered translucent crimson berries and grapes with the bloom on them. Each tiny element was in itself an example of virtuoso glass-making. When he had hung the flowers and the fruit, he perched the birds, a red cardinal, a white dove, a black-capped rosy-breasted bull-finch, a blue Australian wren, an iridescent kingfisher, a blackbird with a gold beak, and in the centre, on the crest of the branches, a bird of paradise with golden eyes in its midnight tail, and a crest of flame. Then he hung winter on the remaining branches, decorating sharp black twigs with filigree leaf skeletons, flounces of snow, and sharp icicles, catching the light and making rainbows in the air. This, he said breathlessly, was his master's world as it would be if the Princess consented to be his wife, a paradise state with all seasons in one, and the tree of life flowering and fruiting perpetually. There is bleak winter, too, said the Princess, setting an icicle in motion. The envoy looked soulfully at her and said that the essential sap of trees lived through the frost, and so it was with the tree of life, of which this was only an image.

The Princess did not leave the tree for the rest of the day. Look, she said to Hugh, at the rich patterning of the colours, look at the way the light shines in the globes of the fruit, the seeds of the pomegranate, the petals of the flowers. Look at the beetles in the clefts of the trunk, like tiny jewels, look at the feathers in the spun-glass tail of the bird. What kind of a man would have made this?

"Not a prince, a craftsman," said Hugh, a little jealous. "A prince merely finds the best man, and pays him. A prince, at most, makes the metaphor, and the craftsman carries it out."

"I make my own weaving," said the Princess. "I design and I weave my own work. It is possible that a prince made the castle, the hive, and the tree."

"It is possible," said Hugh. "A prince with a taste for extravagant metaphor."

"Would you prefer a necklace of bears' claws," asked the ice-woman, "if you were a woman? Would you?"

"A man and his gifts are two things," said Hugh. "And glass is not ice."

"What do you mean?" asked the Princess. But Hugh would say no more.

The princes arrived, after a month or two, in person. Five had made the journey, Prince Boris, the plump dusky prince who had sent the pearls, the precise, silk-robed prince who had sent the silk robe, the curly, booted, and spurred prince who had sent the chess game, and Prince Sasan, who arrived last, having travelled furthest. Prince Boris, the King thought, was a fine figure of a man, strong like an oak tree, with golden plaits and a golden beard. His pale-blue eyes were icy pools, but there were wrinkles of laughter in their corners. Prince Sasan rode up on a fine-boned, delicate horse, black as soot, and trembling with nerves. He insisted on seeing to its stabling himself, though he was accompanied by a meagre retinue of squires with the same sallow skins and huge brown eyes as the envoys. His own hair was black, like his horse, and hung, fine and dry and very straight, in a dark fringe, and a dark curtain, ending at his shoulders.

He was a small man, a little shorter than Fiammarosa, but his shoulders were powerful. His face was narrow and his skin dark gold. His nose was sharp and arched, his brows black lines, his lashes long and dark over dark eyes, deeper-set than the envoys'. Prince Boris had a healthy laugh, but Prince Sasan was catlike and silent. He made his bows, and spoke his greetings, and then appeared content to watch events as though he was the audience, not the actor. He took Fiammarosa's hand in his thin hand, when he met her, and lifted it to his lips, which were thin and dry. "Enchanted," said Prince Sasan. "Delighted," said the icewoman, coolly. That was all.

The visits were the occasion of much diplomacy and various energetic rides and hunting expeditions, on which, since it was high summer, the Princess did not join the company. In the evenings, there were feasts, and musical entertainments. The island prince had brought two porcelain-skinned ladies who played exquisite tinkling tunes on xylophones. The curly prince had a minstrel with a harp, and Prince Boris had two huntsmen who played a rousing, and bloodcurdling, duet on hunting horns. The Princess was sitting between Boris and the curly prince, and had been hearing tales of the long winters, the Northern Lights, the floating icebergs. Prince Sasan beckoned his squire, who unwrapped a long black pipe, with a reed mouthpiece, from a scarlet silk cloth. This he handed to the Prince, who set it to his own lips, and blew one or two tentative notes, reedy, plangent, to set the pitch. "I based this music," he said, looking down at the table, "on the songs of the goatherds." He began to play. It was music unlike anything they had ever heard. Long, long, wavering breaths, with pure notes chasing each other through them; long calls which rose and rose, trembled and danced on the air, fell, whispered, and vanished. Circlings of answering phrases, flights, bird cries, rest. The Princess's mind was full of water frozen in mid-fall, or finding a narrow channel between ribs and arches of ice. When the strange piping came to an end, everyone complimented the Prince on his playing. Hugh said, "I have never heard such long phrases ride on one breath."

"I have good lungs," said Prince Sasan. "Glassblower's lungs."

"The glass is your own work?" said the Princess.

"Of course it is," said Prince Sasan.

The Princess said that it was very beautiful. Prince Sasan said:

"My country is not rich, though it is full of space, and I think it is beautiful. I cannot give you precious stones. My country is largely desert: we have an abundance only of sand, and glassblowing is one of our ancient crafts. All Sasanian princes are glassblowers. The secrets are handed on from generation to generation."

"I did not know glass was made from sand," said the Princess. "It resembles frozen water."

"It is sand, melted and fused," said Prince Sasan. His eyes were cast down.

"In a furnace of flames," said Hugh, impulsively. "It is melted and fused in a furnace of flames."

The Princess trembled slightly. Prince Sasan lifted his gaze, and his black look met her blue one. There were candles between them, and she saw golden flames reflected in his dark eyes, whilst he saw white flames in her clear ones. She knew she should look away, and did not. Prince Sasan said:

"I have come to ask you to be my wife, and to come with me to my land of sand dunes and green sea waves and shores. Now I have seen you, I—"

He did not finish the sentence.

Prince Boris said that deserts were monotonous and hot. He said he was sure the Princess would prefer mountains and forests and rushing cold winds.

The Princess trembled a little more. Prince Sasan made a deprecating gesture with his thin hand, and stared into his plate, which contained sliced peaches, in red wine, on a nest of crushed ice.

"I will come with you to the desert," said the Princess. "I will come with you to the desert, and learn about glassblowing."

"I am glad of that," said Prince Sasan. "For I do not know how I should have gone on, if you had not."

And amidst the mild uproar caused by the departure from protocol, and the very real panic and fear of the King and Queen and Hugh, the two of them sat and looked steadily across the table at the reflected flames in each other's eyes.

Once it became clear that the Princess's mind was made up, those who loved her stopped arguing, and the wedding took place. Fiammarosa asked Hugh to come with her to her new home, and he answered that he could not. He could not live in a hot climate, he told her, with his very first note of sharpness. Fiammarosa was glittering, restless and brittle with love. Hugh saw that she could not see him, that she saw only the absent Sasan, that dark, secret face imposed on his own open one. And he did not know, he added, having set his course, how she herself would survive. Love changes people, Fiammarosa told him in a small voice. Human beings are adaptable, said the icewoman. If I use my intelligence, and my willpower, she said, I shall be able to live there; I shall certainly die if I cannot be with the man on whom my heart is set. He will melt you into a puddle, Hugh told her, but only silently, and in his mind. She had never been so beautiful as she was in her wedding gown, white as snow, with lace like frost crystals, with a sash blue as thick ice, and her pale face sharp with happiness and desire in the folds of transparent veiling.

The young pair spent the first week of their marriage in her old home, before setting out on the long journey to her new one. All eyes were on them, each day, as they came down from their bedchamber to join the company. The housemaids whispered of happily bloodstained sheets—much rumpled, they added, most vigorously disturbed. The Queen observed to the King that the lovers had eyes only for each other, and he observed, a little sorrowfully, that this was indeed so. His daughter's sharp face grew sharper, and her eyes grew bluer and clearer; she could be seen to sense the presence of the dark Sasan behind her head, across a room, through a door. He moved quietly, like a cat, the southern prince, speaking little, and touching no one, except his wife. He could hardly prevent himself from touching her body, all over, in front of everyone, Hugh commented to himself, watching the flicker of the fine fingers down her back as the Prince bent to bestow an unnecessary kiss of greeting after a half-hour absence. Hugh noticed also that there were faint rosy marks on the Princess's skin, as though it had been scored, or lashed. Flushed lines in the hollow of her neck, inside her forearm where the sleeve fell away. He wanted to ask if she was hurt, and once opened his mouth to do so, and closed it again when he saw that she was not listening to him, that she was staring over his shoulder at a door where a moment later Sasan himself was to appear. If she was hurt, Hugh knew, because he knew her, she was also happy.

Fiammarosa's honeymoon nights were indeed a fantastic mixture of pleasure and pain. She and her husband, in a social way, were intensely shy with each other. They said little, and what they said was of the most conventional kind: Fiammarosa at least heard her own clear voice, from miles away, like that of a polite stranger sharing the room in which their two silent selves simmered with passion. And Sasan, whose dark eyes never left hers when they were silent, looked down at the sheets or out of the window when he spoke, and she knew in her heart that his unfinished, whispered sentences sounded as odd to him as her silver platitudes did to her. But when he touched her, his warm, dry fingers spoke to her skin, and when she touched his nakedness she was laughing and crying at once with delight over his golden warmth, his secret softness, the hard, fine arch of his bones. An icewoman's sensations are different from those of other women, but Fiammarosa could not know how different, for she had no standards of comparison; she could not name the agonising bliss that took possession of her. Ice burns, and it is hard to the warm-skinned to distinguish one sensation, fire, from the other, frost. Touching Sasan's heat was like and unlike the thrill of ice. Ordinary women melt, or believe themselves to be melting, to be running away like avalanches or rivers at the height of passion, and this, too, Fiammarosa experienced with a difference, as though her whole being was becoming liquid except for some central icicle, which was running with waterdrops that threatened to melt that too, to nothing. And at the height of her bliss she desired to take the last step, to nothing, to nowhere, and the next moment cried out in fear of annihilation. The fine brown fingers prised open the pale-blue eyelids. "Are you there?" asked the soft whisper. "Where are you?" and she sighed, and returned.

When the morning light came into the room it found them curled together in a nest of red and white sheets. It revealed also marks, all over the pale cool skin: handprints round the narrow waist, sliding impressions from delicate strokes, like weals, raised rosy disks where his lips had rested lightly. He cried out, when he saw her, that he had hurt her. No, she said, she was part icewoman, it was her nature, she had an icewoman's skin that responded to every touch by blossoming red. Sasan still stared, and repeated, I have hurt you. No, no, said Fiammarosa, they are the marks of pleasure, pure pleasure. I shall cover them up, for only we ourselves should see our happiness.

But inside her a little melted pool of water slopped and swayed where she had been solid and shining.

The journey to the new country was long and arduous. Fiammarosa wrapped herself in a white hooded cloak, to reflect the sunlight away from her, and wore less and less inside it, as they rode south, through dark forests, and out onto grassy plains. They embarked, in a port where neither of them spoke the language, in the Sasanian boat that had been waiting for them, and sailed for weeks across the sea, in breezy weather, in a sudden storm, through two days and nights of glassy calm. Sasan enjoyed the voyage. He had a bucket with a glass bottom which he would let down into the green water to watch the creatures that floated and swam in the depth. He wore no more than a wrap round his narrow hips, and during the calm, he went overboard and swam around and under the boat, calling out to Fiammarosa, who sat swathed in white, wilting a little, on the deck, and answered breathlessly. He would bring glasses and buckets of the seawater on deck, and study the bubbles and ripples. He liked also to look at the sleek sea-surface in the moonlight, the gloss on the little swellings and subsidings, the tracks of phosphorescence. Fiammarosa was happier in the moonlight. It was cooler. She sat in a thin gown in the night air and smiled as her husband displayed his drawings and discoveries of translucency and reflection. He played his strange flute, and she listened, rapt. They sailed on. Every day was a little warmer. Every day the air was a little thicker, a little hotter.

When they came to the major port of Sasania, which was also its capital city, they were welcomed into the harbour by a flotilla of small boats bearing drummers and flautists, singers and cymbal-clashers. Fiammarosa nearly fell, when her foot touched land; the stone of the harbour steps was burning to the touch, and the sun was huge and glaring in a cobalt-blue sky with no clouds and no movement of air. She made a joke about the earth moving, after the movement of the waves, but the thought she had was that her temperate summers, with their bright flowers and birdsong, had no connexion to this hot blue arch in which a few kites wheeled, slowly. The people had prepared a curtained litter for their delicate new queen, and so she was able to subside, panting, onto cushions, wondering if she would survive.

The palace was white and glistening, as though it was moulded from sugar. It had domes and towers, plain and blind and geometrically simple and beautiful. It was designed to keep out the sun, and inside it was a geometric maze of cool corridors, tiled in coloured glass, lit only by narrow slits of windows, which were glazed in beautiful colours, garnet, emerald, sapphire, which cast bright flames of coloured light on the floors. It was a little like a beehive, and inside its central dome a woven latticework of coloured light was spun by tiny loopholes and slits in the surface, shifting and changing as the sun moved in the dark bright sky outside. Optimism returned to Fiammarosa when she saw these dark corridors, these dim spaces. Icewomen like bright light, bright cold light, off-white; and darkness and confinement oppress them. But the molten heat outside oppressed her more. And there was so much in the palace to delight her senses. There was fruit on glass dishes, pearly and iridescent, smoky amber, translucent rose, and indigo. There were meditative flute players dropping strings of sound all day into the still air from little stools under the loopholes on the turns of the stairs. There were wonderful white jugs of latticino work, with frivolous frilled lips, containing pomegranate juices or lemonade, or swaying dark wine. Her own apartment had a circular window of stained glass, a white rose, fold on fold, on a peacock-blue ground. Within the heavy doors hung curtains of tiny glass beads of every conceivable colour, shimmering and twinkling. Round the walls were candleholders, all different, a bronze glass chimney, an amethyst dish full of floating squat candles, a candelabra dripping with glass icicles. And her loom was there, ready for her, and a basket of wools in all the subtle shades she loved.

In the long days that followed, Fiammarosa found that her husband worked hard, and was no sedentary or sportive prince. Sasania was, he told her, a poor country. The people lived on fish which they caught in the sea, and vegetables irrigated in little plots from the river whose mouth had formed the harbour of the city. Beyond the city, and a few other towns on the coastal strip, Sasan told her, there was nothing but desert—he described dunes and oases, sandstorms and dancing mirages with the passion of a lover describing the woman he loved. Ah, the space of the bare sand, under the sun, under the stars, said Sasan. The taste of dates, of water from deep cool wells. The brilliance of the shimmering unreal cities in the distance, which had given him many ideas for cityscapes and fantastic palaces of glass. Fiammarosa stretched her imagination to conceive what he was describing, and could not. She connected the distant shimmering to her imaginations of lost glaciers and untrodden snowfields. Sasan explained, enthusiastically (they were talking more easily now, though still like two tentative children, not the man and woman whose bodies tangled and fought at night)—Sasan explained the connexion of the desert with the glass, which

Sasania despatched in trading ships and caravans to the corners of the known world. Glass, Sasan said, was made of the things which they had in abundance—the sand of the desert, three parts, lime, and soda which they made from the wracks, or seaweeds, which clung to the rocks round their coasts. The most difficult, the most precious part, he said, was the wood, which was needed both for the furnaces and for potash. The coastal woods of the country all belonged to the King, and were cared for by rangers. Glass, according to legend, had been found by the first Prince Sasan, who had been no more than an itinerant merchant with a camel train, and had found some lumps and slivers of shining stuff in the cinders of his fire on the seashore. And yet another Sasan had discovered how to blow the molten glass into transparent bottles and bowls, and yet another had discovered how to fuse different colours onto each other. In our country, Sasan said to his wife, princes are glassmakers and glassmakers are princes, and the line of artists runs true in the line of kings.

Every day he brought back from his dark workroom gifts for his bride. He brought crystal balls full of the fused scraps of coloured canes left over from his day's lamp work. Once, Fiammarosa ventured to the mouth of the cavern where he worked, and peered in. Men stripped to their waists and pouring sweat were feeding the great furnaces, or bending over hot lamps, working on tiny scraps of molten glass with magnifying glasses and sharp tweezers. Others were turning the sullen, cooling red glass with large metal pincers on clattering wheels, and one had a long tube raised to his mouth like a trumpet of doom, blowing his breath into the flaming, molten gob at the end of it which flared and smoked, orange and scarlet, and swelled and swelled. Its hot liquid bursting put the pale Princess in mind of the ferocity of her lovemaking and she opened her mouth, in pleasure and pain, to take in such a blast of hot, sparking wind, that she fell back, and could barely stagger to her room. After that, she spent the long hot days lying on her bed, breathing slowly. Sasan came in the cool of the evening; she took pleasure, then, in food, candle-flames, transparency and shadows. Then they made love. She put it to herself that she was delighting in extremity; that she was living a life pared down to extreme sensations. Dying is an ancient metaphor for the bliss of love, and Fiammarosa died a little, daily. But she was also dying in cold fact. Or in warm fact, to be more precise. She thought she was learning to live for love and beauty, through the power of the will. She was to find that in the end these things are subject to the weather—the weather in the world, and the tourbillons and sluggish meanders of the blood and lymph under the skin.

There was another, growing reason for the sickness against which she threw all her forces. When she understood this, she had a moment of despair and wrote to Hugh, begging him to reconsider his decision. I am not well, she wrote, and the days, as you knew they would be, are long and hot, and I am driven by necessity to languish in inactivity in the dark. I believe I am with child, dear Hugh, and am afraid, in this strange place amongst these strange people, however kind and loving they are. I need your cool head, your wisdom; I need our conversations about history and science. I am *not unhappy,* but I am not well, and I need your counsel, your familiar voice, your good sense. You foresaw that it would be hard—the heat, I mean, the merciless sun, and the confinement which is my only alternative. Could you, best of friends, at least come on a visit?

She despatched this letter, along with her regular letter to her parents, and almost at once regretted it, at least partly. It was a sign of weakness, an appeal for help she should not need. It was as though, by writing down her moment of weakness and discontent, she had made it into a thing, unavoidable. She felt herself becoming weaker and fought against a more and more powerful demon of discontent. Sasan was making her a series of delicate latticino vases. The first was pencil-slender, and took one rose. It was white. The next was cloudy, tinged with pink, and curved slightly outwards. The third was pinker and rounder, the fourth blushed rosy and had a fine blown bowl beneath its narrow neck. When the series of nine was completed, cherry pink, rose red, clear red, deep crimson, and almost black with a fiery heart, he arranged them on the table in front of her, and she saw that they were women, each more proudly swollen, with delicate white arms. She smiled, and kissed him, and ignored the fiery choking in her throat.

The next day a letter came from Hugh. It had crossed with her own—she could by no means yet expect an answer. It began with the hope that she would, far away as she was, share his joy, at least in spirit. He had married Hortense, the chamberlain's daughter, and was living in a state of comfort and contentment he had never imagined or hoped for. There followed, in a riddling form, the only love letter Fiammarosa had ever had from Hugh. I cannot, he said, hope to live at the extremes of experience, as you can. No one who has ever seen you dance on the untrodden snow, or gather ice flowers from bare branches, will ever be entirely able to forget this perfect beauty and live with what is pleasant and daily. I see now, said Hugh, that extreme desires extreme, and that beings of pure fire and pure ice may know delights we ordinary mortals must glimpse and forgo. I cannot live in any of your worlds, Princess, and I am happy in my new house, with my pretty woman, who loves me, and my good chair and sprouting garden. But I shall never be *quite* contented, Princess, because I saw you dance in the snow, and the sight took away the possibility of my settling into this life. Be happy in your way, at the furthest edge, and remember, when you can, Hugh, who would be quite happy in his—if he had never seen you.

Fiammarosa wept over this letter. She thought he would not have written so, if it was not meant to be his last letter. She thought, her own letter would cause him pain, and possibly cause him to despise her, that she could so easily and peremptorily summon him, when things were hard. And then she began to weep, because he was not there, and would not come, and she was alone and sick in a strange land, where even the cool air in the dark corridors was warm enough to melt her a little, like a caress given to a snow figure. When she had wept some time, she stood up, and began to walk somewhat drunkenly through the long halls and out across a courtyard full of bright, dazzling air in which the heat currents could be seen to boil up and weave their sinuous way down, and up again, like dry fountains. She went slowly and bravely, straight across, not seeking the shadow of the walls, and went into the huge, echoing, cavelike place where Sasan and his men were at work. Dimly, dazzled, she saw the half-naked men, the spinning cocoons, like blazing tulips, on the end of the pontils, the iron tweezers. Sasan was sitting at a bench, his dark face illuminated by the red-hot glow from a still-molten sphere of glass he was smoothing and turning. Beside him, another sphere was turning brown, like a dying leaf. One hand to her belly, Fiammarosa advanced into the heat and darkness. As she reached Sasan, one of the men, his arms and shoulders running with sweat, his brow dripping, swung open the door of the furnace. Fiammarosa had time to see shelves of forms, red and gold, transparent and burning, before the great sunlike rose of heat and light hit her, and she saw darkness and felt dreadful pain. She was melting, she thought in confusion, as she fell, slowly, slowly, bending and crumpling in the blast, becoming hot and liquid, a white scrap, moaning in a sea of red blood, lit by flames. Sasan was at her side in an instant, his sweat and tears dripping onto the white, cold little face. Before she lost consciousness Fiammarosa heard his small voice, in her head. "There will be another child, one who would never otherwise have lived; you must think of *that* child." And then, all was black. There was even an illusion of cold, of shivering.

After the loss of the child, Fiammarosa was ill for a long time. Women covered her brow with cloths soaked in ice water, changing them assiduously. She lay in the cool and the dark, drifting in and out of a minimal life. Sasan was there, often, sitting silently by her bed. Once, she saw him packing the nine glasses he had made for her in wood shavings. With care, she recovered, at least enough to become much as she had been in her early days as a girl in her own country, milky, limp, and listless. She rose very late, and sat in her chamber, sipping juice, and making no move to weave, or to read, or to write. After some months, she began to think she had lost her husband's love. He did not come to her bedroom, ever again, after the bloody happening in the furnace room. He did not speak of this, or explain it, and she could not. She felt she had become a milk-jelly, a blancmange, a Form of a woman, tasteless and unappetising. Because of her metabolism, grief made her fleshier and slower. She wept over the plump rolls of creamy fat around her eyelids, over the bland expanse of her cheeks. Sasan went away on long journeys, and did not say where he was going, or when he would return. She could not write to Hugh, and could not confide in her dark, beautiful attendants. She turned her white face to the dark blue wall, wrapped her soft arms round her body, and wished to die.

Sasan returned suddenly from one of his journeys. It was autumn, or would have been, if there had been any other season than immutable high summer in that land. He came to his wife, and told her to make ready for a journey. They were going to make a journey together, to the interior of his country, he told her, across the desert. Fiammarosa stirred a little in her lethargy.

"I am an icewoman, Sasan," she said, flatly. "I cannot survive a journey in the desert."

"We will travel by night," he replied. "We will make shelters for you, in the heat of the day. You will be pleasantly surprised, I trust. Deserts are cold at night. I think you may find it tolerable."

So they set out, one evening, from the gate of the walled city, as the first star rose in the velvet blue sky. They travelled in a long train of camels and horses. Fiammarosa set out in a litter, slung between mules. As the night deepened, and the fields and the sparse woodlands were left behind, she snuffed a rush of cool air, very pure, coming in from stone and sand, where there was no life, no humidity, no decay. Something lost stirred in her. Sasan rode past, and looked in on her. He told her that they were coming to the dunes, and beyond the first dunes was the true desert. Fiammarosa said she felt well enough to ride beside him, if she might. But he said, not yet, and rode away, in a cloud of dust, white in the moonlight.

And so began a long journey, a journey that took weeks, always by night, under a moon that grew from a pared crescent to a huge silver globe as they travelled. The days were terrible, although Fiammarosa was sheltered by ingenious tents, fanned by servants, cooled with precious water. The nights were clear, empty, and cold. After the first days, Sasan would come for her at dusk, and help her onto a horse, riding beside her, wrapped in a great camel-hair cloak. Fiammarosa shed her layers of protective veiling and rode in a pair of wide white trousers and a flowing shift, feeling the delicious cold run over her skin, bringing it to life, bringing power. She did not ask where they were going. Sasan would tell her when and if he chose to tell her. She did not even wonder why he still did not come to her bed, for the heat of the day made everything, beyond mere survival, impossible. But he spoke to her of the hot desert, of how it was his place. These are the things I am made of, he said, grains of burning sand, and breath of air, and the blaze of light. Like glass. Only here do we see with such clarity. Fiammarosa stared out, sometimes, at the sand as it shimmered in the molten sunlight, and at her husband standing there in the pure heat and emptiness, bathing himself in it. Sometimes, when she looked, there were mirages. Sand and stones appeared to be great lagoons of clear water, great rivers of ice with ice floes, great forests of conifers. They could have lived together happily, she reflected, by day and night, in these vanishing frozen palaces shining in the hot desert, which became more and more liquid and vanished in strips. But the mirages came and went, and Sasan stood, staring intently at hot emptiness, and Fiammarosa breathed the night air in the cooling sand and plains.

Sometimes, on the horizon, through the rippling glassy air, Fiammarosa saw a mirage which resembled a series of mountain peaks, crowned with white streaks of snow, or feathers of cloud. As they progressed, this vision became more and more steady, less and less shimmering and dissolving. She understood that the mountains were solid, and that their caravan was moving towards them. Those, said Sasan, when she asked, are the Mountains of the Moon. My country has a flat coast, a vast space of desert, and a mountain range which forms the limit of the kingdom. They are barren, inhospitable mountains; not much lives up there; a few eagles, a few rabbits, a kind of ptarmigan. In the past, we were forbidden to go there. It was thought the mountains were the homes of demons. But I have travelled there, many times. He did not say why he was taking Fiammarosa there, and she did not ask.

They came to the foothills, which were all loose scree, and stunted thorn trees. There was a winding narrow path, almost cut into the hills, and they climbed up, and up, partly by day now, for the beasts of burden needed to see their way. Fiammarosa stared upwards with parted lips at the snow on the distant peaks beyond them, as her flesh clung to her damp clothes in the heat. And then suddenly, round a rock, came the entrance to a wide tunnel in the mountainside. They lit torches and lanterns, and went in. Behind them the daylight diminished to a great O and then to a pinprick. It was cooler inside the stone, but not comfortable, for it was airless, and the sense of the weight of the stone above was oppressive. They were travelling inwards and upwards, inwards and upwards, trudging steadily, breathing quietly. And they came, in time, to a great timbered door, on massive hinges. And Sasan put his mouth to a hole beside the keyhole, and blew softly, and everyone could hear a clear musical note, echoed and echoed again, tossed from bell to bell of some unseen carillon. Then the door swung open, lightly and easily, and they went into a place like nowhere Fiammarosa had ever seen.

It was a palace built of glass in the heart of the mountain. They were in a forest of tall glass tubes with branching arms, arranged in colonnades, thickets, circular balustrades. There was a delicate sound in the air, of glass bells, tubular bells, distant waterfalls, or so it seemed. All the glass pillars were hollow, and were filled with columns of liquid—wine-coloured, sapphire, amber, emerald, and quicksilver. If you touched the finer ones, the liquid shot up, and then steadied. Other columns held floating glass bubbles, in water, rising and falling, each with a golden numbered weight hanging from its balloon. In the dark antechambers, fantastic candles flowered in glass buds, or shimmered behind shades of figured glass set on ledges and crevices. As they moved onwards through the glass stems, all infinitesimally in motion, they came to a very high chamber miraculously lit by daylight through clear glass in a high funnelled window, far, far above their heads. Here, too, the strange pipes rose upwards, some of them formed like rose bushes, some like carved pillars, some fantastically twined with glass grapes on glass vines. And in this room, there were real waterfalls, sheets of cold water dropping over great slabs of glass, like ice floes, into glassy pools where it ran away into hidden channels, water falling in sheer fine spray from the rock itself into a huge glass basin, midnight blue and full of dancing cobalt lights, with a rainbow fountain rising to meet the dancing, descending mare's tail. All the miracles of invention that glittered and glimmered and trembled could not be taken in at one glance. But Fiammarosa took in one thing. The air was cold. By water, by stone, by ice from the mountaintop, the air had been chilled to a temperature in which her icewoman's blood stirred to life and her eyes shone.

Sasan showed her further miracles. He showed her her bedchamber, cut into the rock, with its own high porthole window, shaped like a many-coloured rose and with real snow resting on it, far above, so that the light was grainy. Her bed was surrounded by curtains of spun glass, with white birds, snow birds, snowflowers, and snow crystals woven into them. She had her own cooling waterfall, with a controlling gate, to make it more, or less, and her own forest of glass trees, with their visible phloem rising and falling. Sasan explained to her the uses of these beautiful inventions, which measured, he said, the weight, the heat, the changes of the ocean of elementary air in which they moved. The rising and falling glass bubbles, each filled to a different weight, measured the heat of the column of water that supported them. The quicksilver columns, in the fine tubes within tubes, were made by immersing the end of the tube in a vessel of mercury, and stopping it with a finger, and then letting the column of quicksilver find its level, at which point the weight of the air could be read off the height of the column in the tube. And this column, he said, varied, with the vapours, the winds, the clouds in the outer atmosphere, with the height above the sea, or the depth of the cavern. You may measure such things also with alcohol, which can be coloured for effect. Fiammarosa had never seen him so animated, nor heard him speak so long. He showed her yet another instrument, which measured the wetness of the incumbent air with the beard of an oat or, in other cases, with a stretched hair. And he had made a system of vents and pulleys, channels and pipes, taps and cisterns, which brought the mountain snow and the deep mountain springs in greater and lesser force into the place, as the barometers and thermometers and hygrometers indicated a need to adjust the air and the temperature. With all these devices, Sasan said, he had made an artificial world, in which he hoped his wife could live, and could breathe, and could be herself, for he could neither bear to keep her in the hot sunny city, nor could he bear to lose her. And Fiammarosa embraced him amongst the sighing spun glass and the whispering water. She could be happy, she said, in all this practical beauty. But what would they live on? How could they survive, on glass, and stone, and water? And Sasan laughed, and took her by the hand, and showed her great chambers in the rock where all sorts of plants were growing, under windows which had been cut to let in the sun, and glazed to adjust his warmth, and where runnels of water ran between fruit trees and seedlings, pumpkin plants and herbs. There was even a cave for a flock of goats, hardy and silky, who went out to graze on the meagre pastures and came in at night. He himself must come and go, Sasan said, for he had his work, and his land to look to. But she would be safe here, she could breathe, she could live in her own way, or almost, he said, looking anxiously at her. And she assured him that she would be more than happy there. "We can make air, water, light, into something both of us can live in," said Sasan. "All I know, and some things I have had to invent, has gone into building this place for you."

But the best was to come. When it was night, and the whole place was sleeping, with its cold air currents moving lazily between the glass stems, Sasan came to Fiammarosa's room, carrying a lamp, and a narrow package, and said, "Come with me." So she followed him, and he led her to a rocky stairway that went up, and round, and up, and round, until it opened on the side of the mountain itself, above the snow line. Fiammarosa stepped out under a black velvet sky, full of burning cold silver stars, like globes of mercury, onto a field of untouched snow, such as she had never thought to see again. And she took off her slippers and stepped out onto the sparkling crust, feeling the delicious crackle beneath her toes, the soft sinking, the voluptuous cold. Sasan opened his packet, which contained the strange flute he had played when he wooed her. He looked at his wife, and began to play, a lilting, swaying tune that ran away over the snowfields and whispered into the edges of silence. And Fiammarosa took off her dress, and her shawls and her petticoat, stood naked in the snow, shook out her pale hair, and began to dance. As she danced, a whirling white shape, her skin of ice crystals, that she had believed she would never feel again, began to form along her veins, over her breasts, humming round her navel. She was lissom and sparkling, she was cold to the bone and full of life. The moon glossed the snow with gold and silver. When, finally, Sasan stopped playing, the icewoman darted over to him, laughing with delight, and discovered that his lips and fingers were blue with cold; he had stopped because he could play no more. So she rubbed his hands with her cold hands, and kissed his mouth with her cold lips, and with friction and passion brought his blood back to some movement. They went back to the bedchamber with the spun-glass curtains, and opened and closed a few channels and conduits, and lay down to make love in a mixture of currents of air, first warm, then cooling, which brought both of them to life.

In a year, or so, twin children were born, a dark boy, who resembled his mother at birth, and became, like her, pale and golden, and a pale, flower-like girl, whose first days were white and hairless, but who grew a mane of dark hair like her father's and had a glass-blower's, flute player's mouth. And if Fiammarosa was sometimes lonely in her glass palace, and sometimes wished both that Sasan would come more often, and that she could roam amongst fjords and ice-fells, this was not unusual, for no one has everything they can desire. But she was resourceful and hopeful, and made a study of the vegetation of the Sasanian snow line, and a further study of which plants could thrive in mountain air under glass windows, and corresponded—at long intervals—with authorities all over the world on these matters. Her greatest discovery was a sweet blueberry, that grew in the snow, but in the glass garden became twice the size, and almost as delicate in flavour.

HEAVENLY BODIES

She sailed into the sky without annunciation, around the winter solstice. She had been assembled in space, like a pontoon bridge, from a series of tiny satellites, carrying light-emitting polymers and mirrors, and when she was ready, she was unfurled over forty or so kilometres, twinkling and glittering. She went into a non-geostationary orbit, riding calmly round the earth seven and a half times in twenty-four hours, and could be clearly seen with the naked eye to be a reclining woman, full-breasted, narrow-waisted, with a cloud of shimmering hair and shapely legs in diaphanous harem pants, ending in sequinned stiletto-heeled shoes. She appeared to be as large as a jumbo jet on its descent. She lay along the sky, reclining, flying, floating. One arm was curled so that her hand rested on her swelling hip. The other was thrust out in front of her, bearing a huge mirror which reflected the light of the sun so intensely that it created a simulacrum of daylight in the cities she travelled over. It streamed with white rays like the Columbia Motion Pictures totem. The polymers were made with great cunning to create waves and ripples of coloured light, green, violet, lemon yellow, pale red, over her body; indeed she wriggled her hips and jounced the diamondlike facetted light in her navel.

Although there had been no publicity before her appearance, an orchestrated stream of information appeared in all the media immediately after it. Her name, it was revealed, was Lucy Furnix, which was also the name of a singer who was associated with Brad Macmamman, the tycoon, one of the few people powerful and rich enough to assemble a skywoman without fear of international complaints about light pollution, or advertising controls. Touching stories appeared about how the couple had sat together on a Caribbean island, quoting Juliet's desire to take Romeo and "cut him out in little stars," and Brad had had the idea of making his own Lucy immortal in the sky with diamonds. Her light, it was also said, was environmentally useful, as it would increase crop productivity in cold and dark wastes on the earth. And she was socially useful, as she lit up all dark alleys and sordid corners, thus reducing the risk of muggings and rapes. Astronomers had no need to complain about interference with starlight; they had radio telescopes based in deep space, which were perfectly adequate.

A spate of very cheap telescopes—some only plastic tubes with lenses—appeared on the market, patented as Lucy-tubes. With the aid of these watchers could see her finer points as she swept across their skies. She was a miracle of ingenuity—through the tubes she could be seen to have a pouting mouth, partly open to show sparkling teeth, with a plump upper lip. Her eyes were huge, with sapphire blue irises and thick fringes of yellow lashes. Her nose was pert and her cheekbones pronounced. She had mauve nail varnish. She wore multicoloured beads in multiple rows above her softly heaving breasts, and a braided sash above the harem pants. She wore also a diagonal sash, like a bandolier, or the guerdon of Miss World, crossing between the uptilted nipples, patterned with the logo of Brad Macmamman's product, which was a round eye completely surrounded by spiky lashes. Brad Macmamman, in a discreet single interview, referred to her as "The Lady with the Lamp" and said he was a romantic at heart, which was quite likely true. She was popularly known as the Usherette. Graffiti appeared : "See Lucy's boobs, with Lucy-tubes."

People gathered on hilltops, and in parks, and at the tops of buildings, at first, to watch her rise above the horizon and sail to the zenith. Thin outbreaks of scattered clapping greeted her arrival in Sydney, Bogotá, and Helsinki. A kind of indulgent and cheery smile—at first—was the normal response to her frequent returns. Children had Lucy-watching parties, and cultural studies pundits talked about a new age of feminine values.

But after a time her rapidly reiterated appearances began to be greeted with indifference, and then with irritation, and then with increasing distaste and loathing. She was too big, too bright, too artificial. She seemed somehow to interpose her mundane curves between human beings and space, closing the earth off from the sky. Various illnesses, dementias, and aberrations began to be ascribed to her baleful influence, from milk souring to muggings. "Lucy-craziness" became a serious defence in cases of affray and motorway madness. In prosperous countries in the direct path of her spangling glare she caused odd tremors in the housing markets, as people tried to move to where darkness was more or less intact. Brad Macmamman and the singer were quiet on their Caribbean island, which was not in her orbit. Governments, and even the United Nations, began to discuss the dismantling or shooting down of the steadily smiling object, but this was found to be impossibly expensive or dangerous, and Macmamman said he neither could nor would remove her. So she sailed on and on.

Graffiti began to appear. "Watchman, what of the night? Watchman, what of the night?"

It was, ironically, children with Lucy-tubes who noticed the first signs of the new perturbations in the heavens. Swarms of small gold and silver lights were seen travelling across the sky, like self-propelled shooting stars, before and after Lucy's dismally regular appearances. These lights darted and wheeled, like shoals of silvery fishes, or swarms of golden bees. For a time this was all they did, small and delicate and erratically mobile, increasing in number. Astronomers, and the public, began to train larger telescopes on them, and the swarms were seen to be made up of winged creatures in many shapes and sizes. Some were bird-winged—the stubby wings of finches, the powerful wings of albatrosses, the fine wings of swallows, the filigree wings of birds of paradise, the wheeling wings of vultures. Some were insect-winged—dragonflies, damselflies, butterflies, and moths, from skippers to moon moths, from swallowtails to morphos. There were lacewings and beetle cases, jewelled flies and darting wasps. There were fish-forms also, pipefish and medusas, seahorses made of light and writhing eels, nautilus and leaping salmon. They could be seen to expand and diminish, and after a time they could also be seen to metamorphose into other forms, all composed of pure light, it seemed, fingered vines which were snakes, plummeting birds which were flowers. They were most active at Lucy's rising and setting and after a time began to cluster round her, surrounding her in a bright cloud of shimmering forms, dancing and twirling on her limbs and garments. After a time they were seen to be nipping and sipping at her, pulling at her with claws made of fire, sucking away her substance with bee mouths and fish lips, gathering and swarming into the darkness with fragments which they spat out, or tossed away.

Hundreds of humans gathered on hills and at windows with Lucy-tubes to watch the events in the heavens. Lucy began to look nibbled and bedraggled but still sailed on smiling; she was solid and the light-creatures were ephemeral. Then, after a time light began to gather and form in the night sky into larger forms, though those with good telescopes could see that these larger forms were somehow made up of congregations of the smaller ones, like cells or atomies. Over several weeks a large Scorpion assembled itself—its claws and its rearing tail were composed of what looked like swarms of celestial fire ants, who bristled and spun in their own tiny orbits within its form as it advanced, slowly, slowly, across the plains of heaven. When it reached Lucy Furnix it stretched out its formidable, brilliant pincers and sheared away her painted toes. Then it turned and crawled away into outer space, bearing the baubles.

The legs of the Archer's horse-half formed first, gleaming hooves oscillating and prancing. Then the cannon bones, the knees, the hocks, and the gleaming flanks streaming with light made up of millions of racing and leaping elemental beasts, fawns and cheetahs, weasels and wolves. The human head swirled with a crest, or mane, of silver curling locks, which obscured the face, but not the muscular arms, containing twining tree trunks and gripping roots, and brandishing the bow which spanned a great arc of the visible sky. All this was very slow, added piecemeal with an inexorable heavenly patience, and the creatures on earth watched with an analogous patience, which seemed to be required of them—no panic, no rushing to hide, no prophecies of doom. Just a grave and complete attention at the end of optic tubes and from heights and viewing points. When the Archer had come into being he raised the great bow and loosed a sudden two-day-long stream of darting white arrows, using Lucy Furnix's beads, and the logos on her sash, for a mercilessly accurate target practice. One by one the beads went out and fell away. Her sash floated loose, blinked and went dull and then null. The people set up a mild cheer. The Archer tossed his mane and cantered away with rippling muscles of light.

The Goat bounded up from below the horizon, all in one piece, tossing its silver head and its silver toes, butting at space with wicked curved slender horns. It had a majestic silver beard and gold eyes with dark barred pupils. It curvetted and danced and pranced, advancing on Lucy Furnix, jumping back, in teasing syncopated rhythms, for months and then suddenly put down its bright head, charged, and carried away her legs on its horntips in a rush into the depths. Its tail flicked on its elegant rump and the female calves above its head were brandished and taken into blackness.

The humans speculated mildly about how the other creatures would manifest themselves. It was better, and stranger, than a firework display, but had the same quality of ephemeral brilliance and unreality. They were deeply distressed if cloudy weather interrupted their vision of any night's work, which went on whether or not they were looking. The Water-carrier was largely put together in cloudy weather, a figure like a standing waterfall, shimmering with moving light that was at once veil, cloud, and fountain—like the Archer it was faceless. It stood behind and above Lucy Furnix and fell on her in a cascade of shimmering ripples which dissolved into darkness and carried away the harem pants, the exiguous brassiere, and her well-coiffeured waves. Out of the final expanding ripples of the

Aquarian pool rose a whole shoal of silver and golden fishes, finned and scaly, with round bright eyes and every conceivable shape of body—undulating rays, bony pike, seahorses, dolphins with beaks, sea-wolves and basking sharks. This sea of forms shone dappling and struggling, with bright slivers of glitter and moony runnels of shadow, round the lower half of the skywoman, nudging her bottom, eating away her buttocks and sex, such as it was. When they flashed away into their profound depths, vanishing to a network of points, Lucy Furnix was decidedly the worse for wear.

The curly fleece of the Ram floated together in tight spirals of creamy light, and massed itself into a muscular rectangle which then grew four stocky, golden legs, fine bronze cloven hooves, a magnificent pendulous sex, and a bright, weighty head which evolved curling, spiralling horns, ribbed and sharp at the tips. It advanced with a steady, dignified walk, slowly increased its pace to a trot, and then to a gallop. When it reached Lucy it lowered the shining bulk of its head, and with a purposeful hooked pair of tossing movements, bore off her tapered hands, with their painted nails, leaving her light somehow unconnected to the stump of her arm, but still in orbit. The light Jovial Bull, on the other hand, trotted purposefully into view, over the horizon. Its horns were lyre-shaped; there were garlands of starflowers around its neck; its eyes under broad brows were lustrous and gleaming. Its substance was also, under scrutiny, flower-flesh, petal-forms, florets, grasses intertwined like rushing waves. It ran lightly up to the depleted usherette, lowered its brow, and transfixed the mirror of her now dull lamp between its horns. Then it bore it away, at a canter, over the hill of the brightening world edge, into oblivion.

The Twins, who Western watchers expected to see as cherubic infants, took their initial form as complicated repeating diagrams of points and parallel lines which slowly became sword belts and plumed helmets of no known design. The burnish on the swords arrived very lengthily, sparkle by sparkle, whilst intricate devices grew and wreathed and were replaced on the crests of the helmets and the pommels. The two figures were far apart, and the stumps and smiling face of Lucy Furnix lay sacrificially between them, equidistant as they embellished themselves from streams of starlight. They made themselves flowing cloaks, with rippling folds, and intricate hooked spurs, glittering and cruel. Then they made themselves ghostly bodies—also faceless like the Water-carrier and the Archer, their shadowy features lost in swirls of dust and foam of feathers like the Milky Way. They strode at Lucy, in rhythm, in step, from each side, and raised the swords synchronically and sliced off her arms, leaving her trunk and hairless head to progress, with no diminution of her anodyne smile, around and again around.

The heavens darkened and became a shore, a scalloped line of delicately frilled water eternally breaking on a gleaming expanse of pale, bright, grains of sand. The expanse of space that was not shining grew deep indigo, patterned with the rocking motion of crested waves breaking and rolling in. The Crab advanced out of the water onto the sand, sideways with a ripple of synchronised, feathery legs, heaving its monstrous claws, raised and snapping. It was neither gold nor silver but darker blue than midnight, so dark that it gave the optical illusion of being a pit, a crustacean-shaped keyhole into the abyss. The starry water broke over its blue-black carapace. It came forward slowly, very slowly, trailing lines of bright waterlight on the grainy glitter. It was not made up of any other small forms or substances, but of absence and emptiness, with the most beautiful outline, and spherical, quivering burning eyes on stalks above its fluttering mouth. Behind it was a trail of vacancy. When it reached the dimmed truncated remnants of Lucy, it reared back, reached out with both claws simultaneously, the greater and the lesser, and surgically removed her jutting breasts. The watchers could almost feel the tearing in their own bodies. Then, its trophies raised high, it danced slowly sideways back to the rim of the ocean and submerged itself, always slowly, slowly, creating ripples and whirls in the surface. Lucy's boobs bobbed for a moment on a sea of brightness and sunk without trace. The sea swirled and shone on.

Over the next few months there were rains of shooting stars and whizzings of comets, ruddy and dark gold. The sky was a turmoil of movement, amongst which the remnants of Lucy tumbled and shuddered. After a time the comets and stars began to coalesce like giant Catherine wheels into a curling pelt and a lashing tail that brushed the horizon. A mane made up of hissing and swirling circles of fire came next, and last four legs made out of continually rushing fire-arrows and a great cat head with teeth of star-ice, blue-silver, in a mouth opening on a gullet like a tunnel into the pit.

The crescent claws were curved and sharp and icy as the teeth. The great beast's loins were narrow and his chest immense and magnificently draped with a fire-pelt of fiery wheels in turmoil. He arrived in bounds, crouching and lashing his tail, leaping and stretching, yawning and stepping delicately, taking his time. He was couchant for a time, staring at Lucy with great, motionless golden eyes, in which a dark pupil grew and grew. When all his eye was a black stare he pounced—a muscular arc that took up all the illusory curve of the arch of the heavens, and tore away her head from her body, which he tossed from claw to claw like a celestial kitten toying with its prey. Then he lifted the head in the great mouth—looking briefly, to the astonished earthlings, like a phantasmagoric sphinx—and loped away over a space that had become an infinite desert that seemed to tremble under his pads.

Now Lucy Furnix was nothing but an hourglass-shaped torso, with a cupped navel in which her diamond glittered, vulgar and forlorn. Now the angels began to dance in the heavens, flocks of them, swarms of them, like amoeba and water-fleas in pondwater (all sizes are relative) in every shape and size and colour. They were tiny enough to dance on pinheads in hundreds, they were vast enough that flocks of tiny ones could be seen to be busy inside a little fingernail, or seated along the life line in an outspread palm which took up the whole sky-span. For months and months, in unimaginable depths, human beings watched the skydance, circles of prancing cherubim, choirs of sailing seraphim, shoals of darting rainbow-bright thrones, dominations, and Powers. Human beings began to wait with a kind of glorious sick longing for the night and the next vision; they went through daylight like dreamers, and it seemed, the mild light of their one star, like a ghost-whisper of possible brilliance. Finally they all began to coalesce, and out of the whole host one angel, tall, terrible, and beautiful, began slowly to take on shape and sharpness, a great Creature with a tall spear in one hand, and a swirl of brilliant feathers and flowers in the other. The Angel's face could not be seen, though its great beauty could—it was too bright, too full of constant changes of expression, too lucid to look at. Humans found themselves contemplating details for what seemed like eternities—the cloak which was covered with eyes like a peacock's tail, and with little tongues of burning flames, the bright locks fanned by a breeze from the depths of infinity.

The Angel gestured with its spear, and there was a velvet emptiness which slowly became a great field of flowers, like an infinite tapestry on cloth of gold and silver, which had its own valleys and mountains all spread with cups and stars and flutes and bells of brightness, blue and rose and orange and aquamarine, emerald and periwinkle, crocus and windflower, lily-white and tiger-spotted, carnations, pinks, and daisies of every kind, tulips in butter and flame, snapdragons and honeysuckle and many more and all changing. And after a time this cloth of meadows was seen to be only the outer garment of a figure who sat veiled on a starry rock, with a dark blue robe inside the floral one, and a shimmering veil of light over a face too bright to look at, even through the exquisite transparent layers of the milky star-foam that covered it. There was a suspicion of a crown on her head, a plain circle of moonstones on a silver thread, which caught a fiery light from the Angel and blushed briefly rosy. She held a sheaf of lovely grasses and ears of corn, oats and barley, trembling and golden. She held also a pair of scales, solid, burnished, and bright. She waited, still and calm, with everything round her in motion, visionary wings and grasses and creatures, and the orderly rushing of inanimate space.

Then the Angel lifted its spear and brandished it, and saluted the Virgin, and turned its flaming point downwards, and pierced the diamond of the skywoman and offered it to the seated Lady, who held out her scales. And for a moment the diamond shone dimly in one pan, as stardust poured into the other like snuff, like poppyseed. The weightless stardust took its pan down and down, and the one with Lucy Furnix's diamond shot up and catapulted its tiny light out into the field of flowers where it blinked and was lost forever. And the flowers shone, and the Lady smiled, and the angelic hosts wheeled and danced.

And then they were gone, and it was dark.

And the dazed human beings, in orderly and decorous silence, all over the world, dimmed and put out their artificial lights, and sat in darkness. And into their night came their epiphany. They saw, as they had some of them not seen in their lifetimes, the lovely lights visible from our small planet, the Milky Way, the galaxies, the constellations, the travelling planets and moons, the winking lights and the steady lights, the bluish and the red, the gold and the bright white. They sat in silence and were amazed, briefly and forever.

RAW MATERIAL

He always told them the same thing, to begin with: "Try to avoid falseness and strain. Write what you really know about. Make it new. Don't invent melodrama for the sake of it. Don't try to run, let alone fly, before you can walk with ease." Every year, he glared amiably at them. Every year they wrote melodrama. They clearly needed to write melodrama. He had given up telling them that Creative Writing was not a form of psychotherapy. In ways both sublime and ridiculous it clearly was, precisely, that.

The class had been going for fifteen years. It had moved from a schoolroom to a disused Victorian church, made over as an Arts and Leisure Centre. The village was called Sufferacre, which was thought to be a corruption of *sulfuris aquae.* It was a failed Derbyshire spa. It was his home town. In the 1960s he had written a successfully angry, iconoclastic, and shocking novel called *Bad Boy.* He had left for London and fame, and returned quietly, ten years later. He lived in a caravan in somebody's paddock. He travelled widely, on a motorbike, teaching Creative Writing in pubs, schoolrooms, and arts centres. His name was Jack Smollett. He was a big, shuffling, smiling, red-faced man, with longish blond hair, who wore cable-knit sweaters in oily colours, and bright scarlet neckerchiefs. Women liked him, as they liked enthusiastic Labrador dogs. They felt, almost all—and his classes were predominantly female—more desire to cook apple pies and Cornish pasties for him, than to make violent love to him. They believed he didn't eat sensibly. (They were right.) Now and then, someone in one of his classes would point out, as he exhorted them to stick to what they knew, that they themselves were what he "really knew." Will you write about *us,* Jack? No, he always said, that would be a betrayal of confidence. You should always respect other people's privacy. Creative writing teachers had something in common with doctors, even if—yet again—creative writing wasn't therapy.

In fact, he had tried unsuccessfully to sell two different stories based on the confessions (or inventions) of his class. They offered themselves to him like raw oysters on pristine plates. They told him horror and bathos, daydreams, vituperation and vengeance. They couldn't write, their inventions were crude, and he couldn't find a way to perform the necessary operations to spin the muddy straw into silk, or turn the raw bleeding chunks into a savoury dish. So he kept faith with them, not entirely voluntarily. He did care about writing. He cared about writing more than anything, sex, food, beer, fresh air, even warmth. He wrote and rewrote perpetually, in his caravan. He was rewriting his fifth novel. *Bad Boy,* his first, had been written in a rush just out of the sixth form, and snapped up by the first publisher he'd sent it to. It was what he had expected. (Well, it was one of two scenarios that played in his young brain, immediate recognition, painful, dedicated struggle. When success happened it appeared blindingly clear that it had always been the only possible outcome.) So he didn't go to university, or learn a trade. He was, as he knew he was, a Writer. His second novel, *Smile and Smile,* had sold six hundred copies, and was remaindered. His third and his fourth—frequently rewritten—lay in brown paper, stamped and re-stamped, in a tin chest in the caravan. He didn't have an agent.

Classes ran from September to March. In the summer he worked in literary festivals, or holiday camps on sunny islands. He was pleased to see the classes again in September. He still thought of himself as wild and unattached, but he was a creature of habit. He liked things to happen at precise, recurring times, in precise, recurring ways. More than half of most of his classes were old faithfuls who came back year after year. Each class had a nucleus of about ten. At the beginning of the year this was often doubled by enthusiastic newcomers. By Christmas many of these would have dropped away, seduced by other courses, or intimidated by the regulars, or overcome by domestic drama or personal lassitude. St. Antony's Leisure Centre was gloomy because of its high roof, and draughty because of its ancient doors and windows. The class themselves had brought oil heaters, and a circle of standard lamps with imitation stained-glass covers. The old churchy chairs were pushed into a circle, under these pleasant lights.

He liked the lists of their names. He liked words, he was a writer. Sometimes he talked about how much Nabokov had got out of the list of names of Lolita's classmates, how much of America, how strong an image from how few words. Sometimes he tried to make an imaginary list that would please him as much as the real one. It never worked. He would write allusive equivalents—Vicar, say, for Parson, Gold for Silver, and find his text inexorably resubstituting the precise concatenation that existed. His current class ran:

Abbs, Adam
Archer, Megan
Armytage, Blossom
Forster, Bobby
Fox, Cicely
Hogg, Martin
Parson, Anita
Pearson, Amanda
Pygge, Gilly
Secrett, Lola
Secrett, Tamsin
Silver, Annabel
Wheelwright, Rosy

He consulted this for pointless symmetries. Pygge and Hogg. Pearson and Parson. The prevalence of As and absence of Es and Rs. He had kept a register, for a time, of surnames reflecting ancient, vanished occupations—Archer, Forster, Parson, Wheelwright. Were there more in Derbyshire than in other places?

Then there was the list of the occupations, also a flawed microcosm.

Abbs	deacon in the C. of E.
Archer	estate agent
Armytage	vet
Forster	redundant bank teller
Fox	eighty-two-year-old spinster
Hogg	accountant
Parson	schoolmistress
Pearson	farmer
Pygge	nurse
Secrett, Lola	intermittent student, daughter of
Secrett, Tamsin	living on alimony (her own phrase)
Silver	librarian
Wheelwright	student (engineering)

The most recent work they had produced was:

Adam Abbs	A tale of the martyrdom of nuns in Rwanda
Megan Archer	A story of the prolonged rape and abduction of an estate agent
Blossom Armytage	A tale of the elaborate torture of two Sealyham dogs
Bobby Forster	A tale of the entrapment and vengeful slaughter of an unjust driving examiner
Cicely Fox	How we used to black-lead stoves
Martin Hogg	Hanging, drawing, and quartering under Henry VIII
Anita Parson	A tale of unreported, persistent child abuse and Satanic sacrifice
Amanda Pearson	A tale of a cheating husband hacked down by his vengeful wife with an axe

Gilly Pygge	Clever murder by a cruel surgeon during an operation
Lola Secrett	The nervous breakdown of a menopausal woman with a beautiful and patient daughter
Tamsin Secrett	The nervous breakdown of a feckless teenager with a wise but powerless mother
Annabel Silver	A sadomasochistic initiation of a girl sold into white slavery in North Africa
Rosy Wheelwright	A cycle of very explicit lesbian love poems involving motorbikes.

He had learned the hard way not to involve himself in any way in their lives. When he first moved into the caravan he had had a conventional enough vision of its warm confinement as a secret place to take women, for romping, for intimacy, for summer nights of nakedness and red wine. He had scanned his new classes, fairly obviously, for hopefuls, measuring breasts, admiring ankles, weighing pink round mouths against wide red ones against unpainted severe ones. He had had one or two really good athletic encounters, one or two tearful failures, one overkill which had left him with a staring, shivering watcher every night at the gate of his paddock, or occasionally peering wildly through the caravan window.

Creative writers are creative writers. Descriptions of his bed linen, his stove, the blasts of wind on his caravan walls, began to appear, ever more elaborated, in the stories that were produced for general criticism. Competitive descriptions of his naked body began to be circulated. Heartless or cowering males (depending on the creative writer) had thickets, or wiry fuzzes, or fur soft as a dog fox, or scratchy-bristly reddish outcrops of hair on their chests. One or two descriptions of fierce thrusting and pubic clamping were followed by anticlimax, both in life and in art. He gave up—ever—taking women from his classes onto his unfolded settee. He gave up, ever, talking to his students one at a time or differentiating between them. The sex-in-a-caravan theme wilted and did not resuscitate. His stalker went to a pottery class, transferred her affections, and made stubby pottery pillars, glazed with flames and white spray. As the folklore of his sex life diminished he became mysterious and authoritative and found he enjoyed it. The barmaid of the Wig and Quill came round on Sundays. He couldn't find the right words to describe her orgasms—prolonged events with staccato and shivering rhythms alternating oddly—and this teased and pleased him.

He sat alone in the bar of the Wig and Quill the evening before his class, reading the "stories" that were to be returned. Martin Hogg had discovered the torture which consists of winding out the living intestines on a spindle. He couldn't write, which Jack thought was just as well—he used words like "gruesome" and "horrible" a lot, but was unable, perhaps inevitably, to raise in a reader's mind any image of an intestine, a spindle, pain, or an executioner. Jack supposed that Martin was enjoying himself, but even that was not very well conveyed to his putative reader. Jack was more impressed by Bobby Forster's fantasy of the slaughter of a driving examiner. This had some plot to it—involving handcuffs, severed brake cables, the removal of signs indicating quicksands, even an unbreakable alibi for the mild man who had turned on his tormentor. Forster occasionally produced a sharp, etched sentence that was memorable. Jack had found one of these in Patricia Highsmith, and another, by sheer chance, in Wilkie Collins. He had dealt with this plagiarism, rather neatly, he thought, by underlining the sentences and writing in the margin, "I have always said that reading excellent writers, and absorbing them, is essential to good writing. But it should not go quite so far as plagiarism." Forster was a white-faced, precise person, behind round glasses. (His hero was neat and pale, with glasses which made it hard to see what he was thinking.) He said mildly, on both occasions, that the plagiarism was unconscious, must have been a trick of memory. Unfortunately this led Jack to suspect automatically that any other excrescent elegance was also a plagiarism.

He came to "How We Used to Black-lead Stoves." Cicely Fox was a new student. Her contribution was handwritten—with pen and ink, not even felt-tip. She had given the work to him with a deprecating note.

"I don't know if this is the sort of thing you meant when you said, 'Write what you really know about.' I was sorry to find that there were so many lacunae in my memory. I do hope you will forgive them. The writing may not be of interest, but the exercise was pleasurable."

How We Used to Black-lead Stoves

It is strange to think of activities that were once so much part of our lives that they seemed daily inevitable, like waking and sleeping. At my age, these things come back in their contingent quiddity, things we did with quick fingers and backs that bent without precaution. It is today's difficult slitting of plastic wraps, or brilliantly blinking microwave LED displays, that seem like veils and shadows.

Take black-leading. The kitchen ranges in the kitchens of our childhood and young lives were great, darkly gleaming chests of fierce heat. Their frontage was covered with heavy hasped doors, opening on various ovens, large and small, various flues, the furnace itself, where the fuel went in. Words are needed for extremes of blackness and brightness. Brightness included the gold-glitter of the rail along the front of the range, where the tea towels hung, and the brass knobs on certain of the little doors which had to be burnished with Brasso—a sickly yellowish powdery liquid—every morning. It included also the roaring flame within and under the heavy cast-iron box. If you opened the door, when it was fully burning, you could hear and see it—a flickering transparent sheet of scarlet and yellow, shot with blue, shot with white, flashing purple, roaring and burping and piffing. You could immediately see it dying in the rusty edges of the embers. It was important to close the door quickly, to keep the fire "in." "In" meant *contained,* and also meant, alight.

There were so many different blacks around that range. Various fuels were burned in it, unlike modern Agas which take oil, or anthracite. I remember coal. Coal has its own brightness, a gloss, a sheen. You can see the compacted layers of dead wood—millions of years dead—in the strata on the faces of the chunks of good coal. They shine. They give out a black sparkle. The trees ate the sun's energy and the furnace will release it. Coal is glossy. Coke is matt, and looks (indeed is) twice-burned, like volcano lava; the dust on coal glitters like glass dust, the dust on coke absorbs light, is soft, is inert. Some of it comes in little regular pressed cushions, like pillows for dead dolls, I used to think, or twisted humbugs for small demons. We ourselves were fed on charcoal for stomach upsets which may explain why I considered the edibility of these lumps. Or maybe even as a small child, I saw the open mouth of the furnace as a hell-hole. You were drawn in. You wanted to get closer and closer; you wanted to be able to turn away. And we were taught at school, about our own internal combustion of matter. The ovens behind other doors of the range might conceal the puffed, risen shapes of loaves and teacakes, with that best of all smells, baking yeast dough, or the only slightly less delightful smell of the crust of a hot cake, toasted sugar, milk, and egg. Now and then—the old ranges were temperamental—a batch of buns in frilled paper cups would come out black and smoking and stinking of destruction, ghastly analogies of the cinder-cushions. From there, I thought, came the cinders that fell from the mouths of bad children in fairy tales, or stuffed their Christmas stockings.

The whole range was bathed in an aura of kept-down soot. In front of our own, at one time, was a peg-rug made by my father, by hooking strips of colourful scraps of cloth—old flannel shirts, old trousers—through sacking, and knotting them. Soot infiltrated this dense thicket of flags or streamers. The sacking scalp was stained sooty black. The crimsons and scarlets, the green tartans and mustard blotches all had a grain of fine, fine black specks. I sometimes thought of the peg-rug as a bed of ribbon seaweed. The soot was like the silted sand in which it lay.

Not that we did not brush and brush ceaselessly, to cleanse our firesides of this falling, sifting black dust. It rises lightly, and falls where it was, it whirls briefly, when disturbed, and particles may settle on one's own hair and scalp, a soot-plug for every pore in the skin of the hands. You can only collect so much; the rest is displaced, volatile, recurring. This must be the reason why we spent so much time—every morning—making the black front of the black stove blacker with black-lead. To disguise and tame the soot.

"Black-lead" was not lead, but a mixture of plumbago, graphite, and iron filings. It came as a stiff paste, and was spread across, and worked into all the black surfaces, avoiding the brassy ones of course, and then buffed and polished and made even with brushes of different densities, and pads of flannel. It was worked into every crevice of every boss on that ornate casting, and then removed again—the job was very badly done if any sludge of polish could be found encrusted around the leaves and petals of the black floral swags along the doors. I remember the phoenix, who must, I think, have been the trademark of that particular furnace. It sat, staring savagely to the left, on a nest of carved crossed branches, surrounded by an elaborate ascending spiral of fat flames with pointed tongues. It was all blackest black, the feathered bird, the burning pyre, the kindled wood, the bright angry eye, the curved beak.

The black-lead gave a most beautiful, subtle, and gentle sheen to the blackness of the stove. It was not like boot-blacking, which produced a mirror-like lacquer. The high content of graphite, the scattering of iron filings, gave a silvery leaden surface—always a *black* surface, but with these shifting hints of soft metallic lightness. I think of it as representing a kind of decorum, a taming and restraining both of the fierce flame inside and the uncompromising cast iron outside. Like all good polishing—almost none of which persists in modern life, for which on the whole we should be grateful—the sheen was built up layer by infinitesimal layer, applied, and almost entirely wiped away again, only the finest skin of mineral adhering and glimmering.

The time is far away when we put so much human blood and muscle into embellishing our houses with careful layers of mineral deposits. Thinking of black-lead made me think of its opposite, the white stone and ground white-stone powder with which we used, daily, or more often, to emphasise our outer doorsteps and windowsills. I remember distinctly smoothing the thick pale stripe along the doorstep with a block of some stone, but I cannot remember the name of the stone itself. It is possible that we simply called it "the stone." We were only required to stone the step when we didn't have a maid to do it. I thought of holystone, blanching stone (perhaps a fabrication) and a run through the *Oxford English Dictionary* added whetstone and sleekstone, a word I hadn't known, which appears to refer to something used on wet clothes in the laundry. Finally I found hearthstone, and hearthstone powder, a mixture of pipeclay, carbonate of lime, size, and stoneblue. "Hearthstone" was sold in chunks by pedlars with barrows. I remember the sulphur in the air from the industrial chimneys of Sheffield and Manchester, a vile, yellow, clogging deposit, which smeared windows and lips alike, and stained the brave white doorsteps almost as soon as they were stoned. But we went out, and whitened them again. We lived a gritty, mineral life, with our noses and fingers in it. I have read that the black-lead was toxic. I thought of the white-lead with which Renaissance ladies painted their skins and poisoned their blood. "Let her paint never an inch thick, to this favour shall she come." I remember the dentists, giving us gobbets of quicksilver in little corked test-tubes, to play with. We spread this on our play-table with naked fingers, watching it shiver into a multitude of droplets, rolling it back together again. It was like a substance from an alien world. It adhered to nothing but itself. Yet we spread it everywhere, losing a silvery liquid bead here, under a splinter of wood, or there, in the fibres of our jumpers. Quicksilver too is toxic. No one told us.

Hearthstone is an ancient and ambiguous idea. In the past, the hearth was a synecdoche for the house, home, or even family or clan. (I cannot bring myself to use that humiliated and patronised word "community.") The hearth was the centre, where the warmth, the food and the burning were. Our hearth was in front of the black-leaded range. We had a "sitting room," but its grate (also regularly black-leaded) was always empty, for no one visited formally enough to sit in its chilly formality. Yet the hearthstone was applied to what was in fact the lintel or *limen*, the threshold. Northerners keep themselves to themselves. The hearthstone stripe on the flagstone step was a limit, a barrier. We were fond of a certain rhetoric. "Never cross my threshold again." "Don't darken my door." The shining silvery dark and the hidden red and gold roar were safely inside. We went out, as my mother used to say, feetfirst, on our final crossing of that bar. Nowadays, of course, we all go into the oven. Then, it was back to the earth out of which all these powders and pomades had been so lovingly extracted.

Jack Smollett realised that this was the first time his imagination had been stirred by the writing (as opposed to the violence, the misery, the animosity, the shamelessness) of one of his students. He went eagerly to his next class, and sat down next to Cicely Fox, whilst they waited for the others to arrive. She was always punctual, and always sat alone in the pews in the shadow out of the multicoloured light of the lampshades. She had fine white hair, thinning a little, which she gathered in a soft roll at the back of her neck. She was always elegantly dressed, with long, fluid skirts, and high-necked jumpers inside loose shirt-jackets, in blacks, greys, silvers. She wore, invariably, a brooch on her inner collar, an amethyst in a circle of seed pearls. She was a thin woman; the flowing garments concealed bony sharpness, not flesh. Her face was long, her skin fine but paper-thin. She had a wide, taut mouth—not much lip—and a straight, elegant nose. Her eyes were the amazing thing. They were so dark, they were almost uniformly black, and seemed to have retreated into the caverns of their sockets, being held to the outer world by the most fragile, spiderweb cradle of lid, and muscle, all stained umber, violet, indigo as though bruised by the strain of staying in place. You could see, Jack thought fancifully, her narrow skull under its vanishing integument. You could see where her jawbone hung together, under fine vellum. She was beautiful, he thought. She had the knack of keeping very still, with a mild attentive almost-smile on her pale lips. Her sleeves were slightly too long and her thin hands were obscured, most of the time.

He said he thought her writing was marvellous. She turned her face to him with a vague and anxious expression.

"*Real* writing," he said. "May I read it to the class?"

"Please," she said, "do as you wish."

He thought she might have difficulty in hearing. He said:

"I hope you are writing more?"

"You hope . . . ?"

"You are writing *more*?" Louder.

"Oh yes. I am doing wash day. It is therapeutic."

"Writing isn't therapy," said Jack Smollett to Cicely Fox. "Not when it's good."

"I expect the motive doesn't matter," said Cicely Fox, in her vague voice. "One has to do one's best."

He felt rebuffed, and didn't know why.

He read "How We Used to Black-lead Stoves" aloud to the class. He read contributions aloud, anonymously, himself. He had a fine voice, and often, not always, he did more justice to the writing than its author might have done. He could also, in the right mood, use the reading as a mode of ironic destruction. His practice was not to name the author of the piece. It was usually easy enough to guess.

He enjoyed reading "How We Used to Black-lead Stoves." He read it *con brio,* savouring the phrases that pleased him. For this reason, perhaps, the class fell upon it like a pack of hounds, snarling and ripping at it. They plucked merciless adjectives from the air.

"Slow." "Clumsy." "Cold." "Pedantic." "Pompous." "Show-off." "Over-ornate." "Nostalgic."

They criticised the movement, equally gaily. "No drive." "No sense of urgency." "Rambling." "All over the place." "No sense of the speaker." "No real feeling." "No living human interest." "No reason for telling us all this stuff."

Bobby Forster, perhaps the star pupil of the class, was obscurely offended by Cicely Fox's black-lead. His *magnum opus,* which was growing thicker, was a very detailed autobiographical account of his own childhood and youth. He had worked his way through measles, mumps, the circus, his school essays, his passions for schoolgirls, recording every fumbling on every sofa, at home, in the girls' homes, in student lodgings, the point of the breast or the suspender he had struggled to touch. He sneered at rivals, put imperceptive parents and teachers in their place, described his reasons for dropping unattractive girls and acquaintances. He said Cicely Fox substituted things for people. He said detachment wasn't a virtue, it just covered up inadequacy. Come to the point, said Bobby Forster. Why should I care about a daft toxic cleaning method that's thankfully obsolete? Why doesn't the writer give us the feelings of the poor skivvy who had to smear the stuff on?

Tamsin Secrett was equally severe. She herself had written a heartrending description of a mother lovingly preparing a meal for an ingrate who neither turned up to eat it nor telephoned to say she was not coming. "Tender succulent al-dente pasta fragrant with spicy herbs redolent of the South of France with tangy melt-in-the-mouth Parmesan, rich smooth virgin olive oil, delicately perfumed with truffle, mouth-wateringly full of savour . . ." Tamsin Secrett said that description for its own sake was simply an *exercise,* every piece of writing needed an *urgent human dimension,* something *vital at stake.* "How We Used to Black-lead Stoves," said Tamsin Secrett, was just mindless heritage-journalism. No bite, said Tamsin Secrett. No bite, agreed her daughter, Lola. Memory Lane. Yuk.

*

Cicely Fox sat rigorously upright, and smiled mildly and vaguely at their animation. She looked as though all this was nothing to do with her. Jack Smollett was not clear how much she heard. He himself, unusually, retaliated irritably on her behalf. He said that it was rare to read a piece of writing that worked on more than one level at once. He said that it took skill to make familiar things look strange. He quoted Ezra Pound: "Make It New." He quoted William Carlos Williams: "No ideas but in things." He only ever did this when he was fired up. He was fired up, not only on Cicely Fox's behalf, but more darkly on his own. For the class's rancour, and the banal words in which it expressed that rancour, blew life into his anxiety over his own words, his own work. He called a coffee break, after which he read out Tamsin Secrett's cookery-tragedy. The class liked that, on the whole. Lola said it was very touching. Mother and daughter kept up an elaborate charade that their writings had nothing to do with each other. The whole class colluded. There was *nothing* worse than dried-up overcooked spag, said Lola Secrett.

The classes tended to end with general discussions of the nature of writing. They all took pleasure in describing themselves at work—what it was like to be blocked, what it was like to become unblocked, what it was like to capture a feeling precisely. Jack wanted Cicely Fox to join in. He addressed her directly, raising his voice slightly.

"And why do you write, Miss Fox?"

"Well, I would hardly say I do write as yet. But I write because I like words. I suppose if I liked stone I might carve. I like words. I like reading. I notice particular words. That sets me off."

This answer was, though it should not have been, unusual.

Jack himself found it harder and harder to know where to begin to describe anything. Distaste for the kind of words employed by Tamsin and Lola made him impotent with revulsion and anger. Cliché spread like a stain across the written world, and he didn't know a technique for expunging it. Nor had he the skill to do what

Leonardo said we should do with cracks, or Constable with cloud forms, and make the stains into new, suggested forms.

Cicely Fox did not come to the pub with the rest of the class. Jack could not offer to drive her home, for the idea of her frail bony form on his motorbike was impossible. He realised he was trying to think of ways to get to talk to her, as though she had been a pretty girl.

The best he could do was to sit next to her in the coffee break in the church. This was hard, because everyone wanted his attention. On the other hand, because of her deafness perhaps, she sat slightly separate from the others, so he could move next to her. But then he had to shout.

"I was wondering what you read, Miss Fox?"

"Oh, the old things. They wouldn't interest you young people. Things I used to like as a girl. Poetry increasingly. I find I don't seem to want to read novels much anymore."

"I'd put you down as a reader of Jane Austen."

"Had you?" she said vaguely. "I suppose you would," she added, without revealing whether or not she liked Jane Austen. He felt snubbed. He said:

"*Which* poems, Miss Fox?"

"These days, mostly George Herbert."

"Are you religious?"

"No. He is the only writer who makes me regret that for a moment. He makes one understand grace. Also, he is good on dust."

"Dust?" He dredged his memory and came up with "Who sweeps a room as for thy laws / Makes that and the action fine."

"I like *Church Monuments.* With death sweeping dust with an incessant motion.

> "Flesh is but the glass, which holds the dust
> That measures all our time; which also shall
> Be crumbled into dust.

"And then I like the poem where he speaks of his God stretching 'a crumme of dust from Hell to Heaven.' Or . . .

> "O that thou shouldst give dust a tongue to cry to thee
> And then not heare it crying.

"He knew," said Cicely Fox, "the proper relation between words and things. Dust is a good word."

He tried to ask her how this fitted into her writing, but she appeared to have retreated again, after this small burst of speech, into her deafness.

Wash Day

In those days, washing took all the week. We boiled on Monday, starched on Tuesday, dried on Wednesday, ironed on Thursday, and mended on Friday. Besides all the other things there were to do. We washed outside, in the washhouse, which was an out-house, with its own stone sink, hand pump, copper with a fire beneath it, and flagged floor. Other implements were the mon-strous mangle, the great galvanised tubs, and the ponch. Our washhouse was made of stone blocks with a slate roof, and house-leeks growing on the roof. Its chimney smoked, and its windows steamed over. In winter, the steam melted the ice. It was full of extremes of watery climate. As a child, I used to put my face against the stones and find them hot to touch, or anyway warmish, on wash day. I pretended it was the witch's cottage in fairy tales.

First there was sorting and boiling. You boiled whites in the copper, which was a huge rounded vat with a wooden lid. All the wood in the washhouse was soap-slippery, both flaked apart and held together by melted and congealed soap. You boiled the whites—sheets, pillowcases, tablecloths, napkins, tea towels and so on, and then you used the boiled water, let down a bit, in the tubs, to wash the more delicate things, or the coloured things which might run.

You had heavy wooden pincers and poles to stir the whites in the boiling water; steam came off in clouds, and a kind of grey scum formed on the surface. When they were boiled they went through various rinses in tubs. There was a hiss and a slopping as the hot cloth hit the freezing water in the tubs. Then you ponched it. The ponch was a kind of copper kettle–like thing on a long pole, full of holes like a vast tea infuser, or closed colander. It soughed and sucked at the cloth in the water, leaving little bosses of pulled damask or cotton where it had impressed itself and clung. Then with pincers—and your bare arms—you hoisted all the weight of the sheets from one tub to another tub to another. And then you folded the streaming stuff and wound it through the wooden jaw-rollers of the mangle. The mangle had red wheels to turn the rollers, and a polished wooden handle to turn the wheel. It sluiced soapy water back into an under-tub, or splashed it on the floor. You were also always pumping more water—yanking the pump-handle, winding the mangle-handle. You froze, you were scalded. You stood in clouds of steam and breathed an air which was always full of a thick sweat—your own sweat, with the effort, and the odour of the dirt from the clothes that was being released into the air and the water.

Then there were the things you had to pull the washed clothes through, or soak them in. There was Reckitt's Blue. I don't know what that was made of. Because we lived in Derbyshire I always associated it with blue john, from the Peaks, which I know is quite wrong, but is a verbal association which has lingered. It came in little cylindrical bags, wrapped in white muslin, and produced an intense cobalt colour when the little bags were swirled in the blue rinsing water. What went through the blue water (which was always cold) were the whites. I don't know by what optical process this blue staining made the whites whiter, but I can clearly remember that it did. It wasn't bleach. It didn't remove recalcitrant stains of tea, or urine, or strawberry juice—you had to use real bleach for that, which smelled evil and deathly. The Reckitt's Blue went out into the water in little clouds and fibrils, and tendrils of colour. Like fine threads of glass in glass marbles. Or blood, if you put a cut finger in a dish of water. You couldn't see it very well in the galvanised tubs, but on days when there wasn't too much we used to do the blueing in a white enamel panshon, and then you could see the threading cloud of bright blue going into the clear water, and mingling, until the water was blue. Then you swirled the cloth in the blue water—swirled it, and squashed it, and punched and *mashed* it, until it was impregnated with blue, until all the white glistened in pale blueness. As a very little girl, I used to think the white cloth and the blue water were like clouds in the sky, but this was silly. Because in fact in the sky, the white watery clouds stain the blue, not the other way round. It was an inversion, a draining. For when you held up the sheets, and took them from the blue water to drain them, you could see the blue run away and the white whiter, blue-white, a different white from cream, or ivory, or scorched-yellow white, a white under blue dripping liquid that had been changed, but not dyed.

Then there was starch. Starch was viscous and gluey, it thickened the washing water like gruel. I suppose it was a kind of gruel, if you think of it. Farinaceous molecules expanding in heat. Starch was slippery and reminded all of us of substances we didn't like to think of—bodily fluids and products—though in fact, it is an innocent, clean, vegetable thing, unlike soap, which is compressed mutton fat, however perfumed. Cloth slipped into starch, and was coated with it. There were degrees of starching. Very dense, glutinous starch for shirt collars. Light, spun-glass starch for delicate nightdresses and knickers. When you hoisted a garment out of a bath of starch it stiffened and fell into flutes like a carving—or if by mistake you left it lying around, anyhow, and it dried out, it would become solid crumples and lumps, like pleated stones where the earth had folded on itself. Starch had to be ironed damp. The smell of the hot iron on the jelly was like a parody of cooking. Gluten, I suppose. You could smell scorching as you could smell burning cakes. You had a nose for things not as they should be.

Clothes in the process of being cleansed haunted our lives. They were accompanying angels, souls washed white in the blood of the Lamb, surrounding us with their rustle and their pale scent. In the eighteenth century, I imagine, wash days happened once or twice a year, but our time was obsessed with cleansing and had not invented mechanical helpers. We went through an endless cycle of bubble, toil, and trouble, surrounded by an only too visible inanimate host. They danced in the wind, fluttering vain arms, raising full-bellied skirts to reveal vacancy, coiling round each other like white worms. Indoors, they hung in the kitchen on long racks, winched up to the ceiling, from where they then dangled, stiff as boards, like shrouded hanging men. They lay neatly folded, before and after ironing, like dead choirboys in effigy, fluted and frilled. Under the hot iron (on Thursdays) they writhed and winced and shrank. My great-aunt's huge shapeless rayon petticoats flared all colours of the rainbow, spectral, sizzling russets and air-force blues, shot with copper, shot with peacock blue. They melted easily, gophering into scabs which resolved themselves into pinholes and were unredeemable. The irons were filled with hot coals from the kitchen range. They were heavy; they had to be watched for soot-smears which would condemn a garment to an immediate return to the washpot. Inside them the coals of fire smouldered, spat, and dimmed. The kitchen was full of the smell of singeing, a tawny smell, a parody of the good golden cooking smells of buns and biscuits.

It was hard work, but work was life. Work was coiled and woven into breathing and sleeping and eating, as the shirtsleeves coiled and wove themselves into a tangle with nightdress ribbons and Sunday sashes. In her old age my mother sat beside a twin-tub washing machine, a mechanical reduction of all those archaic containers and hoists and pulleys, and lifted her underwear and pillowcases from wash to rinse to spin with the same wooden pincers. She was arthritic and bird-boned, like a cross seagull. She was offered a new machine with a porthole, which would wash and dry a little every day, and, it was thought, relieve her. She was

> appalled and distressed. She said she would feel dirty—she would feel *bad*—if she had no wash day. She needed steam and stirring to convince her that she was alive and virtuous. Towards the end, the increasing number of soiled sheets defeated her, and perhaps even killed her, though I think she died, not from overexertion, but from chagrin when she finally had to admit she could no longer wield her ponch or lift a bucket. She felt unnecessary. She had a new white nightdress which she had washed, starched, ironed, and never worn, ready to shroud her still white flesh in her coffin, its Reckitt's Blue glinting now livelier than the shrunken, bruised yellow-grey of her eyelids and lips.

The creative writing class liked this slightly sinister study of cleanliness no better than its predecessor. They introduced the word "overwritten" into their remorseless criticisms. Jack Smollett reflected, not for the first time, that there was an element of kindergarten regression in all adult classes. Group behaviour took over, gangs formed, victims were selected. There were intense jealousies over the teacher's attention, and intense resentments of any show of partiality from the teacher. Cicely Fox was becoming a "teacher's pet." Nobody had much spoken to her in the coffee breaks before Jack's enthusiasm for her work became apparent, but now there was deliberate cutting, and cold-shouldering.

Jack himself knew what he ought to do, or have done. He should have kept his enthusiasm quiet. Or quieter. He was not quite sure why it mattered to him so much to insist that Cicely Fox's writings were the real thing, the thing itself, to the detriment of good order and goodwill. He felt he was standing up for something, like an ancient Wesleyan bearing witness. The "something" was writing, not Miss Fox herself. She dealt with the criticism of her adjectives, the suggestions for livening things up, by smiling vaguely and benignly, nodding occasionally. But Jack felt that he had been teaching something *muddy,* an illegitimate therapy, and suddenly here was writing. Miss Fox's brief essays made Jack want to write. They made him see the world as something to be written. Lola Secrett's pout was an object of delighted study: the right words *would be found* to distinguish it from all other pouts. He wanted to describe the taste of the nasty coffee, and the slope of the headstones in the graveyard. He loved the whirling nastiness of the class because—perhaps—he could write it.

He tried to behave equitably. He made a point of *not* sitting next to Cicely Fox in the coffee break of the "Wash Day" session, but went and talked to Bobby Forster and Rosy Wheelwright. His new remorseless writer's conscience knew that there was something wrong with all Bobby Forster's sentences, a limping rhythm, an involuntary echo of other writers, a note like the clunk of a piano key when the string is dead. But he was interested in Bobby Forster, his mixture of jauntiness and fear, his intense interest in every event of his own daily activities, which was, after all, writerly. Bobby Forster said he'd sent away for the entrance forms for a competition for new writers in the literary supplement of a Sunday paper. There was a big prize—£2000—and the promise of publication, with the further promise of interest from publishers.

Bobby Forster said he thought he stood a pretty good chance of getting some attention. "I've been thinking I ought to move on from being a literary Learner Driver, you know." Jack Smollett grinned and agreed.

When he got home, he typed up "How We Used to Black-lead Stoves" and "Wash Day" and sent them to the newspaper. The entries had to be submitted under a pseudonym. He chose Jane Temple for Cicely Fox. Jane for Austen, Temple for Herbert. He waited, and in due course received the letter he had never really expected not to receive—all this was *fated*. Cicely Fox had won the competition. She should get in touch with the newspaper, in order to arrange printing, prize giving, an interview.

He was not sure how Cicely Fox would react to this. He was by now somewhat obsessed by the idea of her, but did not feel that he knew her, in any way. He dreamed of her, often, sitting in the corner of his caravan with her neat hair, scarfed neck, and fragile, cobweb skin, studying him with her darkly hooded eyes. She was judging him for having abandoned, or not having learned, his craft. He knew that he had called up, created, this unnerving Muse. The real Cicely Fox was an elderly English lady, who wrote to please herself. She might well regard his actions as impermissible. She came to his class, but did not submit herself to his, or its judgment. But she judged. He was sure she judged.

The prize he had so to speak put her in the way of winning was a propitiatory offering. He wanted—desperately—that she should be pleased, be happy, admit him to her confidence.

He got on his motorbike and drove for the first time to Miss Fox's address, which was in a road called Primrose Lane, in a respectable suburb. The houses there were late Victorian semi-detached, and had a cramped look, partly because they were built of large blocks of pinkish stone, and there was something wrong with the proportions. The windows were heavy sash-windows, in black-painted frames. Cicely Fox's windows were all veiled in heavy lacy curtains, not blue-white, but creamy white, he noticed. He noticed the pruned rose bushes in the front garden, and the donkey-stoned sill of the front step. The door was also black, and in need of repainting. The bell was set in a brass boss. He rang. No one answered. He rang again. Nothing.

He had worked himself up to this scene, the presentation of the letter, her response, whatever it was. He remembered that she was deaf. The gate to the side alley round the house was open. He walked in, past some dustbins, and came into a back garden, with a diminutive lawn and some ragged buddleia. And a rotary clothes drier, with nothing hanging from it. There was a back door, also standing above white-lined stone steps. He knocked. Nothing. He tried the handle, and the door swung inwards. He stood on the threshold and called.

"Miss Fox! Cicely Fox! Miss Fox, are you there? It's Jack Smollett."

⋆

There was still no reply. He should have gone home at that point, he thought, over and over, later. But he stood there undecided, and then heard a sound, a sound like a bird trapped in a chimney, or a cushion falling from a sofa. He went in through the back door, and crossed a gaunt kitchen, of which he had afterwards only the haziest recollection—dingy wartime "utility" furniture, a stained sink, hospital-green cupboards, an ancient gas-cooker, one leg propped unsteadily on a broken brick. Beyond the kitchen was a hall, with a linoleum floor, and a curious smell. It was a smell both human and musty, the kind of smell overlaid in hospitals by disinfectant. There was no disinfectant here. The hall was dark. Dark, narrow stairs rose into darkness inside ugly boxed-in banisters. He went on tiptoe, creaking in his biking leathers, and pushed open a door into a dimly lit sitting room. Opposite him, in a chair, was a moaning bundle with huge face, grey-skinned, blotched, furred with down, above which a few white hairs floated on a bald pink dome. The eyes were yellow, vague, and bloodshot and did not seem to see him.

In the opposite corner was an overturned television. Its screen was smeared with something that looked like blood. Next to it he saw a pair of naked feet, at the end of long, stringy, naked legs. The rest of the body was bent round the television. Jack Smollett had to cross the room to see the face, and until he saw it, did not think for a moment that it belonged to Cicely Fox. It was turned into the worn sprigged carpet, under a mass of dishevelled white hair. The whole naked body was covered with scars, scabs, stripes, little round burn marks, fresh wounds. There was a much more substantial wound in the throat. There was fresh blood on the forget-me-nots and primroses in the carpet. It was not nice. Cicely Fox was quite dead.

The old creature in the chair made a series of sounds, a chuckle, a swallowing, a wheeze. Jack Smollett made himself go across and ask her, what has happened, who . . . is there a telephone? The lips flapped loosely, and a kind of twittering was all the answer he got. He remembered his mobile phone, and went out, precipitately, into the back garden, where he phoned the police, and was sick.

The police came, and were diligent. The old woman in the chair turned out to be a Miss Flossie Marsh. She and Cicely Fox had lived together in that house since 1949. Miss Marsh had not been seen for many years, and no one could be found who remembered her having spoken. Nor, despite all the efforts of police and doctors, did she speak, then, or ever. Miss Fox had always been briskly pleasant to her neighbours, but had not encouraged contact, or invited anyone in, ever. No one ever found any explanation for the torture that appeared to have been applied to Cicely Fox, clearly over a considerable period of time. Neither lady had any living relatives. The police found no sign of any intruder, other than Jack Smollett. The newspapers reported the affair briefly and ghoulishly. A verdict of murder was brought in, and the case lapsed.

Jack Smollett's class were temporarily subdued by Miss Fox's fate. Jack's miserable face made them uneasy. They fetched him coffee. They were kind to him.

He couldn't write. Cicely Fox's death had destroyed his desire to write, as surely as the black-lead and the wash day had kindled it. He dreamed repeatedly, and had waking visions, of her poor tormented skin, her bleeding neck, her agonised jaw. He knew, he had seen, and he couldn't get down, what had happened. He wondered if Miss Fox's writing had in fact been a desperate therapy for an appalling life. There were layers and layers of those old scars. Not only on Miss Fox, on the mute Flossie Marsh also. He *could not* write that.

The class, on the other hand, buzzed and hummed with the anticipated pleasure of writing it up, one day. They were vindicated. Miss Fox belonged after all in the normal world of their writings, the world of domestic violence, torture and shock-horror. They would write what they knew, what had happened to Cicely Fox, and it would be most satisfactorily therapeutic.

A STONE WOMAN

(FOR TORFI TULINIUS)

At first she did not think of stones. Grief made her insubstantial to herself; she felt herself flitting lightly from room to room, in the twilit apartment, like a moth. The apartment seemed constantly twilit, although it must, she knew, have gone through the usual sequences of sun and shadow over the days and weeks since her mother died. Her mother—a strong bright woman—had liked to live amongst shades of mole and dove. Her mother's hair had shone silver and ivory. Her eyes had faded from cornflower to forget-me-not. Ines found her dead one morning, her bloodless fingers resting on an open book, her parchment eyelids down, as though she dozed, a wry grimace on her fine lips, as though she had tasted something not quite nice. She quickly lost this transient lifelikeness, and became waxy and peaked. Ines, who had been the younger woman, became the old woman, in an instant.

She busied herself with her dictionary work, and with tidying love away. She packed it into plastic sacks, creamy silks and floating lawns, velvet and muslin, lavender crêpe de Chine, beads of pearl and garnet. People had thought she was a dutiful daughter. They did not imagine, she thought, two intelligent women who understood each other easily, and loved each other. She drew the blinds because the light hurt her eyes. Her inner eye observed final things over and over. White face on white pillow amongst white hair. Colourless skin on lifeless fingers. Flesh of my flesh, flesh of her flesh. The efficient rage of consuming fire, the handfuls of fawn ash which she had scattered, as she had promised, in the hurrying foam of a Yorkshire beck.

She went through the motions, hoping to become accustomed to solitude and silence. Then one morning pain struck her like a sudden beak, tearing at her gut. She caught her breath and sat down, waiting for it to pass. It did not pass, but strengthened, blow on blow. She rolled on her bed, dishevelled and sweating. She heard the creature moaning. She tried to telephone the doctor, but the thing shrieked raucously into the mouthpiece, and this saved her, for they sent an ambulance, which took the screaming thing to a hospital, as it would not have taken a polite old woman. Later they told her she had had at most four hours to live. Her gut was twisted and gangrenous. She lay quietly in a hospital bed in a curtained room. She was numb and bandaged, and drifted in and out of blessed sleep.

The surgeon came and went, lifting her dressings, studying the sutures, prodding the walls of her belly with strong fingers, awakening sullen coils of pain somewhere in deep, yet less than mothlike on the surface. Ines was a courteous and shamefast woman. She did not want to see her own sliced skin and muscle.

She thanked him for her life, unable to summon up warmth in her voice. What was her life now, to thank anyone for? When he had gone, she lied to the nurses about the great pain she said she felt, so they would bring drugs, and the sensation of vanishing in soft smoke, which was almost pleasure.

The wound healed—very satisfactorily, they said. The anaesthetist came in to discuss what palliatives she might be allowed to take home with her. He said, "I expect you've noticed there's no sensation around the incision. That's quite normal. The nerves take time to join again, and some may not do so." He too touched the sewed-up lips of the hole, and she felt that she did not feel, and then felt the ghost of a thrill, like fine wires, shooting out across her skin. She still did not look at the scar. The anaesthetist said, "I see he managed to construct some sort of navel. People feel odd, we've found, if they haven't got a navel."

She murmured something. "Look," he said, "it's a work of art."

So she looked, since she would be going home, and would now have to attend to the thing herself.

The wound was livid and ridged and ran the length of her white front, from under the ribs to the hidden places underneath her. Where she had been soft and flat, she was all plumpings and hollows, like an old cushion. And where her navel had been, like a button caught in a seam at an angle, was an asymmetric whorl with a little sill of skin. Ines thought of her lost navel, of the umbilical cord that had been a part of her and of her mother. Her face creased into sorrow; her eyes were hot with tears. The anaesthetist misinterpreted them, and assured her that it would all look much less angry and lumpy after a month or two, and if it did not, it could be easily dealt with by a good plastic surgeon. Ines thanked him, and closed her eyes. There was no one to see her, she said, it didn't matter what she looked like. The anaesthetist, who had chosen his profession because he didn't like people's feelings, and preferred silence to speech, offered her what she wanted, a painkiller. She drifted into gathered cloud as he closed the door.

Their flat, now her flat, was on the second floor of a nineteenth-century house in a narrow city square. The stairs were steep. The taxi driver who brought her home left her, with her bag, on the doorstep. She toiled slowly upwards, resting her bag on the stairs, clinging to the banisters, aware of every bone in knee and ankle and wrist, and also of the paradox of pain in the gut and the strange numb casing of the surface skin. There was no need to hurry. She had time, and more time.

Inside the flat, she found herself preoccupied with time and dust. She had been a good cook—she thought of herself in the past tense—and had made delicious little meals for her mother and herself, light pea soups, sole with mushrooms, vanilla soufflés. Now she could make neither cooking nor eating last long enough to be interesting. She nibbled at cheese and crusts like a frugal mouse, and could not stay seated at her table but paced her room. The life had gone out of the furnishings and objects. The polish was dulled and she left it like that: she made her bed with one crumpled pull. She had a sense that the dust was thickening on everything.

She did what work she had to do, conscientiously. The problem was, that there was not enough of it. She worked as a part-time researcher for a major etymological dictionary, and in the past had been assiduous and inventive in suggesting new entries, new problems. Now, she answered those queries which were sent to her, and they did not at all fill up the huge cavern of space and time in which she floated and sank. She got up, and dressed herself carefully, as though she was "going out to work." She knew she must not let herself go, that was what she must not do. Then she walked about in the spinning dust and came to a standstill and stared out of the window, for minutes that seemed like hours, and hours that seemed like minutes. She liked to see the dark spread in the square, because then bedtime was not far away.

The day came when the dressings could, should, be dispensed with. She had been avoiding her body, simply wiping her face and under her arms with a damp face cloth. She decided to have a bath. Their bath was old and deep and narrow, with imposing brass taps and a heavy coil of shower hosing. There was a wide wooden bath-rack across it, which still held, she saw now, private things of her mother's—a loofah, a sponge, a pumice stone. Her mother had never needed help in the bathroom. She had made fragrant steam from rosewater in a blue bottle, she had used baby talc, scented with witch-hazel. For some reason these things had escaped the postmortem clearance. Ines thought of clearing them now, and then thought, what does it matter? She ran a deep lukewarm bath. The old plumbing clanked and shuddered. She hung her dressing gown—grey flannel—on the door, and very carefully, feeling a little giddy, clutching the rim, climbed into the bath and let her bruised flesh down into the water.

The warmth was nice. A few tense sinews relaxed. Time went into one of its slow phases. She sat and stared at the things on the rack. Loofah, sponge, pumice. A fibrous tube, a soft mess of holes, a shaped grey stone. She considered the differences between the three, all essentially solids with holes in. The loofah was stringy and matted, the sponge was branching and vacuous, the pumice was riddled with needle holes. She stared, feeling that she and they were weightless, floating and swelling in her giddiness. Biscuit-coloured, bleached khaki, shadow-grey. Colourless colours, shapeless shapes. She picked up the sponge, and squeezed cooling water over her bust, studying the random forms of droplets and tricklings. She did not like the sponge's touch; it was clammy and fleshy. The loofah and the sponge were the dried-out bodies, the skeletons, of living things. She picked up the pumice, a light stone tear, shaped to the palm of a hand, felt its paradoxical lightness, and dropped it into the water, where it floated. She did not know how long she sat there. The water cooled. She made a decision, to throw away the sponge. When she lifted herself, awkwardly, through the surface film, the pumice chinked against her flesh. It was an odd little sound, like a knock on metal. She put the pumice back on the rack, and touched her puckered wound with nervy fingers. Supposing something should be left in there? A clamp, a forceps, a needle? Not exactly looking she explored her reconstructed navel with a fingertip. She felt the absence of sensation and a certain glossy hardness where the healing was going on. She tapped, very softly, with her fingernail. She was not sure whether it was, or was not, a chink.

The next thing she noticed was a spangling of what seemed like glinting red dust, or ground glass, in the folds of her dressing gown and her discarded underwear. It was a dull red, like dried blood, which does not have a sheen. It increased in quantity, rather than diminished, once she had noticed it. She observed tiny conical heaps of it, by skirting boards, on the corners of Persian rugs—conical heaps, slightly depressed, like anthill castings or miniaturised volcanoes. At the same time she noticed that her underwear appeared to be catching threads, here and there, on the rough, numb expanse of the healing scars. She felt a kind of horror and shame in looking at herself spread with lumps and an artificial navel. As the phenomenon grew more pronounced, she explored the area tentatively with her fingertips, over the cotton of her knickers. Her stomach was without sensation. Her fingers felt whorls and ridges, even sharp edges. They disturbed the glassy dust, which came away with the cloth, and shone in its creases. Each day the bumps and sharpness, far from calming, became more pronounced. One evening, in the unlit twilight, she finally found the nerve to undress, and tuck in her chin to stare down at herself. What she saw was a raised shape, like a starfish, like the whirling arms of a nebula in the heavens. It was the colour—or *a* colour—of raw flesh, like an open whip wound or knife slash. It trembled, because she was trembling, but it was cold to the touch, cold and hard as glass or stone. From the star-arms the red dust wafted like glamour. She covered herself hastily, as though what was not seen might disappear.

The next day, it felt bigger. The day after, she looked again, in the half-light, and saw that the blemish was spreading. It had pushed out ruddy veins into the tired white flesh, threading sponge with crystal. It winked. It was many reds, from ochre to scarlet, from garnet to cinnabar. She was half-tempted to insert a fingernail under the veins and chip them off, and she could not.

She thought of it as "the blemish." She thought more and more about it, even when it was covered and out of sight. It extended itself—not evenly, but in fits and starts, around her waist, like a shingly girdle pushing down long fibrous fingers towards her groin, thrusting out cysts and gritty coruscations towards her pubic hair. There were puckered weals where flesh met what appeared to be stone. What *was* stone, what else was it?

One day she found a cluster of greenish-white crystals sprouting in her armpit. These she tried to prise away, and failed. They were attached deep within; they could be felt to be stirring stony roots under the skin surface, pulling the muscles. Jagged flakes of silica and nodes of basalt pushed her breasts upward and flourished under the fall of flesh, making her clothes crackle and rustle. Slowly, slowly, day by quick day, her torso was wrapped in a stony encrustation, like a corselet. She could feel that under the stones her compressed inwards were still fluid and soft, responsive to pain and pressure.

She was surprised at the fatalism with which she resigned herself to taking horrified glances at her transformation. It was as though, much of the time, her thoughts and feelings had slowed to stone-speed, nerveless and stolid. There were, increasingly, days when a new curiosity jostled the horror. One day, one of the blue veins on her inner thigh erupted into a line of rubious spinels, and she thought of jewels before she thought of pustules. They glittered as she moved. She saw that her stony casing was not static—points of rock salt and milky quartz thrust through glassy sheets of basalt, bubbles of sinter formed like tears between layers of hornblende. She learned the names of some of the stones when curiosity got the better of passive fear. The flat, a dictionary-maker's flat, was furnished with encyclopaedias of all sorts. She sat in the evening lamplight and read the lovely words: pyrolusite, ignimbrite, omphacite, uvarovite, glaucophane, schist, shale, gneiss, tuff.

Her inner thighs now chinked together when she moved. The first apparition of the stony crust outside her clothing was strange and beautiful. She observed its beginnings in the mirror one morning, brushing her hair—a necklace of veiled swellings above her collarbone which broke slowly through the skin like eyes from closed lids, and became opal—fire opal, black opal, geyserite, and hydrophane, full of watery light. She found herself preening at herself in her mirror. She wondered, fatalistically and drowsily, whether when she was all stone, she would cease to breathe, see, and move. For the moment she had grown no more than a carapace. Her joints obeyed her, light went from retina to brain, her budded tongue tasted food that she still ate.

She dismissed, with no real hesitation, the idea of consulting the surgeon, or any other doctor. Her slowing mind had become trenchant, and she saw clearly that she would be an object of horror and fascination, to be shut away and experimented on. It was of course, theoretically, possible that she was greatly deluded, that the winking gemstones and heaped flakes of her new crust were feverish sparks of her anaesthetised brain and grieving spirit. But she didn't think so—she refuted herself as Dr. Johnson refuted Bishop Berkeley, by tapping on stone and hearing the scrape and chink of stone responding. No, what was happening was, it appeared, a unique transformation. She assumed it would end with the petrifaction of her vital functions. A moment would come when she wouldn't be able to see, or move, or feed herself (which might not matter). Her mother had not had to face death—she had told herself it was not yet, not for just now, not round the next corner. She herself was about to observe its approach in a new fantastic form. She thought of recording the transformations, the metamorphic folds, the ooze, the conchoidal fractures. Then when "they" found her, "they" would have a record of how she had become what she was. She would observe, unflinching.

But she continually put off the writing, partly because she preferred standing to sitting at a desk, and partly because she could not fix the process in her mind clearly enough to make words of it. She stood in the light of the window morning and evening, and read the stony words in the geological handbooks. She stood by the mirror in the bathroom and tried to identify the components of her crust. They changed, she was almost sure, minute by minute. She had found a description of the pumice stone—"a pale grey frothy volcanic glass, part of a pyroclastic flow made of very hot particles; flattened pumice fragments are known as fiamme." She imagined her lungs full of vesicles like the frothy stone, becoming stone. She found traces of hot flows down her own flanks, over her own thighs. She went into her mother's bedroom, where there was a cheval glass, the only full-length mirror in the house.

At the end of a day's staring she would see a new shimmer of labradorite, six inches long and diamond-shaped, arrived imperceptibly almost between her buttocks where her gaze had not rested.

She saw dikes of dolerites, in graduated sills, now invading her inner arms. But it took weeks of patient watching before, by dint of glancing in rapid saccades, she surprised a bubble of rosy barite crystals, breaking through a vein of fluorspar, and opening into the form known as a desert rose, bunched with the ore flowers of blue john. Her metamorphosis obeyed no known laws of physics or chemistry: ultramafic black rocks and ghostly Iceland spar formed in succession, and clung together.

After some time, she noticed that her patient and stoical expectation of final inertia was not being fulfilled. As she grew stonier, she felt a desire to move, to be out of doors. She stood in the window and observed the weather. She found she wanted to go out, both on bright days, and even more in storms. One dark Sunday, when the midday sky was thick and grey as granite, when sullen thunder rumbled and the odd flash of lightning made human stomachs queasy, Ines was overcome with a need to be out in the weather. She put on wide trousers and a tunic, and over them a shapeless hooded raincoat. She pushed her knobby feet into fur boots, and her clay-pale hands, with their veins of azurmalachite, into sheepskin mittens, and set out down the stairs and into the street.

She had wondered how her tendons and musculature would function. She thought she could feel the roll of polished stone in stony cup as she moved her pelvis and hips, raised her knees, and swung her rigid arms. There was a delicious smoothness to these motions, a surprise after the accommodations she was used to making with the crumbling calcium of arthritic joints. She strode along, aimlessly at first, trying to get away from people. She noticed that her sense of smell had changed, and was sharper. She could smell the rain in the thick cloud blanket. She could smell the carbon in the car exhausts and the rainbow-coloured minerals in puddles of petrol. These scents were pleasurable. She came to the remains of a street market, and was assailed by the stink of organic decay, deliquescent fruit mush, rotting cabbage, old burned oil on greasy newspapers and mashed fishbones. She strode past all this, retching a little, feeling acid bile churning in a stomach sac made by now of what?

She came to a park—a tamed, urban park, with rose beds and rubbish bins, doggy lavatories and a concrete fountain. She could hear the water on the cement with a new intricate music. The smell of a rain squall blew away the wafting warmth of dog shit. She put up her face and pulled off her hood. Her cheeks were beginning to sprout silicone flakes and dendrite fibres, but she only looked, she thought, like a lumpy old woman. There were droplets of alabaster and peridot clustering in her grey hair like the eggs of some mythic stony louse, but they could not yet be seen, except from close. She shook her hair free and turned her face up to the branches and the clouds as the rain began. Big drops splashed on her sharp nose; she licked them from stiffening lips between crystalline teeth, with a still-flexible tongue tip, and tasted skywater, mineral and delicious. She stood there and let the thick streams of water run over her body and down inside her flimsy garments, streaking her carnelian nipples and adamantine wrists. The lightning came in sheets of metal sheen. The thunder crashed in the sky and the surface of the woman crackled and creaked in sympathy.

She thought, I need to find a place where I should stand, when I am completely solid, I should find a place *outside,* in the weather.

When would she be, so to speak, dead? When her plump flesh heart stopped pumping the blue blood along the veins and arteries of her shifting shape? When the grey and clammy matter of her brain became limestone or graphite? When her brainstem became a column of rutilated quartz? When her eyes became—what? She inclined to the belief that her watching eyes would be the last thing, even though fine threads on her nostrils still conveyed the scent of brass or coal to the primitive lobes at the base of the brain. The phrase came into her head: Those are pearls that were his eyes. A song of grief made fantastic by a sea change. Would her eyes cloud over and become pearls? Pearls were interesting. They were a substance where the organic met the inorganic, like moss agate. Pearls were stones secreted by a living shellfish, perfected inside the mother-of-pearl of its skeleton to protect its soft inward flesh from an irritant. She went to her mother's jewel box, in search of a long string of freshwater pearls she had given her for her seventieth birthday. There they lay and glimmered; she took them out and wound them round her sparkling neck, streaked already with jet, opal, and jacinth zircon.

She had had the idea that the mineral world was a world of perfect, inanimate forms, with an unchanging mathematical order of crystals and molecules beneath its sprouts and flows and branches. She had thought, when she had started thinking, about her own transfiguration as something profoundly unnatural, a move from a world of warm change and decay to a world of cold permanence. But as she became mineral, and looked into the idea of minerals, she saw that there were reciprocities, both physical and figurative. There were whole ranges of rocks and stones which, like pearls, were formed from things which had once been living. Not only coal and fossils, petrified woods and biohermal limestones—oolitic and pisolitic limestones, formed round dead shells—but chalk itself, which was mainly made up of microorganisms, or cherts and flints, massive bedded forms made up of the skeletons of Radiolaria and diatoms. These were themselves once living stones—living marine organisms that spun and twirled around skeletons made of opal.

The minds of stone lovers had colonised stones as lichens cling to them with golden or grey-green florid stains. The human world of stones is caught in organic metaphors like flies in amber. Words came from flesh and hair and plants. Reniform, mammilated, botryoidal, dendrite, haematite. Carnelian is from carnal, from flesh. Serpentine and lizardite are stone reptiles; phyllite is leafy green. The earth itself is made in part of bones, shells, and diatoms. Ines was returning to it in a form quite different from her mother's fiery ash and bonemeal. She preferred the parts of her body that were now volcanic glasses, not bony chalk. Chabazite, from the Greek for hailstones, obsidian, which, like analcime and garnet, has the perfect icositetarahedral shape.

⋆

Whether or not she became wholly inanimate, she must find a place to stand in the weather before she became immobile. She visited city squares, and stood experimentally by the rims of fountains, or in the entrances of grottoes. She had read of the hidden wildernesses of nineteenth-century graveyards, and it came to her that in such a place, amongst weeping angels and grieving cherubs, she might find a quiet resting place. So she set out on foot, hooded and booted, with her new indefatigable rolling pace, marble joint in marble socket. It was a grey day, at the end of winter, with specks between rain and snow spitting in the fitful wind. She strode in through a wrought-iron gate in a high wall.

What she saw was a flat stony city, house after house under the humped ripples of earth, marked by flat stones, standing stones, canted stones, fallen stones, soot-stained, dropping-stained, scum-stained, crumbled, carved, repeating, repeating. She walked along its silent pathways, past dripping yews and leafless birches and speckled laurels, looking for stone women. They stood there—or occasionally lay fallen there—on the rich earth. There were many of them, but they resembled each other with more than a family resemblance. There were the sweetly regretful lady angels, one arm pointing upwards, one turned down to scatter an arrested fall of stony flowers. There were the chubby child angels, wearing simple embroidered stone tunics over chubby stone knees, also holding drooping flowers. Some busy monumental mason had turned them out to order, one after the other, their sweetly arched lips, or apple-cheeks, well-practised tricks of the trade. There was no other living person in that place, though there was a great deal of energetic organic life—long snaking brambles thrust between the stones for a place in the light, tombstones and angels alike wore bushy coats of gripping ivy, shining in the wind and the wet, as the leaves moved very slightly. Ines looked at the repeated stone people. Several had lost their hands, and lifted blind stumps to the grey air. These were less upsetting than those who were returning to formlessness, and had fists that seemed rotted by leprosy. Someone had come and sliced the heads from the necks of several cherubs—recently, the severed edges were still an even white. The stony representations of floating things—feathered wings, blossoms, and petals—made Ines feel queasy, for they were inert and weighed down, they were pulled towards the earth and what was under it.

Once or twice she saw things which spoke to her own condition. A glint of gold in the tesserae of a mosaic pavement over a house whose ascription was hopelessly obscured. A sarcophagus on pillars, lead-lined, human-sized, planted with spring bulbs, and, she thought, almost certainly ancient and pagan, for it was surrounded with a company of eyeless elders in Etruscan robes, standing each in his pillared alcove. Their faces were rubbed away, but their substance—some kind of rosy marble?—had erupted into facets and flakes that glinted in the gloom like her own surfaces.

She might take her place near them, she thought, but was dissuaded by the aspect of their neighbours, a group of the theological virtues, Faith, Hope, and Charity, simpering lifeless women clutching a stone cross, a stone anchor, and a fat stone helpless child. They had nothing to do with a woman who was made up of volcanic glass and semiprecious stones, who needed a refuge for her end. No, that was not true. They were not nothing to do with her, for they frightened her. She did not want to stand, unmoving, amongst them. She began to imagine an indefinite half-life, looking like them, yet staring out of seeing eyes. She walked faster.

Round the edges of the vast field of stones, within the spiky confine of the wall, was a shrubbery, with narrow paths and a few stone benches and compost bins. As she went into the bushes, she heard a sound, the chink of hammer on stone. She stood still. She heard it again. Thinking to surprise a vandal, she rounded a corner, and came upon a rough group of huts and a stack of stony rubble.

One of the huts was a long open shelter, wooden-walled and tile-roofed. It contained a trestle table, behind which a man was working, with a stonemason's hammer and chisel. He was a big muscular man, with a curly golden beard, a tanned skin, and huge hands. Behind him stood a gaggle of stone women, in various states of disrepair, lipless, fingerless, green-stained, soot-streaked. There was also a heap of urns, and the remains of one or two of the carved artificial rocks on which various symbolic objects had once been planted. He made a gesture as if to cover up what he was doing, which appeared, from the milky sheen of the marble, to be new work, rather than restoration.

Ines sidled up. She had almost given up speech, for her voice scratched and whistled oddly in her petrifying larynx. She shopped with gestures, as though she was an Eastern woman, robed and veiled, too timid, or linguistically inept, to ask about things. The stonecutter looked up at her, and down at his work, and made one or two intent little chips at it. Ines felt the sharp blows in her own body. He looked across at her. She whispered—whispering was still possible and normal—that she would like to see what he was making. He shrugged, and then stood aside, so that she could look. What she saw was a loose-limbed child lying on a large carved cushion, its arms flung out, its legs at unexpected angles, its hair draggled across its smooth forehead, its eyes closed in sleep. No, Ines saw, not sleep. This child was a dead child, its limbs were relaxed in death. Because it was dead, its form intimated painfully that it had once been alive. The whole had a blurred effect, because the final sharps and rounds had not been clarified. It had no navel; its little stomach was rough. Ines said what came into her stone head.

"No one will want that on any kind of monument. It's dead."

The stonecutter did not speak.

"They write on their stones," Ines said, "he fell asleep on such a day, she is sleeping. It's not sleep."

"I am making this for myself," he said. "I do repair work here, it is a living. But I do my own work also."

His voice was large and warm. He said:

"Are you looking for any person's grave here? Or perhaps visiting—"

Ines laughed. The sound was pebbly. She said, "No, I am thinking about my own final resting place. I have problems."

He offered her a seat, which she refused, and a plastic cup of coffee from a thermos, which she accepted though she was not thirsty, to oil her voice and to make an excuse for lingering. She whispered that she would like to see more of his work, of his own work.

"I am interested in stone work," she said. "Maybe you can make me a monument."

As if in answer to this, he brought out from under his bench various wrapped objects, a heavy sphere, a pyramid, a bag of small rattling objects. He moved slowly and deliberately, laying out before her a stone angel head, a sculpted cairn, a collection of hands and feet, large and small. All were originally the typical funereal carvings of the place. He had pierced and fretted and embellished them with forms of life that were alien and contradictory, yet part of them. Fingers and toes became prisms and serpents, minuscule faces peered between toes and tiny bodies of mice or marmosets gripped toenails or lay around wrists like Celtic dragons. The cairn—from a distance blockish like all the rest—was alive with marine creatures in whose bellies sat creatures, whose faces peered out of oyster shells and from carved rib cages, neither human faces nor inhuman. And the dead stone angel face had been made into a round mass of superposed face on face, in bas-relief and fretwork, faces which shared eyes and profiles, mouths which fed two divergent starers with four eyes and serpents for hair. He said:

"I am not supposed to appropriate things which belong here. But I take the lost ones, the detached ones without a fixed place, I look for the life in them."

"Pygmalion."

"Hardly. You like them?"

"Like is the wrong word. They are alive."

He laughed. "Stones are alive where I come from."

"Where?" she breathed.

"I am an Icelander. I work here in the winter, and go home in the summer, when the nights are bright. I show my work—my own work—in Iceland in the summer."

She wondered dully where she would be when he was in Iceland in the summer. He said:

"If you like, I will give you something. A small thing, and if you like to live with it, I will perhaps make you that monument."

He held out to her a small, carved head which contained a basilisk and two mussel shells. When she took it from him, it chinked, stone on stone, against her awkward fingertips. He heard the sound, and took hold of her knobby wrist through her garments.

"I must go now," she breathed.

"No, wait, wait," he said.

But she pulled away, and hurried in the dusk, towards the iron gate.

That evening, she understood she might have been wrong about her immediate fate. She put the stone head on her desk and went into the kitchen to make herself bread and cheese. She was trembling with exertion and emotion, with fear of stony enclosure and complicated anxiety about the Icelander. The bread knife slipped as she struggled to cut the soft loaf, and sliced into her stone hand, between finger and thumb. She felt pain, which surprised her, and the spurt of hot blood from the wound whose depth she could not gauge. She watched the thick red liquid run down the back of her hand, onto the bread, onto the table. It was ruddy-gold, running in long glassy strings, and where it touched the bread, the bread went up in smoke, and where it touched the table, it hissed and smoked and bored its hot way through the wood and dripped, a duller red now, onto the plastic floor, which it singed with amber circles and puckering. Her veins were full of molten lava. She put out the tiny fires and threw away the burned bread. She thought, I am not going to stand in the rain and grow moss. I may erupt. I do not know how that will be. She stood with the bread knife in her hand and considered the rough stripes her blood had seared into the steel. She felt panic. To become stone is a figure, however fantastic, for death. But to become molten lava and to contain a furnace?

She went back next day to the graveyard. Her clashing heart quickened when she heard the tap of hammer on stone, as she swung into the shrubbery. It was a pale blue wintry day, with pewter storm clouds gathering. There was the Icelander, turning a glinting sphere in his hand, and squinting at it. He nodded amiably in her direction. She said:

"I want to show you something."

He looked up. She said:

"If anyone can bear to look, perhaps you can."

He nodded.

She began to undo her fastenings, pulling down zips, unhooking the hood under her chin, shaking free her musical crystalline hair, shrugging her monumental arms out of their bulky sleeves. He stared intently. She stripped off shirt and jogging pants, trainers and vest, her mother's silken knickers. She stood in front of him in her roughly gleaming patchwork, a human form vanishing under outcrops of silica, its lineaments suggested by veins of blue john that vanished into crusts of pumice and agate. She looked out of her cavernous eye sockets through salty eyes at the man, whose blue eyes considered her grotesque transformation. He looked. She croaked, "Have you ever seen such a thing?"

"Never," he said. "Never."

Hot liquid rose to the sills of her eyes and clattered in pearly drops on her ruddy haematite cheeks.

He stared. She thought, he is a man, and he sees me as I am, a monster.

"Beautiful," he said. "Grown, not crafted."

"You said that the stones in your country were alive. I thought you might understand what has happened to me. I do not need a monument. I have grown into one."

"I have heard of such things. Iceland is a country where we are matter-of-fact about strange things. We know we live in a world of invisible beings that exists in and around our own. We make gates in rocks for elves to come and go. But as well as living things without solid substance we know that rocks and stones have their own energies. Iceland is a young country, a restless country—in our land the earth's mantle is shaped at great speed by the churning of geysers and the eruption of lava and the progress of glaciers. We live like lichens, clinging to standing stones and rolling stones and heaving stones and rattling stones and flying stones. Our tales are full of striding stone women. We have mostly not given up the expectation of seeing them. But I did not expect to meet one here, in this dead place."

She told him how she had supposed that to be petrified was to be motionless. I was looking for a place to rest, she told him. She told him about the spurt of lava from her hand and showed him the black scar, fringed with a rime of new crystals.

"I think now, Iceland is where I should go, to find somewhere to—stand, or stay."

"Wait for the spring," he said, "and I will take you there. We have endless nights in the winter, and snowstorms, and the roads are impassable. In summer we have—briefly—endless days. I spend my winters here and my summers in my own country, climbing and walking."

"Maybe it will be over—maybe I shall be—finished—before the spring."

"I do not think so. But we will watch over it. Turn around, and let me see your back. It is beautiful beyond belief, and its elements are not constant."

"I have the sense that—the crust—is constantly thickening."

"There is an idea—for a sculptor—in every inch of it," he said.

He said that his name was Thorsteinn Hallmundursson. He could not keep his eyes off her though his manner was always considered and gentle. Over the winter and into the early spring, they constructed a friendship. Ines allowed Thorsteinn to study her ridges and clefts. He touched her lightly, with padded fingers, and electricity flickered in her veining. He showed her samples of new stones as they sprouted in and on her body. The two she loved most were labradorite and fantomqvartz. Labradorite is dark blue, soft black, full of gleaming lights, peacock and gold and silver, like the aurora borealis embedded in hardness. In fantomqvartz, a shadowy crystal contains other shadowy crystals growing at angles in its transparent depths. Thorsteinn chipped and polished to bring out the lights and the angles, and in the end, as she came to trust him completely, Ines came to take pleasure in allowing him to decorate her gnarled fingers, to smooth the plane of her shin, and to reveal the hidden lights under the polished skin of her breasts. She discovered a new taste for sushi, for the iodine in seaweed and the salt taste of raw fish, so she brought small packs of these things to the shelter, and Thorsteinn gave her sips of peaty Laphroaig whisky from a hip flask he kept in his capacious fleecy coat. She did not come to love the graveyard, but familiarity made her see it differently.

It was a city graveyard, on which two centuries of soot had fallen. Although inner cities are now sanctuaries for wild things poisoned and starved in the countryside, the forms of life amongst the stones, though plump, lacked variety. Every day the fat pigeons gathered on the roof of Thorsteinn's shelter, catching the pale sunlight on their burnished feathers, mole grey, dove grey, sealskin grey. Every day the fat squirrels lolloped busily from bush to bush, their grey tails and faces tinged with ginger, their strong little claws gripping. There were magpies, and strutting crows. There was thick bright moss moving swiftly (for moss) over the stones and their carved names. Thorsteinn said he did not like to clean it away, it was beautiful. Ines said she had noticed there were few lichens, and Thorsteinn said that lichens only grew in clean air; pollution destroyed them easily. In Iceland he would show her mosses and lichens she could never have dreamed of. He told her tales, through the city winter, as the cold rain dripped, and the cemetery crust froze, and cracked, and melted into mud puddles, of a treeless landscape peopled by inhuman beings, laughing weightless elves, hidden heavy-footed, heavy-handed trolls. Ines's own crust grew thicker and more rugged. She had to learn to speak all over again, a mixture of whistles and clicks and solo gestures which perhaps only the Icelander would have understood.

Winter became spring, the dead leaves became dark with rain, grass pushed through them, crocuses and snowdrops, followed by self-spread bluebells and an uncontrollable carpet of celandine, pale gold flowers with flat green leaves, which ran over everything, headstones and gravel, bottle-green marble chips on recently dug graves, Thorsteinn's heap of rubble. They lasted a brief time, and then the gold faded to silver, and the silver became white, transparent, a brief ghostly lace of fine veins, and then a fallen mulch of mould, inhabited by pushy tendrils and the creamy nodes of rhizomes.

The death of the celandines seemed to be the signal for departure. They had discussed how this should be done. Ines had assumed they would fly to Reykjavík, but when she came to contemplate such a journey, she saw that it was impossible. Not only could she not fold her new body into the small space of a canvas bucket seat that would likely not bear her weight. She could never pass through the security checks at the airport. How would a machine react to the ores and nuggets scattered in her depths? If she were asked to pull back her hood, the airport staff would run screaming. Or shoot her. She did not know if she could now be killed by a bullet.

Thorsteinn said they could go by sea. From Scotland to Bergen in Norway, from Bergen to Seydhisfjördhur in East Iceland. They would be seven days on the ocean.

They booked a passage on a small trading boat that had four cabins for passengers, and a taciturn crew. They put in at the Faroe Islands and then went out into the Atlantic, between towering rock faces, with no shore, no foam breaking at the base. In the swell of the Atlantic the ship nosed its way between great green and white walls of travelling water, in a fine salt spray. The sky changed and changed, opal and gunmetal, grass green and crimson, mussel blue and velvet black, scattered with wild starshine. Thorsteinn and Ines stood on deck whenever they could, and looked out ahead of them. Ines did not look back. She tasted the salt on her black-veined tongue, and thought of the biblical woman who had become a pillar of salt when she looked back. She was no pillar. She was heaving and restless like the sea. When she thought of her past life, it was vague in her new mind, like cobwebs. Her mother was now to her flying dust in air, motes of bonemeal settling on the foam-flowers in the beck where she had scattered her. She could barely remember their peaceful meals together, the dry wit of her mother's observations, the glow of the flames in the ceramic coal in the gas fire in the hearth.

She opened her tent of garments to the driving wind and wet. She had found her feet easily and did not feel seasick. Thorsteinn rode the deck beside her like a lion or a warhorse, smiling through his beard.

She was interested in his human flesh. She found in herself a sprouting desire to take a bite out of him, his cheek or his neck, out of a mixture of some sort of affection and curiosity to see what the sensation would be like. She resisted the impulse easily enough, though she licked her teeth—razor-sharp flinty incisors, grim granite molars. She thought human thoughts and stone thoughts. The latter were slow, patchily coloured, textured and extreme, both hot and cold. They did not translate into the English language, or into any other she knew: they were things that accumulated, solidly, knocked against each other, heaped and slipped.

Thorsteinn, like all Icelanders, became more animated as they neared his island. He told tales of early settlers, including Saint Brendan, who had sailed there in the fifth century, riding the seas in a hide coracle, and had been beaten back by a huge hairy being, armed with a pair of tongs and a burning mass of incandescent slag, which he hurled at the retreating monks. Saint Brendan believed he had come to Ultima Thule; the volcano, Mount Hekla, was the entrance to Hell at the edge of the world. The Vikings came in the ninth century. Thorsteinn, standing on deck at night with Ines, was amazed to discover that the back of her hands was made of cordierite, grey-blue crystals mixed with a sandy colour, rough and undistinguished but which, held at a certain angle, revealed facets like shimmering dragon scales. The Vikings, he told her, had used the way this mineral polarised light to navigate in the dark, using the Polar Star and the moonlight. He made her turn her heavy hands, flashing and winking in the darkness, as the water drops flashed on ropes and crest curls of wake.

Her first vision of Iceland was of the wild jagged peaks of the eastern fjords. Thorsteinn packed them into a high rugged trucklike car, and they drove south, along the wild coast, past ancient volcanic valleys, sculpted, slowly, slowly, by Ice Age glaciers. They were under the influence, literally, of the great glacier Vatnajökull, the largest in Europe, Thorsteinn said, sitting easily at the wheel. Brown thick rivers rushed down crevices and into valleys, carrying alluvial dust. They glimpsed the sheen of it from mountain passes, and then, as they came to the flatlands of the south, they saw the first glacial tongues pouring down into the plains, white and shining above the green marshes and under the blue sky. Thorsteinn alternated between a steady silence and a kind of incantatory recitation of history, geography, time before history, myth. His country appeared to her old, when she first saw it, a primal chaos of ice, stone silt, black sand, gold mud. His stories went easily back to the first and second centuries, or the Middle Ages, as though they were yesterday, and his own ancestors figured in tales of enmity and banishment as though they were uncles and kinsmen who had sat down to eat with him last year. And yet, the striking thing, the decisive thing, about this landscape, was that it was geologically young. It was turbulent with the youth and energy of an unsettled crust of the earth. The whole south coast of Iceland is still being changed—in a decade, in a twinkling of an eye—by volcanic eruptions which pour red-hot magma from mountain ridges, or spout up, boiling, from under the thick-ribbed ice.

This is a recent lava field, said Thorsteinn, as they came to the Skaftáhraun, this was made by the eruption of the Lakagìgar in 1783, which lasted for a year, and killed over half the population and over half the livestock. Ines stared impassively at the fine black sand drifts, and felt the red-hot liquid boil a little, in her belly, in her lungs.

They travelled on, over the great black plain of Myrdalssandur. This, said Thorsteinn, was the work of a volcano, Katla, which erupted under a glacier, Myrdalsjökull. There is a troll woman connected to this volcano, he told her. She was called Katla, which is a feminine version of *ketill,* kettle, and she was said to have hidden a kettle of molten gold, which could be seen by human eyes on one day of the year only. But those who set out to find it were troubled by false visions and strange sights—burning homesteads, slaughtered livestock—and turned back from the quest in panic. Katla was the owner of a pair of magic breeches, which made her a very fleet runner, leaping lightly from crag to crag, descending the mountain-scree like smoke. They were said to be made from human skin. A young shepherd took them once, to help him catch his sheep, and Katla caught him, killed him, dismembered him, and hid his body in a barrel of whey. They found him, of course, when the whey was drunk, and Katla fled, running like clouds in the wind, over to Myrdalsjökull, and was never seen again.

Was she a stone woman? asked Ines. Her stony thoughts rumbled around heavy limbs made supple by borrowed skin. Her own human skin was flaking away, like the skins snakes and lizards rub off against stones and branches, revealing the bright sleekness beneath. She picked it away with crystal fingertips, scratching the dead stuff out of the crevices of elbow, knee joint, and her nonexistent navel.

Thorsteinn said there was no mention of her being stone. There were trolls in Iceland who turned to stone, like Norse trolls, if the sun hit them. But by no means all were of that kind. There were trolls, he said, who slept for centuries amongst the stones of the desert, or along the riverbeds, and stirred with an earthquake, or an eruption, into new life. There were human trolls, distinguishable only by their huge size from farmers and fishermen. "Personally," said Thorsteinn, "I do not think you are a troll. I think you are a metamorphosis."

They came to Reykjavík, the smoky harbour. Ines was uneasy, even in this small city—she strode, hooded and bundled behind Thorsteinn, as he showed her the harbour. Something was to happen, and it was not here, not amongst humans. New thoughts growled between her marbled ears: Thorsteinn wandered in and out of chandlers' and artists' stores, and his uncouth protégée stood in the shadows and more or less hissed between her teeth. She asked where they were going, and he said—as though she should have read his thoughts—that they were going to his summer house, where he would work.

"And I?" she said, grumbling. Thorsteinn stared at her, assessing and unsmiling.

"I don't know," he said. "Neither of us can know. I am taking you where there are known to be creatures—not human. That may be a good or a bad thing, I am a sculptor not a seer, how can I know? What I do hope is that you will allow me to record you. To make works that show what you are. For I may never see such a thing again."

She smiled, showing all her teeth in the shadow of her hood.

"I agree," she said.

They drove west again, from Reykjavík, along the ring road. They saw wonders—steam pouring from mountainsides, hot blue water bubbling in stony pots in the earth, the light sooty pumice, the shrouded humped black form of Hekla, hooded and violent. Thorsteinn remarked casually that it had erupted in 1991 and was still unusually active, under the earth and under the ice. They were heading for the valley of Thorsmork, Thor's Forest, which lay inaccessibly between three glaciers, two deep rivers, and a string of dark mountains. They crossed torrents, and ground along the dirt road. There were no other humans, but the fields were full of wildflowers, and birds sang in birches and willows. Now it is summer, said Thorsteinn. In the winter you cannot come here. The rivers are impassable. You cannot stand against the wind.

Thorsteinn's summer house was not unlike his encampment in the graveyard, although it was likely that the influence was the other way. It was built into a hillside, walled and roofed with turf, with a rough outbuilding, also turf-roofed, with his long worktable. It was roughly furnished: there were two heavy wooden bedsteads, a stone sink through which spring water ran from a channelled pipe in the hill-side, a table, chairs, a wooden cupboard. And a hearth, with a stove. They had a view—when the weather was clear—across a wide valley, and a turbulent glacial river, to the sharp dark ridges of the mountains and the distant bright sheen of the glacier. The grassy space in front of the house looked something between a chaos of boulders and a half-formed stone circle. Ines came to see that all the stones, from the vast and cow-sized to clusters of pebbles and polished singletons, were works in progress, or potential works, or works finished for the time being. They were both carved and decorated. A discovered face peered from under a crusty overhang, one-eyed, fanged, leering. A boulder displayed a perfectly polished pair of youthful breasts, glistening in circles of golden lichen. Cracks made by ice, channels worn by water, mazes where roots had pushed and twisted, were coloured in brilliant pinks and golds, glistening where the light caught them. Nests of stony eggs made of sooty pumice, or smooth thulite, were inhabited by crystal worms and serpentine adders.

The stonecarver worked with the earth and the weather as his assistants or controllers. A hunched stone woman had a fantastic garden of brilliant moss spilling from her lap and over her thighs. An upright monolith was fantastically adorned with the lirellate fruiting bodies of the "writing lichens." On closer inspection, Ines saw that jewels had been placed in crevices, and sharpened pins like mediaeval cloak brooches had been inserted in holes threaded in the stone surface. A dwarfish stone had tiny, carved gold hands where its ears might have been expected to be.

Thorsteinn said that he liked—in the summer—to add to the

durable stones work that mimicked and reflected the fantastic succession of the weathers of that land. He suspended ingenious structures of plastic string, bubble wrap, polyurethane sheeting, to make ice, rain floods, the bubbling of geysirs and mud baths. He made rainbows of strips of glass, and bent them above his creatures, catching the bright blue light in the steely storm-light and the wet shimmer of enveloping cloud in their reflections.

There were many real rainbows. There could be several climates in a day—bright sun, gathering storm, snowfall, great coils and blasts of wind so violent that a man could not stand up—though the stone woman found herself taking pleasure in standing against the turbulent air as a surfer rides a wave, when even Thorsteinn had had to take shelter. There were flowers in the early brief summer—saxifrages and stonecrops, lady's bedstraw and a profusion of golden angelica. They walked out into soft grey carpets of *Cetraria islandica,* the lichen that is known as "Iceland moss." Reindeer food, human food, possible cancer cure, said Thorsteinn.

He asked her, rather formally, over a fireside supper of smoked lamb and scrambled eggs, whether she would sit to him. It was light in the northern night: his face was fiery in the midnight sun, his beard was full of gold, and brass, and flame-flickering. She had not looked at herself since they left England. She did not carry a mirror, and Thorsteinn's walls were innocent of reflecting surfaces, though there were sacks of glass mosaic tesserae in the workshop. She said she did not know if she any longer differed from the stones he collected and decorated so tactfully, so spectacularly. Maybe he should not make her portrait, but decorate her, carve into her, when . . . When whatever was happening had come to its end, she left unsaid, for she could not imagine its end. She tore at the tasty lamb with her sharp teeth. She had an overwhelming need for meat, which she did not acknowledge. She ground the fibres in the mill of her jaws. She said, she would be happy to do what she could.

Thorsteinn said that she *was,* what he had only imagined. All my life I have made things about metamorphosis. *Slow* metamorphoses, in human terms. Fast, fast in terms of the earth we inhabit. You are a walking metamorphosis. Such as a man meets only in dreams. He raised his wineglass to her. I too, he said, am utterly changed by your changing. I want to make a record of it. She said she would be honoured, and meant it.

Time too was paradoxical in Iceland. The summer was a fleeting island of light and brightness in a shroud of thick vapours and freezing needles of ice in the air. But within the island of the summer the daylight was sempiternal, there was no nightfall, only the endless shifts in the colour of the sky, trout-dappled, mackerel-shot, turquoise, sapphire, peridot, hot transparent red, and, as the autumn put out boisterous fingers, flowing with the gyrating and swooping veils of the aurora borealis. Thorsteinn worked all summer to his own rhythm, which was stubborn and earthy—long, long hours—and rapid, like waterfalls, or air currents. Ines sat on a stone bench, and occasionally did domestic things with inept stony fingers, hulled a few peas, scrubbed a potato, whisked a bowl of eggs. She tried reading, but her new eyes could not quite bring the dancing black letters to have any more meaning than the spiders and ants which scurried round her feet or mounted her stolid ankles. She preferred standing, really. Bending was harder and harder. So she stood, and stared at the hillside and the distant neb of the glacier. Some days they talked as he worked. Sometimes, for a couple of days together, they said nothing.

He made many, many drawings of her face, of her fingers, of her whole cragged form. He made small images in clay, and larger ones, cobbled together from stones and glass fragments and threads of things representing the weather, which the weather then disturbed. He made wreaths of wildflowers, which dried in the air, and were taken by the wind. He came close, and peered dispassionately into the crystal blocks of her eyes, which reflected the red light of the midnight sun. She made an increasing number of solitary forays into the landscape. When she returned, once, she saw from a great distance a standing stone that he had made, and saw that through its fantastic crust, under its tattered mantle, it was possible to see the lineaments of a beautiful woman, a woman with a carved, attentive face, looking up and out. The human likeness vanished as she came closer. She thought he had *seen* her, and this made her happy. He saw that she existed, in there.

But she found it harder and harder to see him. He began to seem blurred and out of focus, not only when his human blue eye peered into her crystal one and his beard fanned in a golden cloud round the disk of his face. He was becoming insubstantial. His very solid body looked as though it was simply a form of water vapour. She had to cup her basalt palm around her ear to hear his great voice, which sounded like the whispering of grasshoppers. She heard him snore at night, in the wooden bed, and the sound was indistinguishable from the gurgle of the water, or the prying random gusts of the wind.

And at the same time she was seeing, or almost seeing, things which seemed to crowd and gesture just beyond the range of her vision, behind her head, beyond the peripheral circle of her gaze. From the deck of the ship she had seen momentary sea creatures. Dolphins had rushed glistening amongst the long needles of air caught in the rush of their wake. Whales had briefly humped parts of guessed-at bulks through the wrinkling of the surface, the muscular span of a forked tail, the blast of a spout in a contracting air hole in an unimaginable skin. Fulmars had appeared from nowhere in the flat sky and had plummeted like falling swords through the surface which closed over them. So now she sensed earth bubbles and earth monsters shrugging themselves into shape in the air and in the falling fosses. Fleet herds of light-footed creatures flowed round the house with the wind, and she almost saw, she sensed with some new sense, that they waved elongated arms in a kind of elastic mockery or ecstasy. Stones she stared at, as Thorsteinn worked on her images, began to dimple and shift, like disguised moor birds, speckled and splotched, on nests of disguised eggs, speckled and splotched, in a wilderness of stones, speckled and splotched. Lichens seemed to grow at visible speeds and form rings and coils, with triangular heads like adders. Clearest of all—almost visible—were the huge dancers, forms that humped themselves out of earth and boulders, stamped and hurtled, beckoned with strong arms and snapping fingers. After long looking she seemed also to see that these things, the fleet and the portentous, the lithe and the stolid, were walking and running like parasites on the back of some moving beast so huge that the mountain range was only a wrinkle in its vasty hide, as it stirred in its slumber, or shook itself slightly as it woke.

She said to Thorsteinn in one of their economical exchanges:

"There are living things here I can almost see, but not see."

"Maybe, when you can see them," he said equably, scribbling away with charcoal, "maybe then . . ."

"I am very tired, most of the time. And when I am not, I am full of—quite *abnormal*—energy."

"That's good?"

"It's alarming."

"We shall see."

"Do humans in Iceland," she asked again, conscious that *something* was staring and listening—uncomprehending, she believed—to the scratch of her voice, "do humans turn into trolls?"

"Trolls," said Thorsteinn. "That's a human word for them. We have a word, *tryllast,* which means to go mad, to go berserk. Like trolls. Always from a human perspective. Which is a bit of a precarious perspective, here, in this land."

There was a long silence. Ines looked at his face as he worked, and could not focus the eyes that studied her so intently: they were charcoal blurs, full of dust motes. Whereas the hillside was alive with eyes, that opened lazily within fringing mossy lashes, that stared through and past her from hollows in stones, that flashed in the light briefly and vanished again.

Thorsteinn said:

"There is a tale we tell of a group of poor men who went out to gather lichens for the winter. And one of them climbed higher than the others and the crag above him suddenly put out long stony arms, and wound them round him, and lifted him, and carried him up the hillside. The story says the stone was an old troll woman. His companions were very frightened and ran home. The next year, they went there again, and he came to meet them, over the moss carpet, and he was grey like the lichens. They asked him, was he happy, and he didn't answer. They asked him what he believed in, was he a Christian, and he answered dubiously that he believed in God and Jesus. He would not come with them and we get the impression that they did not try very hard to persuade him. The next year he was greyer and stood stock-still staring. When they asked him about his beliefs, he moved his mouth in his face, but no words came. And the next year, he came again, and they asked again what he believed in, and he replied, laughing fiercely, *Trunt, trunt, og tröllin í fjöllunum.*"

The English scholar who persisted in her said, "What does it mean?"

" *'Trunt, trunt'* is just nonsense, it means rubbish and junk and aha and hubble bubble, that sort of thing, I don't know an English expression that will do as a translation. Trunt trunt, and the trolls in the fells."

"It has a good rhythm."

"Indeed it does."

"I am afraid, Thorsteinn."

He put his bear-arm round the knobs and flinty edges that were where her shoulders had been. It felt to her lighter than cobweb.

"They call me," she said in a whisper. "Do you hear them?"

"No. But I know they call."

"They dance. At first it looked ugly, their rushing and stamping. But now—now I am also afraid that I can't—join the circle. I have never danced. And there is such wild energy." She tried to be precise. "I don't exactly *see* them still. But I do see their dancing, the furious form of it."

Thorsteinn said, "You will see them, when the time comes. I do believe you will."

As the autumn drew in she grew restless. She had planted small gardens in the crevices of her body, trailing grasses, liverworts. Creatures ran over her—insects first, a stone-coloured butterfly, indistinguishable from her speckled breast, foraging ants, a millipede. There were even fine red worms, the colour of raw meat, which burrowed unhindered. She began to walk more, taking these things with her. In September, they had several days of driving rain, frost was thick on the turf roof, the glacial rivers swelled and boiled and ice came down them in clumps and blocks, and also formed where the spray lay on the vegetation. Thorsteinn said that in a very little time it would be unsafe to stay—they might be cut off. He watched her brows contract over the glittering eyes in their hollow caves.

"I can't go back with you."

"You can. You are welcome to come with me."

"You know I must stay. You have always known. I am simply gathering up courage."

When the day came, it brought one of those Icelandic winds that howl across the earth, carrying away all unsecured objects and creatures, including men if they have no pole to clutch, no shelter built into the rock. Birds can make no way in such weather, they are blown back and broken. Snow and ice and hurtling cloud are in and on the wind, mixed with moving earth and water, and odd wreaths of steam gathered from geysirs. Thorsteinn went into his house and held on to the doorpost. Ines began to come with him, and then turned away, looking up the mountainside, standing easily in the furious breakers of the moving air. She lifted a monumental arm and gestured towards the fells and then to her eyes. No one could be heard in this wailing racket, but he saw that she was signalling that now she saw them clearly. He nodded his head—he needed his arms to hang on to the doorpost. He looked up the mountain and saw, no doubt what she now saw clearly, figures, spinning and bowing in a rapid dance on huge, lithe, stony legs, beckoning with expansive gestures, flinging their great arms wide in invitation. The woman in his stone-garden took a breath—he saw her sides quiver—and essayed a few awkward dance steps, a sweep of an arm, of both arms. He heard her laughter in the wind. She jigged a little, as though gathering momentum, and then began a dancing run, into the blizzard. He heard a stone voice, shouting and singing, *"Trunt, trunt, og tröllin í fjöllunum."*

He went in, and closed his door against the weather, and began to pack.

THE NARROW JET

FOR C. D-L

There were two old men, who made a project to defy gravity. The old knight, Sir Tor, had spent his life securing borders, incarcerating malefactors, protecting widows, reforming crop rotation, sending his sons into the world, marrying his daughters, and mourning his three wives, all dead in childbed, all arrested in youth and beauty. The old architect—he was much more of a master mason—Hew, had built manor houses and a courthouse, funerary monuments and bridges, sunken gardens and the odd hermitage. His wife was not dead, and had never loved him. He had suffered because of this, and now did not. His only son was dead (he was eleven years old) and Hew suffered this death daily.

The two old men sat by the deep carp basin, which was fed by a rush of water from a stone gutter let into the hillside by a much earlier people. The water drained away through various gullies, back into the hillside. They watched a fish rise in the evening light to catch flies. Suddenly it shot up—not very far—bending its fat silver body in an arc over the dark surface, snapping, flickering a tailfin, falling again with a slap and letting the water close over it.

Sir Tor said, "Hup, he defies gravity."

"It gives automatic pleasure," said Hew. "I wonder why."

"Lifts the spirit," said Sir Tor. "Sleek and shining, going *up*."

They watched the ring of water slop, wrinkle, and flatten.

There was a creature, also watching, moving softly across the murky bed of the pool, a creature both long and fat, consisting of a rope of sleek segments, fringed by a large number of hairlike, flickering legs. It had a forked, whisking tail, and a heavy flat head, with constantly working mandibles, a horny surface, and large, uniformly dark treacle-coloured flat eyes, made for peering diligently in shadows and sifting silt. She was clever at avoiding beaks and jaws, clever at finding flakes and fragments of dead flesh amongst weed skeletons and soft black mud. She could not see herself, naturally, and had not seen one of her kind for a long time. She moved slow and wavering but she could see fast movement, and had seen the fish go past, the tremble of its fin, the flick of its muscle, the turmoil of its disappearance in pale bubble and the reconstruction of its underwater shape in the closing cleft of its reappearance. She was interested in the surface.

"I always wanted a fountain," said Sir Tor. "But it was never the moment. Too much to do. Might be the moment now."

Hew dropped a pebble into the olive-brown water and watched it eddy downwards, not heavy enough to sink like a plummet.

The creature saw it appear above her, a smooth solid, with a capsule of underwater air that dissipated upwards. She awaited its landing, snaked over, put out a feeler, saw that although it moved it was unlive and inedible. She felt in her body the vagaries of its fall, the soft thud of its landing in the silt.

"They say those old people had a whole system of fountains just here. One basin feeding another. Fed from up in the hills. Great jets, in the basins. They say the whole hill is mined and channelled inside, draining the rainwater down, feeding it into gullies and pipes. We've lost the art."

"I want a beautiful fountain," said Sir Tor, dreaming. "I want a siren, leaping like that fish, holding a jet in her little fist, like a, like a, not a trident, not a lance, like a rainbow."

Hew said, "You'd need a stone carver, to make her."

She stood in their mind's eye, aspiring and supple, made of golden stone. In Sir Tor's mind's eye, she snapped a muscular fishtail, like a salmon. In Hew's head she was double-tailed, her two halves winding round each other like a gymnast round a rope. In

Tor's mind she smiled blindly. In Hew's she frowned, young and resolute.

"First things first," said Sir Tor. "Before she can stand there, the water must be in place. We have this steady plashing, that comes over the lip, and runs away through the drain, into the hill somewhere. But there are many dry mouths which I think ran with water in the old days. Old lizard-face, under that bluff, and that noseless water god with the ground-down hair. And you find segments of pipe and broken spouts lying in the water and in the heather up the hill. You're the master builder. Where do you think the water ran?"

"I think it soaked into the hills—from rain, and little streams in the fields. I've heard that there are caves in the hill, and that the old folk went into the caves with ropes and even with boats, and built channels from the deep pools in the dark there, and directed the flow—"

"We are maybe too old for clambering inside mountains, or diving in pools in caverns—"

"We are too old for everything," said Hew. "There is no need for us to *be,* at all, anymore. We are redundant. I think we might look into the hillside and see what we can see. And if we need younger and stouter legs and muscles, we can find them. We need a young man, to make the mermaid, too. With blood in his veins, not water."

"I have blood," said Sir Tor. "But it runs thin. And fierce in its way, because its channels are narrow."

They took their time, exploring the hillside, although they knew they had not so much time to take. They set off on horseback, in the grey morning light, left the horses in hillside meadows, and ventured into the earth, through rifts and crannies that lay under the heather and wound into the golden stone. Most of their entries turned out to be culs-de-sac—"like stumbling down a great *sock,*" said Sir Tor, breathing wheezily, "and finding the toe stub." But they also found sand-lined gullets that wound in and down, and finally one that did indeed open into a large cavern, lit from above by a natural chimney, which had no floor, but a deep pool of dark water, quite still, which lapped between stone outcrops and stretched away into a further cavern. Hew lit a torch, and the fire glittered on the inky liquid. Sir Tor gazed towards the further arch and said, "Here we have need of that little boat you spoke of." And Hew, swooping the flame this way and that, said, "Here is where they came. There are marks cut in the stone, and look, here is an iron ring set in it. And another. There must have been a rope."

"Or a mooring."

"We will come back with a boat," said Hew.

"And a boatman," said Sir Tor. "I'd rather not drown before I see our siren."

Though something in him thought it would not matter greatly if he did.

"I shall go in the boat, of course," he said. "We need to see to this ourselves. Given that there is no *need* for any of it."

They carried a narrow boat up the hillside, slung like a litter between their horses, to the great surprise of a shepherd girl and some inquisitive black-faced sheep. In the end they hadn't brought servants. This was their own project, their folly. Creaking and panting they pushed and pulled the boat along the cavern, and tipped it into the black water. The ripples ran away from the wooden shell into the dark. Hew and Sir Tor made the boat fast to the ancient people's moorings, and stepped down into the shell, with their package of torches wrapped in oiled silk, and their bread and meat, and their paddles. They cast off cautiously, listening to the slippery echoes of the displaced water, staring across the grey pool they were floating on, through the arch into the dark. They dipped a cannikin into the water, and tasted it. It was stony-cold, and tasted mineral, not brackish. Pure water. There was no slime. They pushed down with a paddle and could not touch bottom. It was deep. Slowly they paddled through the twilight towards the dark, beyond which was an inky shimmer. It was possible, Hew thought, that the water simply fell hundreds of feet down into the bowels of the hill, over some silent lip of stone. Then he thought no, you would hear the rush of it, the echo, the movement of mass. This was still water, still as death. Maybe they would slide into a dark river of forgetfulness.

Sir Tor back-paddled, as they came under the arch, and Hew lit one of his torches, which lit up high black walls, and fine fiery lines of disturbed water, as far as they could see. He lashed the torch to the rowlocks—the boat dipped, and the lines of light rushed out over the water, and over the roof of the cavern, which was the colour of the hide of black swine, not jetty, but with iron-grey or thick smoke somewhere in it.

They went on, for some time, further out and further out, and there was no change. Then they began to hear trickling sounds, sounds of an inflow, or an overflow, which? They were suddenly wetted now by falling strings of water drops which could be heard all over, dropping into the lake. Very slowly they went on. They came to a wall of stone, in which was a narrow outlet, through which some of the water poured away, quite fast. They edged along the wall and came to other crevices and channels, down which the water was almost silently pouring. It was moving swiftly, as they ascertained when they trailed their fingers in front of the stone mouths. Beside one of these they found another mooring ring, let into the rock face. And then Hew caught his breath. His torch lit up a tiny figure, a doll, sitting on what looked like a natural ledge, a doll with a featureless face, and big breasts, and a coiled fishtail. He couldn't keep his flare steady enough to see her very clearly but she had pigment on her mouth and tresses, he thought.

"That's where we should look," he said to Sir Tor. "That might be our carp water. Or not. It may drain into some more infernal pond that no one can reach."

"How do we tell?" asked Sir Tor, shifting his bones, moving his leathery fingers in the soft dark movement of the water.

"We need dyes," said Hew. "We put packets of dye in all these drains and see if colour appears anywhere near the carp pool, or the stone mouth, or maybe the village stream, who knows."

So they went home and prepared packets of vegetable dye in porous linen bags, asking the village weaver for the secret of durable blues, and yellows, and reds. They stewed rose madder and macerated woad and prepared a brilliant and evil-looking yellow from a kind of lichen that grew in the churchyard. Then they went back to their boat, and their lakes, and rowed out again, over the ink, under the cold drip, and dropped their little packets into the open mouths of the outlets, and watched them bob and twirl away down into the dark, and out of sight.

"Now we wait," said Hew.

"How long?" said Sir Tor.

"Maybe forever. Maybe nothing will emerge," said Hew.

And the weeks passed, and at first they inspected the ponds and the runnels daily, but all remained thickly brown in the lake, and weed green elsewhere.

The creature in the depths could see—did at least see—only a limited range of colours. Her pleasures were more those of taste, and feeling. She liked the sensation of burrowing through loose layers of decaying cellulose and fishy spines, the rustle and ripple of her own muscles and the tiny endlessly testing pads on the ends of her multitudinous hair-legs. She had a particularly energetic ripple of her whole length, from snout, through all her elastic joints, to the flickering sensors at the end of the fork of her tail. She would exaggerate this motion, just for the pleasure of it, letting her plump ribbon float up on a sluggish current, and using all her strength to drive down again, letting water trickle through her hairs and over her chitin. She loved eating, too. She was a scavenger. She watched for the falling flesh of the dead—a minnow rigid in its last struggle, an earthworm, bloodless and falling away from a hook, little delicious chunks of very high duck flesh, mashed with feathers, clinging to shreds of bone. She had avoided being eaten. She could whirl away from a questing, snapping bird mouth, and she could lie, still, still, indistinguishable from the mud itself, her own odour masked by its pungency, whilst the trout, and the carp, and the pike floated by.

She was curious about the smell of the sharp vegetable molecules and the bitter lichen tea that wound their way past her towards the surface. She went towards the bubbles in the mud and sniffed, and tasted, and tested, and recoiled slightly. She closed her nostrils briefly, and backed away. Later she thought of these odd smells as the beginning. Somewhere, even, they troubled her eyes with unaccustomed frequencies, a ghost of a red glare, a rush of bluish shadow, a yellow stain.

Sir Tor was polishing his collection of spyglasses when he saw it. He was sitting in the sun, and held up a spyglass to look at where the siren was not, on the sullen sheen of the carp pond. And there they were, three entwined ribbons of slow colour, red, blue, and yellow, circling each other on the surface, rising in globules from the depths. He did not move, but called Hew.

"What do you see?"

Hew came over and peered under his thin hand.

"I can see dyes in water. Just where we should most hope they might be. They are coming *up,* Tor. From some source *in the centre of the lake.* There's a way through. And all that weight of water behind it."

They were too old to be excitable, but not too old to be very satisfied.

"First," said Hew, "we must find the outlet in the pond. Then we must trace the watercourse, back from where it drains in from the hill. Then we must design—or discover—for who knows what those old folk had already built—the hydraulics of the thing, the narrow pipes and channels through which the water must be forced. We must capture and confine it, so that it goes up, with its release."

There was a mad moment when they contemplated draining the pool. They sat in the evening light, by their balustrade, with beakers of red wine, and looked out over the water. On the far side the sedge swayed and feathered. A heron stood where it often stood, resting one leg, peering down the long spike of its beak into the dark liquid.

Ducks of many kinds paddled from clump to clump, mallards and pochards, glistening drakes and warm brown ducks, and an erratic necklace of fluffy golden ducklings. There were coots and moorhens and a carpet of water lilies, creamy cups and rosy cupolas on green plates. The edge of the pool nearest the manor had a stone rim, where Sir Tor had stood since he was a toddling infant and thrown crumbs to the fat carp, who came soundlessly to the surface and opened and shut their lax mouths with a fleshy popping. There were minnows and sticklebacks, darting into the thickets of green weed, and leaping frogs, and crested newts with flaming breasts and agile fingers and toes. And the water boatmen, and the beetles, carrying bubbles in their arms, to make their nests, and the dragonflies and the clouds of midges in the heat. Sir Tor saw his drained pool as a muddy prospect of gasping and slimy death and saw that he could not do it. Some of the carp were known (how?) to be hundreds of years old. They had been fed by his father and his grandfather before him.

"How?" he said to Hew, staring at the quiet water and the surface of his wine.

"By diving down?" said Hew. "I was—I am—a strong swimmer. Can you think of a way a man might see underwater?"

"A spyglass would fill with mud."

"You might strap a glass to a man's brow—so it was watertight. It would be cumbersome. A man might feel his way—initially—with toes and fingers."

"How deep is the water in the midst?"

"I don't know. The silt on the floor of it must be thick. We cannot know if we do not look."

"I shall dive too," said Sir Tor. "It is my pool, she is my siren."

"You are not so steady on your legs as I am, if I may say so. And your belly is large and loose."

"It will weight me down. And float me up again."

"Both at once?"

"Flesh is versatile, Hew. You can command it. Until the day you cannot."

So out they went, two old men in a kind of coracle, naked because who was there to see, let alone take an interest in, their leathery shanks and wavering buttocks, Sir Tor's mountain belly or Hew's mottled skin through which his pelvis foreshadowed his skeleton?

The creature saw them descending through the thick sliding curtain of greenish light. She saw the horny soles of their feet and the four trampling pistons of their legs, and between them the bobbing tubelets of their sex, and the water bubbles in the hair around them, like nests of eggs. She backed away under a flat stone. The pale light of Sir Tor's belly wrinkled and swayed above her. Their arms flailed but she did not know what arms were and stared at the wild perturbation they caused. There were three arms. Sir Tor was grasping his nose with the fourth. Slowly the four splayed feet bounced across the silt, the toes gripping and stirring. The creature clicked her nostrils shut. She heard the roar and gasp as they blew out between their flubber lips and saw the blocks of their bodies rise up in the water, up and up, turning the thick lentil of the surface into a boiling of bubbles. Just as she was whisking out to inspect they were descending again, plunging, bounding, trampling, bubbling.

Two things happened at once. Hew's big toe hit a man-made disk of stone or metal and a ring, in which for a moment his toe caught, so that he had to battle himself free, his lungs bursting. His toe was bleeding. The creature sipped the blood he left on the stone. Simultaneously Sir Tor was seized by cramps, along his calves, his thighs, his backside, which caused him to float and flounder, gasping, like a beached whale. Hew saw his eyes roll up, swam over, and held the lolling old head above water by grasping the hair and beard. It was some time—during which Hew clung to the coracle and to Sir Tor—before the old knight had the energy to tumble himself back into its shell. He lay there, staring at the sky, while Hew paddled to the rim.

Hew said, "I trod on a thing like a well cover. With a ring, that could be twisted."

Sir Tor said, "Good man."

"Can you get back to the house?"

"With pauses, yes. We are a couple of fools."

"Indeed we are. If I went down headfirst, I could twist it loose with my hands."

"We should employ a younger man."

"I don't like to. This is my task. So to speak. Our task."

Now they undertook more active construction work. They went down again and explored the outlet—Hew did the exploring, with his toes and fingers; Sir Tor, who insisted on participating, carried down implements to scrape and twist—a spike, a clawed hammer, finally a length of lead tubing, which Hew forced into a kind of stone nozzle he had found down there.

The creature, curiously attracted by the invading flesh and blood, wound her body round and round the bubbling and seething hill water, made little darts into the swirling muck to investigate the hands and feet and their traces. She picked up flakes of skin from between Hew's twisted toes, and turned them in her pincers before swallowing them. She prowled around the new piece of lead pipe and snuffed up the stains of blood and salt sweat. Most other creatures had retreated to the outer reaches of the lake. Only this one felt invigorated by the contact with the unwater, plunged into water.

It was time, Sir Tor said, to embark on the carving of the siren. They now had a decorous, but definitely vertical jet, rising through the narrow pipe above the surface, wavering in the air, and falling. We need a stone carver, said Sir Tor. One with imagination.

There was a young man called Rob, said Hew, who had taken over carving saints and coats of arms and such, for the churches and the municipalities. "His virgins all have the same face," said Hew. "They look like real women. Well, *a* real woman. Serene," he ended, looking for an accurate word, rejecting both pretty and beautiful, though the carvings were both, from different angles.

"Sound him out," said Sir Tor.

Rob was a hairy, squat young man, who had no talent for speaking. The two old men showed him the jet of water, and explained the idea of the siren, with some contradictions as to number of tails, and how she related to the water. Rob said there was not a lot of pressure behind the jet. Hew said, ah, but there *would* be, he himself was going to follow it back into the mountain, and narrow the passages it came through, so it would be forced higher. And higher. He had planned a sequence of variable spigots to make different gushes and forces of water. Rob took charcoal, and drew a picture of how the tube and the jet could be contained in the body of the woman, and be held in her hand like a bow of water. He drew arrows of water rushing, and hasps and staples, and sketched round them the ghosts of carved flesh, the pure curve of a breast, a hip metamorphosing to a tail, a stony ringlet on a long neck.

Rob said he would need a model. He didn't have a whole siren in his head. He knew a young girl. She worked in an inn. She was a good girl. She let him—

Hew said he had seen the virgins. The siren would naturally be mother-naked.

Rob said he didn't know if. He really didn't know if.

"Sound her, sound her, sound the young woman," said Sir Tor. "You can have my muniments room for the duration," he added. "Guaranteed no peeking and prying. She'll be respected."

Rob grunted.

He came back a few days later with the girl, whose name, he said, was Corrie. She was younger than the virgins appeared to be, fifteen or sixteen, with a classically regular face, bright ginger hair, held in a snood, and a body wrapped in a heavy skirt and a shawl. She looked vaguely at the two old men, who stood in the hall and considered her.

"We need," said Sir Tor.

"We need to see the shape," said Hew, "of the body."

The young woman wordlessly took off the shawl, and dropped it round her hem. She was wearing a shapeless blouse, but young, uptilted breasts could be seen through the coarse cloth.

Sir Tor said, "And the bum. We need to know about the bum."

The young woman showed no sign of taking off her skirt, so Rob travelled round and round her, pulling it tight and smoothing it over the solid youthful curve of the buttocks, putting his hands round her waist so that the old men could vaguely see the way the flanks sprang out of it, the way the midriff narrowed. Rob intimated that Corrie might be persuaded to take her boots off. Sir Tor said briskly that there was no need, ankles and feet were quite irrelevant.

"What do you think?" Sir Tor asked Hew.

Hew thought that the virgins were gravely beautiful and that the living face looked vacant. He also thought that since Rob had made the virgins beautiful he could do the same for the siren.

"Very good," said Hew. "Most excellent. Just what we can use."

"When can you start?" asked Sir Tor. He was asking the couple. "Don't matter," said Corrie. It was the first thing she had said. Monday, said Rob, clearly at random. Done, said Sir Tor.

Over the ensuing winter, many events took place. A block of the golden stone from the hillside was wheeled into the manor on an oxcart. It had been destined to be either a Madonna or a funereal monument, but neither had been required, and it stood, stained with rain, in Rob's yard. He set to work in the muniments room—whose shelved volumes were draped with bedsheets. A fire was lit, as the winter grew colder, to warm the taciturn Corrie. Sir Tor would go in of an evening, when Rob and Corrie had departed, to see how far the siren had emerged from the rock. It was as though the sculptor was unwrapping a female and a knotted snake from heavy coverings. He chipped and chiselled, and made something like a body in a sack, with stiff folds. After more work, arms and fins could vaguely be seen under a surface covered with tiny runnels, like a knitted mail surcoat, and then like a very thick woollen tunic. After more time, the covering began to be thin, like lawn, and the creature could be seen to have breasts and nipples, a navel and a sinuous scaled lower half. At this stage she had no face, only a rough oval block, over a hideously thick neck, which slowly vanished to reveal lavish tresses on smooth shoulders, and a veiled face, with nose, chin, and mouth.

Some days, Sir Tor thought no work had been done, and then found odd patches of fine carving—the beginnings of fine fingers, the detail of the meeting of human flesh and fish. He had imagined her holding her arm, with the jet in it, straight up towards the sky, above her head. But Rob had stretched it in front of her, on an upwards curve, the hand roughly cupped.

As the cutting away of the stone integument gave form to the siren, boatloads of stone were dropped into the carp pond to make an island, above the water, for her to sit on. These invasions of falling blocks and rubble from the unwater disturbed the creature, who had to swim out of their way, and found the water she breathed full of alien dust. She took to curling round the outlet of the jet, which Hew had carefully protected with a leaden rim, so that the fountain should not be accidentally blocked. At first, she had not liked the inflow of cold mountain water. She liked mulch, and organic warmth, and matter transforming into other matter. But something new in her enjoyed wallowing in the spring water. She sipped it, she expanded and contracted in its flow.

Hew was busiest of all. He followed the mountain water back into the hillside, with the help of a water-diviner, an arrogant, smelly man in a hooded robe who talked a deal of nonsense about contact with underground spirits and his own divine gift of sensing their presence with fingertips and forked willow. When Hew found the gullies and pipes the old people had made, he set to work drawing plans to narrow them, to concentrate the flow. The bubbling over the lake, amongst the rubble which surrounded the outlet, grew higher.

Sometimes, coming home in the dusk from his measurings and fittings, Hew stood on the far side of the carp pond, and stared at its glossy black surface for half an hour, or even more. There were now neither dragonflies nor mayflies nor midges. No birds sang in the willows or the sedge. Occasional gaggles of geese landed briefly on their way south, but they never stayed. The unseen fish were sluggish. Hew watched the evening light, shafts of dull rose and peacock, reflected dim and shadowy, on the lucid black. And then the light dimmed, and the black grew blacker and blacker, and something in Hew wanted to lie down and go quietly under and be still. At exactly the same time he thought he had never seen such subtle colour, such resplendent black, he had never been so alive to the complex evanescent movements of air on water. He must come out, he thought, and stand here in moonlight. When he made the attempt, he was near weeping at the silver sphere reflected in the ink, and the snakelets of silver that ran away from the feet of a solitary moorhen. If I had thousands of years, he thought, it would not be enough to understand all this, or even to see it well. Realistically, he supposed, he had maybe five more years. Five by twelve moons, five winters, five springs, five summers. They seemed like ungraspable riches. How *interesting* it all was.

He was half sorry they had disturbed the centre of the lake, with their crashing and shouting. And then he thought of the stone hand that would hold the water, and he smiled.

There came a day when the siren was pronounced finished. Sir Tor and Hew stood in the muniments room and considered her critically. She had hollow passages, to make space for the water pipes, which would be closed with shaped blocks of the golden stone, like the lids of sarcophagi. Sir Tor looked at these, not quite comprehending. He had seen her already in his mind's-eye. He said,

"I don't want the jet coming *out* of her, you understand. I don't want her spitting water, or pissing water, or leaking water out of her nipples, or any of that nonsense. I want her *holding* water."

Hew and Rob, who had designed the system together, explained that the one fine jet would indeed spring over and above her cupped hands. But her body could be used to conceal and support the jet before it burst free. Its outlet was concealed in the tresses of hair on her shoulders. And from there the water would—if all went well—rise like a spring from waterweed. One hand, holding hair and water, directed the jet up and through the other high hand. As though she was bathing. Water would run down over her hair and body, as well as up and out in the jet. Hew said it might not work, of course. The water pressure had to be just so. He had put in various taps and nozzles along its passage, to change its force.

Sir Tor changed tack. He had really an unbounded confidence in Hew's capacity to solve difficult problems. The water would flow where it should. He said,

"Also, in my opinion, she looks a bit smug."

Hew, fearful of artistic temperament, touched his arm and held him back. Corrie said she thought the siren had a *nice* expression, she was satisfied.

"She should be *joyous,*" persisted Sir Tor.

Rob took his chisel and began to widen the curve of the siren's slightly parted stone lips. More of a dark gap appeared between them, almost a grin. It was a tiny adjustment. It changed her expression from smug to gleeful.

"Hey," said Sir Tor, "a wonderworker."

Corrie pouted, compressing the fleshy lips as the stone ones curled back.

"You can see she enjoys life," said Sir Tor. "She's a muscular brute. Look at the strength in those coils."

He had won over the number of fishtails the siren possessed. She had two, twisted around each other, ending in flirtatiously perked fins.

In past years, the creature had hibernated. She had no clear memory of this process, but she noticed various promptings in her joints, as the water in the lake cooled, and the light grew cloudier, and the dark times longer. She nuzzled down into the mud, and curled her body round her nose, and waited for sleep, and twitched, and trembled, and did not sleep. It was a mild winter. There was little ice, only the finest wafers of it stiffening and softening, perpetuating a water-wrinkle as a fine line for an evening, and melting away in midmorning. The creature conceded to herself that she was not sleeping, and was restive. She uncurled, and set off on her rippling legs, round the periphery of Hew's lead circle, running her whiskers along it, snapping up fragments and spitting them out. She had somehow become obsessed with the strong flow of the water from the mountain, which was oxygenated and full of slivers of pricking minerals, which were enlivening. Instead of hibernating she dragged a kind of bed of weed and half-decayed sedge, and tiny frail bones of fish and frogs and newts into the rim of the outlet, so that the bulk of her body rested on a mattress of stuff through which the spring water seeped and bubbled. In it she tasted pure air, which she had never known. Although in the summer it was colder than the still pond water, in winter it was slightly warmer, and certainly livelier. She came restlessly out of her lair and dabbled in the diverted currents she had made, blocking some, strengthening others. She waited for the large creatures from the unwater to recur, as she supposed they must, since she expected them daily. She took more interest in the curve of the underwater horizon, in the rainbow wavings of those things that still moved above and through it, reeds, sinuous bird-necks full of glittering bubbles, webbed feet marking time.

The siren was ready in the spring. She was wheeled on a trolley to the shore, and transferred to a specially-constructed raft, where she lay couchant, her arms rigidly stretched out. There was a bad moment when it looked as though the raft might not float—though the siren was lapped around with webbings and strings so she could be hauled upright on the island, and back from the depth of the pond, if need be. But the raft only settled in the water a little and Sir Tor and Hew paddled their coracle to the pipe that protruded from the inlet, pulling the raft after them, with the surface water lapping brown-green over it, wetting the siren for the first time. Rob and Corrie also went along, in a rowing boat, to help push and shove. Neither could swim, and Corrie had no intention of trying. Rob wore scarlet flannel drawers and the two old men had baggy linen pants, as a concession to the decent female eye. They managed to push and lever the siren onto the new island, and with Hew and Rob half standing, half treading water, to get her more or less upright. Rob had a bucket of rough cement, to hold her to her perch, and

Hew had plugs and connexions to direct the jet. But the jet was not flowing as it used to. It appeared to be blocked, and a cloud of dense mud lay around it in the water below.

Hew dived down and his fingers and toes became enmeshed in the tangle of weed over the aperture. He felt that the nozzle he had placed over it had slipped and was missing, so he surfaced, and went down again with a fishing net, into which he bundled handsful of the stems and sediment that had been woven over the outlet. He felt it pulse and wriggle. He surfaced, grasping the net, his lungs bursting, and tipped it over the side of the moving boat. It was in this way that the creature, entangled in her nest, was revealed to the humans, and the humans were revealed to her.

What they saw was snaky chitin and leathery connecting tissue, feebly wavering legs and feelers, and the blunt head with its apparatus of pincers and feelers and its great round dark eyes, honeycombed with lenses.

What she saw was a rocking unstable mass of new colours, and the weird texture of dryness in the unwater—no gloss, no gleam. She saw Hew's huge finger approach to prod her, smelled the salt of his sweat and the tang of his blood and the residue of plumskin under his fingernail from lunch. She looked up and out and saw the pale unimaginable blue of the spring sky—she had never really seen blue—and the gold light flaming palely from the new green leaves of the trees that rimmed the carp pond. She heard a shrill breathing sound, which was in fact Corrie, screaming that the thing was disgusting, kill it, kill it, it's a monster. Then she saw a wonder, a pale blue roundel, round a widening black pinhole, fringed with slaty stubs not unlike her fringe of legs. And somehow she saw that this thing was an intelligent eye, bigger than a carp's eye, and unpleasantly slung in bags of skin, but an eye, that more or less met *her* eye.

Corrie shrilled on.

Hew hooked his fingers under the creature, and she dangled, twisting, in air. Breathing was hard, but the touch of air was a kind of unimagined bliss, even as it began to dry her armour.

Huw said, "I've never seen a monster like this. Maybe the floor of the pool is crawling with them."

"Kill it," said Corrie. "It's nasty."

"Nonsense," said Hew. "It's a living being, with lovely eyes, look at them, like jet, like faceted gems."

With his other hand he found his lost nozzle in the flung debris of the creature's nest.

"Come on," he said to her. "Back down. We'll fix it." And holding the creature in one hand and the nozzle in the other, he went down again, in a pillar of bubble and mud. He put the creature down by the fountain, and she backed away between the new stones of the false island, rattling her segments to wetten them, staring at Hew, who was reattaching the nozzle to the pipe where it entered the island. He had arranged various pipes and tributary inlets, to intensify the jet when it was in place, all with their mouths and stopcocks. The creature had investigated them all, during her sleepless winter. She had even attempted to enter those that were temporarily open, not blocked, but they were too narrow.

It took the efforts of both half-naked old men to push the siren into her upright position on the island. There was a ludicrous moment when both were leaning athwart her coiling tails like ancient tritons trying to rape her. They fixed wires, they fixed tubing, they slapped down cement. Up she rose, the two levels of her arms golden against the blue sky, the stone hair spilling over the stony shoulders. Up and up, tremulous, then steady.

The moment came to set the jet in motion. There she sat, the siren, with her gleeful grin, holding a brass spout. Ceremoniously, kneeling on the coils of her tail, Hew opened it. Up came water, in a slow plashing, damping her hands, dripping down over the carp pond. Corrie sniggered. Hew clambered down, and reentered the water, where he adjusted various spigots in his system of pipes. And suddenly up it went, like a fine blade, like a spiralling wire, the high jet, up, up, wavering in the air, breaking, and sprinkling the shoulders of the siren with spray as the jet broke up at its zenith. Hew adjusted the tap in her hand, and the water suddenly rose directly above her, falling now directly on her head, streaming down over eyebrows, nose, and lips, past breasts and into her lap and the swelling of her scaly extremity. Sir Tor sat back on the coracle and waved his arms, which caused him to topple over into the water. He did not surface for some time—Hew went down to drag him up, for the second time—and when he came up he was in the midst of a voluminous nosebleed, so that his skin was glistening with scarlet streaks in the green slime of the water. Below, in the dark, the creature swam into the dissipating smoke of blood, and sipped, and savoured, and was curious.

They had a good summer, contemplating their achievement. They sat at the edge of the pond, with beakers of wine, and stared at the fine water shooting up, wavering, breaking, and descending in blown droplets. We did it, they said to each other, remembering what they had done as *one whole thing*—the mountain climbing, the cave with its black lake, the bags of dye, the siren emerging from the stone as from rough clothing, and then from fine lawn, the pipes, the spigots, the weak fountain, the high jet. We did it, they said. When Hew said "We did it" his knot of memory, irrelevantly, included the twisting coil of the creature in his fingers, as he returned it to its muddy origin. They congratulated Rob and each other on the amazing height of the jet.

Corrie, tramping back to the village with Rob, said they were daft old creatures, who couldn't get anything of themselves to stand up or spout out anymore, and had to make do with water. Corrie and Rob, impassioned by the naked stone and warmed by the fires of the muniment room, had touched timidly, clasped passionately, and, over the months, increased their anatomical knowledge and skills exponentially. Corrie was proud and obsessed. Rob was wonderful, the old men were silly, she felt the world from one position. That wouldn't last. She contained already the curled, fishlike creature who would change her and her world forever. There would be a fierce mouth at those breasts she offered to Rob's reverent fingers.

Rob didn't like her sneering at the old men. They were men, they were old, they had made something, and it would be good to be making something at that age and not simply creaking and moaning, Rob thought. Sixty years later he remembered them quite clearly when his own hands were too crippled to wield a chisel, too clumsy to model clay. He invented a way of painting walls with a brush on a pole. He made sweeps of green and gold and blue in intricate patterns, which looked like the weeds and trees in and round the circle of the carp pond, or like the woven order of illuminated manuscripts, done large and from a distance. His grandchildren mixed the paint, and Corrie washed their hands afterwards.

It occurred to Hew that Sir Tor had been living for the moment when the jet went up, and that now that moment was in the past tense. It was true, it went up every day, and that he could cunningly vary its force with his spigots. Sir Tor liked to sit out and watch it, most of all in the evening light, but also at noon, on hot days, when the sun and the water were both at their highest. Hew talked to the old knight, who seemed shrunken in his armchair, about the building of the great cathedrals.

"I think over and over," he said, "about the masons who made those, about the men who drew up the plans, and the men who quarried, and the men who carved the spouts and the angels and the demons in the towers, and the men who finally stood on the high point and tossed their caps in the air. For they weren't the same men. There were hundreds of years between the first drawings and the topping-out."

Sir Tor looked at him speculatively. He did this less and less frequently.

"You are a projector without a project, old friend," he said. "You don't like endings."

Hew nodded, and stared at the water going up.

"I also don't like to begin what I can't complete," said Hew.

"Then you are hard indeed to satisfy," said Sir Tor. "Maybe you could build a kind of summerhouse, so that an old man could stare at a siren under cover in all weathers. It's not much of a project," he added, deprecating. He had not said, "We could build," Hew noticed.

So Hew drew a shelter, making the plan more complicated than it need be, and adding a ramp as it became clear that Sir Tor was having more and more difficulty with the walk between the manor and the pond. There came a day when the gardener and the stable-hand set him in his great chair on the trolley and rumbled him over the gravel and grass. Hew's shelter was now foundations. Sir Tor sat in his chair beside the diggings. His face was mottled. He said, "I should like to die here, watching the water go up." Hew said, "Well, maybe you will have that chance. But not yet, I hope."

"Soon though," said Sir Tor in a small voice. His eyes were wet, and to tell the truth (which he didn't) he saw the whole world through a rainbow haze, like the penumbra of the curve of the jet in the light and the air. He could barely distinguish his high jet from his involuntary tears.

Hew likewise did not tell Sir Tor that when he looked at the jet he saw black forms, coiling lacunae, in the silver rush against the blue. They were like larger projected versions of those strange forms that float or jerk across our eyeballs, causing small children to imagine they see fairies, or magnified microbes, depending on their culture. Hew thought they were the precursors of blindness. They looked like rips in the fabric of things, Hew thought, and were perhaps rips in the jelly of his eye, disintegrations.

He was so sure that Sir Tor would die grandly in his chair, staring out at the siren in her veil of sunlit water, across the dark pond.

But in fact one day Sir Tor turned his face to the wall and would not get up, and began to mutter crossly to himself. And then only his lips moved. He would not turn back, and did not speak again. They moistened his lips with milk and water, and occasionally his tongue crept out and took a little in. He lay curled, face against the wall, for days. And then, between one imperceptible breath and its nonexistent successor, he gave up.

What Hew had seen coiling in the jet was not a space, but a body.

It was the creature, who had rippled and whisked on her hundreds of legs round and round the spigot system that had invaded her mud. She needed to investigate and was rebuffed. Until, one day, she found a gap between a tap and its mouth, and with painful effort wound herself into the dark pipe. Once inside, she ran with the water, scraping her segments against the hard tube, moving imperceptibly up, and up, until at a corner she was suddenly swept up very rapidly by the unnatural upwards thrust of the water. She relaxed, as she would in death, she lay limp in the long ribbons of driven wet, and was extruded—somewhat battered—from the high nozzle, to dance in coils on the jet before tumbling in its shower, resting on a stone shoulder and seeing again the incredible blue of the atmosphere of the unwater. She wriggled and slipped down, over what was to her simply stone ledges and crevices, down over the carved fishtails and back into the water, noting the strangeness of surface from the other side.

The odd thing was, that once she was rested, she could not rest until she had repeated the journey, the dark constriction, the rush upwards, the dizzying tumble in air and water, the moment of life in the unliveable atmosphere, the stare at the light, the line of the surface, the reentry.

What was it like, for those first fish with limbs who heaved themselves out of seawater and lay exhausted on mudflats and tidal sands? Were they dissatisfied with the submarine, or hungry, or so curious that they changed body and life to breathe the unbreathable air?

What shall I do, with the strength that is left, Hew asked himself, after the burial of Sir Tor. He decided to take a journey, to see cathedrals he had never seen, designed by men who had never seen them. He needed to go quickly. He was afraid he was going blind. He went to say farewell to their siren, still gleefully smiling at empty air in a curtain of water. He moved all the spigots, narrowed the jet until it was at its full fine force. Up it went, up in the empty air. And there was a black coil in it. Hew blinked. The thing buckled and twisted and Hew saw suddenly that its writhing was a form that no slit in his eye fabric could create, that it was a living thing, in the power of the jet. He saw it tumble and slide down the golden stone, he saw it as it reached the place where fish and woman met, steady itself, use its fringe of legs to cling, to set off under its own control. He could not imagine the pleasure and pain of the buffeting it had taken, as it could not imagine his presence by the unfinished shelter. But he felt the pleasure humans feel in the survival of other creatures. He felt lifted.

DOLLS' EYES

Her name was Felicity; she had called herself Fliss as a small child, and it had stuck. The children in her reception class at Holly Grove School called her Miss Fliss, affectionately. She had been a pretty child and was a pretty woman, with tightly curling golden hair and pale blue eyes. Her classroom was full of invention, knitted dinosaurs, an embroidered snake coiling round three walls. She loved the children—almost all of them—and they loved her. They gave her things—a hedgehog, newts, tadpoles in a jar, bunches of daffodils. She did not love them as though they were her own children: she loved them because they were not. She taught bush-haired boys to do cross-stitch, and shy girls to splash out with big paintbrushes and tubs of vivid reds and blues and yellows.

She wondered often if she was odd, though she did not know what she meant by "odd." One thing that was odd, perhaps, was that she had reached the age of thirty without having loved, or felt close, to anyone in particular. She made friends carefully—people must have friends, she knew—and went to the cinema, or cooked suppers, and could hear them saying how nice she was. She knew she was nice, but she also knew she was pretending to be nice. She lived alone in a little redbrick terraced house she had inherited from an aunt. She had two spare rooms, one of which she let out, from time to time, to new teachers who were looking for something more permanent, or to passing students. The house was not at all odd, except for the dolls.

She did not collect dolls. She had over a hundred, sitting in cosy groups on sofas, perching on shelves, stretched and sleeping on the chest of drawers in her bedroom. Rag dolls, china dolls, rubber dolls, celluloid dolls. Old dolls, new dolls, twin dolls (one pair conjoined). Black dolls, blond dolls, baby dolls, chubby little boys, ethereal fairy dolls. Dolls with painted surprised eyes, dolls with eyes that clicked open and closed, dolls with pretty china teeth, between pretty parted lips. Pouting dolls, grinning dolls. Even dolls with trembling tongues.

The nucleus of the group had been inherited from her mother and grandmother, both of whom had loved and cared for them. There were four: a tall ladylike doll in a magenta velvet cloak, a tiny china doll in a frilly dress with forget-me-not painted eyes, a realistic baby doll with a cream silk bonnet, closing eyes and articulated joints, and a stiff wooden doll, rigid and unsmiling in a black stuff gown.

Because she had those dolls—who sat in state in a basket chair—other dolls accumulated. People gave her their old dolls—"We know you'll care for her." Friends thinking of Christmas or birthday presents found unusual dolls in jumble sales or antique shops.

The ladylike doll was Miss Martha. The tiny china doll was Arabel. The baby doll was Polly. The rigid doll was Sarah Jane. She had an apron over her gown and might once have been a domestic servant doll.

Selected children, invited to tea and cake, asked if she played with the dolls. She did not, she replied, though she moved them round the house, giving them new seats and different company.

It would have been odd to have played with the dolls. She made them clothes, sometimes, or took one or two to school for the children to tell stories about.

She knew, but never said, that some of them were alive in some way, and some of them were only cloth and stuffing and moulded heads. You could even distinguish, two with identical heads under different wigs and bonnets, of whom one might be alive—Penelope with black pigtails—and one inert, though she had a name, Camilla, out of fairness.

There was a new teacher, that autumn, a late appointment because Miss Bury had had a leg amputated as a result of an infection caught on a boating holiday on an African river. The new teacher was Miss Coley. Carole Coley. The head teacher asked Fliss if she could put her up for a few weeks, and Fliss said she would gladly do so. They were introduced to each other at a tea party for incoming teachers.

Carole Coley had strange eyes; this was the first thing Fliss noticed. They were large and rounded, dark and gleaming like black treacle. She had very black hair and very black eyelashes. She wore the hair, which was long, looped upwards in the nape of her neck, under a black hairslide. She wore lipstick and nail varnish in a rich plum colour. She had a trim but female body and wore a trouser suit, also plum. And glittering glass rings, quite large, on slender fingers. Fliss was intimidated, but also intrigued. She offered hospitality—the big attic bedroom, shared bath and kitchen. Carole Coley said she might prove to be an impossible guest. She had two things which always came with her:

"My own big bed with my support mattress. And Cross-Patch."

Fliss considered. The bed would be a problem but one that could be solved. Who was Cross-Patch?

Cross-Patch turned out to be a young Border collie, with a rackety eye patch in black on a white face. Fliss had no pets, though she occasionally housed the classroom mice and tortoises in the holidays. Carole Coley said, in a take it or leave it voice, that Cross-Patch was very well trained.

"I'm sure she is," said Fliss, and so it was settled. She did not feel it necessary to warn Carole about the dolls. They were inanimate, if numerous.

Carole arrived with Cross-Patch, who was sleek and slinky. They stood with Fliss in the little sitting room whilst the removal men took Fliss's spare bed into storage, and mounted with Carole's much larger one. Carole was startled by the dolls. She went from cluster to cluster, picking them up, looking at their faces, putting them back precisely where they came from. Cross-Patch clung to her shapely calves and made a low throaty sound.

"I wouldn't have put you down as a collector."

"I'm not. They just seem to find their way here. I haven't *bought* a single one. I get given them, and people see them, and give me more."

"They're a bit alarming. So much staring. So still."

"I know. I'm used to them. Sometimes I move them round."

Cross-Patch made a growly attempt to advance on the sofa. Carole raised a firm finger. "*No,* Cross-Patch. *Sit. Stay.* These are not your toys."

Cross-Patch, it turned out, had her own stuffed toys—a bunny rabbit, a hedgehog—with which she played snarly, shaking games in the evenings. Fliss was impressed by Carole's authority over the animal. She herself was afraid of it, and knew that it sensed her fear.

Carole was a good lodger. She was helpful and unobtrusive. Everything interested her—Fliss's embroidery silks, her saved children's books from when she was young, her mother's receipts, a bizarre Clarice Cliffe tea set with a conical sugar shaker. She made Fliss feel that she was *interesting*—a feeling Fliss almost never had, and would have said she didn't want to have. It was odd being looked at, appreciatively, for long moments. Carole asked her questions, but she could not think up any questions to ask in return. A few facts about Carole's life did come to light. She had travelled and worked in India. She had been very ill and nearly died. She went to evening classes on classical Greece and asked Fliss to come too, but Fliss said no. When Carole went out, Fliss sat and watched the television, and Cross-Patch lay watchfully in a corner, guarding her toys. When Carole returned, the dog leaped up to embrace her as though she was going for her throat. She slept upstairs with her owner in the big bed. Their six feet went past Fliss's bedroom door, pattering, dancing.

Carole said the dolls were beginning to fascinate her. So many different characters, so much love had gone into their making and clothing. "Almost loved to bits, some of them," said Carole, her treacle eyes glittering. Fliss heard herself offer to lend a few of them, and was immediately horrified. What on earth would Carole want to borrow dolls for? The offer was *odd.* But Carole smiled widely and said she would love to have one or two to sit on the end of her big bed, or on the chest of drawers. Fliss was overcome with nervous anxiety, then, in case Cross-Patch might take against the selected dolls, or think they were toys. She looked sidelong at Cross-Patch, and Cross-Patch looked sidelong at her, and wrinkled her lip in a collie grin. Carole said,

"You needn't worry about her, my dear. She is completely well-trained. She hasn't offered to touch any doll. Has she?"

"No," said Fliss, still troubled by whether the dog would see matters differently in the bedroom.

When they went to bed they said good night on the first floor landing and Carole went up to the next floor. She borrowed a big rag doll with long blond woollen plaits and a Swiss sort of apron. This doll was called Priddy, and was not, as far as Fliss knew, alive. She also borrowed—surprisingly—the rigid Sarah Jane, who certainly was alive. I love her disapproving expression, said Carole. She's seen a thing or two, in her time. She had painted eyes, that didn't close.

Other dolls took turns to go up the stairs. Fliss noticed, without formulating the idea, that they were always grown-up or big girl dolls, and they never had sleeping eyes.

Little noises came down the stairs. A cut-off laugh, an excited whisper, a creak of springs. Also a red light spread from the door over the sage-green stair carpet.

One night, when she couldn't sleep, Fliss went down to the kitchen and made Horlicks for herself. She then took it into her head to go up the stairs to the spare room; she saw the pool of red light and knew Carole was not asleep. She meant to offer her Horlicks.

The door was half open. "Come in," called Carole, before Fliss could tap. She had put squares of crimson silk, weighted down with china beads, over the bedside lamps. She sat on the middle of her big bed, in a pleated sea-green nightdress, with sleeves and a high neck. Her long hair was down, and brushed into a fan, prickling with an electric life of its own. Cross-Patch was curled at the foot of the bed.

"Come and sit down," said Carole. Fliss was wearing a baby blue nightie in a fine jersey fabric, under a fawn woolly dressing gown. "Take that off, make yourself comfortable."

"I was—I was going to—I couldn't sleep . . ."

"Come here," said Carole. "You're all tense. I'll massage your neck."

They sat in the centre of the white quilt, made ruddy by light, and Carole pushed long fingers into all the sensitive bits of Fliss's neck and shoulders, and released the nerves and muscles. Fliss began to cry.

"Shall I stop?"

"Oh no, don't stop, don't stop. I—

"This is terrible. Terrible. I love you."

"And what's terrible about that?" asked Carole, and put her arms around Fliss, and kissed her on the mouth.

Fliss was about to explain that she had never felt love and didn't exactly like it, when they were distracted by fierce snarling from Cross-Patch.

"Now then, bitch," said Carole. "Get out. If you're going to be like that, get out."

And Cross-Patch slid off the bed, and slunk out of the door. Carole kissed Fliss again, and pushed her gently down on the pillows and held her close. Fliss knew for the first time that terror that all lovers know, that the thing now begun must have an ending. Carole said, "My dear, my darling." No one had said that to her.

They sat side by side at breakfast, touching hands, from time to time. Cross-Patch uttered petulant low growls and then padded away, her nails rattling on the lino. Carole said they would tell each other everything, they would *know* each other. Fliss said with a light little laugh that there was nothing to know about her. But nevertheless she did more of the talking, described her childhood in a village, her estranged sister, her dead mother, the grandmother who had given them the dolls.

Cross-Patch burst back into the room. She was carrying something, worrying it, shaking it from side to side, making a chuckling noise, tossing it, as she would have tossed a rabbit to break its neck.

It was the baby doll, Polly, in her frilled silk bonnet and trailing embroidered gown. Her feet in their knitted bootees protruded at angles. She rattled.

Carole rose up in splendid wrath. In a rich firm voice she ordered the dog to put the doll down, and Cross-Patch spat out the silky creature, slimed with saliva, and cowered whimpering on the ground, her ears flat to her head. Masterfully Carole took her by the collar and hit her face, from side to side, with the flat of her hands. "*Bad* dog," she said, "*bad* dog," and beat her. And beat her.

The rattling noise was Polly's eyes, which had been shaken free of their weighted mechanism, and were rolling round inside her bisque skull. Where they had been were black holes. She had a rather severe little face, like some real babies. Eyeless it was ghastly.

"My darling, I am *so* sorry," said Carole. "Can I have a look?"

Fliss did not want to relinquish the doll. But did. Carole shook her vigorously. The invisible eyes rolled.

"We could take her apart and try to fit them back."

She began to pull at Polly's neck.

"No, don't, don't. We can take her to the dolls' hospital at the Ouse Bridge. There's a man in there—Mr. Copple—who can mend almost anything."

"Her pretty dress is torn. There's a toothmark on her face."

"You'll be surprised what Mr. Copple can fix," said Fliss, without complete certainty. Carole kissed her and said she was a generous creature.

Mr. Copple's shop was old and narrow-fronted, and its back jutted out over the river. It had old windowpanes, with leaded lights, and was a tiny cavern inside, lit with strings of fairy lights, all different colours. From the ceiling, like sausages in a butcher's shop, hung arms, legs, torsos, wigs, the cages of crinolines. On his glass counter were bowls of eyeballs, blue, black, brown, green, paperweight eyes, eyes without whites, all iris. And there were other bowls and boxes with all sorts of little wire joints and couplings, useful elastics and squeaking voice boxes.

Mr. Copple had, of course, large tortoiseshell glasses, wispy white hair, and a bad, greyish skin. His fingers were yellow with tobacco.

"Ah," he said, "Miss Weekes, always a pleasure. Who is it this time?"

Carole replied. "It was my very bad dog. She shook her. She has never done anything like this before."

The two teachers had tied Polly up into a brown paper parcel. They did not want to see her vacant stare. Fliss handed it over. Mr. Copple cut the string.

"Ah," he said again. "Excuse me."

He produced a kind of prodding screwdriver, skilfully decapitated Polly, and shook her eyes out into his hand.

"She needs a new juncture, a new balance. Not very difficult."

"There's a bite mark," said Carole gloomily.

"When you come back for her, you won't know where it was. And I'll put a stitch or two into these pretty clothes and wash them out in soapsuds. She's a Million Dollar Baby. A Bye-Lo baby. Designed by an American, made in Germany. In the 1920s."

"Valuable?" asked Carole casually.

"Not so very. There were a large number of them. This one has the original clothes and real human hair. That puts her price up. She is meant to look like a real newborn baby."

"You can see that," said Carole.

He put the pieces of Polly into a silky blue bag and attached a label on a string. *Miss Weekes's Polly.*

They collected her the next week and Mr. Copple had been as good as his word. Polly was Polly again, only fresher and smarter. She rolled her eyes at them again, and they laughed, and when they got her home, kissed her and each other.

Fliss thought day and night about what she would do when Carole left. How it would happen. How she would bear it. Although, perhaps because, she was a novice in love, she knew that the fiercer the passion, the swifter and the harsher the ending. There was no way they two would settle into elderly domestic comfort. She became jealous and made desperate attempts not to show it. It was horrible when Carole went out for the evening. It was despicable to think of listening in to Carole's private calls, though she thought Carole listened to her own, which were of no real interest. The school year went on, and Carole began to receive glossy brochures in the post, with pictures of golden sands and shining white temples. She sat looking at them in the evenings, across the hearth from Fliss, surrounded by dolls. Fliss wanted to say "Shall we go together?" and was given no breath of space to do so. Fliss had always spent her holidays in Bath, making excursions into the countryside. She made no arrangements. Great rifts and gaps of silence spread into the texture of their lives together. Then Carole said,

"I am going away for a month or so. On Sunday. I'll arrange for the rent to be paid while I'm away."

"Where," said Fliss. "Where are you going?"

"I'm not sure. I always do go away."

Can I come? could not be said.

So Fliss said, "Will you come back?"

"Why shouldn't I? Everyone needs a bit of space and time to herself, now and then. I've always found that. I shall miss the dolls."

"Would you like to take one?" Fliss heard herself say. "I've never given one away, never. But you can take one—"

Carole kissed her and held her close.

"Then we shall both want to come back—to the charmed circle. Which doll are you letting me have?"

"Any of them," cried Fliss, full of love and grief. "Take anyone at all. I want you to have the one you want."

She did not expect, she thought later, that Carole would take one of the original four. Still less, that of those four, she would choose Polly, the baby, since her taste had always been for grown girls. But Carole chose Polly, and watched Fliss try to put a brave face on it, with an enigmatic smile. Then she packed and left, without saying where she was going.

Before she left, in secret, Fliss kissed Polly and told her, "Come back. Bring her back."

Cross-Patch went with them. The big empty bed remained, a hostage of a sort.

Fliss did not go to Bath. She sat at home, in what turned out to be a dismal summer, and watched the television. She watched the *Antiques Roadshow,* and its younger offshoot, *Flog It!,* in which people brought things they did not want to be valued by experts and auctioned in front of the cameras. Fliss and Carole had watched it together. They both admitted to a secret love for the presenter, the beautiful Paul Martin, whose energy never flagged. Nor, Fliss thought, did his kindness and courtesy, no matter what human oddities presented themselves. She loved him because he was reliable, which beautiful people, usually, were not.

And so it came about that Fliss, looking up idly at the screen from the tray of soup and salad on her knee, saw Polly staring out at her in close-up, sitting on the *Flog It!* valuing table. It must be a complete lookalike, Fliss thought. The bisque face, with its narrow eyes and tight mouth, appeared to her to have a desperate or enraged expression. One of the most interesting things about Polly was that her look was sometimes composed and babylike, but, in some lights, from some angles, could appear angry.

The valuer, a woman in her forties, sweetly blond but sharp-eyed, picked up Polly and declared she was one of the most exciting finds she had met on *Flog It!* She was, said the purring lady, a real Bye-Lo Baby, and dressed in her original clothes. "May I look?" she asked sweetly, and upended Polly, throwing her silk robe over her head, exposing her woollen bootees, her sweet silk panties, the German stamps on her chubby back, to millions of viewers. Her fingernails were pointed, and painted scarlet. She pulled down the panties and ran her nails round Polly's hip joints. Bye-Lo Babies were rarer, and earlier, if they had jointed composition bodies than if they had cloth ones, with celluloid hands sewn on. She took off Polly's frilled ivory silk bonnet, and exclaimed over her hair—"Which, I must tell you, I am ninety percent sure is *real human hair,* which adds to her value." She pushed the hair over Polly's suspended head and said, "Ah, yes, as though we needed to see it." The camera closed in on the nape of Polly's neck. "COPR. BY GRACE S. PUTNAM // MADE IN GERMANY."

"Do you know the story of Grace S. Putnam and the baby doll?" scarlet-nails asked the hopeful seller and there was Carole, in a smart Art Deco summer shirt in black and white, smiling politely and following the movements of the scarlet nails with her own smooth mulberry ones.

"No," said Carole into Fliss's sitting room, "I don't know much about dolls."

Her face was briefly screen-size. Her lipstick shone, her teeth glistened. Fliss's knees began to knock, and she put down her tray on the floor.

Grace Story Putnam, the valuing lady said, had wanted to make a *real* baby doll, a doll that looked like a real baby, perhaps three days old. Not like a Disney puppet. So this formidable person had haunted maternity wards, sketching, painting, analysing. And never could she find the perfect face with all the requisite qualities.

She leaned forwards, her blond hair brushing Carole's raven folds.

"I don't know if I should tell you this."

"Well, now you've started, I think you should," said Carole, always Carole.

"It is rumoured that in the end she saw the perfect child being carried past, wrapped in a shawl. And she said, wait, this is the one. But that baby had just died. Nevertheless, the story goes, the determined Mrs. Putnam drew the little face, and this is what we have here."

"Ghoulish," said Carole, with gusto. The camera went back to Polly's face, which looked distinctly malevolent. Fliss knew her expression must be unchanging, but it did not seem like that. Her stare was fixed. Fliss said, "Oh, Polly—"

"And is this your own dolly?" asked the TV lady. "Inherited perhaps from your mother or grandmother. Won't you find it very hard to part with her?"

"I didn't inherit her. She's nothing to do with me, personally. A friend gave her to me, a friend with a lot of dolls."

"But maybe she didn't know how valuable this little gift was? The Bye-Los were made in great numbers—even millions—but early ones like this, and with all their clothes, and real human hair, can be expected to fetch anywhere between £800 and well over £1,000—even *well over,* if two or more collectors are in the room. And of course she may have her photo in the catalogue or on the website . . ."

"That does surprise me," said Carole, but not as though it really did.

"And do you think your friend will be happy for you to sell her doll?"

"I'm sure she would. She is very fond of me, and very generous-hearted."

"And what will you do with the money if we sell Dolly, as I am sure we shall—"

"I have booked a holiday on a rather luxurious cruise in the Greek islands. I am interested in classical temples. This sort of money will really help."

There is always a gap between the valuation of an item and the showing of its auction. Fliss stared unseeing at the valuation of a hideous green pottery dog, a group of World War I medals, an album of naughty seaside postcards. Then came Polly's moment. The auctioneer held her aloft, his gentlemanly hand tight round her pudgy waist, her woolly feet protruding. Briefly, briefly, Fliss looked for the last time at Polly's sweet face, now, she was quite sure, both baleful and miserable.

"Polly," she said aloud. *"Get her. Get her."*

She did not know what she wanted Polly to do. But she saw Polly as capable of doing something. And they were—as they had always been—on the same side, she and Polly.

She thought, as the bidding flew along, a numbered card flying up, a head nodding, a row of concentrated listeners with mobile phones, waiting, and then raising peremptory fingers, that she herself had betrayed Polly, but that she had done so out of love and goodwill. "Oh, Polly," she said, *"Get her,"* as Carole might have said to Cross-Patch.

Carole was standing, composed and beautiful, next to Paul Martin, as the tens turned into hundreds and the hundreds to thousands. He liked sellers to show excitement or amazement, and Carole—Fliss understood her—showed just enough of both to keep the cameras happy, but was actually rigid inside, like a stone pillar of willpower and certainty. Polly went for £2,000, but it was not customary to show the sold object again, only the happy face of the seller, so, for Fliss, there was no moment of goodbye. And you were not told where sold objects were going.

All the other dolls were staring, as usual. She turned them over, or laid them to sleep, murmuring madly, get her, get her.

She did not suppose Carole would come back, and wondered if she should get rid of the bed. The headmistress at the school was slightly surprised when Fliss asked her if Carole was coming back—"Do you know something I don't?" Then she showed Fliss a postcard from Crete, and one from Lemnos. "I go off on my own with my beach towel and a book and lie on the silver sand by the wine-dark sea, and feel perfectly happy." Fliss asked the headmistress if she knew where Cross-Patch was, and the headmistress said she had assumed Fliss was in charge of her, but if not, presumably, she must be in kennels.

A week later, the head told Fliss that Carole was in hospital. She had had a kind of accident. She had been unconscious for some time, but it was clear, from the state of her nervous system, and from filaments and threads found on her swimsuit and in her hair, that she had swum, or floated, into a swarm of minute stinging jellyfish—there are *millions* out there, this summer, people are warned, but she liked to go off on her own.

Fliss didn't ask for more news, but got told anyway. Carole's eyes were permanently damaged. She would probably never see again; at best, vestigially.

She would not, naturally, be coming back.

The headmistress looked at Fliss, to see how she took this. Fliss contrived an expression of conventional, distant shock, and said several times, how awful, how very awful.

The headmistress said, "That dog of hers. Do you think anyone knows where it is? Do you think we should get it out of the kennels? Would you yourself like to have it, perhaps—you all became so close?"

"No," said Fliss. "I'm afraid I never liked it really. I did my best as I hope I always shall. I'm sure someone can be found. It has a very uncertain temper."

She went home and told the dolls what had happened. She thought of Polly's closed, absent little face. The dolls made an inaudible rustling, like distant birds settling. They *knew,* Fliss thought, and then unthought that thought, which could be said to be odd.

THE LUCID DREAMER

When he woke, the room was full of light. It was a white room. The blinds were white but he never closed them, because he liked to be woken by daylight. He uncoiled under the crisp white heap of his duvet, and the down moved with him, and held him. Incomprehensible happiness flooded him, too much happiness, tinted with relief. He tried to think. He had been tensed against disaster. He had been dreaming, one of those dense dreams which appear to offer no way out, which mock you with the idea that they are not dreams at all. What had he been dreaming? He began to remember and could not, not quite, but he felt the rare surprise and delight of those who discover that disaster was, after all, only a dream. He was in the light and he was let off.

His clock told him it was 6:00 a.m., which meant that he could drift back into sleep for an hour before needing to get up. He closed his eyes against the light and settled his body.

When he woke, there was even more light. Something was wrong. He closed his eyes, briefly, and panic climbed up in him. He was going to be made to remember. Remembering was more bearable if he was standing, so he scrambled out of bed and braced himself. He had tamed the mnemonics so that each could be suffered briefly and put aside. The policewoman's frightened face at the door when he opened it. Clumsy hands on his resistant shoulder. A ludicrous phrase—"undertaking a pantechnicon." "She was at fault." A ragged spike of glistening raw bone protruding through skin. Fools saying, "We must be grateful for her life." He could spin through this dire sequence briskly now, but could not avoid its recurrence. It was not so bad, not so bad, as the memory of the smell of her hair, lightly floral after washing, warmly animal in bed.

He was enraged that he had been trapped into a lying dream that had given him a momentary relief. These dreams were known as false awakenings. He knew a bit about dreams and had studied them. He had even joined a group that practised "lucid dreaming." With practise, you could know in the dream that you were dreaming, you could open doors and walk through walls into new landscapes. You could avoid certain horrors, or familiarise others. As a young man, before he met her, he had kept a dream diary, trying to read rhythms and meanings into what might be merely random. He believed he had dreamed he was going to meet her before she walked into his life. When they were first together he had dreamed repeatedly that he had lost her, that he was seeking her everywhere, over hills and fields, along endless shores, through dusty streets. He told her about these dreams, and she said easily that dreams went by contraries, that here she was and here she would stay. He was—as a professional dreamer—interested in what he imagined her to be, in her imagined absences in the dreams. What was he looking for? A blue dress that resembled nothing she ever wore. A giant, just over the horizon, a pygmy under the hill. When he woke, she was there, "just right"—a phrase that came from Goldilocks's usurpation of the smallest bear's bed in the forest.

Their friends tried to help him, afterwards, and mostly only enraged him. He cleared away her things—her hairwash choked him—he took down every photograph and put them in a trunk. The dead spill over, in these days, into the daily lives of the living. The Internet was infested with the mockery of her voice, her face, her words. He did not believe in ghosts and found memories simply and only painful. Sudden uncontrolled encounters dragged them up, like mud from a pond bottom, and then he braced himself against the policewoman, the bone, the undertaken pantechnicon. He had no concept of working through his grief—indeed he avoided even that word. He felt comforting as deceit. He got a new job, with new colleagues, and he went only to places where they had never gone together.

Some time after "it happened"—he avoided the words accident, death, which were intolerable—a taxi took him unexpectedly past the place, the road, the railings. He could not even bring himself to ask the driver not to go there. He simply sat stiffly and waited to be past. Someone had mounted a white ghost bike on the railings, and hung it with long streamers of black and white silk ribbon. He was moved by that. The solidity of absence. He dreamed once or twice of the ghost bike, chained to the railings, its decorations fluttering with a false life.

He never dreamed of her. He could not control his waking thoughts, but he could fence his dreams against any mocking wraith, any fictive encounter, any journey or gathering or sinking to sleep where relaxation of will could allow her image to slide in and damage him. He could not, he thought, survive either her unreal presence or waking to find that he had dreamed her. Once or twice, in dreams, there were inviting paths in woods he willed himself not to follow, not even naming to himself what he feared to find at the end. Once someone opened a door to him and the figure would not settle, it shivered and tried to shape itself as hers, and he willed it to become his schoolteacher, who glowered at him and then told him he was a good boy. He wondered at first if the effort of will would exhaust him, would sap his energy, but he thought on balance that it did not, that it just about made it possible for him to live. He changed his job, he became formal and distant with his friends, he was a kind of automaton. The dream world was where he lived. He wrote it down more and more intensively, recalling colours and distances and details that would vanish if he waited until he had dressed and drunk his coffee before recording them. He recorded dreams of seeking along halls and corridors, endless stairs opening on more endless stairs. He recorded dreams of being embarrassingly naked at interviews, or standing in a meadow and watching his teeth drop one by one like petals on the grass. He sat in examination rooms and searched fruitlessly for a piece of paper six inches wide and four feet long, without which he was not permitted to begin writing. There were menacing clocks that ticked and moved stiff fingers. Often he could say to himself in the dream, this is one of those dreams, you have been here before. Once he painted an abstract masterpiece in brilliant reds and purples, golds and indigo and almost wept as the pattern dissolved before he could recall it to set it down to remember. He didn't interpret meanings. He simply recorded his dreaming life.

He found he was shaking when he sat down to write his bright, white false awakening. He wrote, "I dreamed I was awake after a nightmare. I was not awake, and it was not a nightmare." He could not go on.

The next day he could not recall his dreams. He attributed this to the shock of the false awakening, and waited patiently for the dream world to be restored. But the next day, and the next day, and the next, his mind was an even, dun-coloured blank.

It was possible that he was dreaming and not remembering. It was possible—though surely unlikely—that he had ceased to dream at all.

The absence of dreams changed his waking self. He found he was creeping rather than striding. He felt heavy and pale and conspicuous, as though his features, glimpsed in shopwindows, had lost their light and shadow, were plain and pasty. He felt he was a simulacrum, made of dough or wet clay.

He began to see dreams in his waking life. He saw a pavement flowing with a dense crowd of lemmings, and was not surprised quickly enough. He saw bicycles out of the corner of his eye, taking forbidden turnings, mounting the pavements with balletic abandon, cavorting like circus horses, upright on a hind wheel. Some of the riders were hooded, some would not cohere into apprehensible forms.

He got in touch with one of his old acquaintances from the lucid dreaming group, from the time before he had known her. He explained to this man, a hospital nurse, that he was experiencing sudden loss of all dreams. He described it as an interesting phenomenon, worth study perhaps. The nurse said maybe he needed counselling. He rejected that idea with considerable firmness, saying oddly that he felt lids should stay on cans of worms. What he needed was to be sure whether he was dreaming and not remembering, or whether he was truly not dreaming at all. Would his friend sit by his bed one night and wake him regularly and ask what he was dreaming? He would be truly grateful, he said rather formally.

So they drank a glass or two of wine together and talked about odd dreams they had had, and why some were remembered in toto, and some only for one vivid detail, and whether the hinterland beyond the detail existed or not. The friend said that his own view was that dreaming went on all the time, like the circulation of the blood. He had learned, he believed, to retrace lost paths in subsequent dreams, to reconstruct faces and places.

He went to bed as he usually did, in his pyjamas, under the buxom white quilt. He said to his friend that all this was making him so exhausted that he was sure he would have no trouble getting to sleep. The friend, in sweater and jeans, sat by the bed in an armchair with a new pad of paper and a pen, waiting to write. He did indeed sleep immediately and easily. The friend woke him during periods of rapid eye movement and during periods of heavy slumber when his face was still. He repeated, each time, "Did you dream?" And each time the answer—sometimes irritable, sometimes weary, occasionally anxious was, no, he could not recall any dream.

They discussed the problem over breakfast in the morning, before the friend went home to sleep. Some people, the friend said, didn't mind not dreaming, or not knowing, at least, what they had dreamed. Maybe if he just waited a bit, patiently, the memories of his dreams would come back. Or he could ask for help, go for counselling.

He said he didn't want that, above all he didn't want that.

After the experiment the waking dreams got worse. A lot worse. He started to write a report in his office and found that he could not write—the computer only produced incomprehensible symbols, and when he tried to retrieve its original state it began to issue red warnings of total breakdown. He called for help, for a technician, who typed and tested and said nothing was wrong, he could not see what the problem was. Then he saw his own hands on the keyboard and they were wrinkled things with long claws, like raptors. The lucid dreaming group had explained that looking at your own hands is a good way of telling whether you are in or out of a dream. So that time he waited for the return of his own pink bitten fingernails, which did indeed return. Much worse was a moment when he was called before his manager to explain why he was suddenly working so much more slowly. When the manager began to speak his tie undid itself, and then his shirt buttons flew open, his vest crawled up his chest, his padded stomach burst open and began to pour out blood and guts. Again there was a slow moment when he believed what he was seeing. He managed to speak to the burst manager in a normal voice, saying he felt unwell, would come back later. The man's head was gross and leonine, carved out of some kind of granite. He remarked drily in his normal peevish voice that this seemed to be happening more and more often. Perhaps help was needed, perhaps he should see a doctor. Or a counsellor. He was pouring with sweat, and did not know if the sweat—which was far more than he had ever known—was real or dreamed.

Out of doors he was trailed and preceded by white bicycles. They came up behind buses he was riding, swaying as they overtook them with bursts of speed. They dangled from lampposts, with dripping manes of ribbons. They lay in the gutter, leaned against postboxes, travelled silent and menacing through red lights and over zebra crossings. He closed his eyes and flinched when it seemed inevitable that they would run him down and opened them to find they were not there at all.

He went back to his dream-group friend. He asked whether the friend knew anything about hypnotism. The friend said he had once been very successful at hypnotising people, so much so that he had given up, after upsetting some people. He didn't appear to want to expatiate. The dreamer said that nevertheless he should be grateful if they could try. He was hideously embarrassed by having to explain his state, even to a dream expert.

He said, "Do you think that you could suggest—tell me—to dream at night, and asleep—and not to dream in the day?"

The friend said he had always enjoyed lucid dreaming by day, himself.

"Not these dreams, believe me."

So they were back in the white bedroom and the friend was dangling a string of green glass beads before his eyes. They had always worked the best in the old days, he said. Transparency added to the effect of the shine and shimmer.

He went under. He sat with an empty mind. How good it felt as it emptied itself. How good to be simple and inane.

The friend woke him, with a snap of the fingers. He said, "I told you you will dream tonight, and not in the daytime. We shall see what happens."

He had a hard time going to sleep that night. He read a bit, and drank a nightcap, and tried not to think about what would happen if he resisted the suggestion. In the end, uneasily, he slept.

When he woke, the white room was full of light. He uncoiled under the crisp white heap of his duvet, and the down moved with him, and held him. Incomprehensible happiness flooded him, too much happiness, tinted with relief. He tried to think. He had been tensed against disaster. He had been dreaming, one of those dense dreams which appear to offer no way out, which mock you with the idea that they are not dreams at all.

He looked at his clock. It was 6:00 a.m. He could drift back into sleep for another hour or so. He closed his eyes against the light and settled his body.

SEA STORY

He was born beside the sea—almost literally, for his mother's birth pangs began when she was walking along the shoreline under a pale sun gathering butterfly shells. He was born in Filey, on the East Yorkshire coast, a fishing town with a perfect sweep of pale golden beach, crumbling grassy cliffs, and the unique Filey Brigg, a mixture of many rocks, beginning at Carr Naze, and stretching out in a long peninsula into the North Sea, full of rock pools and rivulets, harsh and tempting at once. His father was an oceanographer, the son of an oceanographer who studied the deep currents of the North Sea. His mother taught English at a high school and wrote fierce little poems about waves and weather. They took him walking along the beach, and scrambling on the Brigg and fishing from rocks and with lines over the side of rowing boats. The family had almost a collection of bottles picked up by sailing vessels and along coastlines. Several of these were numbered bottles, sealed and weighted to bob along the seabed, designed by the Marine Science project to map the movement of currents around the coast. One—a rather sinister-looking early-twentieth-century medicine bottle—contained a lined sheet of paper. This read "Dear Mary" and was followed by the repeated phrase "I love you, I love you, I love you" on both sides of the paper. It was meticulously signed Robert Fisher, with an address in Hull; the house turned out to have been demolished by bombs in 1944.

His mother recited poems to him. They would emerge from under the tunnel-like underpass which led from the town to the beach. The wind would blast them or wrap itself round them, and his mother would quote Masefield. "I must go down to the seas again, to the lonely sea and the sky."

"I must go down to the seas again, for the call of the running tide
Is a wild call and a clear call that may not be denied;
And all I ask is a windy day with the white clouds flying,
And the flung spray and the blown spume, and the sea-gulls crying.

I must go down to the seas again, to the vagrant gypsy life
To the gull's way and the whale's way where the wind's like a whetted knife . . ."

It was something set in motion by that poem, more than any other, which led him to follow his mother, to study English literature, and to teach. His days in Oxford were the first he had spent away from the sea and its absence was peculiarly painful. He could not quite imagine how it might feel to have been born inland. The space inside his skull was composed of an almost abstract form—the sweep of sand, the black protuberance of the Brigg with the waves licking it or crashing over it, and most of all the huge curve of the horizon. It was an empty line, and it signified the inhuman. That is, it was the limit of human vision. Beyond and beneath it were spaces and moving things unknown to men, not controlled by humans, unseen and unimaginable. In Oxford the stone colleges, the perfectly composed gardens and trimmed lawns were human and had been so for centuries. The river was a place for punts and rowing boats. The Filey horizon was inordinate and its menace delighted him. He needed this danger. He understood the Filey fishermen, who would not learn to swim and sank quickly in their boots if their boats capsised. They acknowledged that the sea was too much for them.

From his Oxford days he kept a kind of anthology of the sea. There was a moment of pure glee when he read for the first time

Chapter 58 of *Moby-Dick.* This is the chapter about brit, "the minute yellow substance upon which the Right Whale largely feeds." The chapter describes the peaceable whales like mowers in a golden meadow. It ends with a rhetorical comparison of the land and the sea. The land is "this green, gentle and most docile earth." The sea is violent, dangerous, inimical. "Panting and snorting like a mad battle steed that has lost its rider, the masterless ocean overruns the globe."

When he fell in love it was an immediate shock which was at once absorbed into his inner landscape. He was fishing from his boat, beyond the end of the Brigg when she rose up beside him, a pale woman in a sleek black wetsuit, like a seal, her long, lovely face streaming with seawater. She trod water and smiled mildly at him and stayed to speak about the weather, the beauty of the bay. Her name was Laura and she had just sat her final exams in marine biology in Aberdeen. She was on a holiday with a group of fellow students staying in the Three Tuns pub. He could see that under her cap her hair was long and white-gold. She was mild, she was sunny. Love at first sight was not something he had believed in until it happened. His own side of their conversation was shocked and hesitant. He feared to say anything that would break the spell or cause her to frown. He drew in his line, so as not to entangle her when she dived again. He went of course to the Three Tuns that evening, although this demanded an effort of courage. There they were, the students, drinking in a bay window. More courage was required to greet her, but she smiled, and room was made for him at their table. She spoke less than the others, mostly to agree with what they were saying. They were a mixture of men and women. He watched anxiously to see if she was attached in any way to any of the men, and concluded she was not. He thought she would never know how witty he was, how eloquent, in the classroom and out of it, unless he broke his charmed silence, but he could not. Everything she did was delightful, the way she tossed her hair, the aquamarine brooch at her throat, the way she listened calmly to what was said.

He became part of their group, in the pub at least. He was full of desire and yet hardly dared to imagine making love to her. He felt, unlike Marvell's lover, that he had world enough and time to take her in slowly. It was somehow not possible to ask her out separately from the group. He stalked the pub decorously and in the end was rewarded by seeing her leave, alone, an unposted letter in her hand. He fell in step with her, easily. She smiled.

She said, "I've just been offered my dream job. I'm going to be part of a team studying the life cycle of eels. This letter is my acceptance. I'm off to the Caribbean next week."

"But," he said. "But."

"But?"

"I've only just got to know you."

"I'll be back, some time."

"Can I write?" he said.

She looked startled and then smiled. "Of course." She took out a notebook and scribbled an address. She added an email address. Then she said goodbye and walked away.

He wrote her love letters in his mind, studded with quotations. He wrote a painfully ordinary letter, posted it, and had no reply, which was unsurprising, for the address she had given him was Scottish and she was in the Caribbean. The emails he sent were returned to him as undeliverable. He dreamed obsessively of her, kind, unkind, naked, wet-suited, inviting, frowning, vanishing. One day he remembered the love letter in the drift bottle on his mantelpiece: I love you, I love you, I love you. On an impulse he put pen to paper, writing her name at the top, and adding,

Laura
I love you.

As fair art thou my bonnie lass
So deep in luve am I
And I will love thee still, my dear,
Till a' the seas gang dry

Till a' the seas gang dry, my dear
And the rocks melt wi' the sun:
I will luve thee still my dear
While the sands of life shall run.

He signed the letter and added his address. Then he rolled the message and put it into a Perrier bottle. The green plastic was lovely and Perrier had been Laura's preferred drink in the Three Tuns. He did not know whether casting his love away into the sea was an attempt to drive his love from his life, or a hope for some improbable luck. In order to show himself that the gesture was serious he added his great grandfather's cornelian signet ring and some threads of his own hair. Then he closed the bottle tightly, and rowed out in his boat to where he knew, from his grandfather's work, that the currents could possibly take the message as far as the Sargasso Sea. He held it up to the light, solemnly, and then dropped it into the water, where it moved, apparently purposefully, away.

In fact, it travelled far. It rode south to North Anglia, and was then carried north past Holland to head round Denmark, past Norway to the Arctic Ocean. It survived the wet and the cold and lost some of its brilliant greenness, becoming smeared with a thick brown algal slime. In the Arctic it was arrested for a time, and moved in circling swirls before being blown again back onto the current which took it south and then round the coast of Greenland. It bobbed and slopped across the Atlantic Ocean, past Newfoundland and Nova Scotia; it was snapped at by seabirds off the coast of Massachusetts, where a stream of cold water took it south into the Caribbean. Here it was arrested at the fringe of a slowly swirling carpet of floating fragments. They were all shapes and sizes and some of them were in jewelled colours, emerald, opalescent, crimson, cobalt, ultramarine. But the overall colour was a colourless all-colour of stained whiteness, deathly pale. This was the Atlantic Gyre, or the Caribbean Trash Vortex. It is said to be the size of Texas and moves slowly in the ocean. It is composed of human plastic waste, and beneath it, hidden under the movement of the sea surface, vast curtains of tiny particles hang fathoms deep. It is like a pop painting, containing white plastic forks and beakers, shoals of toothbrushes, phantom threads of ghostly ropes and lines, bottles and jars. It contains also a silt of threads and fragments from the sumps of the world's washing machines. It could be likened to Melville's sea of golden brit where the whales fed—but the crustaceans, copepods, and fingerling fish that composed the brit are being replaced, little by little, by nurdles, the tiny plastic spheres made by manufactured microbeads of polyethylene thermoplastic, or by rubbed fragments of plastic debris, poetically known as mermaids' tears.

The bottle came to rest, then sidled between an ethereal shopping bag and a cracked shoehorn, was sucked down and spat up, its green sides glittering in the sun. A mollymawk snapped at it. It was beginning to disintegrate, its walls furring and feathering. The mollymawk tore at it, and carried away a smeared strip to feed to its chicks, who would die with bellies distended by this stuff. The cap detached itself, and was swallowed by a green turtle which mistook it for a glass eel. When this turtle choked and died, the cap was picked from its remains by another turtle, which also choked. The signet ring was heavy enough to plummet down to the ocean floor, where a hagfish lunged at it, swallowed it, and choked. A fat eel took the letter with its weeping words, and excreted it. Paper decays, the letter decomposed itself. The body of the bottle separated into shreds of green-grey floaters. Some of these were mistaken for small squid by hungry fish and swooping gannets, whose guts were already swollen with waste. What remained was washed and rubbed into nurdles which joined the mass of other pale beads.

Parts of this mess did in fact reach their intended destination. Many of the nurdles were caught in vast trailing micronets, attached to boats, once designed to study plankton, now part of a long and painstaking experiment to examine the bulk of nurdles and the diminishing bulk of the plankton. There she was, Laura, sleekly black-clad, bright-haired like some marine goddess gathering in the tears, the beads, the microscopic living things. Some of the Perrier nurdles were amongst those she looked at in a glass dish under a strong microscope. The message she read was the human occupation and corruption of the masterless ocean.

Harold married a fellow poet, had three daughters whom he loved, strode along Filey Beach collecting plastic bags and debris, retired and died. Laura had died long ago, caught in the micromeshes of her netting when her boat capsised. The planet became more and more inimical to human life, as fires raged and floods drove through streets and houses. The sempiternal nurdles, indestructible, swayed on and under the surface of the sea.

PERMISSIONS ACKNOWLEDGEMENTS

Selected pieces originally appeared in the following:

"The July Ghost" in *Firebird 1,* edited by T. J. Binding (Penguin, 1982) and collected in *Sugar and Other Stories* (Vintage Books, 1992)
"Sugar" in *The New Yorker* (January 12, 1987) and collected in *Sugar and Other Stories* (Vintage Books, 1992)
"Precipice-Encurled" in *Encounter* (April 1987) and collected in *Sugar and Other Stories* (Vintage Books, 1992)
"Racine and the Tablecloth" in *Sugar and Other Stories* (Vintage Books, 1992)
"Medusa's Ankles" in *Woman's Journal* (September 1990) and collected in *The Matisse Stories* (Vintage Books, 1996)
"The Chinese Lobster" in *The New Yorker* (October 26, 1992) and collected in *The Matisse Stories* (Vintage Books, 1996)
"Dragons' Breath" in *Index on Censorship* (September–October 1994) and collected in *The Djinn in the Nightingale's Eye* (Vintage Books, 1998)
"The Djinn in the Nightingale's Eye" in *Paris Review* (Winter 1994) and collected in *The Djinn in the Nightingale's Eye* (Vintage Books, 1998)
"A Lamia in the Cévennes" in *Atlantic Monthly* (July 1995) and collected in *New Writing 5,* edited by Christopher Hope and Peter Porter (Vintage Books, 1996)
"Christ in the House of Martha and Mary" in *You Magazine* featured in *The Mail on Sunday* (May 31, 1998) and collected in *Elementals* (Vintage Books, 2000)
"Cold" in *Elementals* (Vintage Books, 2000)
"Heavenly Bodies" in *Sunday Times* (December 20, 1998)
"Raw Material" in *Atlantic Monthly* (April 2002) and collected in *Little Black Book of Stories* (Vintage Books, 2003)
"A Stone Woman" in *The New Yorker* (October 13, 2003) and collected in *Little Black Book of Stories* (Vintage Books, 2003)
"The Narrow Jet" in *Paris Review* (Spring 2005)
"Dolls' Eyes" in *The New Uncanny*, edited by Ra Page and Sarah Eyre (Comma Press, 2008)
"The Lucid Dreamer" in *New Statesman* (June 23, 2011)
"Sea Story" in *The Guardian* (March 15, 2013)